A Valentine Kiss

THERESE BEHARRIE
JENNIE ADAMS
CHRISTY McKELLEN

MILLS & BOON

First Published in Great Britain 2019
by Mills & Boon, an imprint of HarperCollins*Publishers*
1 London Bridge Street, London, SE1 9GF

A VALENTINE KISS © 2019 Harlequin Books S. A.

A Marriage Worth Saving © 2017 Therese Beharrie
Tempted by Her Tycoon Boss © 2016 Jennie Adams
The Unforgettable Spanish Tycoon © 2017 Christy McKellen

ISBN: 978-0-263-27478-3

0219

MIX
Paper from
responsible sources
FSC® **C007454**
FSC
www.fsc.org

This book is produced from independently certified FSC™
paper to ensure responsible forest management.

For more information visit: www.harpercollins.co.uk/green

Printed and bound in Spain
by CPI, Barcelona

A MARRIAGE
WORTH SAVING

THERESE BEHARRIE

To my husband, Grant. Thank you for showing me what a strong relationship is. It's knowing that we can face whatever comes our way that has helped me to write about a relationship that survives after the unthinkable. You are my inspiration. I love you.

And for the incredibly strong women in my family. Your courage in facing the most heartbreaking of losses inspired this story. Your determination in facing the future inspired these characters.

I hope it brings you a measure of comfort.

PROLOGUE

JORDAN THOMAS COULDN'T take his eyes off his event planner.

Well, he supposed he couldn't exactly call her 'his' when his father had been the one to hire her. But since he had inherited his mother's half of the vineyard—which he would have gladly traded to have her back—he figured his father's decision went for the both of them.

'Are you going to keep staring at her, or are you going to introduce yourself?'

His father, Gregory, barely glanced at him as he said the words. The serious tone Greg had used would have alarmed anyone who didn't know him—would have made him seem almost angry—but at twenty-seven years old Jordan knew the nuances of his father's voice. Greg was baiting him.

'I'm still thinking about it. I'm not sure I want to bother her an hour before the event,' Jordan answered.

When his father didn't reply, he sighed.

'Maybe you should call her over so that I can introduce myself, Dad.'

His father nodded his approval. 'Mila! Would you come over here for a second?'

The minute she started walking towards them, Jordan's heart raced. She was absolutely beautiful, he thought as he took in the perfectly designed features of her face. A small nose led to luscious lips, pink as a cherry blossom and which curved into a smile when she saw his father. The smile kicked his heart up another notch even though her brown eyes watched him carefully, surrounded by the fullest, darkest eyelashes he had ever seen.

He wondered idly if they were like that with help from cosmetic enhancements, but something told him that everything about her was natural. She made him think of the fields where his grapes grew in the vineyard—of the vibrancy of their colours and the feeling of home he always felt looking at it.

He didn't have time to ponder the unsettling thought when she stopped in front of them.

'Mila, you haven't had the chance to meet my son yet.' Greg nudged Jordan, and if Jordan hadn't been so mesmerised by the woman in front of him, he might have wondered at his father pushing him towards her.

But all thoughts flew out of his head the minute he introduced himself and she said, 'Mila Dennis,' and took his outstretched hand.

He'd thought there would be heat—a natural reaction to touching someone he found attractive. But he hadn't expected the heat to burn through his entire body. He hadn't expected the longing that curled in his stomach, the desire to make her his. But most of all he hadn't expected the pull that he felt towards her—a connection that went beyond the physical.

She pulled her hand away quickly, tucking a non-existent piece of hair behind her ear, and he knew she had felt it, too.

'It's lovely to meet you, Mr Thomas.'

Her voice sounded like music to him and he frowned, wondering at his reaction to a woman he hadn't even known for five minutes.

'Jordan, please. Mr Thomas is my father.' He shoved

his hands into his pockets and watched as a smile spread across Greg's face. Jordan felt his eyebrows raise.

'Actually, Mila doesn't call me that,' Greg said, and Jordan realised Greg's smile was aimed at Mila. It was a sign of affection that made their relationship seem more than that of employer/employee. It was almost…*familial*. Almost, because Greg didn't even share his smiles—a rare commodity—with his family. With his son.

He would have to ask his father about it, Jordan thought when Mila's lips curved in response. But then she looked at Jordan and the smile faltered.

'Well, I think it's best that I get back. We have hundreds of people coming today. It was a great idea to host a Valentine's Day Under the Stars event.'

'It was mine.' Jordan wasn't sure why he said it, but he wanted her to know that *he* was responsible for the idea that had brought the two of them together.

He had a feeling it would be significant.

'Well, it was a great one.' She frowned, as though she wasn't sure how to respond to him. 'I'll see you both a little later then. Greg…' She smiled at Jordan's father, but again it faltered when she turned her attention to him. 'Jordan…'

She said his name carefully, as though it was a minefield she was navigating through. He watched her, saw the flash of awareness and then denial in her eyes, and something settled inside him.

'What was *that*?'

His father had waited for Mila to leave before asking, and Jordan turned to him, noting the carefully blank expression on Greg's face.

'I think I've just met the woman I'm going to spend the rest of my life with.'

Greg's eyebrows rose so high they disappeared under the hair that had fallen over his forehead. And then came another nod of approval.

'I *knew* you were a smart boy,' he said, and a warm feeling spread through Jordan's heart at what he knew was high praise coming from his father.

Meeting Jordan Thomas had unsettled Mila so much that she'd almost lost her headline act.

When she heard the commotion in the tent they'd set up behind the amphitheatre stage—and saw the sympathetic look Lulu, her assistant and long-time friend, shot her on her way towards the sound—Mila knew she was about to walk into a drama.

'Why would you do this to me on Valentine's Day?' Karen, the pretty singer that the whole of South Africa had been raving about since she'd won the biggest singing competition in the country, was wailing. 'You couldn't wait *one day* before breaking up with me? And right before a performance, too!'

Wails turned into heart-wrenching sobs—the kind that could only come from a teenage girl losing her first love— and Mila felt the telltale tickling of the start of a headache. She took in the chagrined look on Karen's guitarist's face and realised he was responsible for the tears.

She sighed, and then strode to the little crowd where the scene was unfolding.

'What's going on?'

'Kevin broke up with me!' Karen said through her sobs, and Mila wondered why she had decided that hiring a fresh young girl to perform at one of the biggest events she had ever planned—for one of the most prominent clients she had ever worked for—had seemed like a good idea.

And then she remembered the voice in the online videos she'd watched of Karen, and the number of views all those videos had got, and she sighed again.

'On *Valentine's Day*, Kevin?' Mila asked, instead of voicing the 'What were you thinking?' that sat on the tip of her tongue. Best not to rock the boat any further, she thought. Kevin, who looked to be only a couple of years older than the girl whose heart he had broken, shifted uncomfortably on his feet.

'Well, ma'am, there was this—'

He cut himself off when Mila held up her hand, affronted that he was calling her 'ma'am' even though she was only a few years older than him. Four, max. She'd also realised that whatever Kevin had been about to say would have caused Karen even more distress.

'Okay, everyone, the show is over. Can we all get back to what we need to be doing? Our guests are starting to arrive,' Mila called out and then waited until everyone had scattered, eyeing those who lingered so that they eventually left, too.

When she was alone with Karen, she turned and took the girl's hand. 'Have you ever been broken up with before, Karen?'

Red curls bounced as Karen shook her head, and Mila suddenly felt all the sympathy in the world for her.

'It sucks. It really does. Your heart feels like it's been ripped into two and your stomach is in twists. It doesn't matter when it happens—that feeling is always the same. Stays there, too, if you let it.'

Mila thought about when she had been Karen's age—of how moving from foster home to foster home had meant that she'd never had someone to tell her this the first time a boy had broken *her* heart—and said what she'd wished she'd known then.

'But, you know, the older you get, the more you realise that the less it meant, the less it will hurt. And, since Kevin over there seems like a bit of a jerk, I'm thinking you'll be over this in a week…maybe two.'

'Really?' The hope in Karen's eyes made Mila smile.

'I'm pretty sure. And, you know, the best revenge is to prove to him that it didn't really matter that much after all.'

'But how…? Oh, if I perform with him, he'll think that I've got over it. Maybe he'll even want me back!'

She said the words with such enthusiasm that Mila resisted rolling her eyes. 'Sure… Why not?'

She watched Karen run to the bathroom to freshen up, feeling both relieved that Karen was going to perform and annoyed that she didn't seem to have heard a word Mila had told her.

'That was pretty impressive.'

The deep, intensely male voice sent shivers up Mila's spine, and she turned slowly to face its owner. Jordan Thomas's eyes were the most captivating she had ever seen—a combination of gold and brown that made her think of the first signs of autumn. They made the masculine features of his face seem ordinary though she knew that, based on the way he made her feel distinctly female, he was anything *but* ordinary. Light brown hair lay shaggy over his forehead, as though he had forgotten to comb it, but it added a charm to his face that might have been otherwise lost under the pure maleness of him.

She took a moment to compose herself, and then she smiled at him.

Because she was a professional and he was a client.

And because she needed to prove that the effect he'd had on her when they'd first met had been a fluke.

'Thanks. All a part of the job.'

'Consoling teenage girls is a part of your job?'

The smile came more naturally now. 'When the teenage girl is the headline act at my event, yes.'

He shoved his hands into his pockets and the action drew her attention to the muscles under the black T-shirt he wore. Heaven help her, but she actually thought about running her hands over them before she could stop herself.

'It looks great.'

She blinked, and then realised that he was talking about the event. She nodded, and then peeked out of the tent to where people were beginning to fill the seats of the amphitheatre.

'It's come along nicely.' She noted that the wine stalls were already busy, and she could smell the waft of food from the food vendors. 'You should pat yourself on the back. It *was* your idea after all.'

She glanced back at him, saw the slow, sexy smile spread on his face, and thought that she needed to get away from him as she had almost fanned herself.

'It may have been my idea to host the event here at the vineyard, but I could never have arranged a concert *and* a movie screening in one night.'

'It pulls in fans for the concert and romantics for the movie,' she said, as she had to Greg Thomas so many times before. 'Who can resist either of those events—or any event, really—under the stars, with delicious Thomas Vineyard wines on tap, on the most romantic day of the year?'

His eyes sparkled, as though her words had given him some kind of idea, and then he smiled at her. A full smile that was more impactful than a thousand of his slow, sexy ones.

'I need to check everything one more time. If you'll excuse me?'

Jordan nodded, and then said, 'I'll find you later.'

She frowned as she walked away, wondering what on earth he'd meant by that.

When the movie was about ten minutes in, she found out.

He had come to her and claimed that there was a problem with the wine delivery for those who had pre-ordered boxes to take home with them. Like a fool she had followed him, her mind racing to a million different ways of solving the problem. Only when he led her through a gate past the Thomas house did it occur to her that there might not be an emergency.

'What is this?' she asked quietly, even though they were far enough away from the guests that no one would hear her.

'It's a picnic. Under the stars.'

A part of her melted at that—the pure romance of it made her feel as giddy as a girl on her first date. But it didn't change the way her heart raced in panic as she took in the scene in front of her.

A blanket was spread out overlooking the vineyard, and in the moonlight she could see the shadow of the mountains. For a brief moment she wondered what it would look like during the day, with its colours and its magnitude and the welcoming silence.

She shook her head and looked at what was spread on the blanket. A bottle of wine—she couldn't read the label, though she thought she saw the Thomas Vineyard crest—cooled in an ice bucket with two glasses next to it. A variety of the foods that she hadn't had time to taste accompanied the wine.

Although she really didn't want to, she found herself softening even more, her heart racing now for completely different reasons than a man expressing interest in her.

'Are you going to stay or run?'

She looked up at him, and though his words sounded playful, his expression told her otherwise.

'Are those my only two options?'

'I could offer you another.'

She saw the change in his eyes and her body heated.

'What would you do if I ran?' she asked, hoping to distract him.

'I'd run with you.'

She resisted the urge to smile at his charm, and wondered why someone like Jordan Thomas would be interested in her? First, she was his employee. And second, she didn't have much to offer him. What could a woman with no family and no foundation offer a man like Jordan Thomas of the Thomas Vineyard?

Still, she found herself saying, 'Pour me a glass of wine, Jordan.'

He handed her a glass with a smile that had her shaking her head.

'You don't agree with my methods?'

'You mean lying to get me to share a drink with you?'

'Yes.' He grinned. 'But you can't tell me this isn't a welcome change to having to run around all day?'

'No, I can't.' She sighed, and took a sip from her wine. 'Drinking wine after a long day with a handsome man should be the only way to unwind.'

She didn't realise what she'd said until she saw him smiling at her, and then she blushed furiously.

Where had that come from?

'I didn't mean—'

'To tell me I'm handsome?'

She set her wine down. 'Yes. It's been a long day.'

'So I could ask you anything now and you would answer it?'

'Maybe,' she said softly, caught by the expression in his eyes.

And then she wondered who this person who was flirting with this gorgeous man was. Because surely it couldn't be tame, safe Mila. How often had she heard those comments from boys she had dated? From her foster siblings, who'd had no interest in hanging out with a girl who couldn't bring herself to try drugs or go out drinking every night, no matter how desperately she'd wanted to be liked?

She closed her eyes at the pain, and picked up her wine

glass again. It must have been the stress of the event that had her thinking about a past she'd thought she'd left behind.

But before she could drink her wine, Jordan took the glass out of her hand and she froze.

'Do you have a boyfriend?' he asked her, and she realised he was a lot closer than he'd been a few moments ago. Her throat dried at the woodsy smell that filled her senses, and suddenly she wished she hadn't flirted with him.

'No,' she answered quickly, her breathing becoming more heavy than she thought could be healthy.

'Good. That makes this much easier.'

'What are you talking about?' She couldn't take her eyes off him, and knew she should be worried that the realisation only caused the slightest bit of alarm in her.

'Us.' He pulled the clip out of her hair so that it fell to her shoulders. 'I'm glad you won't have to break another man's heart so that we can be together.'

'That's presumptuous of you,' she replied, though for the life of her, she couldn't think of one reason why that was a problem. Even when he had her speaking her mind without the filter she usually employed with every word.

He didn't respond immediately, and she wondered if she'd said something wrong.

And then her heart stopped completely when his hand stilled on her neck and he said, 'It should be. Everything inside me is saying that feeling this way about someone without even knowing them is crazy. And yet I can't help myself.'

His hand moved to her face, and she thought that even if the sky fell down on them she wouldn't be able to look away from him.

'So tell me whether I'm being presumptuous when I say I know you feel it, too?'

She couldn't speak because the pieces that had been floating around in her head since they'd met—and the feelings that had become unsettled the moment he'd introduced himself—told her there was truth to his words.

'You did all of this to…to see if I felt the same way?'

'No.' He smiled, and tucked a piece of hair behind her ear. 'I did this to make you realise that you *did*.'

'Jordan, I—'

His lips were suddenly on hers, and she felt herself melt, felt her resistance—her denial—fade away. Because as his mouth moved against hers, her heart was telling her that it wanted to be with him. She ignored the way her mind told her she was being ridiculous, and instead ran her hands over the muscles she had admired earlier.

With one arm he moved everything that was on the blanket away and she found herself on her back, with Jordan's body half over hers. But she pulled away, her chest heaving as though she'd run a marathon.

'This is crazy,' she said shakily, but didn't move any further.

'Yes, it is,' he replied, his eyes filled with a mixture of desire and tenderness.

She raised a hand to his face, pushing his hair back and settling it on his cheek. He turned his head and kissed her hand. And in that moment, under the stars that sparkled brightly on Valentine's Day, she realised that she might have just fallen in love with a man she had only known for a few hours.

Even as her mind called her foolish she was pulling his lips back down to hers.

CHAPTER ONE

Two years later

JORDAN STOOD OUTSIDE his childhood home and grief—and guilt—crashed through him.

The house was like many he had seen in the Stellenbosch wine lands—large and white, with a black roof and shutters. Except he had grown up in this house. He'd played on the patio that stretched out in front of the house, with its stone pillars that had vines crawling up them. He and his father had spent Sunday evenings watching the sun set—usually in silence—on the rocking chairs that stood next to the large wooden door.

He turned his back on the house and the memories, and looked out to the gravel road that led to the rest of the vineyard.

Trees reached out to one another over the road, the colour of their leaves fading from the bright green of summer to the warm hues of autumn. From where he stood he could see the chapel where he'd married Mila just three months after they'd met.

He shook his head. He wouldn't think about that now.

Instead he looked under the potted plants that lined the pathway to the front door for the key he knew his father had kept there. When he found it he began to walk to his father's house—except that wasn't true any more. He clenched his jaw at the reminder of the new ownership of the house—the house he had grown up in—and the reason he was back, and turned the key in the lock.

He heard it first—the crackling sound of fire blazing—and he set his bags down and hurried to the living room where he was sure he would find the house burning. And slowed when he realised that the fire was safely in the fireplace.

He turned his head to the couch in front of the fire, and his heart stopped when he saw his ex-wife sitting in front of it.

'What are *you* doing here?' he demanded before he could think, the shock of seeing her here, in his childhood home, forcing him to speak before he could think it through.

She jumped when she heard him, and shame poured through him as the glass of wine in her hand dropped to the ground and the colour seeped from her face.

'Jordan… What…? I…'

In another world, at another time, he might have found her stammering amusing. Now, though, he clamped down the emotions that filled him and asked again, 'What are you doing here, Mila?'

Her fingers curled at her sides—the only indication that she was fighting to gain her composure. He waited, giving her time to do so, perhaps to make up for startling her earlier.

'What are *you* doing here?' she asked him instead, crossing her arms and briefly drawing his attention to her chest. He shook his head and remembered how long it had taken him to realise that she took that stance whenever she felt threatened.

'You want to know why *I'm* here? In *my* father's home?'

'It's not your father's home any more, Jordan.'

His heart thudded. 'Is that why you're here? Because you'll own part of this house soon?'

She winced, and it made him think that maybe he wasn't the only one unhappy with his father's will.

'No, of course not. But I do live here.'

'What?'

The little colour she had left in her face faded, but her eyes never left his. If he hadn't been so shocked he might have been impressed at her guts. But his mind was still very much focused on her revelation.

'I live here,' she repeated. The shakiness in her voice wasn't completely gone, but the silken tone of it came through stronger. The tone that sounded like music when she laughed. That had once caressed his skin when she said, 'I love you.' The tone that had said 'I do!' two years ago as though nothing could touch them or their love.

How little they had known then…

He pushed the memories away.

'I heard that. I want to know why,' he said through clenched teeth, his temper precariously close to snapping.

'Because your father asked me to move in with him after…after everything that happened.'

The reminder of the past threatened to gut him, but he ignored it. 'So after we got divorced you thought it would be a good idea to move in with my father?'

'No, *he* did,' she said coldly, and again shame nudged him for reasons he didn't understand. 'He wanted—he *needed* someone around when you left.'

'And you agreed?'

'After his first heart attack, yes.'

Her words cut right through to his heart, and he asked the question despite the fact that everything inside him wanted to ignore it. 'His first? You mean his *only*.'

Something flashed through her eyes, and he wondered if

it was sympathy. 'No, I mean his first. The one that killed him was his third.'

Jordan resisted the urge to close his eyes, to absorb the pain her words brought. He wondered how he had gone to his father's funeral, how he had spoken to the few friends Greg had had left, and was only hearing about this now.

But then, was it any wonder? a voice asked him. His father had always kept his feelings to himself, not wanting to burden Jordan with them. An after-effect of *that* night, Jordan thought. But there was a part of him that wondered if Greg hadn't told him as punishment for Jordan leaving, even after his father had warned him that it would destroy his marriage—which it had. After Jordan had decided that limited contact with his father during the year he'd been gone—grief snapped at him when he thought that it had actually been the year before his father's death—was the only way he would be able to forget about what had happened...

'Why didn't you tell me?' he asked, determined not to get sucked in by his thoughts.

'He didn't want you to know.'

It was like a punch to the gut—and it told him that his father wanting to punish him might not have been such a farfetched conclusion.

'He told you that, or *you* decided it?'

Mila's face was clear, but when she spoke her voice was ice. 'It was Greg's decision. Do you think your father's friends would have kept quiet about it for *me*?'

She waited for his answer, but it didn't come. He was too busy processing her words.

'He didn't want you to come home until *you'd* decided to.'

'You should have called me,' he said, his voice low, dangerous.

'If you hadn't been so determined to put as much distance between us as possible—if you hadn't let it cloud your judgement—you would have *known* that you should have come home even though I didn't call you.'

Her voice was a mirror of his own thoughts, and if her words hadn't pierced his heart Jordan might have taken a moment to enjoy—perhaps a better word was *admire*—this new edge to Mila. But he was too distracted by the emotion that what she'd said had awoken in him.

Had his desire to escape the pain of his marriage blinded him to what he should have known? That he should have come home?

'So you're back because of the will?'

Her question drew him out of his thoughts—drew his attention to her. He took a moment before he answered her.

'Yes, that sped up my return to Cape Town. But I'm here for good.'

Jordan watched as her left hand groped behind her, and he moved when he realised she was looking for something to keep her standing. He caught her as she staggered back, his arm curved around her waist. His heartbeat was faster than it had been in a long time, and somewhere in the back of his mind he wondered if he'd really wanted to stop her from falling, or if he'd put himself in this awkward situation because...

He stopped thinking as he looked into those hauntingly beautiful eyes of hers that widened as they looked up at him. The love that had filled them a long time ago had been replaced by such a complexity of emotion that he could only see surprise there. And caution.

Her brown curls were tied back into a ponytail, making her delicate features seem sharper than they'd once been. But maybe that was because her face had lost its gentle rounding, he thought, and saw for the first time that she'd lost weight. Pressed against hers, his body acknowledged that her body felt different from what he remembered. The curves he'd enjoyed during their marriage were now more toned than before.

He wished he could say he didn't like it, but the way his body tightened told him that he would be lying if he did. The lips he had always been greedy for parted, and his eyes lowered. Electricity snapped between them as he thought about tasting her, about quenching the thirst that had burned inside him since they'd been apart…

They both pulled away at the same time, and again Jordan heard the smash of glass against the floor. Pieces of a wine bottle lay mingled with pieces of the glass Mila had dropped earlier, and Jordan belatedly realised that he'd knocked it over when he'd moved back.

'I'll get something for that,' she said, hurrying away before he could respond. But she didn't move fast enough for him to miss the flush on her face.

He stared at the mess on the floor—the mess they'd made within their first minutes of reuniting—and hoped it wasn't an omen for the rest of the time they'd spend together.

Mila grabbed the broom from the kitchen cupboard, and then stilled. She should take a moment to compose herself. Her hands were still shaking from the shock of seeing Jordan, and now her body was heated from their contact.

She hated that reminder of what he could do to her. Hated it even more that he could *still* do it to her, even after everything that had happened between them.

Why had he touched her anyway? She hadn't been going to fall—she was pretty sure about that. It had just been the prospect of him staying—her stomach still churned at the thought—that had shaken her balance. And then, before she'd known it, she'd been in his arms, feeling comfort— and something else that she didn't care to admit—for the first time since the accident that had ruined their lives.

She took a deep breath and, when she was sure she was as prepared as she could be to face him again, she returned to the living room.

And felt her breath hitch again when she saw him standing there.

He was leaner now, though his body was still strong, with muscles clearly defined beneath his clothing. Perhaps there were more muscles now, whatever excess weight there had been once now firm. His hair was shorter, though it was still shaggy, falling lazily over his forehead as though begging to be pushed aside. And then there was his face…those beautiful planes drawn into the serious expression she was becoming accustomed to.

'We need to do something about the house,' he said when he saw her, and moved to take the cleaning items away from her.

But he stopped when he saw the expression in her eyes—the coldness she had become so used to aiming at him to protect herself from pain—and she bent to pick up the pieces of glass.

'I'll be leaving in the morning,' she said, grateful that he couldn't see her face as she tidied up.

The idea of going back to the house that reminded her of all that she'd had—and all that she'd lost—made her feel sick. But what choice did she have?

After Jordan had left, she hadn't been able to be alone in the place where it had all happened. So she'd escaped to their beach house in Gordons Bay for a few months, before Greg had asked her to move in with him. But the divorce meant that she no longer had any right to stay there, and since she had been renting before they'd got married the only thing she had was the house she'd lived in with Jordan. It was in *her* name after all.

But what did that matter when she couldn't bring herself

to *think* about what had happened there, let alone *live* there and having to face the memories over and over again…?

'That wasn't what I meant,' he said.

Sure that she had got to all the pieces of glass that could be picked up by hand, she stood. 'Not the *only* thing, maybe.'

She wondered how she could speak so coolly when her insides were twisted. But then, she was used to saying things despite her feelings. How many times had she bitten her tongue or said the thing people wanted to hear instead of saying what she really thought? The only difference now was that she was actually being honest.

'Fine.' The word was delivered through clenched teeth. 'There is something else. Did you put him up to the ridiculous conditions of his will?'

Anger whipped through her, and she barely noticed her hand tighten on the dustpan.

'No, Jordan, I didn't. I don't want to own a house with you, and I don't want to plan an event with you.'

I just want to move on with my life.

He didn't say anything immediately. 'I don't want that either.'

'But we'll have to.'

'Because you want your half of the house, the vineyard?'

'Because if we don't you'll lose your half of both, too.'

He didn't deny her words, though she knew by the way his face tightened that he wanted to. It wasn't so much at the truth of what she said, but at the fact that it *was* the truth. How could Jordan explain the fact that his father had left his house—and his share of the vineyard—to *both* his son and ex-daughter-in-law? For someone who valued logic as much as Jordan did, having no explanation for something this important must be eating at him.

'I'm going to contest the will.'

The part of herself that Mila had felt softening immediately iced.

'Based on what?'

'On anything I can find. I won't just accept this.'

And yet you just accepted it when I told you to give me space.

'And if I *don't* succeed in contesting the will…will you…will you sell your shares to me without any of the conditions?'

Pain sat on her chest at the question—the one she knew he'd wanted to ask since he had arrived—and forced words from her lips. 'Yes, Jordan. If that's possible, and if that's what you want, I'll do it.'

Unspoken words filled the air—memories of when he had said much the same thing to her at the end of their marriage—and she closed her eyes against them. When she was sure her emotions were in check—when she was sure that she was strong enough to look at him—she did.

And realised how different he was from the man she'd known…and loved.

She hadn't noticed any of it when she'd seen him four months ago at his father's funeral. He hadn't looked at her then, she thought, too consumed by the grief of losing his only surviving parent—the man who had raised him—despite their complicated relationship. Or maybe because of it. She wasn't even sure he knew she had only gone to the church and graveyard, not being able to bear spending time socialising after the death of the only man she'd ever thought of as a father.

After losing the last of the family she had.

Suddenly she felt incredibly weary.

'I think it's best if I go to bed now,' she said, as the shock of seeing him finally caught up with her.

'Wait,' he said, and took her arm before she could walk out of the room.

She looked down at his hand as heat seared through her body at his touch, and quickly moved away. She didn't want to think about the physical effect he had on her. The emotional one was already too much.

He cleared his throat. 'I've arranged for a meeting with Mark Garrett in the morning. To see if I have grounds to contest. Since you're willing to sell, I was hoping you would come with me.'

Her eyebrows rose. 'You've made an appointment with your family lawyer? The executor of your father's will?' When he nodded, she said, 'And you're only telling me this now? When it's beneficial to you?'

He looked at her, those golden eyes carefully blank of emotion. 'I didn't think you needed to be there.'

'Because my inheritance doesn't concern me, right? No, it's fine. I get it.' She shook her head when he opened his mouth to respond. 'You've been making decisions for the both of us since we got married. Why stop now that we're divorced?'

She didn't wait for a response, but walked past him, hating the way her body longed to be held in his arms.

Hating the way her life was once again in turmoil because of Jordan Thomas.

Mila got up at five in the morning, her muscles hard with tension after a restless night. She got dressed and did the thing that always helped to keep her mind busy—she cooked. First she made a batch of scones and then muffins and pancakes. When that was done she scrambled eggs, made bacon and toast, and eventually, as the sun peeked through the kitchen windows, put on the kettle for coffee.

'What's all this?'

The deep voice startled her, even though she knew he was there. She supposed she had already grown so used to being alone in the months since Greg had been gone—her heart ached at the reminder—that anyone's presence, let alone that of the man who unsettled her most in the world, would have frightened her in the quiet of the morning.

'Food,' she said, and wiped her hands on her apron. She stilled, thinking that it made her look nervous. 'I'm going to take it down to Frank and Martha's.'

Frank was the kind-hearted man who'd helped manage the vineyard after Greg had taken ill and Jordan had moved away. She had a soft spot for him and, since cooking was something she did to keep herself calm, often took food to Frank and his wife, Martha's house on the Thomas property to share with the workers at the vineyard during the day.

Though now Mila supposed she should offer some to Jordan. Except that would make it seem as if she had got up that morning specifically to cook for *him*. Just as she had when they were married. So she wouldn't offer him breakfast, but would wait until later to pack up the food and let him get breakfast for himself.

Satisfied with the decision, she asked, 'What time is the appointment?'

To avoid his gaze, she turned to make herself coffee. But she stopped when she realised she was about to take out *two* mugs, her mind already making his as he liked it. So she turned back to him and folded her arms, ignoring the way the sight of his hair, wet from a shower, made her body prickle.

'Eight thirty.'

'In less than an hour,' she confirmed, proud of the fact that her voice wasn't as shaky as she felt. 'I'll go and get ready.'

She nearly ran out of the kitchen, but acting normally was eating at her strength. The last time she had been in that kitchen with Jordan she had been pregnant and happy, with the only true family she'd known—her husband and her father-in-law—around her.

The loss of it all was a physical pain.

She bided her time so that she didn't have to have breakfast with him, only coming out when they had to leave. Her eyebrows barely lifted at his choice of transportation—a sleek blue car she knew was a recent and expensive model—but her heart thawed when he opened the door for her.

The trip was silent and tense, but she consoled herself by repeating that it would be over soon. If she signed her share of the vineyard, of the house, over to Jordan she would be able to move out and move on. It would mark the end of the worst and best years of her life and, though her heart was nostalgic for the best, the worst was enough that if she could, she would sign the papers right there in the car.

When Jordan gave his name to the receptionist at the lawyer's, they were shown into an office where Mila spent another ten minutes of tension with Jordan while waiting for the lawyer to come.

'Good morning, Jordan... Mila.'

Mark spoke softly to her and she gave him a small smile. She had only met him twice—once when she'd signed a prenuptial contract, and again after Greg's death when Mark had come to give his condolences and to drop off her copy of the will. Both times he had been kind, and she'd appreciated that.

Jordan barely waited until Mark was seated before he asked, 'What was going on in my father's head when he made this will, Mark?'

Mark gave him a wry smile. 'I think you would be a better judge of that than me.'

When Jordan didn't return the smile, Mark nodded,

apparently realising Jordan was only in the mood for business.

'Well, you've both read Greg's will by now. It's actually quite simple in its conditions—which I know you both must find hard to believe, considering what it's asking of you. You already own half of the Thomas Vineyard, Jordan, having inherited your mother's share of the property when you were twenty-one. Greg's half has been left, as he states in his will, to his son and his daughter-in-law, on the condition that you both work together to plan an...'

Mark paused and took a closer look at the will.

'An Under the Stars event. Instructions have been left regarding the nature of the event—which, again, both of you will have read—and this event has to take place no later than two months after the last of you received a copy of the will.'

'I received mine two weeks ago,' Jordan interrupted, looking at Mila for confirmation of her date.

'I probably got mine a week before that,' she said, and wished her heart wouldn't beat quite as hard.

'Which would mean that we have just over a month to plan this. *If* we do,' Jordan said, his voice masking all emotion.

'Honestly, Jordan. I don't see you having a choice if you want to keep the vineyard solely in your family. If you don't plan the event, your father's share of the vineyard will be auctioned off and the proceeds will be divided between the both of you.'

'Excuse me, Mark?' Mila said, ignoring the way her stomach jolted as Jordan's eyes zoned in on her. 'The will says that I've been left half of Greg's portion as his "daughter-in-law," right?' When Mark nodded his head, she continued. 'So, since Jordan and I aren't married any more, won't that give Jordan grounds to contest the will?'

And leave me out of it?

Mark's eyebrows rose. 'When did you get divorced?'

'About a year ago.' Jordan spoke now, and his eyes were hopeful when Mila lifted her own to look at his face.

She knew that she shouldn't take it personally—if Greg's will could be contested they would both get what they wanted—but her heart still contracted.

She diverted her attention to Mark, saw him riffling through the papers in front of him, and felt concern grow when he lifted one page, his face serious.

'Is there a problem?' she asked.

'I'm afraid so.' Mark looked at them both and laid the page back down. 'Before we send the beneficiaries copies of a will, we check all the details we can for accuracy. Your marital status was one of them and, well…' He gave them both an apologetic look. 'According to the court records of South Africa, the two of you are still very much married.'

CHAPTER TWO

THE SILENCE THAT stretched through the room was marred only by their breathing.

Jordan tried to use it to compose himself, to control the emotions that hearing he was supposedly still married had drawn from him. But then, how could he compose himself when he knew there had to be some mistake?

'I could check again,' Mark said, when Jordan told him as much, 'but I'm afraid the chances of there being a mistake are quite slim.'

'But I signed the papers.' Jordan turned to Mila. 'You did, too.'

Her eyes, slightly glazed from the shock, looked back at him from a pale face as she nodded her agreement. He fought against his instinct to hold her, to tell her that everything would be okay. It wasn't his job any more. Unless, he realised as his mind shifted to their current situation, it *was*.

'With which law firm did you file the papers? I can have my assistant call them to ask them about it.'

'With *this* law firm,' Jordan said, his voice calm though his insides were in a twist.

Mark frowned. 'Do you know which lawyer?'

'With *you*, Mark. As you're my family lawyer, I filed the papers with you.'

His patience was wearing thin. All he'd wanted when

he'd come back was to sort out his inheritance. Once that bit of unpleasantness was done, he would be able to run his family vineyard.

It was the only way he knew to make up for the fact that he'd left without dealing with any of the unresolved issues with his father. To make it up to his mother, too, he thought, remembering the only thing she had asked of him before she'd died when he was five—that he look after his father.

He forced his thoughts away from how he had failed them both.

'I think there's been a mistake of some kind.' To give him credit, Mark was trying incredibly hard to maintain his professionalism. 'I remember you asked me to draw up divorce papers. But when I met your father to set up his will last year he said that the two of you were choosing to separate—not divorce.'

'Wait—Greg set this will up *last year*?' Mila's voice was surprisingly strong despite the lack of colour in her face. 'When exactly did he do it?'

'August.'

'That was a month after his first heart attack. And two months after I signed the divorce papers.'

'Did they have my signature on them?' Jordan asked, wondering where she was going with this.

'Yes, they did.'

'So you would have been the one to file the papers with Mark?'

If Jordan hadn't seen her looking worse than this once before—the day of her fall—he would have worried about how muted she had become.

'I didn't feel entirely comfortable with that…'

Something in her eyes made him wonder what she meant, but he decided now wasn't the right time to think about it. Not when he saw that she was struggling to keep her voice devoid of the emotion she couldn't hide from him.

'So we are still married,' he said flatly.

'No, no—I was going to drop them here after I'd signed, but then Greg asked me whether I would feel better if *he* did it. Because Mark was *your* family lawyer,' she said quickly, avoiding his eyes—which told him she was lying.

It only took him a moment to realise that she was lying about the reason she'd let Greg take the papers, not about his father's actions.

'Did you follow up with Dad?' he demanded, his anger coating his real feelings about the fact that his father had been there for Mila when he hadn't been. Or the fact that his father had been supportive at all—especially to someone who wasn't his son. Was it just another way Greg had chosen to show Jordan how wrong his choice to leave had been?

'Did *you*?' she shot back, and Jordan stared at her, wondering again where the fire was coming from.

'No, clearly not.'

There was a pause.

'I think that, all things considered, we should probably postpone this meeting until a later point,' Mark said, breaking the silence.

'I don't think that's a good idea with the time frame we're working with, Mark.'

Though denial was a tempting option, Jordan knew that he had to face reality. And it seemed the reality was that he was still married.

'Could you please give us a few moments to talk in private?'

'Yes, of course.'

If he was perturbed by being kicked out of his own office, Mark didn't show it as he left the room.

The minute the door clicked closed, Jordan spoke. 'So,

my father was supposed to give the papers to Mark, who was supposed to file them. And since none of that happened, I think Mark's right—we are still married.'

'Yes, I think so...'

Her eyes were closed, but Jordan knew it was one of the ways she worked through her feelings. Closing herself off from the world—and in those last months they'd shared together closing herself off from *him*—so she could think.

The silence stretched out long enough that he became aware of a niggling inside his heart. One that told him that there was still hope for them if they were married. He didn't like it at all—not when that hope had already been dashed when Mila had accepted the divorce.

He had filed for divorce because he'd thought that it was what she wanted—she hadn't called, hadn't spoken to him once after he'd walked out through the door to a life in Johannesburg. He'd taken it as a sign that she wanted the space she had asked him for to be permanent. And so he'd thought he would make it easier for the both of them by initiating the divorce, half expecting her to call him, to demand that he come home so that they could fix things.

But he'd realised soon enough that that wasn't going to happen—when had she demanded anything from him anyway?—and he'd figured that he had done the right thing. Especially since *he* had been the one to make the decision that had caused the heartbreak they'd suffered in the first place.

'Your father spoke to me about a reunion between the two of us.'

He turned his head to her when she spoke. Her voice held that same music he had heard the first time they'd met.

'In his last few months. He wanted us to be together again.'

She opened her eyes, and Jordan had to brace himself against what the pain he saw there did to him. Against the anguish that disappointment was the last thing his father had felt about him.

He cleared his throat. 'I suppose that gives this situation some meaning. He wanted us to plan an event like the one where we met. He knew that still being married would mean we would have to bend to his will. Unless we can show that he was unfit when he made it.'

'I don't think that will work.'

She shook her head, and he wondered why she kept tying her hair up when those curls were meant to be free.

'He was completely sane—his heart attacks had nothing to do with his ability to make rational decisions.'

'What's rational about *this*?'

She lowered her eyes. 'Nothing. Of course, nothing. But making an emotional decision isn't against the law.'

'It should be.'

'Maybe.' She looked at him stoically. 'But he isn't the first person to do that in this family, so I think we can forgive him.'

Jordan found himself at a loss for words, unsure of what she meant. Was she talking about when she'd asked him to go, or the fact that he had left? Regardless of their meaning, her words surprised him. She hadn't given him any indication that she regretted what had happened between them… But then again, she wasn't exactly saying that now either.

But still, the feeling threw him. And because he didn't like it, he addressed the situation at hand.

'It doesn't seem like we're going to get out of this before our time is up, Mila.'

'Out of this…? You mean out of our marriage?'

Why did the question make him feel so strange?

He cleared his throat. 'Yes. The divorce—the one we thought we had—was supposed to take six weeks, and that's as much time as we have to make sure the will's terms are met. So…' he took a deep breath '…what would you say about putting the divorce off until we've planned the event, and then we can take it from there?'

She briefly closed her eyes again, and then looked at him, her expression guarded. 'Why would I do that?'

'What do you mean?'

'Exactly what I said.'

Her guard had slipped enough for him to see a complexity of emotion that reflected the complexity of their predicament.

'I lose in this situation either way. If I help you, we'll get the inheritance, sure, but I would still have to sell my share to you. So what do I get out of this besides spending time with the man I thought I would never have to see again?'

It took him a moment to process what she was saying, and even then he found it difficult to formulate an answer. 'You'll get money. I'll pay you for the share of the vineyard my father left you.'

'Money? *Money?*' She pulled her head back as though she had been slapped. 'I can't believe that we're still married.'

Her words felt like a slap to him, too, but the shame that ran through him at his own words made him realise that maybe he'd deserved it. He was surprised that she had said it—she would never have done so before—but that didn't make it any less true.

'I'm sorry, Mila, I didn't mean that.' He sighed. 'This has been a shock to me, too.'

She nodded, though the coldness coming from her made him wonder if she really did accept his apology.

'You know money isn't an incentive for me,' she said after a few moments, her voice back to being neutral. 'Especially since selling you my share of the vineyard would mean that I lose the only thing I have left of someone I thought of as family.'

His heart ached at that because he understood it. But the logical side of him—the side that didn't care too much for emotions—made him ask, 'If you didn't want to sell your share of the vineyard to me, why did you say you would?'

'I didn't say I wouldn't sell. I just want you to understand what I'm giving up so that you won't say something so insensitive again.'

He was beginning to feel like a schoolchild who was being taught a lesson. 'What *do* you want, then, Mila?'

'I want—' Her voice was husky, her face twisted in pain. But it disappeared almost as quickly as it came, and she cleared her throat. 'I want to sell the house and the car—everything, really, that was a part of our life together.'

Pain flared through him, and the only way he knew how to control it was to pretend it didn't affect him at all. 'Why?'

'To get rid of everything so that I can move—' She broke off, and then continued, 'Move away.' She said the last two words deliberately, as though she was struggling to formulate them. 'I haven't been able to sort things out since you left. The past year I've been busy. Looking after Greg, planning some events and...'

Getting over you, he thought she might say, and he held his breath, waiting for the words. But they didn't come.

'Your help would be useful so that by the time the vineyard is yours, I'll have something to move on to.'

'Where will you go?' he asked when it finally registered that she wanted to move away.

She raised her eyes to his, and they brimmed with the emotion he thought he carried in his heart.

'I'm still working on that part.'

Hearing her say that she was leaving was more difficult than he could have imagined. He couldn't figure out why that was when he had done the same thing.

'Are you sure you're not sacrificing more than I am?'

She smiled a little at that. 'I'm sure.'

Her smile told him all he needed to know. That he needed to help her so he could help himself. Once this was all over he would have the vineyard his parents had owned and would be able to live up to the promises he'd made to them. Maybe he would even be able to make restitution for the decisions he'd made during his short marriage and finally find some peace.

'So if I agree to help you deal with everything from when we were married, you'll agree to plan the event and then sell your inheritance to me?'

'Yes.'

'And then we'll file for divorce again?'

'We?'

The hope he thought he'd extinguished earlier threatened to ignite again at the uncertainty in her voice. But then he remembered that *he* was the one who had filed for divorce the first time, and she was probably just checking whether that would be the case again.

'You,' he clarified. 'We might as well even the score since we have the chance.'

He could have kicked himself when he saw the way her eyes darkened. He wasn't entirely sure he blamed her since his words seemed callous even to his own ears. But despite that, she nodded.

'I guess we have a deal.'

CHAPTER THREE

THEY DROVE BACK to the house in silence.

Jordan's presence was already turning Mila's life upside down. He reminded her of the things she'd failed at. Of the things she had wanted since she'd realised as a child that she didn't have a family in the way her classmates did.

Her entire class had once been invited to a party and she had begged her foster mother at the time—a perpetually exhausted woman who'd spent all her time catering to her husband instead of the children she'd been charged with caring for—to let her go.

When she'd got there Mila had seen for the first time what a real family was. She'd seen her classmate's parents look at their child with love, with pride. Had watched them take photos together while the rest of her class played on the grass. Had seen the easy affection.

She had spent that entire afternoon watching them, wondering why no one else was when this family was clearly doing something out of the norm. But when Mila had been the last to be picked up, she'd seen the way the other parents had treated their children. She'd realised that *that* was normal, and that *she* was the one with the special circumstances.

Her longing for family had started on that day, spreading through her heart, reminding her of it with every beat. Since she had lost her child, those beats had become heavy with pain, with emptiness. And it would only be worse now that Jordan was back.

Since he was back for good, she would have to leave the house she'd been staying in for almost a year. Though she'd known she couldn't stay there for ever, she *had* hoped for more time than she'd got. Not only because she didn't know where she would go—again, the thought of returning to the house where she'd lost their baby made her feel nauseous—but because it had come to feel like the home she'd never had. But then, Mila had also hoped for more time with Greg—especially since she'd finally managed to pierce that closed-off exterior of his...

But that was the least of her concerns now that she'd found out she and Jordan were still married.

It was the hope that worried her the most. Hope had been her first emotion when she'd heard the news, and it had lingered until Jordan had brought up filing for divorce again. It reminded her of how receiving those papers for the first time had destroyed her hope for reconciliation. And rightly so. She shouldn't be—wasn't—interested in reconciliation, however easy it might be to get lured back into the promise of a life with Jordan.

But that wasn't what he wanted, or he wouldn't have left so easily. And that, she told herself, was exactly why she needed to protect herself from him. That was why she had accepted Jordan's suggestion that *she* be the one to file the divorce papers this time. She needed to remind herself that their life together—at least in a romantic sense—was over.

She didn't want him to know how difficult things had been for her since he'd left, even though she had almost told him about it in Mark's office. About how selling their possessions had nothing to do with moving away and everything to do with moving on. But because she couldn't bear to expose herself to him she'd lied instead. Though now that she thought about it perhaps moving away *was* the first step to moving on...

Either way, she needed his help. She couldn't go back to their house—she would never think of it as hers, even if it was in her name—alone. She couldn't face it by herself. And she *had* to face it. She had spent long enough grieving for the family she was sure she would never have now. She knew the loss of her son would stay with her for ever, but she was determined to make something out of her life. To prove that she would have been a worthy mother...

'Do you want to talk about how everything will work?' Jordan asked, almost as though he knew that she'd been thinking too much and wanted to distract her.

'You mean how we'll plan the event?' she asked, and looked out of the window to the vineyards they were passing.

Stellenbosch had always felt like home to her, even when she hadn't had a home. The minute she had driven down the winding road that offered the most beautiful sights she had ever seen—the peaks that stood above fields and fields of produce, the kaleidoscope of colours that changed with every season—a piece had settled inside her. That had been the first time she had visited the Thomas Vineyard.

'That's part of it, of course. But I was speaking about all the details. Like where you're going to stay, for example.'

She sighed. She had told him that she would leave Greg's house that morning, and when she'd said it she'd thought it was the best way to force herself to face going back to their house. But her deal with Jordan meant that she could delay that a little longer, and immediately the ball in her chest unravelled.

Though that didn't mean she could stay at the farmhouse.

'I can still leave today.'

She could stay at a bed and breakfast, she thought, forcing herself to ignore the pain in her chest. She didn't need to be thinking about how leaving would sacrifice her only connection to Greg—to the memories of family and the love she'd never thought she deserved. She also didn't need to remember that she'd spent little time working since the accident, which meant her bank account was in a sorry state.

'You don't have to,' he said stiffly, and she turned to him.

'What do you mean?'

'It might make more sense for us to stay together.' Jordan's eyes were fixed on the road. 'We have six weeks to sort this event out. Being in the same space will make it a lot easier.'

There was Mr Logical again, she thought, and unexplained disappointment made her say, 'I can't stay in the house with you there, Jordan.'

She saw him frown. 'Why not?'

Because there's too big a part of me that wants to play house with you again, she realised.

'It's too complicated. This whole thing with us still being married…' Her head pounded at the knowledge and what it meant. 'It's a lot to deal with. It would probably be best if you and I lived separately.'

He didn't respond as he turned onto the gravel road that led to the house that would soon be theirs. She used the time to remind herself that she had been at a standstill for a year. She couldn't keep letting the tragedies in her life *or* her dreams for a family hold her back. It was time to move on, and living with Jordan—even if it *was* practical, considering her current financial situation—didn't seem to be the way she would do it.

But then she thought about the deal she had made with Jordan—about how he was going to help her sell all the things from their marriage if she helped him—and she began to wonder if living together and planning the event *was* the way she was going to move on.

As though he knew her thoughts, Jordan repeated, 'I think you should stay. We're planning an event that will happen in the next six weeks. We need to get your house and your car sold—things that might take a lot longer than six weeks—but we can start now. And we can definitely get everything in the house sold before then.'

Which should help her financial problems, she thought.

'Handling all of it will be a lot easier if we could do it from the same place,' he said again.

It made sense, she thought, but cautioned herself not to make a hasty decision.

'I'll think about it,' she said, even though the rational part of her told her she should say no. 'But I'll stay here until I've made a decision.'

'Okay,' he responded politely, and though she didn't look at him, she frowned at his acquiescence.

The Jordan she knew would have pushed or, worse, would have made the decision for her. Was he giving her space just so he'd get what he wanted? Or was it genuine? She couldn't decide, but he had pulled up in front of the house now, and her attention was drawn to the raindrops that had begun to fall lightly on the windshield.

They made a run for the front door.

'Where you'll be staying isn't the only thing we should talk about,' he said, once they were inside the house.

Mila turned to him when she'd taken off her coat. The light drizzle had sprinkled rain through his hair, and her fingers itched to dust the glittering droplets away.

Another reason I should stay away from you.

'Yes, I know.'

She moved to the living room and started putting wood in the fireplace. It had become a routine—a ritual, almost—

and it comforted her. Perhaps because it was so wonderfully normal—so far from what she'd grown up with. 'We need to talk about the event—about how we're going to plan something I did in six months in just over one.'

She saw a flicker in his eyes that suggested that wasn't what he was talking about. She supposed she had known that on some level. Which was why she had steered the conversation to safer ground. To protect herself. Now she just had to remember that for the entire time they spent together...

'Is it possible?' Jordan asked, watching Mila carefully. Something about her was different, and it wasn't only her appearance. Though as she sat curled on the couch opposite him—to be as far away from him as she could, he thought—the cup of tea she had left the room to make a few moments before in her hand, he could see that the old Mila was still there.

His heart throbbed as though it had been knocked, and he found himself yearning for something that belonged in the past. His present—*their* present—involved planning an event to save his family's vineyard. And his family no longer included the woman he had fallen so hard for, despite every logical part of him...no matter what his heart said.

'It's going to be difficult,' she conceded, distracting him from his thoughts.

'What do you think we should start with?' he asked, deciding that the only way he could focus on their business arrangement was by talking about business. But then she shifted, and the vanilla scent that clung to her drifted over to him. Suddenly he thought about how much he had missed it. About how often he'd thought he'd smelled it— had felt his heart racing at the thought that she'd come to find him—only to realise that it had been in his imagination...

'Well, the conditions of your father's will stipulate that we try to replicate the original Under the Stars event as much as possible. But, considering the season…' she looked out at the dreary weather '…I'm not sure how successful that will be.'

As she spoke she ran a finger around the rim of her cup. It was a habit for her—one she reverted to when she was deep in thought. Once, when he'd teased her about it, she'd told him that one of her foster mothers had hated it when she'd done it. The woman had told her that she was inviting bacteria, and that Mila shouldn't think they would take her to the doctor if she got sick.

It was one of the rare pieces of information she had offered him about her childhood, and she had meant for him to be amused by it. But instead it had alerted him to the difficulty of her past. Since he knew how that felt, he had never pushed her for more information.

'I don't think he thought this through,' he said, to stop his thoughts from dwelling further, but only succeeding in shifting them to his father.

'No, I don't think so either,' she agreed. 'He meant well, but in his head this idea was romanticised. We would do an event together, just like the one where we met, and it would remind us of how we felt that first night.'

The dreamy look on her face made his heart accelerate, and for the first time Jordan wondered if his father had been right. But nostalgia wasn't enough to save a broken relationship.

'And then he'd have facilitated our reunion through his death,' she ended, the expression he'd seen only moments before replaced by sadness.

His heart ached. 'He always said he wanted his death to mean something.'

'Especially after your mother's,' she said softy.

His eyes lifted to hers, and the sympathy he saw there stiffened his spine. 'Maybe.'

He didn't speak about his mother's death. He had been five when it had happened and he had spent most of his life till then watching her suffer. Because she hadn't done anything about her cancer soon enough. Because she had chosen *him*.

The memory made him think about whether his father *had* designed his will as a punishment for Jordan. To get justice, perhaps, for the fact that Greg had always blamed Jordan for her death. Something Jordan had only found out years after his mother had passed away. It would be the perfect way for his father to make his death 'mean something,' Jordan thought, especially since Greg had made his will *after* Jordan had left to cope with the loss of his son, of his wife. It was something he knew Greg hadn't approved of, despite the fact that although Greg had been there physically, in all the ways that had mattered, Greg had done the same after Jordan's mother had died…

Jordan lifted his eyes and saw that Mila was watching him in that way she had that always made him think she saw through him. He only relaxed when she averted her gaze.

'We have six weeks to do this—which means that the event is going to happen in winter. And this rain suggests that the weather has already made a turn for the worst.'

He was grateful for the change in subject. 'It also means that the grounds in the amphitheatre won't be suitable for the public.'

'Actually, I don't think that will be a problem. When your father got sick, he couldn't take care of the vineyard as well as he'd used to. So we minimised operations. We closed up the amphitheatre since we wouldn't be using it, and concentrated our efforts on the wine.'

'How did you do that? The area is huge.'

She shrugged. 'I had a connection with a tent and marquee supplier, and he designed one for us. I'll take you to see it tomorrow, if you like…' She trailed off. 'You know, I could probably get him to customise the design so that the top of the marquee is clear. That way the event would still be in the amphitheatre—'

'And still be under the stars,' he finished for her.

'Why do you look so surprised?'

'I'm just…' He was just *what*? Surprised to see her throw herself into a task like this when he couldn't remember the last time she had shown interest in anything?

'I'm good at my job, Jordan,' she said flatly when he didn't continue.

'I wasn't saying that you weren't,' he replied.

The look she shot him burned through him, and he found himself bristling in response. It simmered when he saw a slight flicker in her eyes that made her look almost vulnerable, and he wondered why he couldn't tell what had caused her reaction. He should know her well enough to be able to… Except he didn't, he realised in shock.

'I'll draw up a list of everything that needs to be done and give you a copy once I have,' she said tightly as she stood, and Jordan could see that tension straightened her spine. 'We can discuss things then.'

She walked to the door and grabbed her coat.

'Where are you going?' he demanded, anger replacing the shock of only a moment ago.

'Out,' she replied, and slammed the door on her way out, leaving him speechless.

The woman who had walked out through that door—who had got angry at nothing and left before they could deal with it—was *not* the woman he had married. *Or was she?* a voice mocked him, and briefly he wondered if he was angry at Mila for seemingly acting out of character, or at himself for not knowing his wife well enough to be able to tell.

The thought spurred his feet forward, and he was out the door before she could get far.

'Mila! Mila, wait!'

Her steps faltered, but she didn't turn back. He stopped with enough distance between them that she wouldn't feel crowded, but so she could still hear him.

'Why are you upset?'

She turned and pulled her coat tight around her, determination lining her features. 'I didn't like that you looked surprised about me being good at my job.'

It took him a moment to process her words—especially since he was surprised that she had actually chosen to answer him.

'I wasn't surprised that you're good at your job. I *know* you are.' He watched her, hoping for some indication that she believed his words, but her face was carefully blank. 'You took the spark of an idea I had with the first Under the Stars event and turned it into something I'd never dreamed of. *And* you made it a success. Of course you're good at your job.'

'I *did* do all of that,' she said after a moment. 'I *am* good at my job.'

'Yes, you are,' he reiterated, and thought about the vulnerability he'd thought he'd seen in her eyes earlier. 'But are you trying to convince me of that, or yourself?'

She folded her arms in front of her—but not before he saw her wince. She *was* trying to convince herself, he thought, and wondered how she could even doubt it.

'Don't pretend like you know me.'

Because he was suddenly worried that it was true and he *didn't* know her, anger stirred inside him again. 'It goes both ways, Mila.'

'What?'

'You assumed that I thought poorly of you because of one look you misinterpreted. If you knew who *I* was, then you would have known that couldn't be true.'

'Then tell me the real reason for your surprise.'

Her arms fell to her sides and he watched her straighten her shoulders. As if she was preparing for battle, he thought. But he couldn't answer her question. It would open the door that both of them seemed happy to keep closed—the one that protected them from their past.

When he didn't respond, she shook her head. 'That's what I thought.' She sighed. 'You know, maybe I jumped to the conclusion that you thought I wasn't good at my job because you never told me that I was. But then, we didn't have that kind of relationship, did we?'

She walked away, leaving him wondering what kind of relationship they *had* had.

CHAPTER FOUR

MILA WALKED DOWN the gravel road to the amphitheatre, Jordan beside her, and some of her tension eased. It was home, she thought as she looked at the road shaded by trees, their leaves brown and gold as though they didn't know whether to mourn or celebrate the coming winter. The grass around them had begun to lose its colour, too, though there were still patches that seemed to be fighting to remain as green as in spring.

When she made it through the trees she was standing at the top of a slope that led to the vineyard on the one side, and to the amphitheatre on the other. She had sombrely told Jordan that she would take him there that morning, and thought she needed to get over herself. She'd spent most of her time since their argument thinking about why she'd been upset—the *real* reason, not the one she had made up.

Because as soon as she'd given herself time to think it through—with Jordan's words still in her head—she'd realised her reaction the previous day *had* been because *she* was doubting her skills. It wasn't just about her job either. Jordan's return had reminded her of her failures—at being a wife. At being a mother.

Her heart hiccupped and she laid a hand over her chest, hoping to comfort herself.

Losing her baby when she was barely six months pregnant had only succeeded in amplifying her insecurities. Insecurities that stemmed from growing up without hearing anyone tell her she was good at something—at anything. She could see now that it had led to her believing that she wasn't good *enough*. Certainly not for Jordan when she'd first met him, since he'd had everything she hadn't had in her childhood.

Love, a family, a home.

A little voice had reminded her of that throughout their marriage. It was part of the reason she wished Jordan had told her he was happy with her. Or that he was proud of her. Or that she was a good wife.

But then, they'd never shared things like that during their brief marriage. She had just accepted what he'd said because she'd been afraid to speak up in case it upset him. She hadn't wanted to risk him realising that their relationship was too good to be true. That she wasn't the right person for him.

Now she saw no point in keeping her thoughts to herself—he'd realised all that anyway. And perhaps that had been the reason for Jordan's surprise—she was no longer meek Mila who didn't speak her mind. What had that got her? Nothing but a heart broken by the loss of her husband and her child.

'Nothing beats this view,' Jordan said quietly from beside her, and her heart pounded when she turned and saw him looking at her. But then he nodded towards the vineyard, and she mentally kicked herself. *Of course* he wasn't talking about her—especially since things between them were still tense.

She turned her attention to the vineyard to hide her embarrassment at thinking such a silly thing, and took in the clash of different shades of red and brown. Fields of the colours together was a picture she would never forget—even when it was years in the future and she no longer had any reason to be a part of the Thomas Vineyard. She could see the dam just beyond the fields, large and beautiful, and behind it the hills that made the vineyard look surreal.

Walking the vineyard with him felt like old times. Despite how difficult things were with them now, when they had walked past the chapel where they'd got married, Mila's heart had longed for the people they'd been then. It didn't help that the weather had turned from the rain of the previous day to bright sunshine. It reminded her of her wedding day, almost two years ago.

It had been cold, true to the season, but the sun had been shining just as it was today, as though the gods had approved their union. A fanciful thought, she realised now, indicative of the person she had been then. The person who had fallen in love at first sight and married three months later.

The fact that their wedding anniversary was a few weeks away pained her, and she tried to ignore it. Her mind reminded her that she and Jordan hadn't been together long enough—physically or emotionally—for them to celebrate their *first* anniversary. Now, on their second, they'd be together physically, but emotionally…

'It's more beautiful than I remember,' he said, and she almost smiled at the sincerity in his voice.

'It's become a bit like home to me in the past year,' she murmured, deep in thought, and then her stomach dropped when she realised what she had said. 'Because of Greg,' she added hurriedly, hoping it would make her words seem less like a revelation.

He didn't answer her, and when she looked over he had a blank expression on his face. How was it possible that the tension between them could become worse? she wondered, her insides twisting.

'I have memories of every part of this place,' he said, his face pensive now. 'This is where I last saw my mother. This is where my father raised me.'

Mila frowned. Had he just willingly mentioned his mother? His reaction the previous night when she'd said something about her had been what Mila was used to. A quick brush-off, an unwillingness to respond. She had wanted to know about his mother so badly when they were dating, when they were married, but she'd never had the nerve to push beyond Jordan's resistance. Since she didn't really want to offer information to him either, she'd convinced herself that it didn't matter. That one day, while they watched their children play in front of the house, he would tell her about the woman who had died when he was five, and she would hold his hand and tell him that it was okay.

But that day would never come now.

Jordan turned towards the amphitheatre and she followed him, and then she stopped, her eyes widening when she realised what going to the amphitheatre meant. Why hadn't she realised this earlier, she thought in panic, when she could have done something about it? *Before* she had suggested it, for heaven's sake!

'Are you coming?' Jordan asked her, and she exhaled shakily, forced her legs to move and her mouth to respond.

'Yes…yes, I am.'

'This is great,' Jordan said when he saw the white marquee that covered the amphitheatre. The edges were pinned down between the trees that surrounded the area, and it had done its job for the most part, he noted. Though water ran down the steps, the seats and the stage were still dry, along with most of the ground. It would do for their event, he thought.

'Whose idea was it to do this? It was smart.'

He took the steps as he asked the question, and was about halfway down when he realised Mila hadn't answered him. Nor could he hear her following. When he turned back to look up at her his heart raced at her expression. Her face was white—and so was the hand that clung to the railing that ran down the middle of the stairs. He could see her chest heave—in, out…in, out—and his first instinct was to run to her side and make sure that she was okay.

But somewhere at the back of his mind he realised what was happening, and a picture of her at the bottom of the stairs at their old house, lying deadly still, flashed through his mind.

This is what you left behind, a voice told him, and a ball of grief and guilt drop in his stomach.

Careful to keep his expression blank, even as his heart thrummed, he walked up to her and slid an arm around her waist. She didn't look at him, and he could feel her resistance, so he waited until her hand finally gripped the back of his jacket. Slowly they made their way down to the bottom of the stairs, and with each step the ball of emotion grew inside him.

'Thank you,' she said through tight lips when they got to the bottom, but he could hear the shakiness in her voice—felt it in her body before she stepped back from him.

'Since the accident?' he asked.

She lifted her eyes briefly, and then lowered them again as she straightened her shoulders. 'Yeah. It's not impossible to do. It just takes longer.'

He didn't know what to say. How could he say anything at all? he wondered with disgust. He knew the loss of their son had hurt them both—Jordan lived with it every day, no matter where he was. Every moment of his life since that day still held glimpses of what it would have been like if his son had been alive—images of them as a family in the home where he and Mila used to live crushed his heart each time.

But the reality was that he *wasn't* a father. And, yes,

he had complicated emotions about it—dashed hopes, a broken heart—but his body was fine. Though his heart pained, he could go down a flight of stairs without thinking about the fall that had led to a placental abruption and a premature baby who couldn't survive outside the womb. *His* mind, though still dimmed by grief, wasn't addled by a fear of stairs.

Seeing Mila's reality, seeing the effect losing their baby had had on her, gutted him. The shame and guilt he already felt about the loss of their child pierced him. And the anger—the tension Jordan felt at the fact that Mila hadn't turned to him—flamed inside him.

'Why didn't you tell me?'

She slanted a look at him. 'About…?'

She was giving him a chance to back down, he thought briefly, but he wouldn't do it.

'About the stairs. Is there anything else you're still struggling with?'

'That isn't your business any more, Jordan,' she replied easily, though he could tell that the conversation was anything but easy for her.

'You're my *wife*, Mila.' It didn't matter to him that they had both signed divorce papers and had only found out they were still married the previous day. 'I have a right to know.'

'No, you don't,' she said tersely. 'You gave up that right when you walked out. When you sent me divorce papers. When you didn't come home.' There was a brief pause. 'I'm your wife in name only.'

'You asked me to leave.'

'You should have known you needed to stay!' she shot back, and hissed out a breath.

His eyes widened at the show of temper and his heart quickened at the sight of her cheeks flushed with anger. She still took his breath away, he thought vaguely, and then his mind focused on her words.

'Is that what you really wanted?' he asked softly.

She pursed her lips. 'I don't want to talk about this, Jordan. What's done is done.'

'Clearly it isn't done. Tell me,' he begged. It had suddenly become imperative for him to know what he had walked away from. And whether she had wanted him to walk away at all.

'You made a choice to leave, Jordan.'

She looked up at him, her eyes piercing him with their fire. It wasn't a description he would have used of her before. And perhaps before he wouldn't have found it quite as alluring. But it suited her, he thought.

'We all have to live with the decisions we made then. For now, we need to focus on getting this event done.'

His jaw clenched and tension flowed through his body with his blood. She made it seem as though he had left easily—as though he had *wanted* to leave.

'I left because you asked me to. Why are you punishing me for it?'

She watched him steadily, and for a brief moment, he thought he saw her soften. But it was gone before he was sure, and then she answered him in a low voice.

'You're fooling yourself if you think you left because I asked you to.' She stopped, as though considering her words, and then continued, 'You left because you couldn't handle my grief.'

He felt his blood drain. 'Did my father tell you that?'

Mila frowned. 'Why would you think that?'

Because that was exactly what his father had accused him of in one of their last conversations before he'd left, Jordan thought in shock. After Jordan had told Greg he was leaving—that Mila had asked him to and that he was going to Johannesburg to focus on getting their research institute started—his father had accused him of leaving because Mila's suffering had reminded Jordan of his mother's suffering. And that that meant Jordan was in the same position that his father had been in.

He had ignored the words when his father had said them—had believed the two situations had nothing in common—and had refused to think about it afterwards. But hearing those words come from Mila now brought the memory into sharp focus. But, just as he had then, Jordan shut down his thoughts and feelings about it.

'Do you think your contact would actually be able to make a customised marquee?'

He saw her blink, saw her adjust to his abrupt change in topic. She opened her mouth and closed it again, and then answered.

'Yes, I think he would.'

Her voice was polite. No, he thought, *controlled*.

'I think the more appropriate question would be if he'd be able to do it in such a short period of time.'

She took her phone out and started typing, changing the tone of their conversation. The tension was still there though, he realised, noting the stiff movement of her fingers.

'If he *is* able to do it we'll have solved one of the major problems of this event.'

'I'm sure the others won't be quite as bad,' he said, and walked up the steps to the stage.

He needed space from her, even though she was standing a far enough distance away that her proximity shouldn't have bothered him. The stage was clear of the usual clutter events brought, he saw, with only the large white screen used for movies behind him.

'It's not going to be easy,' she warned. 'We'll have to see if the same food vendors are available, *and* we'll have to find out if Karen can perform...' She trailed off, as though the thought frightened her, and he felt the release of the tension in him at the memory of Mila dealing with the teenage singer.

'Won't *that* be fun for you?'

'I can't wait,' she said wryly. 'We might have to consider someone else if she isn't available. After that, the hardest part is going to be getting people to come. Karen—or whoever we get to perform—will have a huge impact on that, but it's still going to be a challenge.'

'Social media will help,' he said, and walked down the stairs to where she stood. She was taking pictures, and he realised that with the marquee the space was different from what she'd worked with before. 'We can have Karen post something closer to the time. It could even be a pop-up concert.'

'That won't work,' she disagreed. 'Doing that would put us at risk of overcrowding or riots. Of course we can have her post about the event, but we need to sell tickets. That's the only way we can know how many people to expect.'

If he'd thought she wouldn't be insulted by it, he would have complimented her on her professional knowledge. But he'd learned his lesson the previous evening. He hadn't been around before to see her in action, but his father had complimented her often enough. Now Jordan could see why.

'Was it hard work the first time?'

She glanced over at him. 'Yes, but for different reasons. We had to start from scratch then. Design it, figure out what would work, what wouldn't. Now we don't have those problems, but we're working from a blueprint. Which means we're confined. It also puts us at risk of making a loss.'

'Well, regardless of that, we're going to have to plan this.' He stuck his hands into the pockets of his jacket. 'Maybe it's a good thing I wasn't here the first time.'

'Marketing wine in American restaurants does sound more exciting,' she said easily, and his heart knocked at hearing her attempt something remarkably close to banter. Perhaps they should stick to work, he thought.

'Well, seven of the ten restaurants I visited now carry our wines, so I *was* working. Besides, if I'd been here, we probably would have been married a lot earlier—' He broke off, cursing himself for not thinking. He almost saw Mila's walls go up again.

'This event is going to take a lot of work,' she said instead of addressing his slip. 'I might have to give Lulu a call...'

Her face had tightened, and Jordan wondered what he didn't know about Mila's only real friendship.

'Have you spoken to her recently?' he asked, watching the emotions play over her face.

'Now and then,' she answered him. 'Not nearly as often as I should have.'

The admission came as a surprise to him—and to her, too, it seemed.

'I think we've seen all we need to here.' she said quickly. 'The stairs...they're easier going up.'

It was a clear sign that she didn't want any help from him, and he had to clench his fists at his sides to keep himself from doing just that as he watched her painstakingly climb the stairs.

Why couldn't she just ask for help? he thought irritably, and then stilled when a voice asked him why she should need to ask at all.

CHAPTER FIVE

MILA HEARD THE door to the house slam and closed her eyes. Clearly Jordan hadn't returned from their trip to the amphitheatre in a good mood. Not that *she* was feeling particularly cheerful herself. She had let him bait her into lashing out, into revealing things she didn't want him to know.

It was only because she had been feeling particularly vulnerable after hesitating at those stairs. She had always hated that reminder of her accident—any reminder, really. But as she had stood in front of those steps, her heart in her throat, she had hated that the most. Because every time she thought she would be able to take a step she was reminded of the sensation of tumbling to the ground. Pain would flash through her at the memory of lying at the bottom of the steps, her breathing staggered, waiting for someone to help her.

She blamed that feeling for the accusation she had hurled at Jordan from nowhere earlier. She had never intended letting that slip—the *real* reason she thought he'd left—but her tongue no longer seemed to obey the 'think before you speak' rule she had always played by.

Heaven knew she was tired of taking all the blame for him leaving—yes, she *had* asked him for space, but that had been said in grief, in pain. She hadn't meant it, but when he'd packed his bags she hadn't been able to bring herself to ask him to stay. She had wanted him to—every fibre in her being had urged her to stop him—but she had also wanted him to *want* to stay. She had wanted him to refuse to go, to tell her that he needed her, to acknowledge that they needed *each other* to get through the heartbreak of losing their son.

But he hadn't, and she had been forced to admit to herself that their make-believe life—the one where they were playing at being a happy family and where she was a worthy wife—was never *really* going to be her life. Jordan hadn't had any reason to be with her before she had lost their baby, so why would he bother with her now, when she'd proved that she wasn't capable? When she'd proved that she was broken, especially during her grieving?

He must believe that, too, or he would never have asked her if Greg had told her that. Jordan must have said it to Greg at some point, in confidence, and the stunned expression she'd seen on his face must have been because Jordan had thought Greg had broken his confidence…

Hurt beat at her heart, but she set her shaking hands down on the lists of the things she needed to do and the notes from the phone calls she had made at the kitchen counter.

'Hey,' he said, and the deep voice made her heart jump in the same way it had when they'd first met.

She turned and saw the amicable expression on his face. Had she been mistaken about his mood? Perhaps not, she thought as she looked in his eyes.

'Hi,' she replied, determined not to let her emotions get in the way of amicability. If he could do it, so could she. 'You were gone for a while.'

'Yeah, I bumped into Frank and we talked about the vineyard. I got us some food, too.'

She could tell from his voice that something was bothering him, and while her heart wanted to ask him about it, her head told her to keep to the game they seemed to be playing.

'That was nice of you,' she said measuredly, and took the pizza from him.

It had already gone cold, she saw when she opened the boxes, making her wonder if he'd gone somewhere else after picking the food up. But she was distracted when she saw he had got her favourite pizza, and she had to force herself not to be swayed by something as simple as that that only indicated his memory.

'Frank couldn't have told you all that much,' she said, and took out two oven trays to warm the pizza on. 'You two spoke about the place quite often while you were gone.'

'Did he tell you that?'

She looked back at him, and was suddenly struck by how attractive he was. He'd taken off the red winter jacket he had on that morning, and now she was being treated to the sight of the muscles he sported almost lazily under his long-sleeved top. Even his light blue jeans highlighted the strength of his lower body.

She swallowed, and told herself to answer him instead of staring like a fool. 'Frank's mentioned it, yes. But he told your dad first, and Greg told me. I think he thought that if I knew you'd kept in touch, *I'd* get in touch with you.' She closed her eyes briefly as soon as she realised she'd said it. It was being in this kitchen with him, she thought, and desperately changed the topic. 'Do you want to eat now?'

'I'd like to take a shower first, but that shouldn't take too long.'

There was a pause, almost as if Jordan had wanted to say something else and then decided not to. She glanced at him and saw an unreadable expression on his face. That in itself told her something was bothering him, but still she refused to ask him. That wasn't supposed to be her job any more.

'This is different,' he said, abruptly changing the topic.

She followed his gaze and for the first time since Jordan had first brought her to his father's house she saw the brown cupboards and cream countertops. But since that was the part of the kitchen that *hadn't* changed, she knew he was referring to her new additions.

'I thought a little colour might cheer the place up.' She didn't add that she'd hoped it would cheer his father up, as well. Greg had always been a man of a few words, and often she'd thought that it was because of sadness. He hadn't ever spoken much about his wife—like father, like son—but when he had she'd seen that Greg had loved and missed her. And then in his ill health and missing Jordan, his sadness had become grumpiness and sometimes even meanness.

Jordan was watching her when she looked up, a complicated expression on his face, and she wondered if he realised what she hadn't said after all.

'I knew it would be something like that,' he said, and it sounded forced. 'I would never have pegged Dad as a fuchsia kind of guy.' He nodded his head to the curtains and matching utensils that were scattered across the counters.

She smiled a little, felt her guard ease a touch. 'I think he grew fond of it after a while. Though at the beginning he made all sorts of noises.' The smile widened. 'And then he started seeing how the colour lightened up the place, and how the art helped me, and he got much better then.'

The walls were covered with her mosaic artwork—something her doctor had once suggested she do to keep herself busy during a postaccident, postbaby check-up—and she was quite proud of it. It made her remember the simple things she had taken pleasure in before her life had been destroyed.

'How did it help you?'

He said the words so quietly that at first she didn't

register what he'd asked. And then she realised that her guard was down, and her shoulders stiffened in response. *It shouldn't be this easy to slip up in front of him*, she thought. Not when slipping up meant talking to him about the time she was trying to move on from. Not when it meant him prodding her about it *again*.

'It just gave me something to keep busy with while I recovered,' she said firmly, and then turned to put the oven on and slide the trays with the pizzas into it.

She took her time with it, and it didn't take long for Jordan to get the picture. After a few moments, she heard the shower being turned on and she sighed with relief.

He was getting under her skin, she thought. He had always been able to do that to her, from the moment she had first taken that glass of wine from him two years ago. She'd forgotten all her insecurities then—had slipped into those enticing eyes of his and had believed that they would last, that she could be someone he wanted. Someone he needed.

The past didn't matter now, she thought, checking the pizzas. She had been young and completely in love then. Now she knew better. She could protect herself now—she *would* protect herself, regardless of how easy it seemed to be to slip up in front of him. Whether it was out of anger, or out of familiarity, she would control it.

A sharp pain snapped her from her thoughts, and she looked down to see an angry welt spread across her hand where she had reached for the oven tray without a mitt. She rolled her eyes as she ran the hand under cold water, blaming her silly thoughts for distracting her, but grateful that she had only used one hand instead of both, as she usually did.

Once the pain had subsided to a throb, she saw the welt was threatening to blister and rushed to the bathroom to get the first-aid kit and the gel she knew would soothe the burn.

She realised too late that Jordan was still in there, and barely had the chance to move back before the door opened. A cloud of steam followed a muscular body precariously covered by her white-and-pink towel out of the room.

'I'm so sorry! I was just—' She felt her face redden as she tried to avert her eyes from Jordan's half-naked body.

Except every time she tried, her eyes moved back to him of their own accord. She had been right when she'd thought his body was more muscular than she remembered. His broad shoulders were more defined, the muscles in his chest and abs sculpted so perfectly that she wondered if it were possible for her insides to burn, as well. Then she cleared her throat and told herself that she had seen him like this before. There was no reason to panic.

She took a deep breath. 'I'm sorry, I just need to get the first-aid kit.' She gestured to her hand and was quite proud of the way she'd managed to put words together in the calm tone her voice had taken.

Which all went out the window when he immediately walked to her and took her hand in his.

'What happened?'

'I…I burned myself.' Her mind was whirling at the feel of her hand in his, at the contact between them—however minimal. But her heart was the problem—it was thumping at a rhythm she thought she couldn't possibly sustain, merely because of his proximity.

'Still a clumsy cook, I see. Even when you're just heating pizza,' he said softly, and then he led her into the bathroom.

She had no choice but to stand there as he reached for the first-aid kit. He pulled out the soothing gel and spread it gently over her burn, and the heat went from her hand to the rest of her. His body was still warm from the shower, and she could smell his body wash—the same kind he'd used before they had broken up. The same kind that had thrilled her each time she had smelled it.

And suddenly her heart and her body longed for him with an intensity that had her backing away from him.

'It's fine, thanks. I'll finish this up in the kitchen.' She grabbed the kit and almost ran back to the kitchen, not caring if he saw.

All she cared about was putting some distance between them so she could try and convince herself that he *wasn't* affecting her.

'Did you manage to call Lulu?' Jordan asked Mila when he'd finally got his body back under control.

He hadn't expected her to react like that after seeing him in a towel. The look she had given him before she had bolted had been filled with the desire that had marked their entire relationship, and his body had acted accordingly. But that was over now, he told himself, and he was making an effort to forget it. Except that all of a sudden he was noticing the curve of her neck, the faint blush of her cheeks...

'I did,' she replied, her voice husky, and he thought that maybe she wasn't as recovered as she pretended to be. 'She's coming over to the house tomorrow.'

Something in her voice made him forget about the curls that had escaped the clip she'd tied her hair back with. He looked up, saw the shaky hands that handed him his pizza and a glass of wine, and something pulled inside him.

'You're worried.'

'About seeing her?' She picked up her glass and plate, walking past him on her way to the lounge.

He followed, saw that she took one couch, and sat on the other. He didn't need another reason to be distracted by her. He watched as she broke a piece of pizza from the rest, but didn't lift it to her mouth.

'No, I think that's going to be fine,' she said, and lifted her head with a defiant smile.

But he could still see the uncertainty, and he knew that she was pretending. He just didn't know for whom.

'Do you really?'

'Yeah, of course. I mean, we've spoken in the last year.'

She was desperately trying to convince him—or perhaps again convince herself.

'Then why are you worried?' he asked again. 'And don't tell me you aren't because I can see that you are.'

'Honestly, it's nothing,' she replied, picking at her pizza, and he had to force himself not to be annoyed by her denials. He had to force himself not to push her just because he wanted to know. Because he wanted to help.

So he didn't answer her, biting from a slice of pizza that he didn't taste, chewing mechanically, waiting for her to speak. Her hands grew busier, and soon there was a pile of cheese on her plate and her pizza base was nearly bare. Still, he waited, because he could see it unnerved her, and perhaps it would do so enough that she would open up to him.

'I have to apologise.'

The words came out of nowhere, and Jordan felt a short moment of pride that his patience—a trait that maybe he needed more of—had paid off, before reacting to her words.

'Why?'

'I haven't…kept in touch with her like I should have. Not after the baby.'

She didn't look at him, and concern edged into his heart.

'You were in a difficult place.'

'And that's when you're supposed to *turn to* your friends, not push them away,' she said hotly, and then lifted a hand to her mouth as though she was surprised at her own words.

He could believe that, since it was the way he felt, too. Did she mean she shouldn't have pushed *him* away either?

'Maybe Lulu should have understood,' he replied carefully.

'Maybe,' she repeated. 'Maybe I expected her to.'

They were talking about the two of them, he knew, and yet he couldn't bring himself to speak plainly.

'You would have had to say it. How else would she have known?'

'Because she's my friend.'

You were my husband.

'She should have known.'

You should have stayed.

'People don't just know things, Mila,' he said with anger, the only emotion he was ready to accept. 'You have to tell them.'

'Because saying things means so much, right?' she replied calmly.

But he saw the ice in her eyes and he knew the calm was just a front.

'Like when you say things like "until death do us part"? That means you can never go back on it?' She raised her eyebrows, waiting for him to reply.

Just beneath his anger, he felt the guilt. When he had left he *had* gone back on his word. But he wouldn't have if she hadn't done it first.

'You said it, Mila. You have to turn to your friends when you need them, not push them away. *You* were the first one to go back on your word.'

Her eyes widened, and it seemed that for a moment the ice melted as a tear fell down her cheek. She wiped it away and stood.

'This was a mistake. Pretending we could do something as simple as having a meal together without getting into some kind of argument.' She slammed her plate onto the coffee table. 'Neither of us may be innocent in what happened between us, but don't for one moment think I went back on my word. *I* lost our baby. *My* body failed us. So when I asked for space I was racked with guilt. I was *devastated*. But you didn't even fight. You left like it was the easiest decision you ever made.'

'It was the *hardest* decision I ever made,' he shot back, setting his plate next to hers and standing, too, his body riddled with tension, with emotion. 'But it was better for me to focus on my work, on something I could control.' He frowned at the unexpected admission, and shook his head. 'It was the best decision, Mila.'

'For who, Jordan? You or me?'

She wiped at another tear and it pierced his heart.

'This is so silly. I'm going to bed. I'll see you in the morning.'

He couldn't bring himself to ask her to stay—knew that if he did he needed to say something other than the accusations that were coursing through his mind.

When he heard her bedroom door close he flopped down on the couch, thinking about her words. She'd wanted him to stay. The realisation was a blow to his heart that he didn't know he could recover from, and the niggling in the back of his mind—the niggle that had always made him doubt his decision to leave—finally gained ground.

He *had* believed that he was doing the right thing for her. But her words now made him wonder if it had been only for her, or for him, too. His own words seemed to prove that it had.

He thought about how relieved he had been to focus on something he could control, to focus on his work. Unlike the day when Mila had fallen and he'd had no choice but to sign the forms approving the emergency C-section. Unlike the subsequent loss of his son that he'd been unable to do anything about, just as he had been able to do nothing about Mila's grief and suffering.

He froze as his father's accusation about why he'd left played back in his head. For the first time he considered it. If Jordan *had* left Cape Town—had left the wife who'd needed him—because it reminded him of his mother's illness, then Jordan *had* been running. When Mila had asked him for space to deal with the tragedy of losing their child he had run away. From her pain...from his. Because he hadn't wanted to see her suffer—emotionally or physically—as his mother had. Because he didn't want to watch on, helpless, as his father had.

Pain stabbed through him and he rested his head in his hands. Were those the *real* reasons he had left?

CHAPTER SIX

MILA WOULD HAVE liked a day to ignore the world and lick her wounds. To ignore the fact that the tension between her and Jordan was making her feel ill. She knew that she was causing it—that if she could just sit back and agree as she had during their marriage, she wouldn't be in the situation she was.

But words kept pouring from her mouth as if she had no control over them. Maybe because she'd realised control didn't *do* anything. Jordan had still left, even though she had done—and said—everything she'd *supposed* to. She had managed to alienate her best friend—her *only* friend—even though she had always gone out of her way to make sure everyone liked her. To make sure she would always have someone who wanted her.

But when the doorbell rang the next morning she knew that she wouldn't be able to wallow. Not only because she had to meet Lulu, but because the meeting was only a part of what she needed to do for the event.

She'd made some progress—Karen's manager had told her that he would run the event by the singer and confirm after that. Her marquee contact had agreed to the customised design, his complaints about the short timeline quelled by the generous amount of money she'd offered. And on her to-do list that day was getting in touch with the food vendors and checking their availability for the next month. That and Karen would determine the date of the event, and once that was confirmed she would be able to start the marketing process.

Before she could get to that list, though, she needed to face Lulu.

Her hands were shaking as she made her way to the front door. She took a deep breath before she opened it, and then she smiled.

'Hi!' she said, and her eyes swept over Lulu.

Her first thought was that Lulu hadn't changed all that much. Her face was still oval shaped, her hair cut close to her head. Her brown skin was smooth, her light brown eyes careful as she looked at Mila. Her second thought was that none of that mattered when there was something massive that *had* changed.

'You're pregnant…' Mila said through frozen lips, and her heart sped up. Her breath threatened to speed up, too, but she saw the reserve in Lulu's eyes change to concern and forced herself to control it.

It was just one of those annoying reactions she'd had since losing her baby—like the stairs. She was strong enough to deal with the reaction her body had to seeing Lulu pregnant. Strong enough for the emotional one, too. So she ignored the heartache, the emptiness, and clung to the genuine excitement she felt for her friend.

'Congratulations!'

She pulled Lulu into a hug, ignoring the distance that had grown between them since her fall. She also ignored the way the swell of Lulu's belly made her feel incredibly empty.

'How far along are you?'

Lulu squeezed Mila quickly and then pulled back. The concern still gleaming in Lulu's eyes was almost eclipsed by the reserve that had now returned. 'Thank you. I'm twenty-eight weeks. I wasn't sure if I should come because of…'

Her voice grew softer as she spoke, and Mila knew exactly what Lulu was saying.

'Well, I'm glad you came. Please come inside.'

Lulu walked past her and Mila closed her eyes for a second. Lulu had kept her pregnancy from Mila for more than six months because she had been afraid of the way Mila would react. What did that say about her? she thought, and her heart felt bruised at the knowledge. She had never meant for her tragedy to keep her friend from telling her the happy news. It meant Mila had more to atone for than she'd originally thought.

'Is there anything I can get you? Some tea or coffee?'

'Um…no, thank you. I can't stay too long,' Lulu said, and Mila realised that she wouldn't have time to beat around the bush.

She watched Lulu gingerly lower herself onto one of the couches, and briefly thought that she remembered that perfectly. But she shook her head and decided she wasn't going to go down that path.

Instead, she spoke. 'Look, I know things between us aren't like they used to be. Our work has suffered because of…everything that happened to me…and now that I know you're pregnant I feel even worse about not taking on more so we could get commission—'

'I'm not interested in our work, Mila,' Lulu interrupted, her pretty face tense. 'Our *friendship* has suffered.'

Hearing Lulu say that made Mila feel worse. 'I know. I…I should have called.'

'You should have,' Lulu agreed. 'And you shouldn't have pushed me away at all. We've been friends for almost a decade.'

'I know,' Mila said again, and felt herself dangerously close to tears. It was almost the same conversation she had

had with Jordan the previous night. And it was time she admitted the truth of it to herself.

'I just...' She stopped. Took a breath. Tried again. 'I couldn't deal with it. I didn't want people around me who would remind me of the things I'd failed at.'

Lulu didn't respond, and Mila didn't look up to see what her friend's face might tell her. She didn't deserve the benefit of the doubt, she thought harshly.

'How would Jordan and I have done that?' Lulu asked finally, with a slight hitch to her voice that told Mila she was hurt. Her heart panged.

'I wasn't a good enough wife or a good enough mother, Lulu. Can't you see that?' Mila was suddenly desperate to make her understand. 'I should have taken it easy, like Jordan asked me to...' She faltered, but then continued, 'I didn't want Jordan around to remind me of how I had failed.'

'Even if that made sense—which it absolutely does not—why did you push *me* away? I wanted to be there for you.'

A trickle of heat ran down Mila's face. 'I know you did. But I didn't deserve someone around who wanted me to feel better about myself.'

'Oh, Mila...'

Lulu walked to where she was standing and pulled Mila into her arms. On autopilot, Mila returned the hug, too busy thinking about what she had just revealed to her friend—to herself—to be really present in the moment.

'You deserve everything. Happiness...love.' Lulu pulled back, her eyes teary. 'You *are* good enough. You just need to give yourself permission to believe that.'

Though she wanted to, Mila didn't waste her breath on asking how she could do that.

'I'm a mess,' Lulu said suddenly, wiping at her eyes. 'Pregnancy hormones are *very* real.'

'Yes, they are,' Mila replied, smiling, but then the smile faded. 'I'm sorry about everything, Lulu. I shouldn't have… Well, I should have let you be my friend.'

'Yeah, you should have.' Lulu watched her for a moment. 'Friends are *there* for one another, Mila. I don't know how after almost ten years you still don't know I'm not going anywhere.'

Because for almost double that time I didn't have anyone to show me what that meant.

But she simply repeated, 'I'm sorry.'

'Apology accepted,' Lulu said, and then sat down again. 'So—tell me the other reason you called.'

A genuine smile crept across her lips. 'How did you know?'

Lulu gave her a look that had Mila's smile spreading.

'I want to start working again. Seriously, this time. Again, I'm sorry I let the ball drop with all the events we should have been doing—'

'Oh, I've been doing them anyway,' Lulu interrupted.

'You have?'

Lulu shrugged. 'It didn't seem right to let things fall apart just because you needed some time to recover. So I've been responding to emails from the website and I forwarded you some so that you'd have something to do.'

Another smile crept onto Mila's face. 'You've been *managing* me?'

Lulu let out a small laugh. 'Yes, maybe I have. But it's meant that your business hasn't fallen apart.'

'Like my personal life, you mean?' The smile on Mila's face faltered before she reminded herself that she needed to move on. 'Thank you, Lulu. That means more than you know.'

'It wasn't a big deal. All the details, including the financials are in this binder.' Lulu reached into her bag—puffing just a little, since it was on the floor—and handed

Mila the file. She took it, but didn't look inside. She trusted Lulu, and knew everything would be in order.

'I already have our next event,' Mila said, and explained about the event they needed to plan, the timeline and what she'd already done.

She absorbed Lulu's shock at the details, and was immensely grateful when Lulu didn't comment on the fact that she was doing the event with Jordan...or the fact that they were still married. At least that was what she thought.

But after they had spoken about the event in more detail, and just as Lulu was on her way out, her friend said, 'You know, I was with you when you met Jordan *and* when you found out you were pregnant. I saw how happy both of those things made you. How happy being a family made you. Maybe finding out you're still married is a sign for you to try again. A second chance.'

Mila ignored the hope, the fierce desire that sprang up inside her at Lulu's words. 'That's not going to happen.'

'Why not? You still love him. I know you do. And you've always wanted a family, so...' Lulu trailed off.

'That doesn't matter any more, Lulu,' Mila said firmly. 'I just want to move on with my life. Focus on my work. Be a good aunt.' She tried to smile.

Lulu shook her head. 'If that's what you really want, I'll support you. But just make sure it *is* what you really want. And do me a favour?'

Mila looked up at her.

'Give yourself permission to think about what you want *honestly.*'

'Yeah, I will,' Mila responded, and then took the time to enjoy having a moment with the only person who had made her feel loved since she was sixteen.

No, that's not true, she thought, and heard Lulu's words about Jordan, about family, echo in her head.

Was a second chance possible?

No. She clamped down on the thought. She couldn't go down that path. Not if she wanted to survive the task they'd been given.

CHAPTER SEVEN

JORDAN WAS RETURNING from his morning run just as Lulu came out through the front door.

'Hey!' she exclaimed when she saw him, and Jordan grinned, remembering how much fun she had always been.

She and Mila had been a bundle of light together. It bothered him to see how much of that light had dimmed in Mila, he thought as he saw her, too, and his smile faded.

'You look great, Lulu,' he said, focusing his attention on the pretty woman in front of him. And then he saw that she was pregnant and his heart clenched. He suddenly became aware of the way his lungs struggled for air, the way his shoulders felt heavy with grief. He cleared his throat. 'Congratulations.'

'Thanks,' she said softly, and he saw the flash of concern in her eyes.

Because he didn't need it, he forced out, 'You finally managed to find someone who deserves you?'

'Yeah—still my husband.'

She smiled at him kindly and then turned back to Mila, who was watching their exchange with wary eyes.

'Let me know how this afternoon goes. Like I said, most of the vendors will be there. And I'll track down those who aren't.'

'Thanks.' Mila's eyes warmed as she looked at Lulu. 'I'll see you soon.'

They both stood and watched as Lulu walked to her car, and waved at the sound of her horn. When she was no longer in sight Jordan felt his legs go weak, and he walked forward to the chair that stood next to the front door.

'Hey…' Mila crouched down in front of him, and as his heart palpitated and he fought for a steady breath, she took his hand and squeezed. 'Look at me. *Look* at me, Jordan,' she repeated when he didn't respond the first time.

He lifted his eyes.

'You're going to be okay. Just keep breathing.'

She repeated it until finally he could feel his heart falling back into the uncomfortable rhythm it always had around her. He pulled his hand away, embarrassed at his reaction. She stood up, but his hope that she would leave it alone and go inside faltered when she took the seat next to him.

'So it happens to you, too?'

He looked over at her, but she was staring out to where the trees lined the driveway.

'I don't know what you're talking about.'

'Your lungs feel like they don't work any more and your heart feels like it's beating to keep the entire world alive.'

She still wasn't looking at him and he eased. He didn't know why he had reacted to Lulu in that way. He had seen other pregnant women before. Why had this one been any different?

'It's happened to you?' he said hoarsely before he could stop himself.

'Yeah, plenty of times.' She paused. 'It almost happened with Lulu today.'

'Why didn't it?'

'I didn't want her to think I wasn't happy for her.'

He nodded. He understood that. And perhaps for the first time he found himself opening up the door he had locked his feelings about his son's death behind.

'I don't know why this is different.'

'Because she's someone you know. You care about her,' she answered softly. 'It hits harder when it's closer to home.'

'Yeah, probably,' he agreed, but something told him there was something else, as well.

'I know what I said, but it doesn't mean that you're not happy for her.'

He knew she was looking at him, so he nodded, but didn't respond. Pieces were settling in his mind from where he had locked them away. And then he spoke almost without realising it.

'You're right. When I saw Lulu there was a part of me that was happy for her before the doom and gloom set in.' He realised now where the reaction had come from, and for some reason felt comfortable with saying it out loud. He didn't care to examine why.

'And…?' Mila prompted softly.

'And I felt bad about it because when we found out *you* were pregnant…' he couldn't quite believe he was saying it '…I was terrified.'

'What?' The shocked tone of her voice had his heart accelerating.

'Of course, I was happy, too. But I was scared.'

'You never told me that.'

'You were so happy. I didn't want to spoil that.'

'I was scared, too, Jordan.' She let out a little laugh when he looked at her. 'I didn't know the first thing about being a mother. About being in a family.'

His mouth opened in surprise, but before she could see it, he asked, 'Why didn't you tell me?'

'Because *you* were so happy.' She smiled over at him. 'I didn't want you to think I couldn't do it.'

Something bothered him about her answer. It reminded

him of the time she'd thought he was telling her she wasn't good at her job.

'I never thought that,' he said. 'I knew you were going to be a wonderful mother.'

'You would have been a wonderful father, too.'

'Maybe,' he replied.

Or maybe he would have been as emotionally unavailable as his own father had been. He frowned, but didn't ponder it any more. Not when he was thinking about how nice it was sitting with her. The grief he'd felt at seeing the chairs where he'd spent so much time with his father for the first time after Greg's death had faded, and he knew it was because of Mila. She was the only person besides his father that he wanted to be there with.

The realisation unsettled him.

'Why were you scared?' She interrupted his thoughts. 'I mean, I know becoming a parent is scary in general, but was that the only thing?'

No, he thought, but he couldn't bring himself to say it when he was only just beginning to realise the effect his parents had had on him. Like the fact that part of his fear over becoming a parent was because of the way his father had treated him as a child—fear that he would turn out just like that.

'Yeah, that's all.'

He looked over at her and saw that she didn't believe him. Saw the flash of hurt in her eyes because of it, felt the nudge in his heart. And still he couldn't formulate the words.

'It didn't seem like things went poorly with Lulu,' he said instead, hoping for reprieve.

'They didn't,' she replied in a measured tone, and he closed his eyes when he realised he might just have undone the progress they'd made. In their *working* relationship, he clarified to himself.

'So, you guys are friends again?'

'We were never *not* friends, it seems. She's even been doing events for me while I've been…away.'

'That's great,' he said lamely, and felt helpless as the tension seeped back in between them. Silence came with it, giving him enough time to berate himself for spoiling the tentative truce that they'd been starting to forge.

But he couldn't tell Mila why he hadn't told her everything. She didn't know that side of his father, and he didn't want to taint her memories of Greg by telling her about the angry person his father had been in Jordan's youth. About the remnants of that time that had marred his relationship with his father right up to Greg's death. And now Jordan would never get the chance to fix it, or to make up for the past year when he hadn't been in touch…

'Lulu told me about a food fair that's happening this afternoon.' She broke the silence. 'It's at the Johnson High School in town—and most of the vendors who were there for the original Under the Stars are going to be there. I'm leaving in an hour. You can come, if you like.'

'I'd like that very much. I'll go get ready,' he said softly, grateful that she was still trying to be amicable despite his reluctance to open up to her.

As he headed to the bathroom for a shower he thought about it. He hadn't told her much about his childhood. Their relationship had been such a whirlwind at the beginning, and he'd fallen in love with her before he'd known what was happening. And then they'd got married, just three months after meeting—Jordan couldn't remember *ever* making such an impulsive decision—and Mila had fallen pregnant a few months after that.

Things had been so anchored in the future for them that they hadn't considered their past. They hadn't considered how the way they had grown up and how the people in their lives might have an impact on their relationship.

It made him realise that there were pieces between them that had been broken long before they'd lost their child. They hadn't even been able to share the way they'd felt about having a baby, for crying out loud! Each of them hadn't wanted to offend the other with their real feelings. That wasn't a healthy relationship.

The conversation they had just had was the first open one they'd had since they'd met—at least about their pasts. Did that mean things were changing for them? Did he *want* them to? He couldn't deny how being with Mila reminded him of how much he had felt for her. Maybe *still* felt for her...

No! He shut that train of thought down as the water hit his body. There was no point in exploring that now. His marriage was over in every way but legally. He would just focus on the event, on helping Mila, and then on running the vineyard in a way that would have made his parents proud.

He *would* focus on that, Jordan told himself when the hope inside him twinged.

There was no point in hoping after all that had happened between them.

CHAPTER EIGHT

SHE NEEDED TO THINK.

She couldn't turn to the usual activities that helped her to do so since they all involved staying in the house with Jordan, so Mila decided to go to the place that always did.

She grabbed her jacket and walked out into the sunshine that was growing rarer the closer it got to winter. Though the cold air reminded her of the season, it brought a beauty to the vineyard that was underappreciated. *Especially from here*, she thought, standing atop the slope that overlooked the vineyard, just as she had the previous day with Jordan.

It felt as if it were a lot longer than that. So much had happened since then. She'd done a lot for the event, yes, but she had also learned a lot about herself. About how much she wanted to look worthy, and how she had sacrificed her relationships in pursuit of that. About how much what people thought about her affected her behaviour—and how she couldn't bring herself to acknowledge that to herself, or to the people who cared about her.

Perhaps it was because there hadn't been many people who cared about her when she was growing up. She'd had ten different foster families over her years of being in foster care, and she couldn't remember even one of them fostering because they actually *cared* about the children they were looking after.

It meant that she desperately wanted to feel loved, to

feel needed. But it also meant that she didn't know how to turn to people when she needed *them*. Her conversation with Lulu had shown her that those were opposing desires, since the people she wanted to feel loved and needed by needed to feel that, too. And, since she struggled to do that, she only succeeded in pushing them away. It was a vicious cycle, and if she was being honest with herself, it was another reason the loss of her baby had broken her.

When she'd fallen pregnant so quickly, so unexpectedly, she had let herself hope for a family. She was going to have a child—someone who would need her without conditions. Someone who would know that she needed them, too, without her having to say it. That was what family was, wasn't it?

But she had also been scared that she wouldn't be a good mother. And of the way having a baby would change her life. In some ways it had been a remnant of her fears about marriage. Her pregnancy seemed to have sharpened them, causing her to worry that they'd moved too fast.

So she had clung to her job, working just as hard as she had before she'd fallen pregnant to prove to herself that things wouldn't change that much. She'd ignored Jordan's suggestion that she move more slowly, that she take time to adjust to the changes her body and their lives were going through.

And then she'd fallen down the stairs and her baby had been born prematurely, only surviving for seventeen minutes in the world Mila was supposed to have prepared him for. Her mourning had been part grief at her loss, part guilt at the fact that she hadn't slowed down. That she'd put her selfish fears first.

And in her grief she'd realised how unimportant those fears had been. Having a family—having her son—had always been the most important. She'd pushed Jordan, Greg and Lulu away because that realisation had come too late, and she hadn't wanted to be reminded of how stupid she'd been.

So she'd locked her hopes for a family away, convincing herself that she could survive without one. And she would cling to that belief so no one would get hurt again because of her. It didn't matter what Lulu said about second chances and Mila wanting more. Wanting more didn't matter. Not any more.

Besides, she and Jordan just weren't right for each other. She absently rubbed at the ache that throbbed in her chest at the thought as she remembered their interaction earlier. She'd had no idea he was as affected as she was by their baby's death, and she felt awful about it. She could still see the way the colour had leached from his face when he'd realised Lulu was pregnant, could still remember how erratic his breathing had been.

It always gave her an objective glimpse into what other people felt when she went through her own episodes, and it wasn't good. And, though she still felt guilt about it, knowing that he struggled, too, made her feel a little better about how she was coping. It made her feel, for the first time since her life had imploded in front of her, as if she wasn't alone.

But that didn't mean anything other than shared experience, she thought firmly. She and Jordan hadn't even shared the way they'd really felt about having a baby. And then she had told him about why *she* hadn't, about why *she* was scared, and he had still refused to share *his* feelings with her. It reminded her of how little she actually knew about him…

No, she concluded. They weren't right for each other. And no matter what her heart said she couldn't be with someone who didn't want to let her in.

'Going down?' a voice asked behind her, and she turned,

her heart in her throat until she realised that it was Frank, not Jordan behind her.

'No.' She smiled at him and checked her watch. 'I have under thirty minutes before I need to leave to do some work on the event. There's no time for me to get lost in the fields today.'

Frank nodded and just stood behind her, and his steady presence gave her a feeling of calm.

'Something's wrong,' Frank said, still staring out to the fields.

She bit her lip when Frank's lack of eye contact reminded her of how uncomfortable he was talking about anything personal, and answered him. 'Nothing out of the ordinary.'

Not if you counted a will forcing you to reunite with a not-so-ex-husband as ordinary.

'You sure?'

'Yes.' She turned to him now, and saw the concern on his face. 'I'm not going to break down because Jordan is back, Frank.'

Frank sank his hands into his pockets and shifted his weight. He hated interfering, she thought, and her heart warmed even as she wondered why he thought he needed to.

'I know you're a strong, independent woman…'

This time Mila didn't try to hide her smile.

'But that doesn't mean that your ex being back shouldn't bother you in some way.'

Her smile faded and she shrugged. 'I'm not saying it doesn't bother me. But I can handle it.'

'He hurt you pretty bad the last time.'

'Yeah, he did. But I hurt him, too,' she answered without thinking, and lifted a hand to her mouth when she realised it was true. She *had* hurt him when she'd asked him to give her space. The thought left a feeling of discomfort in her stomach.

'I can talk to him if you like.'

She smiled. 'You would hate that.'

Frank returned her smile. 'I would. But I'd do it.'

'I know you would. For Greg, right?' She said it because she knew it must be true. Especially since Greg had asked her to look after the others at the vineyard in the same way.

'Yeah. But for you, too.'

She brushed a kiss on Frank's cheek because she knew he cared for her, and laughed when the action made him blush.

'I'm okay, Frank. I promise.'

She left after that, the brief interaction leaving her steadier. Perhaps it was because she believed what she'd told Frank. She *could* handle Jordan.

Yes, his being back brought back emotions, memories that she wished she could forget. And it stirred up the anger, the accusations she'd wanted to hurl at him the moment she'd got the divorce papers that had made her realise he had given up on them. But the more time she spent with him now also made her realise that there were things between them that had never really been right. With her, with him or in their relationship.

But Frank's presence had reminded her of the promise she'd made to Greg to look after the vineyard. And for the first time she realised the implications of Greg's will on that promise. If she didn't put aside her feelings, she wouldn't be able to plan the event. That would mean that 50 per cent of the vineyard would be auctioned off, which would mean an uncertain future.

If someone horrible became part-owner, it would affect Frank and everyone else on the vineyard that she'd grown to care about. She *had* to do it for them. She needed to plan this event, make sure that it was a success and then sign her share over to Jordan even if the whole process pained her.

And she would do it for the people she cared about.

It seemed to Jordan that he wasn't the only one who had decided to let his feelings take a back seat. Mila had greeted him cordially when she'd seen him waiting for her on one of the chairs on the patio and asked him to drive them to the school. Her tone had been reserved, but not entirely cold, and Jordan had thought that maybe she had decided cordiality was better than letting the emotions of the past interfere again.

He couldn't agree more, and so an unspoken truce had formed between them. He'd waited for Mila to grab some things from her room, and when she'd returned and walked past him the smell of vanilla had followed her. His body had tightened in response, and he'd wondered how difficult this truce would be.

'What's our plan for this?'

'Well, I have the list of all the vendors we used last time. Most of them will be at this food fair—thank goodness Stellenbosch's event industry is small—so we can split up and ask them about their availability and interest in our event.'

He ran his tongue over his teeth, keeping his eyes glued to the road. 'I don't think we should split up. Didn't the will stipulate we do this together?'

She gave him a wry smile. 'I don't think that's what your father meant.'

'Maybe not, but it would probably be a good idea for me to tag along with you. I didn't do any of this the first time, remember?'

He wasn't sure when it had suddenly become so important for him to stay with her—especially since he was sure he could convince a few vendors to come to an event that they would get great publicity and payment for.

'Fine, we can stay together.'

She said it as though she was conceding millions instead of just her company. Was there a reason she didn't want to spend time with him? Maybe it was because she could also feel the slight sizzle that simmered between them whenever they were together.

'It would probably be best if I introduce you as the new owner of the vineyard. It might give some of them more incentive to say yes.'

'And what happens after this?'

'We speak to Karen—she's supposed to contact me to confirm if she can do it.'

He glanced over at her, saw the pained expression on her face, and smiled. 'Brings back bad memories, does it?'

She groaned, and it made him feel lighter than he had in a while. 'I've always thought about her with both pride and despair. Her performance that night was fantastic, but I could have done without the drama.'

'But if she *can* perform…?'

'We'll have to work with her to figure out a date. And then we market.'

They had just pulled up at the school, and were being directed up a road that Jordan remembered led to a sports field. It was ages since he'd been here, he thought idly, and then turned his attention back to Mila when she spoke.

'Did you know she's playing a concert? Saturday at Westgate Stadium. It would be an excellent way to show our support. You up for it?'

His eyebrows rose. 'You want me to go with you?'

'If I have to suffer through a concert with a load of teenagers, then so do you, buddy.'

He grinned, and found himself relaxing for the first time since he'd arrived back home. 'Sounds fair to me.'

They got out after he'd parked, and he took a moment to appreciate the beauty of the surroundings he'd in no way appreciated in his teens. The field he stood on reminded him of the countless rugby matches he'd played there, and though nostalgia was easy to slip into, he found the scene beyond the school to be more compelling.

The hills made it seem almost enclosed by nature, and had been the backdrop to many of his teenage escapades. Large trees were scattered over the grounds, leaves fading from green to orange with the turn of the season. He thought it might only be in Cape Town that even a school was beautiful to look at.

'This place hasn't changed since I was here,' Jordan said as they stood in line to get tickets, and he watched as Mila turned her head to follow his gaze.

'The swimming pool is new,' Mila pointed out, and he looked over and saw she was right.

He wasn't sure how he had missed that, since the school grounds were built at a much lower level than where they were parked.

'How do you know the pool's new?'

'I went to school here, too,' she said, a light blush covering her cheeks.

He wondered why telling him that would embarrass her. He frowned. 'Why didn't we see each other?'

'You would have been four years ahead of me, so we would have only seen each other if I was there in your last year.' She glanced over at him. 'I wasn't.'

'So you came after I had already matriculated.' The timeline had already formed in his head.

'Yeah, and only stayed for a year.'

'And then what?'

'I got moved to another family and another school.'

Her words left him...disconcerted. Perhaps it was because of the reminder of her childhood. Or perhaps it was because she had never spoken about her schooling before. It highlighted another crack in the relationship they'd had before breaking up. Shouldn't he have known this about her, his wife?

'Why didn't I know this?'

She shrugged, though the gesture was made with stiff shoulders, and the relaxation Jordan had felt only a few moments ago slipped away.

'There were a lot of things we didn't talk about, Jordan,' she said.

Exactly what he'd realised over the past few days, he thought. He took out his wallet before Mila could pay when they got to the front of the line, and turned to her as they waited for their tickets.

'It seems a bit strange that we didn't talk about it, doesn't it…?'

He trailed off when he saw that her face had lost its colour. And then he realised why. Because the school was at a lower level, there was a long staircase that led down to another sports field. It was steep, even for him, and he felt her shake even before he saw it.

'I can't do this,' she said, and turned away, her eyes wide and frightened.

Jordan felt the punch to his stomach even as steel lined it. 'You don't have a choice,' he said firmly, and grabbed her hand, leading her to the stairs slowly.

Every step she took—every uncertain, painful step—sliced at his heart, but he knew he had to do this for her. He knew that if he could redeem himself in any way for the decisions he'd made since the day she'd fallen down the stairs, it would be by giving her back her freedom. And he knew her well enough to know that the only way to do that was through tough love.

'Jordan, please…' she whispered, her hand white on

the railing. She had managed one step down the stairs, but had then frozen.

'Mila, look at me.' He waited as she did so, letting those behind him pass as he stood with Mila. 'You *have* to do this. The event depends on it. The vineyard depends on it. For my father.'

It was a low blow and he knew it, and he saw the responding flash of red in her eyes. But the look quickly fizzled out as he took her hand again, and was replaced by a combination of fear and...trust? he thought, and felt that punch in his gut again.

He couldn't ponder why that look had that effect on him now, though, and instead focused on taking another step down, waiting for her to join him. After taking a breath, she did. He saw the temptation in her eyes to freeze again, and decided that distracting her would soften the tough-love approach.

'Do you think it's because we did everything so fast that we didn't talk about our pasts?' he asked her, and patted himself on the back when he saw confusion in her eyes at his change of topic.

'That was a part of it.' Her voice was shaky, but she had taken the next step with his encouragement. 'But definitely not the biggest part.'

'What do you mean?'

She rolled her eyes, and he thought vaguely that his attempt at distraction was working. Except that she was distracting *him*, too.

'We told each other about the most important parts. You knew that I didn't have any family, and that I grew up in foster care, and I knew that your mom had passed away from cancer.'

'And we were just content with that...' he said, more to himself than to her.

Ever since he had realised that there had been things in

their relationship that were broken even before the accident, the more he saw them. Yes, they'd known the basics—like the fact that her father had died before she was born and her mother had died shortly after her birth—but he'd had no idea how that had made her *feel*. Just as she hadn't known how his mother's death had affected him. And how much he blamed himself for it.

'*You* were,' she scoffed, and took another step down, still leaning on him. 'I wanted to know everything about you. About your father, your mother, your childhood... *Everything*,' she repeated. 'But you didn't seem willing to offer the information...'

She took a deep breath, but he knew it had little to do with the fact that she was going down the stairs.

'And I never wanted to push.'

He frowned. 'You didn't *want* to ask me about my life?'

She was silent for a moment. 'I didn't want to push you to give me any information you didn't want to.'

'Why not?'

She looked at him, uncertainty flickering in her eyes. 'Because I didn't want to tell *you* things either.'

It was a strange conversation to be having while she was facing her fears, he thought briefly, but in that moment the only thing that had his attention was what she was saying.

'What didn't you want to tell me?'

He felt her hand tighten, felt her resistance as she tried to pull away from him, but then she stopped. Maybe because she'd realised that pulling away from him would mean she would have to deal with her fear alone. Or maybe because she had chosen to be cordial and her refusal to answer his question would be going against that. But still she didn't say anything.

'Why did it embarrass you to tell me that you went to school here?' he asked, with a sudden urgency lighting up inside him that made it imperative for him to know. The same urgency that told him that whatever she didn't want to tell him about her life was somehow tied to that.

'It didn't,' she replied quickly. Too quickly for someone who had only a few minutes ago stiffened next to him.

'Mila…' It was a plea—one that came from that urgency—and it seemed to make a dent in that defensiveness she'd always had about her past. One he was beginning to realise *he* had, too.

She let out a huff. 'I just didn't want you to think about my crappy unstable childhood when you'd had the complete opposite.'

'That embarrassed you?' he asked incredulously, and a wave of shame washed through him. Had he said something to her that had made her feel embarrassed about her childhood? Did she really think his had been so wonderful?

'Yes, it did,' she said through gritted teeth. 'You had an amazing home—one you could go to every day. You had a father who loved you. I had none of that.'

'Why were you embarrassed by that?'

'Because…' She had reached the bottom of the stairs, but she didn't seem to notice. She took another breath, and said, 'Because it meant that I wasn't worthy of someone like you.'

CHAPTER NINE

THE WORDS HAD already left Mila's lips when she realised
how much they revealed about her. She was annoyed that it
was the second time she had disclosed something to Jordan
that she hadn't wanted him to know, even if it had made
her feel better. Especially since the disturbed look on his
face made her think that he didn't feel like what she'd said.

'Did you really believe that?' he asked softly.

'I did.'

Maybe I still do.

'It doesn't matter any more, though, does it?'

'You're wrong, you know.' He shook his head. 'I haven't
met anyone else I respect more than you. You didn't have
family, but you're more loyal than any family member I
can think of. Even me.'

He paused, and she thought that he was sacrificing his
own comfort to make her feel better. It melted her heart.

'You looked after my father when I couldn't. Thank
you.'

His words made her blush, and she mumbled, 'You
know you don't have to thank me for that.'

'I know you don't think I need to—which just proves
my point. You *are* worthy, Mila. *I'm* the one who isn't worthy of *you*.' He shook his head. 'I didn't have the childhood you thought I did.'

'What do you mean?'

He stuffed his hands into his pockets and looked down. The gesture made him look so defeated she wanted to hold him in her arms, but as she followed his gaze she realised she was looking at grass. She'd made it down the stairs!

'I did it...' she said to herself, not quite believing this victory, especially after the fear had paralysed her for over a year.

'Yeah, you did.'

Jordan smiled at her, and for the first time since he had returned, she could tell that it was completely genuine, despite the look of disconcertion on his face.

'I did it. I really did it.'

She felt like a fool when her eyes started tearing up, but she couldn't help it. A small piece inside her that had broken after she'd lost her son had become whole, and it gave her a sense of peace. She felt relief, a sense of accomplishment, and so many other emotions she couldn't even begin to put her finger on.

When she looked at Jordan, she saw that his frown had cleared, replaced by a look of satisfaction.

He did this purposely, she thought and, ignoring the voice that screamed in her head, she hugged him.

The comfort of it hit her so hard that she had to close her eyes. But that only heightened her senses. The woodsy smell of him was intoxicating—so familiar and masculine that awareness heated inside her. She was moulded to his body, could feel the strength of the muscles she had admired when she'd first seen him after he'd returned. His arms—which had been still at his sides until that moment—wrapped around her and she was pulled in tighter to his body. Her breathing slowed, her heart sped up, and she had to resist the urge to pull his head down so that she could taste his lips.

And then she lifted her head and met his eyes. The heat of longing there was a reflection of her own, and she could feel the world fade as it always did with him. Gooseflesh shot out on her skin, and she considered for a brief moment what would happen if she kissed him.

It would be magical, she knew. The things inside her that had died when he'd left would find life. She would finally feel alive again. *But at what cost?* a voice asked her, and she took a step back from him, knowing that it would take away everything she had rebuilt if she gave in to this temptation.

'Thank you,' she said, and felt the warmth of a blush light her face. But she'd needed to say it, to make sure that he knew why she had hugged him—as a token of gratitude, nothing else. The physical effect the seemingly innocent gesture had awakened was merely an unforeseen consequence.

'It's the least I can do,' he replied in a gravelly voice, and she knew that their contact had affected him, too.

What was more surprising to her was that he looked as though he genuinely meant the words, that he wasn't just saying them automatically.

She cleared her throat. 'So…we should probably start rallying the troops.'

He nodded his agreement, and she forced herself to shift focus. She could be professional. She prided herself on it, in fact. She began to explain her strategy—she would speak to the vendors first, since they knew her, and then introduce them to Jordan as the new owner of the vineyard. Then they would pitch their event, find out if they were interested and available, and hope for the best. Since the will stipulated that they should give evidence of trying their best to find exactly the same service providers for the event, she would record their interactions and use them to show Mark if they needed to find alternatives.

'You've thought of everything, haven't you?'

'That's the job,' she replied, her neck prickling at the admiration she heard in Jordan's voice.

'Where have I heard *that* before?' he muttered, and she remembered she'd said something similar to him the first time they'd met.

She brushed off the nostalgia. 'We'd better get to it.'

They spent almost two hours there. It was time spent waiting for vendors to find a moment to talk to them in between serving people, and eating to fill that time. She found herself growing more comfortable as the minutes went by, the tension that was always inside her around him easing.

He was a wonderful ambassador for the vineyard, she thought as she watched him, and even though all the vendors remembered her and their event—especially since she had used many of them multiple times before—it was Jordan they responded to. He spoke to them with such warmth, with such praise, that she could almost see their spines straighten with pride. He played up his enjoyment of their food so much that sometimes she found herself giggling.

The sound was strange, even to her, and she wondered why it was so easy to relax around him now. Her determination to focus on the event and ignore whatever was between them had been decided just that morning. A few hours later and she had spoken to him about the past, made herself vulnerable by admitting that she hadn't thought she was worthy of him, and had walked down an intimidating staircase. And now she was laughing with him. *At* him.

She knew that at some point he had gone from entertaining the vendors to trying to make *her* laugh. She wasn't sure how she felt about that, but she chose not to ponder it then. Not when for the first time in a long time she felt…free.

'Ice cream?'

She looked at him when she heard his voice, and realised that she had been staring off into space while she thought about the day.

'I'm not sure it's warm enough for ice cream,' she replied, feeling self-conscious now.

'The sun is shining, Mila. We should thank it by offering it the traditional food of appreciation.'

Her lips curved. 'And that's ice cream?'

'Yes, it is.' He smiled back at her and her heart thumped. It was as if they were on a first date, she thought, and then immediately cast the thought aside.

'Besides, we have one more vendor to see,' he continued, 'and he still hasn't returned from his supply run.'

She shrugged off her hesitation. 'Sure—okay.'

She followed him to the ice-cream stand, where they joined a long line.

'Seems like everyone wants to make a sacrifice to the gods,' she said, and smiled at him when he looked at her.

'I told you so,' he replied, and took her hand as though it was the most natural thing in the world.

And the truth was that on that day, after talking, after laughing together, with the winter sun shining on their faces, holding hands *did* seem natural. But it wasn't, she reminded herself, and let go of his hand under the guise of looking for the notepad where she had written down the names of all the vendors and made notes.

'I think we've done pretty well today,' she said, and pretended not to notice the disappointment that had flashed across his face. 'Of the six vendors here, three are interested and are available for two weeks—the end of this month and the beginning of next. It cuts our time in half. Not ideal, but I think it's doable. And if we speak to the owner of the Bacon Bites food truck when he gets back, we could have four.'

'So that means we only have to replace two or three?'

Jordan slipped his hands into the pockets of his jacket,

and she wondered if it was because he was tempted to take her hand again.

Her hand itched at the thought.

'Yes, but we still need to hear from two vendors who aren't here. Lulu said she would follow up on those. But I think we could substitute any who don't come with some of the other vendors here. I chatted to the woman who owns the chocolate truck over there—' she gestured to it with her head '—and she thought our event sounded great. She told me to come over if we were interested.'

'How did you manage to speak to her?'

'Oh, it was between your moan of delight for the meat pies and your groan of appreciation for the burger sliders,' she teased, and saw the tension that had entered his body after she'd let go of his hand fade.

'They have good food here,' he said, with a shrug and a smile.

Before she could respond they were at the front of the line. Behind the glass casing of the van she could see a variety of ice cream flavours that made her mouth water. After a few minutes of looking, she still couldn't decide between the chocolate hazelnut flavour and the vanilla toffee.

'How about you take the chocolate hazelnut and I take the vanilla toffee?' he said when she told him as much, and she smiled at the proposal.

'Perfect!'

She relayed their order to the patient vendor, and watched with delight at he made the sugar cone their ice cream would be served in from scratch.

Her first lick was deliciously creamy, and the thrill of cold ran down her spine. But then she realised that Jordan was watching her—with amusement and something else in his eyes—and she wondered if the thrill *had* come from the cold.

'This is great,' she said to avoid feeling awkward. 'Want some?'

'Sure,' he replied, and moved closer.

He watched her as he tasted the ice cream, and suddenly it was a year ago, when they'd been on honeymoon in Mauritius and had come across an ice-cream stand. It had been perfect for the hot summer's day after they'd been at the beach all morning.

Sharing their ice creams with one another had been... *sensual*, she thought, just as it was now. Shivers went up her spine at the look in his eyes—the look that told her that even though they weren't together any more he still wanted her.

He offered her a lick of his, and as though she was in a trance she leaned forward and tasted it, her eyes still on his. The flavour was just as delectable as she'd thought it would be, but the thought barely registered. Instead she was wondering if their sharing ice cream would end the way it had in Mauritius—with a passion that could have heated the entire resort for a week.

The thought had her moving backwards so quickly she almost stumbled. She regained her balance in time to realise that there was ice cream on her nose. She spent a few seconds trying to figure out how to remove it, and sighed when she saw that neither of them had taken a serviette.

'Do you want some help?' he asked, and she looked up to see that he was watching her—again—this time with an amused expression. And then she thought that she must have been crossing her eyes to look at the spot of ice cream on her nose, and she flushed.

'No, thanks—I'll manage.' She rubbed her nose with her sleeve and quickly turned to look for the vendor they were waiting for, hoping with all her might that he would be there. Relief swamped her when she saw that he was, and she turned back to Jordan, who was now watching her with a guarded expression.

'We should go over there,' she said, and gestured behind her.

He nodded and started walking, and she took a moment to instruct her emotions to stop fluttering around and get into place. When she was sure she had them under control she followed him—and wished with all her might that the roller coaster the two of them were on would stop.

CHAPTER TEN

'WHERE ARE WE GOING?'

They were in the car and supposed to be heading home from the school. But after spending the entire day with Mila, Jordan didn't want it to end.

Yes, they lived together at the moment—he kept waiting for her to tell him she would be leaving—but as soon as they walked through the front door of his father's house Jordan knew that Mila would erect a fence between them. He would be able to see glimpses of her, but he wouldn't be able to get near her, and the thought of that disturbed him.

He didn't think about why—he didn't need to defend himself for the time he spent with the woman who had once been his everything, did he?—but he couldn't bear being kept at a distance any more. Not after he'd seen parts of her today that he hadn't known existed during their marriage.

And now he knew what he had been missing.

'Did you know the Gerbers?'

'The old couple who used to live behind us?'

Mila turned to him, her brows drawn together in a frown, and Jordan's hand itched to reach out and smooth it over. But he tightened his hands on the steering wheel. Just as he had tightened them into fists in his pockets to keep himself from taking her hand again that afternoon. He had done that by mistake, but it had felt so right that he hadn't let go even though his mind had told him to. And then she had done it instead, and disappointment had hit him like water from a burst pipe. He blamed that desire to touch her on that hug she'd sprung on him after making it down those stairs.

His body awoke just at the thought of it.

'Yeah...' He forced himself to speak, forced his body to calm down. 'Did you ever speak to them? Get a look around their property?'

'I... No,' she said, confusion clear in her voice. 'What's going on, Jordan? Where are you taking me?'

He had wanted to keep it a surprise, but he didn't want her to worry. 'I'm taking you to our house.'

'What?'

Was that panic her heard in her voice?

He frowned. 'Is something wrong?'

'No, no,' she replied quickly—too quickly—and looked out of the window. Her hands were clasped so tightly together in her lap that he reached over with one of his.

'What's going on, Mila?'

She blew out a shaky breath and he felt the deliberate relaxation of her hands under his. Taking it as a sign that she didn't want to be touched, Jordan moved his hand away. Even that slight loss of contact made him feel empty.

'It's nothing.'

'Mila...' Again, he found himself pleading.

She sighed. 'I just haven't been there since...since you left.'

'And going back now is...worrying for you?'

She didn't answer, and he glanced over to see her deliberately relaxing again. It made him wonder about why she was reacting this way to something as simple as going back to the house they'd shared. He felt a slight stir in his brain and frowned. He was missing something.

'A reminder of the past,' she finally said softly, and

when he looked at her again he saw that she was still looking out of the window. 'Going back to the house we lived in… Going back together… It's just a reminder of a life that seems worlds away.'

'We were planning to go anyway, weren't we? I have to help you get the stuff out so that you can leave.' Even saying the words sent a flash of pain through his heart.

'Oh, yes, of course,' she said, again more quickly than he thought she needed to, and again he wondered what he was missing.

There had to be something… The stirring in his brain seemed like a distant memory, but he couldn't recall it to verify whether that was the truth, and he didn't know if it had anything to do with what was currently happening between them. But it must—why else did he feel as if he was having a conversation without knowing all the facts?

'It's probably because this is unplanned,' she continued. 'Why are we going there now?'

'I have something to show you,' he replied, forcing himself to ignore the dull thud of unrecalled memories and focus on what his intention had been from the beginning. 'Did you ever see that pathway in the backyard, just next to that huge tree we planned to turn into a tree house for the little grape?'

He heard her sharp intake of breath before he realised he had used the pet name they had given their child after finding out they were having a boy. They had been so happy, he thought, pain tainting the memory. It had been the first time they had considered names for the baby, and he had teased her, calling him 'the little grape' since their child would one day have to take over the vineyard.

Mila had protested, of course, and with each objection had come a splutter of laughter that had warmed Jordan's insides so much that the name had stuck. They'd had a list of real names, of course, but they had never got the chance to decide on what they would call him.

'Yes, I remember,' she said hoarsely, and he reached for her hand, not caring about the unspoken rules that meant he shouldn't.

'I'm sorry, Mila, I didn't mean to—'

'It's okay.' She squeezed his hand. 'I think it's time we weren't afraid to refer to our son.'

He tightened his hand on hers and then let go, unable to keep the contact. His son was always in his thoughts—and always would be. He couldn't escape the way it had felt to hold his dying son in his arms when he'd been barely big enough to fit in Jordan's hands.

But she was right—he *had* been afraid to speak about him. And there was a lot more to it than just the fact that he couldn't bring himself to do it. No, admitting to Mila earlier that he'd been scared when they'd found out she was pregnant was only the tip of the iceberg. It hadn't fully left his mind since their conversation, and he'd realised that, as he'd initially thought, he *had* been scared he would turn out to be the same as his father. And that *was* part of the reason he'd left for Johannesburg.

Jordan knew Greg had loved him, but his childhood had been tainted by his father's grief. Grief that had made Greg into a bitter and sometimes angry man. The years after his mother had died had been filled with tension for Jordan—he'd sometimes felt as if he was walking on eggshells when he was around Greg. As a child, Jordan hadn't understood why his father would never look at him in the eye, or why Greg had spoken *at* him instead of *to* him. If he'd ever spoken to Jordan at all.

He had started behaving badly because of it, which had strained his relationship with Greg even more. It had also led to the night that would be burned in his memory for ever. The night that had changed Jordan—and his father—with only a few words.

Jordan vaguely remembered a time when laughing had been easy for his father. When there had been an open affection between them. But those memories were so faded he wondered if he'd made them up. The memories that were clear were of a steady man—a sombre, reserved and often difficult man. It clearly highlighted the fact that when Jordan had lost his mother, he'd lost his father, as well. And that had led to Jordan not being able to grieve fully for his mother because, frankly, his father had done it for both of them.

He hadn't thought about it until Mila had told him she was pregnant, and then suddenly he'd spent nights worrying about whether that grief for his mother would pop up once Mila had had the baby. Whether that grief would turn him into the kind of angry man his father was and spoil his son's childhood *and* Jordan's marriage.

It had made him worry that they'd rushed into marriage, made him think that he should have considered those possibilities when he'd been able to do something about them.

And when they'd lost the baby his fears had only intensified. He'd lost someone he loved, just as his father had, which surely upped the chances of Jordan turning into Greg. So Jordan had left. Escaped. Or, as he'd recently realised, run away...

'He's not alone, you know,' Mila said suddenly as he pulled into the driveway of their old house. 'The little grape's with our parents.'

He glanced over and saw a tiny smile on her lips. It made her look peaceful, he thought, and a large part inside him settled at the thought. It brought *him* peace, too.

'That's a really lovely thing to think about, isn't it?'

She smiled at him, and something in his heart eased. Was that because she'd smiled at him—a sweet, genuine smile that he had only been privy to that day—or was it because it comforted him to think about two generations of his family together?

'He'll have met your mom,' Mila said softly. 'I always wished I could have met her, you know. Your father used to talk about her sometimes.'

Jordan could tell that Mila was looking at him, but he stared steadily ahead. He didn't want to talk about his mother. That would mean telling her about his father. About his childhood. About his fears.

'She sounded amazing.'

He didn't respond, and then he tilted his head. 'Come on. Before it gets dark.'

He got out of the car, aware of the disappointment that shrouded her, and waited for her to join him as he stood outside the house they'd lived in during their short marriage. The first time he had seen the house he had thought it timeless and elegant—exactly what he had been looking for for his sweet, beautiful bride.

A marble pathway led to large oak doors that looked newly polished yet still antiquated. Large glass windows overlooked the road, and gave the white façade a modern feel. The pathway was lined with palm trees, which had always made him feel as if he was walking into an oasis of some kind. It still looked the same to him now, though all the memories made him feel more than he had the first time he had seen it.

Now he thought about those days when they'd had breakfast on the patio, just as the sun went up. She had always moaned about getting up that early, but the peace on her face when she was curled up on a chair, a cup of coffee in her hand, made him think she'd thought it worth it. He remembered walking hand in hand with her through their garden, where the roses that were planted there were always the perfect gift for her. And he could still see her lying next to the pool, the slight swell of her stomach obvious in her swimming costume. Could still feel the surge of protectiveness that had gone through him when he'd looked at her.

'It looks the same…but it feels different,' she said beside him, and he looked down at her to see a mixture of emotions playing over her face that had him grabbing for her hand.

He could feel that she was shaking, and just like that he realised what he'd been missing in the car—why she'd been anxious about coming back.

'It reminds you of your fall, doesn't it?'

She didn't have to answer him—he could see the truth of his words on her face.

I'm an idiot, he thought, and wondered how he hadn't thought about it before.

His mind had been too focused on showing her the secret he'd kept since he'd found out that she was pregnant. He hadn't wanted today to end, hadn't wanted her guard to come up, and in the process his actions to prevent it had hurt her.

He was a selfish man, he thought in disgust.

'I sometimes still dream about it,' she said quietly, and he immediately wanted to hold her in his arms.

But her words told him that she was forcing herself to face it—it was that fire he'd noticed in her when he'd returned again—and he told himself to be content with holding her hand.

'I can feel myself falling, reaching for a railing that wasn't there for support. And then the impact of rolling down the stairs.' She drew a shaky breath. 'I still feel foolish for falling down five steps.'

'It had been raining,' he said immediately, his heart clenching in pain at the anguish—the guilt—that he heard in her voice.

She ignored him. 'I lay there, my breath gone, with shock keeping me from feeling the true pain of what my body had just gone through, and I felt warmth between my legs and realised...'

Her hand was so tight on his that he could tell there was no blood flowing through it, but that didn't matter to him. Not when he could feel the pain of what she had gone through—what she had never spoken of before. Not when he could hear the quickness of her breath. He drew her in, though she didn't seem to notice.

'I realised that something was wrong...that I had done something wrong...and then I saw you, and your face told me that I was right.'

Tears fell from her eyes and he didn't care this time if he was interrupting her. His arms went around her and she sobbed—heart-wrenching sobs that broke everything inside him each time he heard them.

'I'm sorry, Jordan. I'm sorry I wasn't more careful. I'm sorry I didn't slow down like you asked me to. I'm sorry I didn't look after him like I should have.'

'You didn't do anything wrong, Mila.' He felt his own tears as he said the words. 'I shouldn't have asked you to slow down. It was just...fear. My own. I think I was hoping to slow *us* down.' He paused, held her tightly. 'Everything was happening so quickly.'

He could feel her body shake, knew his words weren't having any effect. So he told her the facts, hoping their simplicity would help her.

'You were walking down stairs we'd both used a million times before. It had been raining—a light summer rain that had come from nowhere. You slipped. It was an accident.'

He said the words over and over again—to himself just as much as to her—until her shaking dissipated and everything went still. They stood in each other's arms longer than was necessary, their grief finally—*finally*—something they shared.

Not completely, a voice reminded him, and he stepped back. His heart thudded painfully in his chest as a reminder of what he needed to tell her—worse now that he knew about the guilt she felt. And the expression on her face—the completely exhausted expression—tempted him to ignore it, to tell her some other time.

But he knew that was just an excuse. He wouldn't ever get to that other time—not when he had been meaning to tell her since the accident. And now she had bared her soul to him he knew he couldn't keep it a secret from her any more.

'There's something I need to tell you.' He said it quickly, afraid that he wouldn't get through it otherwise. 'I had to give them permission to operate on you, Mila. You were bleeding from the abruption, losing consciousness...'

He shook his head.

'Waiting for the bleeding to subside would have put you *and* the baby at risk.' He took a shaky breath, not daring to look at her—not yet. 'I had to approve the C-section knowing there was a chance our baby wouldn't survive. But I couldn't take a chance on losing both of you...'

His voice had gone completely hoarse at this admission of something he had carried with him for what felt like for ever, and he forced himself to look at her before he lost his courage. She was staring at him, those eyes more haunting than ever before, carefully blank of all the emotion he wished he could read in her.

Her hand reached up, and he braced himself for the pain of a slap, but she only brushed away the remnants of her tears from her cheeks. Then she cleared her throat.

'I know.'

He looked at her, his eyes wide. 'What?'

'The doctor told me when I went back for my check-up. And then I asked Greg about it and he confirmed it.'

'Your check-up was…' He sorted through the memories 'I was still here, Mila… Why didn't you tell me you knew?' He couldn't believe that the burden he had been carrying with him for such a long time wasn't a secret after all.

'I was waiting for *you* to tell me.'

The look she aimed at him made him feel like a school-boy.

'I wanted to, but I was afraid—'

'That I would blame you for it?'

He nodded, and she folded her arms.

'I did. I thought it was your fault that I didn't get to see my son alive. Why do you think I asked for space?'

He was dumbfounded, the words of apology, of excuse, he'd prepared were wiped from his mind.

'I thought you would go and stay with your dad for a while, and I would be able to deal with all the feelings. I was raw, hurting and in more pain than I thought possible. I just needed time.'

She looked at him, and he saw her anger.

'But then you left me completely. And instead of space I got divorce papers.'

'You're angry with me…' But he'd known that, he thought. Deserved it.

'Yes, I am. But not about you giving them permission to operate. What choice did you have?' She shook her head. 'We both might not have survived if you hadn't.' She paused, kicked at a stone. 'I *was* angry about it. But only because I wished I could have held him during those seventeen minutes he was alive.'

Her breath caught at that, and Jordan wished he could hold her again.

'And then I thought that if it couldn't be me—and since I was still under anaesthesia then it couldn't have been—

you were the only other person I would have wanted it to be. So after a while I forgave you.' She looked at him stonily. 'It wasn't your fault either, Jordan.'

'I can't believe you've known all along. I've been carrying this with me ever since I...' He trailed off when he saw her jaw set and she looked away. And then he realised that she'd said that she wasn't angry with him about *that* any more. 'Why *are* you angry at me, then?'

'You really don't know?'

He opened his mouth to answer, but she waved him away.

'If you can't figure it out then you don't deserve to know.' She set her jaw. 'Can we just leave now, please?'

'No, we can't.' He felt uncomfortable, but he said it because he'd shared one of his deepest secrets with her, which he wouldn't have done with anyone else, and now she was pulling away. Even though he didn't want to delve any further into emotion—his insides were raw and knotted from what had already been said—he persisted. 'I want you to tell me what else I've done wrong.'

'So you can continue with this victim mentality you seem to have going?'

Anger sparked, deep inside him, and pumped through his body with his blood. 'Excuse me?'

'Every tragedy that's happened to you, you somehow blame yourself for it.'

He could see the anger in her, too, but that only fuelled his own.

'You blame yourself for approving an operation that saved my life—that gave your son his best chance at living—and you blame yourself for your father's death. Oh, did you think I couldn't see the weight of guilt crushing you?'

He kept his face clear of the turmoil he felt—the anger and truth in her words were daggers piercing his insides—

and wondered how she had realised what he felt about his father's death.

'You think that his heart attacks were because you left. Because you didn't keep in touch over the past year. You hate it that he died without fixing whatever was wrong between you.'

'Stop!' he said, his hands clenched into fists at his sides.

'Why?' she demanded, her face flushed from her tirade. '*You* were the one who wanted me to continue, remember?' She didn't wait for his affirmation before continuing, as though she was purging herself of everything that she felt. 'Do you want to know what I'm *really* angry about, Jordan? It's because you ran away when I needed you the most.' She took a shaky breath. 'You made me feel like you left because I had lost our child.'

She was trembling, and he itched to touch her, to comfort her, even as her words shook him. 'Stop saying that! Stop blaming yourself for what happened. It wasn't your fault.' And she'd made him see that it wasn't his either.

'If that's not the reason, then why did you go?'

'I was running—just like you said,' he shot out, and immediately stilled.

'Why?'

'Does it matter?' he said, exasperated. He couldn't deal with the emotion any more. 'I'm back now.'

Her eyes flashed. 'Yes, it *matters*, Jordan. And here's why.'

She grabbed the front of his top, and before he knew it her lips were on his.

CHAPTER ELEVEN

SHE'D DONE IT out of desperation, to pierce through that controlled façade he clung to even though she could see that he felt beneath the surface. She wanted him to feel the earthquake that was happening inside her, to know the emotions that sprang from the hole the quake had opened, and the only way she knew how to do that was to kiss him.

But as she sank into the kiss she thought that she was a fool for being so impulsive, for letting go of the control she'd fought for around him. And then she stopped thinking, pressing her body closer to his as she tasted him.

The same…he tasted the same. Of fire and home and pure man.

Her anger had turned into passion, so there was no gentle sliding back into the heat they had always shared. No, they jumped straight into the fire, greedily taking each other, their hands moving over bodies that had changed yet were somehow still the same.

When he lifted her from the ground she went willingly, her arms around him, refusing to lose contact with him. She barely felt the wall that he pressed her against, her senses captivated by what his hands were doing. He pushed aside the jacket she had on, his tongue playing with hers in a way that had her moaning, and the sound seemed to burn away the last of his patience with her clothing.

He ripped open the shirt she wore, his hands roaming

over her bare skin before she even heard the buttons fall
on the marble path to their home. Though the house was
enclosed, and there was no one who would see them, Mila
didn't think she would have cared if there had been. Her
body was too occupied in being touched by the hands that
had always owned it, her mind too employed by the pleasure only he could make her feel.

She fumbled with his clothes, wanting to touch his skin
as he did hers. Giving up, she slid her hands under his top
and eagerly over his body. The toned, muscular body that
she had wanted since the moment she had seen him. Somewhere she thought about how different touching him felt
now, but the thought was vague, dulled by the passion of
his lips on her skin.

She wanted him, she heard her heart tell her as he kissed
her neck, letting her head fall back to give him better access. And she would have let him have her, she thought
later, had her phone not rung.

The sound was muffled, since the phone was in her
jacket pocket, but it was clear enough to give them both
pause. And the pause allowed her thoughts to spin back
into her mind.

Though most were still muddled and hazy, one came
to her with the clarity of a conscience after confession—
she was giving herself to the man who had broken her
heart. And one more occurred to her after that—he was
still breaking it.

She pushed him away, ignoring the desire that clouded
his face, and with one hand held her torn shirt together.
She walked a short distance away from him, took a deep
breath and answered her phone.

The conversation only lasted a few minutes, but it was
enough for her thoughts to clear and her cheeks to flush
with embarrassment. She was a fool! she thought, keeping
the phone at her ear even though Simon, Karen's manager,

had long since said goodbye. Why had she thought *kissing* him would make him *feel*? The only thing it had done was to awaken her body and alert her mind to the fact that she was still alive. That she was still a woman who needed, who *wanted*. And that both those needs and wants had to do with Jordan.

She shoved the phone back into her pocket, and zipped up her jacket, not wanting to feel any more exposed than she already did.

'Who was that?'

She turned at his voice, hating it that she still remembered the effect it had had on her the day they had met. That it still had an effect now.

'Karen's manager.' Mila didn't look at him, not wanting him to see the emotions she couldn't hide nearly as well as he did. 'She's doing a show at the university's conservatorium tonight. She wants us to come through.'

There was a moment that beat between them, and then he asked, 'What kind of show does a pop star do at a *conservatorium*?'

'A performance for her studies, apparently,' she answered him. 'It's formal, and it starts in an hour and a half. We'd better get going.'

She strode past him, determined not to look at him, and braced herself for contact when out of the corner of her eye she saw his hand lift. But the contact never came and she sighed with relief—*not* disappointment, she assured herself—and got into the car.

It was going to be a long trip home.

Mila stood under the shower, angling her head so that the warm water could hit her body directly. She stayed like that, hoping that it would wash away her actions of that day. She cringed every time she thought about it, and the day wasn't even over yet. Now, after nearly tearing Jordan's clothes off, Mila was going to have to spend who knew how long with him at a classical concert by the winner of a pop competition.

There was no way around it, she thought, shampooing her hair. Simon had told her that Karen wanted to speak to her before making a decision about the event, and this was the only time she could spare to do it.

At least it meant that Mila wouldn't have to go to a teenybopper concert with Jordan. She could only imagine how the girls would swoon around him. Hadn't she just had first-hand experience of that? Her body still trembled from his touch, reminding her of how good that part of their relationship had been. But what good did that do when there were other, more substantial cracks between them?

Mila knew she had made progress with him, getting him to admit that he'd had to give permission for her C-section. But at what cost? He now knew more about her than she'd wanted him to know—he knew she didn't want to go back to the house, that it reminded her of the accident. He knew that she still dreamt about it, and that she was angry at him for leaving. It was a miracle that he'd admitted that he'd run away, but she still couldn't get him to tell her why. She couldn't even get him to talk about his mother.

Everything was so *controlled* with him. Sometimes she wondered where the man who had given her a surprise picnic the day they had met had gone. That impulsive, romantic man who had swept her off her feet and convinced her to marry him. He didn't seem to exist any more, she thought, and got out of the shower. No, he had been replaced by the man who had run away when she'd needed him—the man who never wanted to speak to her about the things that mattered.

And still the man who set her body on fire.

Calm down, she instructed herself. She just needed to get through the event and then she would be moving on with her life, away from Jordan and all the problems he created for her. And to do that she needed to get Karen to set a date so that things could finally move ahead.

Mila would ignore the voice in her head that told her that finding out what Jordan didn't want to tell her was about more than just her. The voice that told her Jordan needed to admit it to himself, too, or he would carry the guilt of his past for the rest of his life. It might have been harsh, but she had meant it when she'd referred to him seeing himself as a victim.

It wasn't her problem, she reminded herself. And even if finding out would mean she would have to sacrifice a part of herself that she had carried for a long time, there was part of her that didn't want to ask for what she wanted. That couldn't. There was no way Mila would do that when there was nothing on the line—no relationship, no family—and she had no guarantee Jordan would do the same for her.

So she focused on getting ready. She took out the only two dresses she had kept when she'd moved in with Greg that were formal enough to work for the event. One was a knee-length loose black dress. Pretty enough to wear to a formal event, but demure enough not to draw attention.

She put it in front of her body and realised that it was no longer something she wanted to wear. It reminded her of someone she no longer seemed to be, and she took a moment to figure out whether she was okay with that. When the thought didn't make her feel anxious something settled inside her, and she pressed her hand to her stomach with a small smile.

Maybe she was changing for the better, she thought, and then put the thought away as something she would take with her when she moved on. And when *that* thought unsettled her she dismissed it completely and looked at the second dress.

It was long and midnight blue, with a lace halter-neck

overlay that led down her arms to form sleeves. It covered the sweetheart neckline designed to show off her bust, and though she would have preferred something *completely* covered after her actions earlier, she put the dress on and chose to feel confident in it. *Another change?* she considered.

She fluffed her hair, sighing when her curls wouldn't play along, and decided to leave it loose. She might as well accept all of herself, she thought, and spent a few minutes on make-up. She looked in the mirror when she was done, told herself to be careful around Jordan, and then grabbed her purse and headed for the front door.

Jordan was already there, and her heart screamed in protest at how handsome he looked. He was wearing a tuxedo that showed off his strong body and looked as if it had been designed to make her breath catch. He had shaved—the five o'clock shadow that had brushed her skin earlier was only a memory now—and had smoothed back his hair, and he looked at her with an unreadable expression that reminded her of a celebrity who was preparing to walk the red carpet.

But as his eyes swept over her his expression slipped enough for her to see his appreciation of her outfit, and she blushed.

'You're wearing your hair down,' he said.

'Yes, I am,' she answered, and resisted the urge to fiddle with it.

'That's the way I remember it.'

Her heart rapped in her chest, like someone desperately knocking at a door, and she forced herself to calm down. What did it matter if that was how he remembered it?

'It's the way I like it,' he said softly, as though he had been privy to her thoughts, and she had to fight against the embarrassment.

'Are you ready to go?' she said, instead of responding

to his comment, and almost turned away from him before she saw the look in his eyes.

Gooseflesh immediately shot out on her skin, and she resisted the urge to pull at the material around her neck to get more air. He was looking at her as though he would have liked to continue from where they had left off earlier, and his eyes pierced her right down to her soul.

After a moment his face went back to being unreadable, and she sighed in relief and grabbed her coat from the rack that stood behind the front door.

Jordan opened the car door for her when they reached it, and she carefully got in, trying to avoid all contact with him. Which was in vain, she realised, when the train of her dress still lay outside her door after she'd sat down and they both reached to get it.

Their hands touched for the briefest moment, and yet the feeling reminded her of the way she had felt when she'd burned herself the day before. She snatched it back and let Jordan tuck her dress into the car, and only exhaled when he closed her door and walked around to get in at his side.

'Do you have *any* idea why a pop star would be studying classical music?'

He spoke without looking at her, and she wondered if he knew how tight his hands were on the steering wheel despite his outward calm.

'Your guess is as good as mine,' she murmured, proud of the aloof tone she had managed.

She made an extra effort not to fold her arms, which would, for sure, give away *her* nerves about spending time with him. Because, as much as she didn't want to be affected by him, she inevitably always was.

The rest of their journey was made in silence, and she tried not to use it as an opportunity to spend more time thinking about everything. Relief hit her right to her bones when the car stopped at the university's conservatorium. It was a large white building, with the word *conservatorium* printed boldly at the top, and the glass doors at the bottom were open to the crowds who, for some reason, were pouring into the venue.

She looked up in surprise when her door clicked open, and realised that the time she had spent ogling the building meant she'd been distracted from climbing out of the car by herself. Now she was faced with the hand Jordan was offering to help her out.

She couldn't say no, she thought, even if that had been her immediate reaction. He was offering an olive branch, she realised when she saw his face.

She braced herself for the contact, but in no way did it help when she took his hand. Heat and memories slid through her like a warm knife through butter, from the hand he now held to the top of her head and right down to her feet. She tightened her hand on his in response, saw the feeling mirrored on his face, and got out so that they wouldn't have to spend any more time touching.

Except the pavement they had parked on was not meant for high heels, and after she'd stumbled for the second time Jordan snaked an arm around her waist and pulled her closer. Her body immediately groaned in delight at the feel of him so close, and her mind was fogged by the intoxicating smell of his body wash and cologne.

She ignored the effects it had on her body and pulled her coat tighter around her, as though the action would somehow protect her. She pulled away from him the moment they were inside the building, ignoring the way her heart protested at the emptiness she felt immediately, and gave her coat to a man with an unnecessarily prudish expression on his face.

'Mila, I'm so glad that you made it!'

Mila turned at the familiar male voice, and opened her arms to return a hug when she saw it was Simon.

'I'm so glad that you invited us, Simon! We appreciate Karen taking the time to speak to us.'

She pulled back and smiled, and then her skin prickled and she realised that Jordan had joined them.

'You've never met my...' She'd been about to say *husband*, but that didn't seem right. 'You've never met Jordan, have you? He owns the vineyard where Karen performed at the event where we met. Jordan—Simon.'

They shook hands, and she noted the way Jordan's 'businessman' expression slid easily onto his face.

'I'm glad to see you both. Unfortunately Karen won't have time until after the performance to talk to you two, but can you come backstage immediately after and we'll discuss the event then?'

'Yes, of course,' Mila answered.

'Great! I've given your names to the guys at the door, so you can go straight through.' Simon brushed a kiss on Mila's cheek, nodded at Jordan and then moved on to whoever was behind them in the line.

'I suppose we can't sneak out now,' she whispered to Jordan as they walked towards the door. She looked at his face when he didn't respond, and was treated to the stormy expression she had seen that first day after he had returned.

'What's wrong?' she asked, but there was only silence.

She sighed and pulled him out of the line they were standing in, not wanting to be overheard.

'Look, I know what happened this afternoon was... wasn't ideal...' she rolled her eyes at her description '...but this is work. This is why we're here. Can you put your feelings aside so we can do this?'

His expression grew darker, and she was about to launch into another lecture about keeping the event and their personal feelings separate when his face grew blank. He gave her a curt nod, and then extended his arm for her to hook hers onto. She hesitated for a moment and then slipped her arm through his. If he was going to put his feelings aside then so could she, she thought, and ignored the spread of warmth through her body at his touch.

CHAPTER TWELVE

'YOU'RE HEARING THE same thing I am, right?'

Jordan glanced over at Mila, and saw that her jaw had dropped. She nodded at his question, and then quickly closed her mouth.

'This is ridiculous,' she whispered back to him, her eyes still riveted on the stage. 'Why do they have her doing those awful pop songs when she can sing like this?'

He chuckled—more at Mila's reaction than at the fact that Karen-the-pop-star was actually Karen-with-the-most-incredibly-beautiful-classical-voice. She was standing alone in front of an orchestra, her usual red curls straightened into a sophisticated updo that, along with her green ballgown, made her look a lot older than she was. More mature, too, he thought—which was probably the point, though not entirely necessary. Not when each note sent a wave of appreciation through the audience.

'Maybe this is so that she won't *have* to do "awful pop songs" any more,' he responded, and received a death glare from a woman in front of him, who looked like the kind of woman who always shushed people.

It was effective, though, and he didn't speak again until Karen's performance was over. She had been one of many performers that night, all of them students who were singing as part of their evaluation for a degree. And, although he knew that was why Karen had been performing that night, he had expected the beauty of her voice almost as much as he had expected that kiss he and Mila had shared that afternoon.

He sighed when he realised that he was thinking about it yet again.

Though how could he not? an inner voice asked him, and his mind played back portions of it. Mila coming towards him with passion in her eyes…the feeling of her lips on his…the desire that had shot through him and had him tearing at her clothes—literally—just about ready to take her against the wall of the house they had once shared…

If she hadn't taken that phone call he wasn't sure he would have been able to help himself, although he definitely should have…

He wasn't sure if he was grateful for that call or annoyed by it.

Since his mind kept slipping back to that afternoon, he was grateful when all the performances were over and they could make their way backstage. Jordan saw Simon standing with Karen, and warned himself against the jealousy that still threatened. When he'd met Simon, Jordan had noted the easiness of the interaction between him and Mila. He'd only vaguely been able to remember a time when things had been that easy between himself and Mila—when they'd been married, probably—and that thought had led to the annoyance that Mila had incorrectly interpreted as anger earlier.

But Jordan had shaken it off now, and he forced himself to remember that as Simon waved them over.

'Karen, I can't believe it was you out there!' Mila pulled the smiling girl in for a hug. 'It can't be only two years since that event. You have grown up *so* much since then!'

'It makes a huge difference when I'm not in leather tights singing about boys breaking my heart, doesn't it?' Karen responded, and Mila laughed.

'Yeah—although I can't disregard the value of the tights *or* the songs. They're the reason we're able to see *this* amazing side of you.'

It still impressed Jordan to see how good Mila was at networking, even though he'd spent the afternoon witnessing it. She had made every vendor feel as though they were her friend, he remembered, asking them about details of their lives that he was sure they had only mentioned to her in passing. And then, when they had been buttered up by the personal conversation, she would segue into the professional.

Now she was complimenting Karen on her current performance but still highlighting their need for the other side of her to perform. It wasn't only a testament to how good she was at networking, he realised suddenly, it was smart, too.

'They're the reason she's here, too,' Simon chimed in. 'Some well-placed donations helped her get in, even though she had missed the application deadline.'

Mila smiled at Simon, though Jordan saw the flash of annoyance in her eyes, and he found himself agreeing. Why would Karen's manager undermine her talent like that?

'I'm sure it didn't take that much convincing with your voice, though,' Mila said smoothly, and Jordan felt warmth radiate from the smile Karen aimed at Mila.

She cared, he thought, though he wasn't sure why he hadn't thought about that before. Since he'd come back Jordan had learned all kinds of things about his wife— and was clearly still learning. He knew more than he'd known before. She was feisty, and he was beginning to realise just how much he liked it. It made her a lot more confident, he thought as he watched it first-hand and felt the tug of attraction.

'Oh, I'm sorry!' Mila turned to him and he realised it

was his turn to perform. 'I don't think you met Jordan the night of the first Under the Stars event, did you?'

'No, I didn't.'

Karen held out her hand, and Jordan smiled at the interest he saw coming from her. She didn't try to hide it, which amused him even more. It seemed she'd grown up a lot from the whiny teen who'd cried at a broken heart, he thought.

'It's lovely to meet you, Karen. Mila was absolutely right about that performance. If you don't get an A for that, then I'm not sure the lecturers were listening properly.'

'How very kind of you to say, Jordan.'

He hid a smile at the flirtatious tone of her voice.

'Simon tells me that you're interested in me performing at an event you're hosting at the vineyard?'

'Yeah, Mila and I are hosting it, actually.'

'You mean she's hosting the event *for* you?' Karen's eyes didn't leave his face.

'No, I mean we're hosting it together.'

Karen didn't know they were married, Jordan thought, and wondered how it would change things if he told Karen they were.

But then he saw the slight shake of Mila's head and continued, 'My father grew quite fond of Mila after the last event, and his dying wish was that we plan one more event in his name.'

It wasn't exactly a lie, was it?

'He essentially requested a replica of the event you performed at a couple of years ago, in fact. Said he couldn't remember hearing someone sing as beautifully as you.' That, he thought, *was* an outright lie. But desperate times called for desperate measures.

'Oh, wow...' Karen breathed, and Jordan realised his earlier assumption hadn't been entirely correct.

She was still a teenager—she had just learned to hide it better.

'Well, I can't see myself saying no to such an amazing offer. I have time towards the end of the year, right, Simon?'

'Actually...' Mila interrupted whatever answer Simon had been about to give '... I mentioned to Simon that the concert will have to happen quite soon. Like before the end of next month.'

Karen frowned. 'Why so soon?'

Mila exchanged a look with Jordan that screamed "Help me!" and words came out of his mouth before he had an opportunity to think about them.

'Well, Mila's moving away at the end of next month to teach in Korea. She won't be able to do anything once she's gone, and I'd like to honour my father before she leaves, since we don't know when she'll be back.'

Mila bit her lip, and he could see she was trying to hide a smile.

'Yes, Karen—I'm going to teach English to little children in Korea, and I need to do this before I leave. Can you help?'

Karen looked at Simon. 'Tonight was my last exam, but I'll be going on tour in a few weeks and then I won't be available.'

'The proceeds will be going to charity,' Jordan said suddenly, inspired by his fear of losing Karen's performance and the repercussions that might have on their event. But now that he'd said it, he realised it wasn't a bad idea.

Mila raised her eyebrows at him, but said, 'An event for charity will have an awesome effect on your public image, Karen. And, Simon, I don't have to tell you how much that can do for Karen's tour.'

Simon waited a beat, and then whipped out his phone and tapped on the screen. 'She has a sold-out concert at West-gate Stadium this Saturday, but the following Saturday—

the one before the tour—we don't have anything booked. It was intended to give her some rest before she leaves on tour. Would you be willing to sacrifice that?' Simon directed the question to Karen.

'Yeah, sure.' Karen turned to them in expectation, and all they could do was look at her with stunned expressions. Mila was the first to recover.

'That's great. Would you mind helping us with the marketing, then? We'll organise the tickets, but support from you on social media will properly ensure that we have an audience for you. *And* enough support for charity.'

'Yeah, of course.' Karen's eyes shifted to someone behind them and she smiled. 'Look, you can chat to Simon about the arrangements—the set, details about soundcheck—and he'll let me know what the deal is. We can take it from there. I'm going to run. It was nice seeing you again, Mila... Jordan.'

Karen fluttered her eyelashes, and then walked over to join a group of giggling girls.

'I'll contact you tomorrow, when I've had more time to look at the schedule, and we can talk about things,' Simon said to them.

'Yeah, that's perfect. Thanks, Simon.'

Mila smiled at him, and Jordan nodded a farewell, his mind too consumed by what Mila had just got them into to be concerned about the interested look Simon threw at Mila as he walked away.

They stood in silence after Simon had left, and then Jordan gathered his wits to ask, 'Did you just agree to holding our event in two weeks' time?'

'I...I think I did,' Mila stammered, not quite believing that it was true. But her instincts had taken over, and the event planner inside her had jumped at the opportunity to secure a performer who would ensure their event was a success.

'What were you *thinking*?' he asked under his breath,

and then gave a polite smile to the man who was returning their coats.

'I was thinking that we need Karen to make the event
a success.'

'But you realise we don't actually need the event to be
a success, right?'

He shot her a frown as he slid his coat on, and then
turned for her to help him when his arm got stuck. Her
hands shook a little, but she forced them to behave and
helped him into the garment, lingering a tad too long at
his shoulders.

'We just need there to *be* an event. Whether we have
five or five hundred people there doesn't matter.'

'*You* were the one who said it was for charity,' she
hissed at him. 'And you heard that she wouldn't be able
to do it before our deadline otherwise. What was I supposed to do?'

'Find another performer?'

'It would have been more of an effort,' she replied, and
he nodded as though he'd thought of that, too.

'You've made this much more difficult for us now,' he
said stonily.

'I know that. But we both knew that this was a possibility when we spoke to the vendors today. It was either
at the end of this month *with* Karen, or the beginning of
next month without her.'

She was trying to convince herself as much as she was
him, but suddenly she knew that she had done the right
thing. That her actions would make the event a success.
She really wanted it to be a success, she thought. And because she had just realised why, she said, 'It'll be the last
thing I do for Greg, Jordan. I want it to go as well as it
possibly can.'

Her stomach knotted at her words. The intimacy of
what she had revealed and the fact that she'd said it out

loud warned her that she was growing too comfortable around Jordan. But up until that point it hadn't occurred to her that she might want to do the event for any reason other than the fact that she had to.

Now she knew she wanted to do it as a thank-you to Greg for all he had done for her—the last one she would be able to give him—and perhaps as a goodbye present to all those she cared about at the vineyard. A successful event would boost the vineyard's image and be a foundation they would be able to use to rebuild everything that had been put on pause over the last year with Greg's illness.

'I'm sorry, I—'

'No, it's fine,' she interrupted him, not wanting his sympathy.

She thanked the man for her coat, and took care to slip it on so that she wouldn't need Jordan's help as he had needed hers. They walked to the car in silence, though Jordan once again put an arm around her waist to keep her steady. She murmured a thank-you when she got into the car, and wondered why the silence was suddenly so bothersome. Maybe it was because she could feel, just beneath the armour she had put around her heart, her need for Jordan become stronger.

And he had only been back for three days.

That was another reason—one that also hadn't occurred to her until now—that she'd agreed to expedite the event. The quicker it happened, the sooner she would be able to get away from the reminder of a life that had never been hers to begin with. She would be free of all the wants and needs that were beyond her grasp, and she would finally be able to move on to a more realistic future, where she would be safe from hurt...

'So, I'm going to teach in *Korea*?' she blurted out, sick of the direction of her thoughts.

Jordan chuckled, and the vibration of his voice sent a

chill up her spine. Or maybe that was just the cold, she told herself desperately.

'One of the fellows at the research institute we started in Johannesburg told me about how his daughter was going to teach there in a few months. For some reason that was what jumped into my head when you sent me the fire signal for help.'

She smiled. 'Fire signal?'

'Your eyes were screaming "Help me!" so loudly I'm surprised no one else heard it.'

'I'm grateful that you came to my rescue—though now I'm wondering if Korea might be a good next step for me.'

She was still smiling, but her words reminded them that she would be leaving after the event. The thought was sobering—for both of them, she thought, when Jordan didn't respond—and again she sought for something to break the tension.

'How did things go with the institute?'

He looked over at her, and she wondered why he seemed to be checking to see if she was asking him seriously.

Because that's the excuse he used to leave the first time, she thought, and shook her head at the fact that everywhere she turned there was a reminder of a life she no longer had and a future that was uncertain.

'It went well,' he said after a moment. 'We had already started the ball rolling by then, so I just went there to finalise the staffing and ensure that the premises were suited for the expected capacity.'

'Was it?'

'Yeah, it was. It's in central Johannesburg, which is a great location, and it has enough space for the research fellows and for research seminars.'

'Worth the hassle of the accreditation process?'

She remembered the hours he'd had to spend on the phone, and the countless meetings when he'd first had the idea for a research institution for wine microbiology. He had wanted to give back—to contribute to the wine industry in some way other than just selling—and setting up an educational institution that would ensure the quality of the wines the Thomas Vineyard made as well as allow continued research into wine production had seemed like the way to do it. But getting accreditation from the Department of Education for some kind of qualification for the fellows had been a mission—as Jordan's facial expression now proved.

'Right now, with twenty fellows, I'm going to say yes.'

'Seems like you did a good thing, then.' She meant it—though she wished it hadn't been at the expense of their relationship. But then again, they'd already established that that hadn't been the real reason—at least not the only one—that he'd left.

'How was living there?' she asked suddenly, thinking that perhaps knowing how Jordan had lived in his year without her would bring her some peace.

He frowned again, his hands still on the steering wheel, and she realised that they were already in front of the house. She waited a few more minutes and then shook her head in disappointment, feeling the cold run through her as she said, 'Don't tell me, then. I'll just add it to the list.'

She opened the car door, happy to escape from the desperate need inside her to know more about him. To know more about the aspects of his life that she hadn't been a part of.

To escape the need to demand to know about them.

'Mila, wait!' he called after her.

But she had already reached the front door and was trying to find her key to get in—to get away from him. The key fell from her hand, and she let out an exasperated breath as he came from behind her and picked it up.

He inserted the key into the door, but didn't turn it. 'I'll tell you,' he said, without looking at her, and she scoffed.

'I'm not pulling your teeth, Jordan. Talking to people is supposed to be natural. Or at least it's supposed to be with your *wife*.'

It was the first time she had referred to herself like that since learning that she *was* still his wife, and it sounded strange—maybe even terrifying—to hear it. But at the same time something came to rest inside her at the term—an acknowledgement of why learning about him had become so important.

She cared about him.

As a friend, she assured herself, not because she had been his wife. But even through her self-assurance she knew she was more hurt than she cared to admit that after all the revelations she'd made to him, he refused to share his own with her.

'I want to tell you,' he insisted. 'I want to talk to you… It's just difficult.'

Her eyebrows rose. 'Why?'

He exhaled sharply, and then turned the key in the lock. He pushed the door open and waited for her to walk through. When she had, she took her coat and hung it on the rack, then looked at him expectantly.

He would tell her this at least, she thought.

He took his jacket off, and then rubbed at his chin, which was already starting to show stubble. She remembered the slight burn on her skin from the friction earlier and her body responded with need.

To combat it, she folded her arms, and waited for him to speak.

'There's a lot I have to deal with. Since I came back here after Dad died…' He stuffed his hands into his pockets. 'It's hard for me to verbalise it. It's…a lot.'

She steeled herself against the softening that inevitably

touched her heart, and said, 'We've both had to deal with "a lot," Jordan.' Her next words were already forming, and she ignored the voice telling her not to say them. 'Don't accuse me of pushing away the people who care about me when *you're* doing exactly the same thing.'

CHAPTER THIRTEEN

SHE HAD A POINT, Jordan thought, even as he wished for the old Mila. The one who would have understood him saying he had a lot to deal with and wouldn't have pushed. But hadn't he, only a few hours earlier, thought about how much he *liked* this new Mila? He couldn't change his mind now, just because she was making him uncomfortable. Especially when she was right.

'Fine—let's talk, then,' he forced himself to say, though he wasn't sure what he was prepared to talk about. 'But let me change first. I'd feel better in comfortable clothes.'

He wasn't sure how true that was, but he wasn't about to bare his soul in a tuxedo. Mila nodded, and he went to his bedroom, already unbuttoning his shirt.

The room hadn't changed much since his childhood, Jordan thought as he pulled on a pair of worn jeans and a long-sleeved shirt. It was still painted the blue his mother had chosen for him when he was younger. It had been one of their last activities together, before she had become too sick to get out of bed.

His memories of her had faded over time, but he still remembered how much time she had wanted to spend with him. He would play in front of the house on the patio, shouting for her to look when he did something that only a four-year-old would find impressive. And she had always sat on those chairs beside the front door, cheering for him, sharing his pride and telling him how happy he made her.

Even when his father had no longer joined her she'd sat there, watching over him. Even when she'd grown frailer, paler, more sickly, with his father hovering around, she'd spent hours with Jordan outdoors. His heart ached at the memories, which suddenly seemed so clear now, and he took a deep breath.

Why was he thinking about this *now*? There was no purpose in rehashing that part of his past. The part that reminded him of his father's anger towards him and, ever since he had learned the truth about his mother's death, his anger towards himself and the guilt he felt.

The thought had already put him on edge, and he forced himself to control it or he knew the conversation he was preparing to have with Mila could only go poorly.

It didn't work, since he found himself considering why he was preparing to have this conversation in the first place. Why had it all of a sudden become so important for her to see him trying? For her to see that he wanted to let her in, to tell her the real reasons behind why he had left?

There was no answer that would pull him away from the edge, and his insides tensed even further.

When he walked into the lounge, he noticed that she had started a fire. And then she walked into the room, a glass of wine in each hand, and his gut tightened.

She had changed, too, into a long-sleeved shirt he recognised as an old one of his. It was worn, and stretched so much that it almost touched her knees, which were clad in tights. She hadn't worn that particular shirt before, but it still reminded him of the times when she would wear his clothes. They smelled like him, she had always said, and he wondered if that was the reason she was wearing the shirt now.

The emotions that thought evoked—and his physical reaction to her—did nothing to make him feel better.

'How was my father before his death?' he asked abruptly, his voice harsher than he'd intended.

Her eyebrows rose in response, and he saw the flash of annoyance before it was replaced with ice.

Back to this again, he thought, but knew he was to blame for her reaction.

She set his glass down on the table in front of him, hard enough that he watched the contents swirl in disruption, and then she said, 'No, I'm not doing this with you when you're in this mood.'

'Mila, I don't have—'

'Whatever you're going to say, I'm sure I've heard it before. You don't feel like talking right now…or you're going through a lot…or can we postpone?' She shook her head. 'We don't have to have this conversation *at all*, Jordan.'

'No.' The word came quickly—something he was sure was a result of the answers he hadn't wanted to consider earlier.

'Are you sure?' She raised her eyebrow, and her sassy look sent a shock of desire through him.

'Yes.'

Both brows rose now, and then she picked up her wine and settled back. 'We can start with something simple. Tell me about your life in Johannesburg.'

'There's not much to say. And I'm not saying that because I don't want to tell you,' he said quickly, when he saw the expression on her face. 'I spent most of my time at the institute. Too much time, probably. But it helped to focus on something other than…'

'Me,' she finished when he trailed off.

He nodded. 'And on everything else that had happened.

I thought that if I could make a success of this, something I could actually control, then my failures at home…'

He was messing it up, he thought. Her finger was tracing the rim of her glass again, so although her face was unreadable he knew she was thinking about what he was saying. But he couldn't tell *what* she was thinking, and it was driving him crazy.

'I get that,' she said finally, and raised her eyes to look at him. 'When your dad got sick and asked me to move in…focusing on him instead of the things going on in my life helped me deal with everything.' She cocked her head. 'Did you have a social life?'

'You mean did I date?'

Her mouth opened slightly at the blunt question, and then she straightened her shoulders. 'I suppose so. Though I was talking about whether or not you had friends.'

His lips curved at the slight blush on her cheeks. But he answered her question,

'No dates, but I did go out for drinks with some of the people from work sometimes. Not often enough to keep in touch outside work now, though.'

She nodded, and sipped from her wine. It gave him a clear view of the line of her throat, and again he felt his need for her run through his blood with the memory of how he had kissed her there that afternoon.

'Can I ask about my father now?' he asked quickly, before the need consumed him and he did something he regretted.

'Of course. What do you want to know?'

'Anything.'

Everything, he thought, but stopped the word before it came out.

'Well, he was devastated about the baby,' she began. 'Not that he would ever have said it. You know how he was.'

Yes, he did. And wasn't that part of why he was absorbing everything she was telling him now?

'I didn't speak to him that first month. Not to anyone, really, as you know. But he eventually told me he'd stayed away because he wanted us to deal with it together.'

Jordan remembered that. His father hadn't visited them much after Mila's fall, and when Jordan had turned up at the vineyard Greg hadn't got involved. Not that Jordan had given him a chance to. Jordan hadn't spoken about it—not the accident, not his wife. The only reason he had been there was because Mila hadn't wanted him around. That was the first time he had noticed the anger seep in, the resentment. The signs that he had it in him to react as his father had after his mother's death.

Jordan reached for his glass of wine at the unsettling thought.

'But then you left.' She looked up at him. 'I'd like to say your father and I helped each other through it, but that isn't true. Like with everyone else...I pushed him away. I wanted nothing to do with him since he only reminded me of you, and of what I'd lost.'

She cleared her throat, as though the admission had taken her by surprise. And since it had surprised *him*, too, he didn't interrupt.

'I was staying at the beach house—I couldn't stay at our place alone, not after what had happened—and I told Greg because I didn't want him to worry. And then I got the divorce papers, and Greg was the only person who would understand...'

She stopped, and he heard her take a shaky breath. He didn't blame her—her story was peppered with anecdotes that he wasn't sure she would have shared with him if they hadn't agreed on having an honest conversation.

'I could see that you leaving had hurt him. I'm not saying that to hurt *you*, Jordan,' she said immediately, and he wondered what it was in his face that had told her he needed reassurance. 'I'm telling you because you need to know to move on. He was hurt, but I think he understood. He didn't blame you.'

'I'm not sure that's true.'

'It is,' she said firmly.

'You didn't know him like I knew him, Mila. And he asked me not to go. Told me I would be destroying our relationship if I did.' He could feel his breathing hitch, and he emptied his wine glass.

'Maybe that's true,' she said when he'd set the wine glass down, and he saw that she was watching him. 'But you didn't know him like *I* did either.'

He wondered what she meant by that—was about to ask—and then she continued, 'He was growing frailer, I saw. At first I thought it was because of everything that had happened over the last months. I'd lost some weight, too, so I didn't think too much of it. And then he had the first heart attack. He was out in the fields with Frank. They had people around them, who rallied round to get Greg to the car, to the hospital, the moment they realised what was happening. He wasn't alone.'

Jordan didn't know if she'd done it purposely, but that piece of information seemed to have settled something inside him.

'I didn't think twice when he asked me to move in after that. It was the only admission of needing help that he would ever give, I knew. So I moved in...helped around the house.'

'How long?'

She took a moment to respond, and then she said, 'The time between his first and second heart attacks was short, and between his second and third even shorter.' She was watching him carefully. 'The whole period was just over seven months.'

Seven months. It was shorter than the time his mother had had to suffer, and that comforted him. They'd found out about her cancer when Jordan was two, and she'd had to suffer for three long, agonising years—two without treatment and one with—before she'd passed away.

He thought of watching his mother suffer, and of how his father had suffered because of the pain he'd seen his wife go through. Felt relief that he hadn't been there to witness what Greg had gone through during the past year, and the overwhelming guilt at the thought. And realised how exactly his childhood had impacted him…

'Was he in pain? My father?'

The words escaped his lips before he'd realised he wanted to know the answer. But knowing the answer would confirm what he had just learned about himself—that he couldn't see anyone he cared about suffer.

The compassion in her eyes sent a blow to his heart. 'Sometimes. It made him miserable, difficult. More so than usual.' She paused. 'But it also made him more honest than usual.'

He raised his eyebrows, but she shook her head. 'I'm not going to tell you about that until you share something with me.'

The calm tone of her voice infuriated him. 'Tit for tat? Are we children?'

'If that's what it takes.' She shrugged, but the gesture was anything but casual.

'You have no right to keep things from me!' he spat, his heart pounding furiously. 'He was my father.'

'And maybe I wouldn't have to keep things from you if you'd been here.'

'Back to this, are we?' He shook his head and thought that he needed to get out of the room.

'Yes, we are. But we wouldn't need to get back to it if you just *told* me why you left,' she shot back.

'Because of *you*,' he said angrily. 'You wouldn't listen to me, just like my mother didn't listen to my father. And where did *that* get her?'

He was breathing heavily, and it took him a moment to compose himself.

'What does that mean?' she asked in a shaky voice when he finally looked at her.

Her face had lost its colour, and it shook him more than he wanted it to. 'It doesn't matter.'

'Yes, it does,' she said, in a voice that twisted his insides. 'Please, Jordan, just let me in for once.'

'You know more about me than anyone else.'

'I don't know *enough*,' she contradicted him. 'There's more—I know there's more. I've shared so much with you,' she said, in a tone that told him that that wasn't necessarily what she had wanted. 'Please, Jordan. I...I...*need* you to tell me.'

'I can't give you more than this, Mila,' he rasped, and pushed up from his seat. He didn't need to see the torment on her face when he had his own to deal with.

He walked out of the room, ignoring the voice that mocked him for running away from her for the second time.

CHAPTER FOURTEEN

MILA WATCHED HIM leave and pain tore through her. She had been honest with him. She had pushed through her reservations about opening up to him and told him she *needed* him.

And he'd rejected her.

She gasped when the pain turned into a burn that consumed her entire body, and sank to her knees. *This* was why she didn't want him back. *This* was exactly what she was afraid of. Showing people the real her, showing *him* the real her, and having them—*him*—reject her.

Though she didn't know how it was possible, this was worse than the first time. Maybe it was because then Jordan hadn't been leaving *her*. Not the real her. No, back then he'd been leaving the person she was pretending to be. The one who didn't believe that she was worth him, who didn't speak her mind, who was waiting—expecting—for him to leave. The one who had failed as a mother, as a wife.

But since he'd come back she had shown him more and more of herself. She hadn't realised how much until right at that moment when she hadn't been able to hide behind the person she showed the world.

A sob escaped, but she clasped a hand over her mouth. She *wouldn't* let him hear her cry for him. She would get through this—she would. She had survived growing up without anyone to care for her.

It didn't matter now that the man she loved didn't care for her enough to be honest with her.

Another sob came when she realised the truth that she'd been running away from since Jordan had come back. She still loved him. She'd never stopped. That was why she had started opening up to him. Why she had told him the truth. Why she had shown him who she was. Maybe even why she wanted the event to go well—so she could show him, prove to him, that she was capable, that she was worthy.

She wanted Jordan to love the real her.

It was a foolish hope, she thought now. Not because she wasn't worthy—she was slowly but surely fighting her way out of *that* pit—but because he didn't want to. She knew he was struggling—she had watched him during their conversation, knew that the information she'd given him about his father had opened up something for him—and now she knew that it had to do with his parents. With his mother. But, whatever it was, he didn't want *her* to be a part of it.

He doesn't need me, she thought, and closed her eyes against the pain.

She'd always thought it was something simple—something childish, even—to feel needed. To want a family who would need her unconditionally. But it wasn't, and she needed to face that. She needed to stop *pretending* that she was okay without having it, and to *really* be okay with it.

The man she loved didn't need her. She wouldn't ever get to have the family she had always wanted. And that was okay, she told herself. She would get through it. She *would* be okay.

But that didn't have to happen right now, she thought as she lowered her head between her knees and let the tears fall silently to the floor.

Jordan got up earlier than he normally would the next day. Not only because he hadn't got any sleep, but because he knew Mila was an early riser and he wanted to be up before her. He wasn't running away, he told himself. He just needed to get out of the house to think.

He sighed when he heard a loud thunderclap, and then the steady pelting of rain on the roof. There would be no walking through the vineyard to clear his thoughts, he thought. But since he was already up he decided to get some coffee. He needed the strength.

He had hurt her. The look on her face when she'd told him she needed him to let her in would be branded in his mind for ever. He wished that he could go back, that he could take it back, so that they could go back to the truce they'd had with one another. But he couldn't, and now all he wanted was to finish the darn event and get it over with so that he could move on with his life.

Because he didn't want to get caught up in the past any more. The last few days had been more than enough for his entire lifetime, and he could do without the memories of his mother, without the regrets he had about his father. *And he could do without Mila.*

His hand stilled midway on its path to bringing the coffee mug to his mouth. That *was* what he was saying, wasn't it? She was the one forcing him to face his past. The last few days had been filled with his past because of *her*. And since he wanted the event over and done with, it meant he wanted things with *her* to be over and done with…right?

Except that the very thought sent an unpleasant frisson through his body. And an even worse one through his heart. The last thing he wanted was to say goodbye to her. Though they'd been difficult for him, the past few days had also been great. He'd started to get to know a side of Mila that he hadn't seen before. In fact, he'd thought he was getting to know a whole different Mila. The feistiness, the speaking her mind suited her in a way he hadn't considered before.

But it was more than that. It was the passion that he could see she had for her job. For her family. Because, although she didn't think she had one, the way she cared about Lulu and his father was more familial than anything he had ever experienced.

She was compassionate even when she didn't want to be, he thought as he remembered the way she had cared for him after his run-in with Lulu. As he thought about how she'd had nothing to gain when his father had asked her to move in with him and yet she had still done it.

It spoke of warmth, of the kindness that was naturally *her*. She was the best person he knew. And he cared about her.

But he couldn't *be* with her.

Not when she needed more from him than he could give her. So he would simply have to be without her. And even though the thought sent pain through him, he knew it was the right thing.

But that didn't mean he didn't have to apologise to her. He'd been a bit of a jerk the previous day, walking out on her like that, and she didn't deserve it. Not when *he* had been the person to suggest they have an honest conversation in the first place.

He started taking out things for breakfast. It was an apology, yes, but he also wanted to see her smile again. He wanted to see the smile that made him feel as if he was the only person in the world. The smile that pierced through his defences and reminded him of why he had fallen in love with her...

Before he could ponder why seeing her smile had become so important, she walked in. She stopped when she saw him there, and he could sense her hesitation. And then she turned around.

'Hey, I'm making breakfast.'

She stopped, and then slowly turned back to him. 'Are we just going to pretend last night didn't happen?'

Her voice was a little husky, her hair still mussed from sleep, and the effect was potent. It was as if his body was reminding him about yet another thing he was leaving behind, and it took a moment for him to recover.

'I'm trying to apologise.'

'Why? What's the point?'

His heart dribbled against his chest when he realised he didn't have an answer for her.

'Because we have an event to plan together,' he finally managed.

'If that's the only reason, apology not accepted. I've worked with people I don't like before. This won't be a first for me.'

She turned away from him again, and his heart skidded to a halt when he realised that she was putting barriers up. Barriers he didn't think would ever come down again. It bothered him and he didn't know why.

'We're doing more than just working together, Mila,' he found himself saying.

'Really?' She folded her arms. 'What else are we doing, then?'

'We're saying goodbye to my father.' That wasn't it, he realised as his stomach sank. But it was good enough to appease her.

'You know where to hit, don't you?' she said as her arms dropped to her sides.

She was right, but he couldn't think of anything else to say. Not when he was still stunned by how all his conclusions earlier had been swept aside the minute he'd seen her. How much the thought that she would push him away again had alarmed him. How much he wanted things between them to be okay.

'How about we start with a cup of coffee?' she said

when he didn't respond, and he nodded, turning away from her.

Why was it suddenly so important for him to stay close to her? He had resigned himself to letting go—of her, of the past—but now he couldn't imagine anything worse.

He took his time making her coffee, ignoring the sudden jittery feeling in his body, and then he handed it to her carefully, so that they wouldn't touch. But her fingers brushed against his anyway, and his body responded.

Except that the physical effect she had on him had little to do with desire. It was a way of confirming what he had just realised. He still had feelings for her. It was the only thing that made his reaction to her logical. What else could make his rational thoughts seem like the most nonsensical things in the world?

He had barely acknowledged his feelings before he was striding towards her. He took the mug from her hands, had the pleasure of seeing her eyes widen and hearing her sharp inhalation, and then with her body against his, he touched his lips to hers.

She tasted of coffee and toothpaste…a combination he would have never thought sexy if he hadn't experienced it himself. She didn't move at first, her lips stiff under his, and he prepared himself to pull back—all but had words of apology ready in his mind before he felt her hands tentatively touch his waist.

Immediately he felt heat at their contact, but he resisted giving in to it. Instead he kept it slow, like the afternoon walks they'd used to take on Sundays, and let the fire simmer. It made him more aware of the connection they shared, of how their kiss was more than just a meeting of their lips, more than just something he was doing to sate his need for her.

It made slow and tender feel as satisfying and as passionate as the desperate kiss they had shared—was it only the previous day?

He didn't spend much time thinking about it—was too consumed by the way her body fitted his in just the right way. By the way her hands tightened on his waist, and then slid up under his shirt to touch his skin. Everywhere they moved heightened the sensation in his body, and he sank deeper into the kiss, using his tongue to remind her of their passion, of their love.

She moaned, pressed herself tighter against him, and he felt her shake. It turned the temperature up between them and his hands found her waist and lifted her up, setting her on the kitchen counter without losing contact. She pulled the hoodie he wore over his head, and he barely felt the sting of cold on his bare body. Not when she was kissing his neck, his shoulders, then his mouth again, as if she had discovered she needed him just as much as he needed her.

The thought gave him pause, and he moved away.

'Do you want this?' he asked, and searched her face for the real answer.

His heart was filled by her beauty in that moment—the flush of her cheeks, her untamed curls framing her face, her chest heaving—but he couldn't ignore the flash of uncertainty, of fear that lit her face.

It was gone in a moment and she nodded and pulled his head closer, but with all the self-control inside him, he resisted.

'You don't, Mila. At least, you're not sure,' he forced himself to say, and braced himself against the pain that flashed through her eyes at his words.

'No, I think *you're* the one who isn't sure,' she told him.

'You have no idea what I'm thinking,' he said, his voice sharp. She was too close to the truth.

'Whose fault is that?' she asked softly, before pushing at his chest.

He took a step back, watched as she lowered herself off the counter and pulled at the shirt that had ridden up to her waist during their passion. But not before he had got a good look at her stomach. The skin was slightly loose over the flat surface, with tiny vertical lines leading to the scar from her C-section—evidence that she had once carried his child—and his hands itched to touch, to feel, to remind himself of better times between them.

'I don't know what to do about you,' she said suddenly, and all his thoughts gave way to one single thought that ripped at his heart.

He was hurting her.

With his words, with his actions. He couldn't do this with her again, he realised. Not until he was sure.

'I'm sorry,' he said, because he didn't know what else he could say.

'We should just stick to the event, Jordan. Everything else…'

She looked at him, her eyes shockingly beautiful in their misery, and he saw for the first time that they were a little swollen, a little red, as if she'd been crying. The thought sent another blow to his heart.

'*Nothing* else will work between us.'

She walked away, leaving him alone in the kitchen. It was sobering to think that he had never felt so alone ever before. He no longer had his mother, his father. He no longer had his wife.

He was pushing her away.

Was it worth it? Was his guilt, his regret over what had had happened in his childhood, over his relationship with his father, over his mother's choices, worth risking the woman he loved?

He ran a hand through his hair and then slid it down his face. Who was he fooling? Thinking he had feelings for Mila was just vague enough to make him feel better about himself. But he should have known the truth would catch up with him. He should have known from the moment he had seen her and fallen for her that he couldn't run away from his feelings for her.

His shoulders stiffened even more at the thought. He needed to stop running. He loved Mila—had never stopped—and he needed to step up for her. Except…he didn't know how. Or even if he could. He had been running away all his life. From the moment his father had told him that his mother had chosen to look after him instead of her own health. From the moment he'd realised his father blamed Jordan for her death.

Even the thought sent waves of hurt through him, and only his hope of love with Mila was keeping them at bay. He knew that if he told her those hurts might overwhelm him, and that if he didn't they would keep nudging at him, causing him to run all his life.

He had to make a choice. And, despite all the things he had been through in his life, despite all the difficult choices he'd had to make, he knew that this one would be the worst.

CHAPTER FIFTEEN

SHE KEPT MAKING the same mistakes, and if she continued down that path it would destroy her. So Mila kept to her word and focused on her work, ignoring the kiss that she'd shared with Jordan that morning—*and* its after-effects.

She called Lulu and explained that their event was now less than two weeks away and they needed to make sure there *would* be an event. She confirmed the details with Simon, informed the marquee supplier about the date, and called to tell the vendors the same thing. She soothed complaints, found alternatives, until eventually she was fairly certain that the event would take place.

She updated Mark, as the executor of the will, and emailed him records of all they had done to keep within the conditions of the will.

And then she braced herself for visiting her house again.

She had decided the previous evening that she would move out of Greg's house. She should have done it the day after Jordan had returned. It would have saved her so much heartache. Now her heart pained her with every beat, and her mind was consumed by grief because he didn't want her.

He wanted her physically, maybe, she thought, flushing at the memory of that morning, but not in any other way. And so, because she couldn't live with the man who reminded her of everything she wanted and couldn't have, she was going to live at the house where they'd started their lives together.

It was better that way, she told herself as she began packing a bag. She would start clearing the house, get it on the market, and once it was sold she would use the money to buy offices for her business.

She and Lulu had used to work out of the flat she'd rented before she got married and at Lulu's home before Mila's fall, but now she wanted something more legitimate. Something that would make her feel steady. Something that was her own.

It was also the only thing she could think of to use the money from the sale of the house *for*—taking it to live a lavish life didn't seem right to her. And she knew Jordan wouldn't want it back—it would be a slap in the face to him if she offered, when she knew that he'd done it because he had wanted to give her something. He had hurt her, yes, but Mila had no intention of doing the same thing to him. She was better than that.

That was another reason why she had decided to sort out the house on her own. Before she'd thought she needed him. That she couldn't do it by herself. But as part of her resolution to move on, to only rely on herself, she *would* do it by herself.

Yes, her heart still thumped at the thought of going back to the house where she had lost her baby, but it was also the house where she had found out she was going to have him. It was the place where she had first felt him kick, where she had spent the only time she'd had with him. And although focusing on those positives almost made her reconsider selling—*almost*—she knew it would be for the best if she did.

And then, when the event was over, she would file for divorce.

She *would* move on from Jordan.

She packed the case with her essentials—she had enough clothing to last her until the event at the house—and dragged the case behind her to the front door. It rattled on the tiles, and then stopped. She turned back, giving it a forceful pull before continuing.

And walked straight into Jordan.

'Hey!' he said, steadying her, and she had a flashback to those hands on her waist, lifting her. 'Where are you going?'

'I'm going to stay somewhere else.' She knew it sounded snappy, but it was better than showing the need that heated her belly at her memories.

She looked up at him and saw the carefully blank look in his eyes.

'You're leaving,' he said flatly.

'I am,' she said in the same tone. 'It's what's best, isn't it?'

She could almost see the gears grinding in his head as he thought, and she wondered what there was to think about. He'd made his choice. She'd made hers. That was it.

That was it, she reminded herself when something inside her lit up—just a little—at the thought of him wanting her to stay.

'Where are you going?'

'Back to the house.'

She saw the twitch in his eyebrow before he schooled his features again. 'I'll take you.'

'No, no,' she said quickly, feeling all her bravado fade at the prospect of going back with him. 'I'm calling a taxi.'

'No, you're not.'

She would have been annoyed by his tone if she hadn't seen that twitch in his brow again. She had grown familiar with his facial expressions when they were married—was even more so now, perhaps—and she knew he was upset, but was trying to hide it.

'Please, just let me do this thing for you.'

The tone had softened, and she hated that her heart did the same. 'Okay…'

She didn't protest when he took the case from her hand, and she followed him to the car, getting in before he could open the door for her. She had had too many lingering touches from him in the past when he'd done that, and she wasn't interested in repeating it now. Not when she was already warning her heart to stay behind the wall she'd erected the previous night after she had finished sobbing. That wall had already been threatened by their kiss that morning, and she refused to put it in danger again.

When they pulled into the driveway at the house she immediately turned to get out—and then froze when she felt his hand on her thigh. It was in no way sexual, but heat seeped through her and she turned back in the hope that if she did he would remove it.

'Are you going to miss it?' he asked, and pulled back his hand as Mila had hoped.

He was staring at the house now, avoiding her gaze, so she sat back and looked at it, too. It *was* beautiful, she thought, and felt a pang in her heart.

'I am,' she said carefully.

'But it's not the vineyard?' he replied and looked at her.

She felt pinned by the look—especially since he had said exactly what she was thinking. The house she had lived in for the past year had begun to feel like more of a home to her than this place, where she had lived in with the man she had married. It was going to be hard to leave all that behind, she thought.

'I walked in here for the first time and I thought this would be a great house for you to come home to. Your first real home. I wanted it to be special for you.'

And just like that his words carved another spot in her heart.

'It *was* special,' she said, 'and it will always be my first home. Thank you.'

She wanted to kiss him in gratitude—a simple peck as she would have given him so often before—but she resisted.

'I'd like to show you something.'

He got out of the car before she could answer and she followed quickly, unsure of what was going on.

'I wanted to show it to you yesterday, but we…er…got a little distracted.'

He locked the car, and then held out his hand to her. It was a simple gesture, almost a reflex, but he stood like that until she walked over to him and carefully took his hand with her own. The warmth immediately gave her comfort, and she almost pulled away. She didn't need to be reminded of how much Jordan made her feel at home. But then she looked up, saw the impact simply taking her hand had had on him, and left it there.

You're hopeless, she berated herself.

But still she followed—perhaps because she thought it was for the last time.

'Where are you taking me?' she asked, to escape her thoughts.

'You'll see,' he replied, and she felt him tighten his grip on her hand.

It made her sad, and she wasn't completely sure why. They walked in silence, and when they reached a gate that Mila had never seen before Jordan took a key out of his pocket.

'Wait—this is the Gerber place.' Mila let go of his hand and placed hers lightly on his arm.

'It used to be,' he answered, and then pushed open the gate.

It didn't make any sound as it opened—confirmation to her that it had been recently put there—and Jordan gestured for her to go through. The plot was vast and green, as though completely unaffected by the coldness of the season, and a bridge led over the stream that ran around the whole property.

He held out a hand to help her cross, even though she saw that the bridge was fairly sturdy. And she took his hand, needing the contact to help her soothe the sudden anxiety in her stomach.

'I don't think this is a good idea.'

'Trust me.'

She stood at the base of the bridge, looked at the sincerity in his eyes, and felt the wall she had prided herself on erecting and then maintaining completely disintegrate. She nodded, unable to speak, and they walked over the wooden bridge together.

She ran her free hand over the railing, forcing herself to focus on its design—anything to keep her mind occupied with something other than how much she loved him. It was a perfect example of the traditional charm that all the Stellenbosch properties had—just as the barn they were walking towards now was.

'Are you going to tell me what's going on?' Mila asked softly.

'This is the latest Thomas property.'

'You *own* this place?'

'Yeah.'

'How? It must be recent, because I didn't once see or suspect that the Gerbers were selling their property.'

'They weren't planning on selling it, but I managed to convince them.'

He stuffed his hands into his pockets, and the gesture made him seem less rich-vineyard-owner and more handsome-husband. Though his words implied that he had very much *played* rich vineyard owner to get the property.

'When?'

'About a year ago.'

'A year ago? But that was—'

'Just before your fall?'

She nodded, and he continued.

'Yes, it was. I was going to surprise you with it after you gave birth.'

'With what? Another property? We didn't need that—'

'With the Thomas Events venue.'

Her mind took a moment to process what he was saying, and the moment she did she felt the heat of tears in her eyes.

'The Thomas Events venue?' she repeated, and hated it that it sounded so right. Hated it even more that Jordan had been trying to make another dream of hers come true.

She wished with all her might that things could have worked out between them. Her life would have been absolutely perfect then! She would have had a place to go home to, a husband who loved her and a baby who needed her and to whom she would have given the world.

'I thought it was time your business had a home,' Jordan said when she didn't say anything. 'I had the barn redone so that you could host events there—weddings, conferences, anything you wanted—and I was going to turn the house into an office. You could meet your clients there, do mock-ups—even turn one of the rooms into a baby's room, if you wanted.'

'I...um... Wow... I...' She took a deep breath, and pulled her hand away from his. 'This is... I don't know what to say, Jordan.'

A tear slid down her face and he took a step forward.

'I didn't want you to be sad. I just wanted to—'

'*What?*' she asked, grasping for anger instead of pain. 'You wanted to show me another thing I don't have?'

'*No!* No, of course not,' he said quickly, his eyes wide.

'I wanted to show you this because it's still yours. I want you to have it.'

'I don't *want* it,' she snapped, and another tear rolled down her face. 'I don't want any reminder of the life we will never have together.'

'Mila—' He stepped forward again, opening his arms, but she took a step back away from him.

'No, Jordan! You don't get it, do you? I can't do this with you any more. I can't pretend that we're friends, or whatever we're pretending to be at the moment.' She took a shaky breath and impatiently wiped at her tears. 'I need to move on. I *am* moving on. The minute this event is over, I'm gone. Far away from this place—' she threw a hand out '—from the house I lived in as your wife and from the vineyard that started this whole thing in the first place.'

She looked up at him and choked out her next words.

'I'm filing for divorce and moving on from *you*.'

She bit her lip, trying to compose herself as the words tore her heart into pieces.

And then she said slowly, 'I don't want you to show me things I'll never get to enjoy. And I don't want you to show me a person I'll never get to be with.'

'No, Mila—wait,' he said when she turned to walk away, and she heard anger and something else coating his voice with gravel. 'You had your say, so now I'm having mine. I showed you this because it's *yours*. I don't care what you call it, or if you accept it or not. I bought this for *you*. So that you can understand how much I care for you and how much I believe in you.'

Care, she thought. Present tense. Before she could caution herself against it, she felt hope reignite.

'You can move on, move away, Mila, but this place will still be here when you get back.' There was a momentary pause, and then he said, 'It'll be waiting for you just like I will be.'

He took a step closer and lifted her chin until she was looking at him.

'I don't care whether it's a year or ten years, whether we're married or not, I'll be waiting for you.'

'Why?' she whispered, before her mind could give her permission to speak.

There was barely a moment before he answered, 'Because I love you.'

He slid an arm around her waist and pulled her in, silencing her protests even before his mouth found hers. It was similar to the way she had kissed *him* two days ago, she thought hazily, and she wondered if his reason was similar, too—to show her that they mattered.

But she was already too lost in the taste of him to think any more about it. Her body was thanking her for something—*someone*—it had longed for but never got in the last year. And yet still she could feel a part of her resist—the sane, rational part of her that wanted to protect her poor already broken heart—and in response she felt his arm loosen around her.

He was giving her an out—telling her that she could leave the embrace if she wanted to.

But that only made her want him more, and barely a beat after he'd offered her a way out, she found herself pressed against him again. His arms went around her, tighter this time, and his mouth took hers more deeply, hungry after the possibility of stopping.

She couldn't breathe, couldn't hear, couldn't think in his arms, and she poured all the love she felt for him into the kiss, turning it from desperate into tender.

He eased away, and then looked down at her, his eyes heavy with need. 'I love you, Mila.'

Hearing the words again was like a slap. 'Stop!' She pulled herself away from him completely and felt the tears come back. 'You don't mean that.'

'Of *course* I mean it,' he said firmly, almost angrily. But the look in his eyes was...*fear.*

'If you really meant that, Jordan, you would stop being afraid of sharing with me and tell me about your childhood. About your mother and your father. You would *want* to tell me about it.'

CHAPTER SIXTEEN

JORDAN OPENED HIS MOUTH, ready to retort, but she had hit him exactly where she knew he was most vulnerable. He closed his mouth again, and before he could think of something to respond with she spoke again.

'This is exactly what I'm talking about. *Why* is it so hard for you to tell me about it?'

'For the same reasons you don't talk to me about *your* childhood in foster care.'

Her head snapped back as though he had hit her, and something inside him warned him to stop. But the words kept sprinting out of his mouth.

'It isn't that easy to talk about when you're on the other side, is it?' he said steadily, and watched the emotions run over her face like a movie reel.

Eventually she replied, 'No, it isn't. But when you love someone you have to make a sacrifice and put your reservations aside.' She took a deep breath. 'I didn't have anyone who needed me when I was growing up, Jordan. I lived with ten different families in eighteen years. It was hard.'

She blew out a shaky breath, and he felt himself shake a little, too. Was she doing what he thought she was?

'I didn't have anyone who needed me, and quite frankly no one wanted me. Lulu was the first person I met who cared about me—and I mean *really* cared—and I was sixteen years old when I met her.'

She wiped at tears he hadn't seen, too captivated by what she was telling him to notice before—and even more so by what it meant.

'Growing up like that made me… It made me someone I don't want to be any more.' She shrugged. 'I wouldn't ever say what I felt or what I thought because I wanted people to like me.'

'Even with me?' he asked, needing to know.

She looked at him through wet lashes that made her eyes all the more piercing. 'Even with you.' She bit her lip, and then said, 'I couldn't… I *thought* I couldn't tell you what I felt. There was a big part of me that felt like being married to you was a dream, and I didn't want to wake up. It didn't matter how I felt about our house, our cars…'

All things *he* had chosen for her, he thought in disgust.

'I had you. And that was enough for me.'

She lifted a hand when he opened his mouth to speak.

'Wait, I'm not done yet. I have to get this out before you say anything.'

Something shifted in her eyes, and panic spread through his body in response.

This is the last time she'll do this, he thought, and his heart pounded at the thought of losing her.

'But that also meant I didn't know how to ask you for help when we lost our child. I was afraid that you blamed me—you'd asked me to slow down and I hadn't. And then I fell down the stairs and I thought that you were right—I *should* have slowed down, enjoyed being pregnant. After that…I felt like a failure. Like every fear of mine had come true.'

Tears shone in her eyes and he took a step forward, wanting to be closer to her, to comfort her.

'It was a confirmation of what I'd feared all along—that I wasn't worthy of you. I always expected you to leave me, so when you did—'

'I proved you right,' he finished for her, stunned.

How could he have been so unaware of what his wife was going through? How had he not noticed that she hadn't ever disagreed with him? How had he been so blind? She had it completely wrong, he thought. *He* was the one who wasn't worthy of *her*.

'Mila, I'm so sorry. I didn't know...'

He trailed off as he realised that she had just told him everything he had ever wanted to know about her. And based on that information—based on the completely raw look in her eyes—he knew how much it had cost her.

'You love me, too.'

He didn't need her to say it because it was suddenly so painfully clear to him. It made the fact that he felt as if he was losing her so much worse. He looked at her, saw the truth in her eyes, and the past year of his life flashed through his mind.

He had always been a loner, but he hadn't ever felt alone. As difficult as his relationship with his father had been, Jordan had always known he had somewhere to go to, someone to talk to if he needed it. But after he had left for Johannesburg he hadn't really spoken to his father. His life had felt emptier than he'd thought possible, and he'd felt more alone than ever.

He had missed Mila with all of him, and now he knew— he *knew*—that his grief at losing his son, at losing his chance of a full family, would have been bearable if he had been with Mila.

It was something her words had only just made him re- alise, and the simple truth of it led him to say, 'My father blamed me for my mother's death.'

When the words were out, he couldn't believe such a simple sentence could convey the thing that had followed him around for his entire life. He stuffed his hands in his pockets and faced the stream. He didn't want to see her face—the compassion he knew would be there—while he told her of his childhood. Not when what he was going to tell her might change her opinion of his father, whom she'd clearly cared about.

He rubbed a hand over his face, wondering where to start, and decided on the part Mila already knew about.

'My mom found out about her cancer when I was two.' He took a steadying breath, then continued, 'She refused treatment. For two years she didn't want to get treatment, even though she was ill most of the time… She wanted to be a normal mother.'

He took another breath, shifted the weight between his feet.

'Her mom had died of the same thing, and they'd caught it earlier. She'd had treatment and it hadn't helped. So she refused. She thought the treatment would only make her sicker, even if only for a little while, and she didn't want to lose any time with me. So she chose to be a mother. She chose *me*.'

Jordan shrugged, the movement heavy with the weight he had been carrying. With the guilt.

'My dad hated her choice. He told me once that he'd begged her every day for those two years to get treatment, until finally he wore her down. And during that time my dad kept me at a distance. He wouldn't sit with her when she watched me play—would only agree to family time if she was there.'

Jordan wondered how his memories of the events he was talking about could be vague, but the feelings they evoked still sharp.

'He helped to take care of me physically—especially when my mom grew weaker, more ill—but he wouldn't be a father to me. Not a real one. But he was the *best* husband, and even at my age I knew that he loved her more than anything. By the time she agreed to treatment it was too late.'

He felt her move closer to him, and welcomed the comfort her presence brought.

'She spent her last year in agony, going through a cycle of chemo and radiation, until finally my dad brought her home and she died in her sleep a few days later.'

'It wasn't your fault,' she said, in a voice thick with emotion.

'I didn't think so until…'

This was probably one of the worst parts, he thought, but he pushed through.

'For years after my mom died, I felt like I was walking on eggshells. My father was testy most of the time, and I just got used to trying to make myself invisible at home. But at school, I acted out. And one day…' He took a deep breath. 'One day I did something I can't even remember any more and my dad got called in to school. I remember he sat there, listening to my teacher, and I saw the tic just above his eye. I didn't know what that meant then, but when I got home…'

He paused, then forced himself to say the words.

'The anger that my dad had built up since my mom had died came spilling out of his mouth.' Jordan's jaw clenched. 'He told me that if it hadn't been for me my mom wouldn't have died. He said that it was *my* fault, that she had foregone treatment because of me, and that it had all been for nothing since I was just a bratty, ungrateful child.'

Jordan stopped for a moment, composing himself.

'He said some other things that night—I think most of them things he blamed himself for. He broke down immediately afterwards and apologised, over and over again. It was grief, mixed with anger and regret, but I've never forgotten how seeing my distant father break down felt. Or…' he turned to her now '…how it affected me.'

He could see the sadness gleaming in her eyes, and he waited for resentment to boil up in him at the sight of it.

But it never came, and he realised that the only thing he felt was her support.

'I always wondered why things were so difficult between you two,' she said after a while, and she walked over until she was next to him and took his hand.

The warmth of her gesture of comfort immediately flowed through him, and he tightened his grip. 'I didn't think you'd noticed.'

She let out a slight laugh. 'It was hard not to. I always thought it was because of him.'

'Why?'

'He was a difficult man, Jordan. He didn't show his emotions, didn't say what he thought, and most of the time when he spoke it sounded like a military command.'

Floored, he looked down at her. 'I thought you *liked* him?'

'I loved him,' she corrected. 'He was kind to me, and in his own way he showed me he cared for me. I *loved* him,' she repeated, and he could hear the grief in her voice, 'but that doesn't mean I didn't see his flaws.'

He nodded, and there was a silence as they both thought about his father. As he thought about the fact that he needed to continue with his story.

'He only became the man you're talking about after that night. But even then he wasn't perfect, and I spent my whole life believing that my mother's death was my fault.'

'Your father was angry, Jordan. He was grieving for a woman he had loved with all of him and for the life he thought he would get to live. He didn't mean what he said, *or* the things he did.'

'But she *did* choose me, Mila,' he said softly.

'Exactly. *She* did. You had absolutely no say over the choices she made, Jordan. Don't keep blaming yourself for something you didn't have any control over.' She wrapped an arm around him. 'It won't help.'

Somewhere in his mind her words resonated, and he said, 'I didn't want to see you suffer like she did.'

She looked up at him, her eyes wide. '*That's* why you left?'

'I didn't think so at first. I thought I was doing the right thing.' He stopped, wondering how he was having all the most difficult conversations of his life within the space of an hour. 'But I've realised over the last few days that that *was* why I left. Why I ran.'

Her arm was still around him, though he could feel it slacken.

You deserve it for being a coward, he thought, but it didn't make the pain of her pulling away any easier.

Still he continued. If she was going to leave—if she was going to move on—it wouldn't be because he hadn't fought for her with all his might.

'It was also because I was...*angry*. I couldn't deal with the loss of our son.'

It was his biggest regret about his father's death—that he hadn't been able to tell Greg that he understood the grieving. He had been too young with his mother, but losing his son... Finally Jordan had understood how irrational grief could be.

'I got angry at you for pushing me away, and it...it scared me. I thought I was turning into my father. Even after the anger had dulled I thought it was for the best that I didn't come back, that I didn't fight for us. Because I didn't want to wake up one day and blame you for something that wasn't your fault. I didn't want to treat you like my father had treated me.'

He paused.

'It wasn't your fault, Mila,' he said again, because he thought she needed to know. 'The fall had nothing to do with you not slowing down. You would have had plenty of time to do that later. We *both* would have.' He turned to her. 'You need to let go of whatever's still inside you that thinks the accident was your fault.'

With eyes full of tears, she nodded, and his heart settled at the knowledge of what they'd just shared. He had finally told her everything, and he hoped he had got her to forgive herself. If she chose to leave now, she would leave free of the weight of the past. But still he wished she wouldn't leave, and his heart sank when she pulled away, convinced that she had given up on him.

So much so that he looked up in surprise when he saw she was in front of him.

She took both of his hands in hers. 'I wish you'd told me about this a long time ago.'

'I couldn't.'

'And I wouldn't have been in the right space to listen,' she agreed, and then took a deep breath. 'It makes sense now. All of it.'

'But does it change anything?' he asked hopefully, and a familiar expression shone in her eyes. One he hadn't seen in almost a year.

'I…I think that depends on you.'

The glimmer of affection in her eyes that he'd seen just before gave way to seriousness.

'Are you still angry at me?'

'No, not any more. I understand why you pushed me away. I understand *you* better, too.'

She gave him a small smile. 'Do you still blame yourself for your mom?'

'I…' He took a breath. 'I think it'll take some time— just like I think it will for you not to blame yourself for the baby—but we'll get there.'

She nodded, gripping his hands tightly. 'You won't turn into your father, Jordan, so I won't even ask if you still believe you will.'

'How do you *know*?'

'Because I know *you*. You're strong, and when you're not afraid…' she squeezed his hand '…you're the most considerate man I know.' She paused, and then dropped his hands to slide her arms around his waist. 'And because you have me, and I will make sure that you don't turn into an angry, bitter person. Our little grape wouldn't have wanted that for his father.'

His heart filled at her words. 'You're staying with me?'

'If you want me, I'd really like to.'

'I don't want you, Mila. I *need* you.' He pulled her in tighter and felt the part of him that had been broken heal. 'I love you so much.'

'I love *you*,' she replied, and when she pulled back her eyes were gleaming with tears.

'Don't cry,' he said gently, wiping her cheeks.

'They're happy tears,' she whispered. 'I didn't dare imagine this was possible when you came back, but my heart hoped it would be.'

'Mine, too,' he said, knowing that his heart was only full when he was with her.

'And we'll face everything we go through now together.'

'I promise.' He stopped, and then said gently, 'I want us to have another baby.'

He watched her, saw the fear.

'Not right now. When we're ready—when we've taken the time to *be* ready. You're going to be a wonderful mother, and I want a chance to be a good father. And a good husband to my pregnant wife.'

He smiled, lifted her chin. Noted that the fear had turned into longing.

'We can be a *family*, Mila.'

Another tear slipped down her face. 'It sounds perfect.' And then she smiled. 'How about we seal this with a kiss?'

He laughed and leaned down to kiss her, vowing that he wouldn't spoil his second chance at love with the woman who had always owned his heart.

CHAPTER SEVENTEEN

MILA FELT JORDAN'S hand tighten on hers and she sent him a grateful smile. It was the morning of their event—just over a week since their reconciliation—and she'd told Jordan that she wanted to visit their son's grave. She'd only ever been to the grave twice—when they'd buried him, and when they'd buried Greg. But after spending the past week talking with Jordan, sharing things that they hadn't shared with anyone else before, rebuilding their trust and fortifying the foundations of their new relationship, she finally found herself ready.

It didn't seem right to go through the event without doing it first, so they'd driven over and were now standing just in front of the path that would take them to the grave.

Except now, of course, her legs felt like lead and she didn't think she could do it.

'We can do this,' Jordan said, and she looked over, wondering if she had spoken out loud.

He threaded his fingers through hers and squeezed again, and she returned the pressure, knowing that he was just as nervous as she was. Probably even more so, since it was the first time he'd been back after his father's funeral, too.

Together they walked down the path that led to the family plot Greg had bought after his wife had died. He'd wanted to make sure that the Thomas family would always be together, even in death.

She slid an arm around Jordan's waist when they stopped in front of the first tombstone—made of the most expensive marble—which told her that Jade Thomas, Jordan's mother, had only lived until she was forty.

Way too young, she thought, thinking about how much time with her Greg had been robbed of…how early Jordan had lost her. She knew from losing her own parents how growing up without them could hurt. Perhaps it hurt even more, she considered, when you actually knew them.

'She would have been proud of you,' she said, leaning her head against Jordan's shoulder.

He lifted his arm and pulled her in closer. 'Even though I didn't look after my dad like she asked?' he said, but it was half-hearted, and she knew it reflected habit more than what he believed now.

'I think she would understand,' Mila replied softly, knowing that the tales she'd told Jordan about his mother—the ones Greg had shared with her in his rare open moments—confirmed her words. Jade had been a lovely woman: stubborn, like all the Thomases, but with just as big a heart as her son.

'I think she would, too,' Jordan said eventually, and they walked a few steps further to the front of Greg's grave. It was identical to Jordan's mother's, except that the words were about Greg.

'"Loving husband and father. You will be missed,"' she read aloud, and smiled. 'It's perfect, Jordan.' Her throat closed, but she smiled up at him. 'He *did* love you. Just in his own way.'

'I know.' Jordan laid a hand on the tomb and she waited, knowing that he needed time. 'I know that you loved me, Dad. I wish we could speak just one more time, so I could tell you I love you, too. So that I could tell you I understand now, and that I forgive you.' He took a shaky breath. 'But I think you already know that.'

Mila's heart broke for him, but she knew that it was healthy. It wouldn't do for him to keep it all in any more.

When he didn't say anything else, Mila said, 'Thank you for everything, Greg.' That was enough, she thought, but then she remembered something else. 'Especially for the will. Seems like your plan was right all along.'

They smiled at each other, and then took a few more moments to say goodbye. The overwhelming grief she had felt since Greg's death dulled to a throb in her heart, and that told her it would be okay. She and Jordan would be okay.

The tiny little tombstone that stood above the grave next to Greg's still broke her heart, though.

The name they'd decided on and had engraved that week was bold in grey against the black marble stone. Below the name was a black-and-white picture of her and Jordan on the day she had given birth—they both had tears on their faces, and were both clearly heartbroken, but she had her son in her arms and it was their only family photo.

The dates on his tombstone were the date they'd found out they were expecting their child and the date they'd lost him. And below that was an inscription.

You were the light of our lives.
A light that will stay in our hearts for ever.

'I still have that image of you in my head—you with our son in your arms...the absolute devastation and love on your face.' He sucked in air, and she felt the sucker punch of his emotions—*their* emotions—right down to her gut.

'Me, too. But with your face.'

She spoke because something inside her compelled her to. Perhaps because it was the first time they could acknowledge it together.

'The dreams I have are about that moment a lot. I had

only just felt him alive inside me, and then when I could see him he wasn't.' She was whispering now, her voice no longer willing to say the words that told her the wound inside her was still fresh. 'I'm so glad you got to hold him while he was still alive.'

They clung to each other, and though she knew she was still healing she felt the glimmer of hope that sharing that moment with the only person who knew what she was going through had brought. Suddenly she was even more grateful for their second chance.

We'll do it right this time, baby, she told her son, and her lips curved even through the tears.

'He knows how much we love him.' Jordan's voice was raw as he spoke, but she saw the hope she felt inside reflected in his eyes.

'He does. I'm sure our parents tell him that every day.' The thought of their family together made her smile widen.

'Yeah…' He looked down at her. 'I think so, too.'

It was a long time before either of them spoke again, but finally Jordan said, 'We should get going. Karen will probably be there for the soundcheck soon.'

They headed back to the car together, and before she climbed in Mila looked back one more time. 'We'll visit them again soon, won't we?'

Jordan kissed her hair. 'Of course.'

She smiled at him, and couldn't help but think that the people they had visited would have loved it that she and Jordan were a family again.

'I'm sweating like a pig,' Lulu said, and fanned herself with the clipboard that she insisted on using for her tasks instead of the tablet Mila was using.

Mila laughed, grabbing a bottle of water from the ice bucket behind the stage that Karen had walked out onto a few minutes ago and handed it to her friend.

'The perks of growing a life inside you!'

Mila found she could say that now, after that morning, without a piercing pain going through her body. It was more like a dull ache in her heart that reminded her of her child, just like her significantly lowered fear of stairs. The necessity of this event had helped her overcome *that* fear, but she knew it was more than that, too. It was knowing that she *could* do it that helped her do it. And because of the person who had helped her reach that realisation.

'No!' Lulu said after gurgling down half the bottle. 'There is *no way* you can tell me that you're not getting as hot as I am.'

'Honey, it's eighteen degrees. We've spent the past half an hour handing out blankets to our guests and setting up the outside heaters. You *know* it's only you.'

'Maybe it's because I've been running around for the past week.'

'And you know I love you for it. Especially when you look at how amazingly it's turned out.'

She peeped out from the tent they had assembled backstage—just as they had for the first event—and a smile spread on her face.

The amphitheatre held about two hundred fifty people, which was about a hundred more than she had been expecting. Most of them were only there for Karen, but that didn't matter since they had all still bought food from the vendors, still purchased wine from the vineyard. They had managed to set up the marquee so that it had more than enough space for everyone, and as she looked up she was treated to a stunning view of the stars.

'It seems like a success.'

A voice broke through her thoughts and she turned to see Mark standing there, with a briefcase in one hand and some papers in the other, with Jordan behind him.

Her heart immediately responded to him being there,

and she smiled at him before nervously asking Mark, 'Did we tick all the boxes?'

Mark pulled his glasses down from the top of his head and read from the paper in front of him. 'Well, your event *is* "under the stars"—excellent improvisation, by the way—and you have the same performer, you're screening the same movie, you have most of the vendors from the original event, and you've provided me with all the documentation for those who couldn't make it, as well as for their replacements. And you've done this all within the time limit.'

Mark removed his glasses.

'So I would say, yes. Congratulations, you two, you're officially the owners of Greg's share of the vineyard. I'll send the paperwork through in the coming weeks.'

Mark excused himself, and as soon as he was gone, Lulu let out a hoot.

'This is wonderful news, you guys!' She hugged them both, then waved a hand. 'But, much as I would like to celebrate with you, my bladder is telling me there are things that take a slightly higher priority at the moment.'

She winked at Jordan before she waddled off, and though that puzzled her Mila jumped into Jordan's arms the minute they were alone.

'We did it!' she said, her body sighing in contentment as soon as it touched his.

'We did.' He pulled back, and the look on his face made her heart thud.

'What's wrong?'

'There's just something… Actually, I can take care of it myself. I'll just run up to the house…'

He was already starting up the stairs by the time she'd processed his words, and in a bit of a panic she followed him.

'Jordan!' she called when they were far enough from the concert that they wouldn't be heard. 'Wait!'

She was out of breath when she finally caught up with him, and she rested her hands against her knees when she saw that he'd stopped.

'Why wouldn't you just wait for me?' she puffed, and then straightened. 'What's the problem—'

She broke off when she saw where they were, and a smile spread across her face.

'You are such a sneaky—'

He cut her off with a quick kiss, and then grinned as he pulled back.

'Surprise!' he said, and pushed open the gate to the place where they'd picnicked that very first night.

A blanket was spread out, just as it had been then, but this time there was a fire burning in the pit that had been created just in front of it. A bottle of Thomas Vineyard red wine was placed next to two glasses, and a variety of foods similar to those he'd had there the first time sat next to that.

'It's perfect,' she said with a smile as she turned towards him—and froze when she saw him kneeling in front of her.

'What are you *doing*?' she gasped. 'I've already told you I wouldn't file the papers.'

'I want to begin our second chance together properly, Mila.'

The teasing glint in his eyes was gone, replaced by a sincerity that sent a tear down her cheek.

'I can't live my life without you. I want you—and I need you—by my side for ever. I want to have a family with you, and I want to love you and our family unconditionally. Will you give me the chance to do that?'

She nodded, unable to speak, and he grinned.

'I'm not done yet.'

He pulled a ring from his pocket, and her heart skipped when she saw it was the one he'd proposed with the first time. The one she had put in a jewellery box the day she'd received the divorce papers and tried never to think about again.

'Be my wife again, Mila. And not only because we're still married.' He smiled. 'Marry me again.'

'Yes, of course—yes!' she said, and he slid the ring onto her finger.

She smiled at its familiar weight.

'I know the perfect time and the perfect place,' she said, and hooked her arms around his neck.

He grinned. 'Me, too. But until then…'

He kissed her, and she melted against him.

EPILOGUE

TWO DAYS LATER, on their second wedding anniversary, Mila stood in a long white dress covered in lace. Lulu beamed at her as she lowered the veil over Mila's face and dabbed at a tear that had fallen down her cheek.

'I'm such a mess!' Lulu said with a hiccup, and Mila smiled teasingly.

'The joys of—'

'Growing a life inside you—I know.' Lulu rolled her eyes and then smiled. 'I'm so happy for you.'

Mila laid a shaky hand on her stomach. 'Me, too.'

They walked the short distance from the house to the chapel where she and Jordan had made their vows two years before. And although she was wearing the same ring and the same dress as the first time they'd got married, *she* was a different person. She was someone who was more confident, who only cared about the opinions of those who loved her. And she was standing on her own this time.

Though she would have done anything to be walking down the aisle with Greg again, being on her own was oddly comforting. It represented the fact that she *could* be on her own if she needed to. But now she was walking towards the man who had promised her that she would never have to be alone again.

She didn't take her eyes off him as she walked down the short aisle, her heart thumping at how handsome he looked in his suit. And then it was just the two of them, standing in front of the altar, making their promises to one another.

'I can't believe how lucky I am to have you in my life again,' she began, and tears welled up in her eyes. 'You have shown me how it feels to be loved, to be needed. You have given me the family I've never had. You have helped me grow into someone I didn't know I could be. Into someone who is willing to hope after hurt, who is willing to open her heart to the possibilities of the future when shutting everyone out would be so much easier.'

She squeezed his hands, felt the tears run down her face now.

'We have been through the worst of times together. But because I look at you now and see how much stronger you are—*we* are—and how our love has grown stronger because of it, I know that we can face anything together. And I believe that the best of times are still to come.'

His eyes gleamed, but he cleared his throat and said, 'Mila, I am a different man because of *you*. You've helped me unload the baggage I came into this relationship with. And what I have left I know you'll help me carry.'

He smiled at her, brushed a hair out of her face, and she leaned into his touch.

'I promise to stay with you through good times and bad. I promise to love you with all that is in me and put our relationship first. You mean the world to me, and I can't wait to have a family with you. To show our children what love's supposed to be. No matter what we go through, I will be there for you. Thank you for giving us a second chance.'

They kissed, and she felt it solidify their promises, their declarations of love for each other.

As they walked out of the chapel Mila leaned over to Jordan. 'Do you think this is what your father wanted all along?'

Jordan smiled down at her, and her heart warmed at

the look in his eyes. 'Absolutely. And I can't thank him enough.'

She laughed when he scooped her into his arms, and as she placed her head on his shoulder she knew she was finally living the life she had dreamed of.

* * * * *

TEMPTED BY HER TYCOON BOSS

JENNIE ADAMS

For my dad. You were my first storyteller
and you'll always remain the best to me.
Love you.

CHAPTER ONE

'GOOD MORNING, CECILIA.' Linc MacKay spoke the greeting as he stepped between shoulder-height hedge shapes bursting from within with raised flowering displays. 'Your second-in-command told me I'd probably find you here.'

'Here' was the feature maze area of the Fleurmazing Plant Nursery on its acreage just outside the Sydney city limits. The Australian sun warmed the air, and the light breeze carried the scents of a summer garden.

Now it had also brought a handsome millionaire, stepping around a corner of the maze to an alcove where a statue of a sun goddess draped in gossamer folds reached her arms upwards as though to bless the world with her light.

Was it the soft look in Linc's eyes as his gaze moved beyond the sun goddess and lingered on her that made Cecilia's breath suddenly catch? A moment later the expression disappeared, if it had ever truly been there at all.

'Linc. Is it that time already?' She focused on projecting professionalism into her words and tried to push those discomforting questions to the back of her mind. 'I'm glad Jemmie was able to point you in the right direction to find me.'

Cecilia placed one final hedge trimming into the basket over her arm and walked towards the plant nursery's owner. If she didn't feel entirely calm she could at least act as though she were.

'This is my favourite part of the maze, to be honest.'

'I can see why.' His gaze took in the maze, its beautiful flowers every shade from creamy white to deepest violet and blue. But then he turned back and took in Cecilia, too, from the top of her honey-blond hair in its high ponytail, over her face, lingering on each feature, and quickly sweeping over the simple strappy sundress that showed off her curves to perfection.

She rarely dressed in her best girly attire for work but, knowing that today she'd be inside most of the day in the office, Cecilia had let her most feminine side have its way.

'It's stunning,' Linc finally said. 'The...ah...the maze.'

'Thank you.' She drew a slightly unsteady breath. 'I'm sorry I wasn't up front, ready to greet you.'

Cecilia glanced at the trimmings in the basket over her arm and hoped by doing so she would disguise her swirling thoughts from him.

'This is a never-ending job.'

'And a very important one at the moment, I can imagine.'

Why, oh, *why* did she have to feel suddenly oh-so-conscious of him? She had much better control than this. Usually...

Wasn't it enough that she'd mistaken his interest once before, years ago?

'The maze needs to look good. Fantastic, in fact.'

She forced the words out and told herself to concentrate on matters at hand. The Fleurmazing plant nursery was the third and most recent of Linc's Sydney plant nurseries that she had managed over the six years she'd been in his employ, but this one was different.

It was *her* brainchild—a holistic nursery that required greater upkeep but offered an enhanced experience for its visitors. At least in this aspect of her life she had it together!

She should keep her focus on that. Now, of all times, Cecilia needed to 'sell' the nursery's virtues to Linc at any opportunity she got. Noticing his character traits or wondering if his attention was caught on her wasn't part of that plan.

'We're logging hundreds of people every day, who all come here specifically because they want to experience the maze. Sales out of that alone are fantastic. And the maze needs to be perfect in time for the part we're playing in Sydney's Silver Bells charity flower show, so I'm giving it a lot of attention at the moment.'

'A masked ball in the middle of a plant maze is ambitious.' One side of his mouth kicked up. 'But I'm sure if anyone can carry it off it'll be you.'

'The Silver Bells organisers have put their faith in me, so I have no choice now.' She said it laughingly, but the importance of it was never far from her thoughts.

She wouldn't have had the opportunity if Linc hadn't agreed to let her take the risk.

'It'll pay off, Linc. Your whole chain of plant nurseries will get good attention out of our participation in the Silver Bells event.'

Linc owned a dozen nurseries across the city, along with bucketloads of real estate and a commodities trading portfolio that, on its own, probably ran into millions. He truly was the quintessential millionaire bachelor, with the world at his feet. They were more than poles apart, which had made her *faux pas* of throwing herself at him six years ago even more embarrassing.

He hadn't been interested. She'd mistaken his charming way for something it wasn't, and then—moments after he'd let Cecilia down as gently as anyone possibly could have—a woman had arrived for her lunch date with him. A sophisticated older woman.

Old news, Cee. Linc played the gentleman that day, apologised that he'd given the wrong impression and went off on his date with Ms Socialite while you went back to digging around in potting mix. And you got over it.

Cecilia had worked hard to impress him professionally since then, and she'd dated. Then she'd found Hugh, and that relationship had lasted almost two years. Linc had no doubt dated lots more versions of Ms Socialite, too, though Cecilia had not heard of him ever being in a serious long-term relationship since she'd known him.

'I appreciate you coming in for the business review. I know you're busy. Actually, I thought you might have sent someone to do it for you.'

'You've earned this opportunity, and I felt I owed

it to you to undertake the review myself.' Sincerity rang in his tone. 'I want to grant you that twenty per cent share in the nursery if I can, and no one else will understand your work here and your vision the way that I do.'

That was true. Even though the bulk of their interactions were over the phone, she'd always reported regularly to Linc.

And she'd negotiated—refusing bonuses over the years in favour of building up to this: a chance to own a share in the nursery. One day she wanted to open her own business.

'I hope the review proves my efforts worthy of your time.'

Linc might have rejected her overtures, but he had been her example since he'd first taken her on and let her manage one of his nurseries six years ago, with no experience and only her determination to get her through. He was proof that a person could achieve anything if they wanted it enough.

What would he be now? Thirty-four? Thirty-five? Still with the same deep timbre to his voice, the same way of wearing his work boots, jeans and chambray shirt with an authority overlaid with a deceptive dose of casual charm.

With a strong chin, short-cut dark hair, those gorgeous shoulders and a way of carrying himself that shouted, *Look out, world!* Linc MacKay was in all ways a force to be reckoned with.

Linc would be making the nursery his base while he undertook the review. They'd be spending quite a bit of time in each other's company. It couldn't be a worse time for that old awareness of him to resurface. Whatever had brought it back, she needed her interest in him *gone*. Now, if not sooner.

Cecilia began the return walk towards the equipment shed and the front office.

'I know I'll see good results here, Cecilia. With each new nursery you've managed, you've improved on the last.' Linc fell into step beside her in the maze. 'I *have* taken it all in, you know—including the way this one has exceeded all expectations. Bringing coach tours in on a daily basis, gaining that whole new layer of tourism clientele…that has shown real vision.'

His words made every moment of her hard work feel doubly worth it. Cecilia couldn't help smiling as she quietly thanked him.

'Our social media presence has made a difference, too. I'm blessed to have Jemmie here, with her skills in photography and videography. Her plants-growing-and-bursting-into-flower videos get a lot of attention online.'

'You found a good asset in her.'

His compliment pleased her, but it was his simple gesture for her to precede him through a narrower section of the maze that brought back that earlier flutter to Cecilia's pulse. It felt *intimate* to her. As though they'd met here for a morning tryst and were returning now to their 'real' lives.

How silly.

Planning for this masked ball must be messing with her brain. Cecilia couldn't come up with a more feasible explanation for her sudden case of hyper-Linc-awareness.

Or perhaps you've simply been out of your rela-

*tionship with Hugh long enough to open your eyes
and look around you?*

If so, she could cast her attention in some other
direction, thank you very much. Because Linc was
not for her and she'd accepted that fact and got over
caring about it a very long time ago.

She *had*, right…?

'Thank you, Linc, for the commitment you've
made to do this review.'

If the words were a little stiff and formal, that
couldn't be helped. Surely that was better than falling all over him, even if only inside her own thoughts.

'I know it's time away from the other demands of
your life.'

'I suspect some of those demands will follow me
here, but I'll do my best not to disrupt you.' A teasing smile came and went.

Cecilia ignored how that smile made her tummy
flutter. It had to be the kind of smile that one friend
might share with another, or a person who'd known
another person for years, or a boss who felt comfortable with his employee. And Cecilia fell into the latter category. Yes, she'd known Linc for years, but
they were work associates with a lot of *professional*
ground walked over in that span of time.

Therefore his smile must be a perfectly normal one
that meant nothing whatsoever outside those bounds.
He couldn't help it if he was cute.

Great avoiding of his appeal, Cee.

He went on. 'I don't want to make a painful time
out of this for you.'

'I'm sure it will be fine.' No matter the outcome,
she knew Linc would be fair in his assessment.

Whether she could eliminate the painful knowledge of her reawakened awareness of him was another challenge altogether.

But it was one that she had to achieve, and she could not let the rest of her life mess with her head, either, while she got through the review. That would be easier said than done, when one part of it gnawed at her ceaselessly and she was still stinging over another part.

Well, no-longer-interested-and-nothing-could-keep-me-here-now Hugh could go and trip over and fall into a duck pond, for all she cared. And the other thing just...*was*.

Cecilia drew a breath.

Her personal life might not be as calm as she would like, but she could manage—and Linc didn't need to know about any of it.

She detoured to leave her plant cuttings and basket in the potting shed, and then led the way to her office. 'Come on in. How long do you think the review will take?'

'Depending on how much I get interrupted, it shouldn't take more than a few days.'

His gaze searched hers just a little bit too keenly for her comfort.

'Great.' She gestured to where a second computer and desk sat at a diagonal angle to her own, and pushed those other thoughts as far back in her mind as she could manage. 'I don't mean it's great that you won't be here more than that. You know what I mean...'

Did he? Was he hearing her words falling over themselves in a way that was quite out of character after her usual modulated approaches to him?

So get over it, Cecilia. You've been to see him at his city office, where the staff all complain that he's hardly ever there but say it fondly, as though they're glad that he gives them the autonomy to do their best for him while he's out spreading his holdings even further. You've been to the warehouse home he shared in the past with his brothers. He's seen you at each of the nurseries you've managed. Multiple times, in fact. This is no different.

'The financials are all on there.' She used her best I've-got-over-it tone, which would at least make sense to her. 'Along with my strategic forecast for the business for the upcoming couple of years.'

The hand she'd been waving around now hid itself in a fold of her sundress's knee-length skirt.

'Thanks.' Again his lips curved into that hint of a smile. 'I'll jump straight in.'

'I'd best get on with my work, too.' Cecilia dropped into her chair. 'I have invoices to get into the system from the weekend's trade.'

She did *not* mention that she'd spent so much time ensuring that the outdoor aspects of the nursery were impeccable in recent days that she'd allowed that invoicing to get somewhat behind.

She'd known Linc would be here and that he'd want her around—at least to start with. This way she could work while she answered any questions he might have.

That's right. You weren't hiding out doing your favourite tasks just because they help you not to think about other things.

Cecilia had a major event coming up for the nursery. She simply didn't have time to think about any-

thing else. Not family stresses, not her abandonment
by Hugh and certainly not this morning's odd noticing of Linc in a way she had stopped herself doing
for years.

Cecilia jabbed the start button of her Slimline computer. 'I'll be here all day in the office to be sure I'm
available for any questions you may have.'

'I appreciate that you're so well organised for the
review, even with a big event looming on the horizon.'

Linc MacKay murmured the words as his plant-
nursery manager shuffled her bottom into her office chair and peered down her nose at the computer
screen in front of her.

She looked beautiful today…a summery woman
with golden skin. Her shoulders were bare but for a
couple of spaghetti straps on the deep red sundress
splashed with a bold floral design, and her lips were
highlighted in a subtle lipstick.

Linc had rejected her innocent overtures six years
ago, even though he'd felt a spark of interest at the
time. It had never truly gone away, and he had felt
that fact keenly today. Seeing her in the beautiful sundress, showing such a feminine side of herself, Linc
felt as though he were seeing her in a whole new light.

And because that awareness wasn't acceptable to
him, he forced his focus to her business acumen.

Cecilia was determined and motivated and very
capable when it came to running a nursery. Her push
to gain a share in this one had impressed him, and
she'd earned that opportunity over the last six years.

She was an intriguing woman, Linc acknowledged
silently, and his glance returned to her once again.

Slender, with shoulder-length hair every shade from ash to dark blond and eyes the colour of bluebonnets…

Where had he been?

Right. Her inner strength and drive impressed him. Linc told himself not to think about how sweet she looked, how he felt as though layers had been pulled from his eyes and he could see her clearly for the very first time.

'I'll review the strategic projections first.' He pushed the knowledge of her appeal to the back of his mind, where it had to remain. 'Those will form a solid basis for the rest of my review. They'll also help me to spot any areas where the business might not yet be living up to its full potential.'

'I'll be keen to discuss any weak areas with you.' Cecilia sat very upright in her chair. 'I pride myself on trying to keep everything strong. I've printed a copy of the projections document for you.'

She pointed to the pile of files beside his computer. The document sat right on top.

'I appreciate it.' He lifted the sheaf of pages and flipped through them before turning back to the first page and lowering his gaze so he could fully concentrate on it.

It took a while, but Linc did immerse himself in the work. Even if he *could* see acres of soft, delicately sun-kissed skin in the periphery of his view.

Cecilia focused studiously on her office work, but out of the corner of her eye she remained very aware of Linc as the hours passed.

She wanted to know how he felt about his findings so far, even though he would have only just scratched the surface at this stage.

Distractingly, she noticed the scent of his after-shave. It made her think about things that had no business being in her mind.

'Cecilia?'

'Yes. No. I mean—' Had Linc asked her a question while she'd been daydreaming about woodsy scents and clear grey eyes? She had no idea—and no business noticing his eyes. Or his shoulders. Or the way his strong nose perfectly matched the firm, sensuous appeal of his lips.

Concentrate, Cee! On something other than how gorgeous he is.

'I might get a bite to eat.' He glanced at the clock on the wall. 'It's getting to be that time of day. Would you like to join me, or can I pick up something for you?'

For a moment blank incomprehension filled her. She fought her way out of it and realised she *was* hungry—but a lunch date with Linc MacKay…?

'Thanks, but I have errands to run on my lunch break.' Fortunately, his invitation had been offhand enough that she didn't need to worry about causing offence by refusing it.

Exactly.

So why had her heart skipped a beat?

'Plus, I brought something to eat from home.' Something dull and ordinary that held no uncertain surprises and certainly wouldn't make her think back to a past time when she had wanted to know Linc better on a personal rather than a business footing. 'But I appreciate the offer.'

He gave a little nod and a half smile and went on his way—which quite put it into perspective, as she should have done from the start. Thank goodness she hadn't sounded as though she were turning him down in a personal way or anything like that.

Cecilia ate her home-packed sandwich at her desk, and then headed for the nearby mall. Her thoughts turned to her sister more and more with each step. Hugh might have dropped Cecilia like the proverbial hot potato when her family life had suddenly gone from slightly troublesome to really concerning, and that still hurt, but it was the rift with Stacey that remained as a constant source of heartache any time Cecilia let the thoughts surface.

Rejection seemed to have formed a bit too much of a repeat cycle in Cecilia's life lately. It was just as well that she had learned to bury her emotions in her work and that she was very *good* at that work.

'Next, please.' The voice of the man behind the counter at the postal outlet drew her from her thoughts.

'Hello. I need to purchase a money order, please.'

'Same name and amount?'

The clerk probably thought he was being helpful, asking that. Instead, it just reminded Cecilia of how many times she had done this. Every Monday for the past five months, and it wasn't over yet.

Not this guy's fault, and not your fault, either, so smile and be normal. Got it?

She was fulfilling a duty, and if that felt like a paltry thing to do, well, the situation wasn't easy—and doing this was a lot more than just duty. She had to continue to hope that things would improve.

'Yes. Thank you.'

Cecilia placed the money order into a pre-stamped envelope and mailed it.

As she returned to work she let her spirits find happiness again. She loved the nursery and loved what she'd achieved here. And if she felt a little lift, knowing she was about to see Linc again, too, that came from knowing that every moment in his presence brought the results of the review and his decision about her share proposition closer. It was that and only that.

If she didn't entirely believe herself, Cecilia ignored the fact.

Her peace lasted until she approached the office and heard Linc speaking.

'I can tell you really want to speak with her, but Cecilia is at lunch just now.' There was a pause. 'Are you in a position where you could call back a bit later?'

'Is that for me? I'll take it now.' She could hardly speak for the buzzing in her ears, and she saw Linc was ending the call even as she spoke.

For a moment after he'd placed the phone back in its cradle, she simply stood there.

'That was a supplier wanting to change an order.'

Linc seemed to be searching her face with a great deal of attention.

It was just a supplier, phoning on the office phone. Your sister only has your cell phone number. You haven't missed a chance to speak with her, and Linc hasn't found out anything about her.

Disappointment and relief fought for supremacy inside Cecilia.

They both won.

'The guy sounded old...grumpy.' Linc gave a what-do-you-do kind of a shrug. 'He didn't want to leave his name or number, only wanted to speak with you, and he ended the call quite abruptly.'

'I think I know which supplier that would have been.' She walked to her desk, sat down. Felt Linc's gaze on her and an added layer of awareness of her that she would swear, despite her admonitions to herself earlier to the contrary, was real.

Did she want to set herself up for further rejection? No.

Exactly, Cecilia. So get your mind back on your work. Now!

But trying to do that just reminded her that her heart had almost stopped for a second or two, and now she was fighting a renewed sense of sadness and loss that she tried to keep distant during work hours.

'I'll call the supplier back a bit later and let him know that a message would be welcome the next time, whether I'm here or not.'

Next time she wouldn't practically fall apart over a silly, perfectly routine, office-related phone call.

Cecilia ignored the reasons why she *would* panic, and why she now felt deflated and sad all over again. Because no cause for panic had actually ensued. She'd ignored the way Linc had made her feel today so far, too. If she ignored that for long enough, she would get it under control.

She turned her attention back to her work. In the end, that was where her focus needed to stay!

CHAPTER TWO

'Is THERE A chance we could move my tour of the facility forward and do it now? I have to disappear for a while later this morning on other business.'

Linc made the request as he and Cecilia met at the front area of the plant nursery the next morning. They'd driven into the staff parking area within seconds of each other.

'I'm sorry for the disruption to our review, but would that be manageable for you?'

'There's no need to apologise. I'm surprised you got through even one day without a disruption, to be honest. And the flower show management team aren't due here until eleven—so, yes, I can do the tour now.'

Cecilia's words and tone were calm. Yet in catching her unawares Linc had glimpsed what had looked like sorrow in her eyes, before she'd shielded her expression and the mantle of 'business manager' came down over her face.

There'd been an awareness of him, too. It had sparked briefly before that mantle had come down. It disturbed him that he had looked and hoped for that very thing. And it disturbed him that she had seemed sad.

He frowned, but a moment later Cecilia spoke with such enthusiasm and apparent focus on her work that he wondered if he had imagined that earlier moment of interest and its preceding sadness.

'It'll be a real pleasure to show you everything here in detail. Just let me stow my things, Linc, and we'll get into the tour.'

Cecilia quickly divested herself of her purse and her lunch, tucked her cell phone into the back pocket of her jeans, and led the way to the first part of the nursery.

She'd been an intriguing young woman at twenty, when she'd fought so hard to get him to let her manage one of his nurseries. With nothing but a community college course and some time spent in customer service in a small plant nursery behind her, she'd gone after her dream of managing one, tenaciously.

Linc would have been a fool not to employ her, so he had done exactly that. But not before she had let him see that she would have welcomed the opportunity to know him better as a *man*, not only as a potential employer.

Her interest then hadn't been one-sided.

And now...?

Now, for his sins, Linc had seen a whole new aspect of her yesterday, and that had not only refreshed the underlying awareness of Cecilia that had never truly left him, but had added to it. *Why?* Was it because there'd been no woman in his life at all lately?

Well, he'd been busy.

Too busy to pick up the phone and invite someone out or to say yes to any of the invitations that came his way?

Was he getting jaded? Or perhaps lonely? Wanting what his brothers had in their marriages?

That last thought came out of nowhere, and Linc shoved it right back there just as quickly. Ridiculous. He was perfectly happy as he was. He ignored any possibility that he might not be.

Linc's gaze was focused on the back of Cecilia's head as she walked along a curved pathway ahead of him, but all that did was draw his attention to her again.

A yellow sleeveless shirt contrasted with denim cut-offs, and both highlighted her soft curves. Today she wore her hair up in that ponytail again, and it bounced with every step of her work-booted feet.

The ponytail made Linc want to kiss her, and while the sensible work attire spoke of her determination, she looked equally as appealing to Linc today as she had yesterday—all feminine curviness and beauty.

Layers had definitely been peeled from his eyes, and Linc wanted to paste them right back on. He needed to do that, because Cecilia wasn't the kind of woman he'd date and forget—the type of woman he had always dated because it was easy to walk away.

He had to set aside this awareness of Cecilia—whether he'd suddenly noticed her on a whole different level or not.

Cecilia glanced over her shoulder. 'Shall we visit the cold storage first?'

'Yes. That would be…ah…great.'

They headed over there, and Linc forced his attention back to the tour. He noticed the amount of empty space surrounding the limited offerings of cut flowers.

'How's the cut-flower trade going?'

'It's going well.'

Her glance seemed only to calculate the empty shelf area. But her cheeks held a hint of pink that couldn't be attributed to their brief walk.

Was she feeling this, too? This interest and curiosity that felt fresh and new and oh-so-tempting to pursue?

'At the moment we're keeping our stock orders tight.' She waved a hand in the general direction of the shelves, and then shoved it into the front pocket of her cut-offs.

She's as aware of it as you are.

Maybe, but that didn't mean she wanted to pursue it any more than he did, Linc reminded himself belatedly.

'Any special reason?' He cleared his throat. 'For keeping the stock orders tight?'

She tipped her head on one side and seemed to consider him for a moment before she responded. 'It's because Valentine's Day is very close and we'll need the space for all the cut roses.'

'Right. It's good that you've thought ahead to make as much of that day as possible.' His voice was so deep it might have come from his boots. 'I should have thought of that straight away.'

'It's a very special day.' The pink in her cheeks deepened. 'For—for the customers, and very much for the nursery.'

And most of all for lovers.

She didn't say that. Instead, she drew a deep breath, as though to try to compose herself.

In Linc's experience women seemed to expect a

very emotional expression of love on that particular day of the year. To show a love that encapsulated exactly the kind of commitment that would never be part of Linc's own life.

He was grateful his brothers had found such love—that their lives had turned out okay in the end. However, Linc would never deserve—

'We'll be getting in red roses, predominantly.'

Cecilia's words drew him back from the dark thoughts as she led the way out of the cold storage area and, once he'd joined her outside, secured it.

'We'll stock other colours of roses, too. There's a growing percentage of buyers who will purchase something other than the classic red—particularly when purchasing for friends or family rather than—'

'The romantic loves of their lives?'

There. He'd said it and the sky hadn't fallen in.

'Yes.' She glanced at him and quickly away again. Her chin tipped up. 'Roses are lovely at any time of the year. My favourites are the creamy white ones. They have a beautiful, subtle scent.'

She led the way through a section of potted seedlings and, as he came to her side, gave him the benefit of a determinedly work-focused gaze.

'Hopefully this year's sales of roses will prove to be as lucrative as last—if not more so.'

The words made Cecilia sound as unromantic as they came, and she *was* a great businesswoman. But one who'd managed to bring romance right to the heart of her working life through her instigation of this year's masked-ball event. Not to mention all the flowers she stocked for Valentine's Day, and the flowering maze she had designed and nurtured to fruition.

'Given your track record over the last six years, I have no doubt that the Valentine's Day trade will exceed all expectations.' He made the comment matter-of-fact, but his thoughts were not pragmatic.

She'd been in a relationship a few months ago. His brother Brent had mentioned that it had ended.

So she's single.

Why would Linc even consider her availability?

She may be hurting and still love the guy.

'Thank you.'

For a moment Linc didn't know what she was thanking him for, and then he remembered. He'd paid her a compliment. A business one, about her ability to do a great job as plant-nursery manager.

Which was true.

'You're welcome.'

They moved between rows of gardening supplies, through arrays of flowering plants and herbs, potting mix and foliage. Linc began to find his focus again, and the colour in Cecilia's cheeks returned to normal.

So it was fine. He'd been foolishly carried away—imagining things, nothing more. Flights of fancy weren't Linc's style. He would make sure it didn't happen again.

Cecilia's love of her work shone through more and more as she talked avidly, explaining the progress and plans that related to each area.

'What's happening in that shed?'

He asked the question as they walked towards a shady path, far into the back section of the nursery. Access to the shed was gained through a locked gate. There were no customers to be seen or heard, and it truly felt secluded and private.

In fact, it was the perfect setting for a man to steal a kiss. Assuming that a man would choose to do something so unprofessional.

So much for him returning his thoughts to nothing but business.

'I'll show you.' Cecilia led the way to this final shed on the property and unlocked and opened the door. The tour with Linc had proved productive so far, but she had been oh-so-conscious of him the entire time.

This sharpened interest towards Linc needed to stop.

She felt a moment of nervous anticipation as she prepared to reveal this part of the business. It was working well, and she was proud of it, but what would Linc think of the concept?

'I hope you'll approve of this aspect of the nursery.' She tried to imbue nothing but confidence into her tone as she went on. 'This is where I work on my repurposing projects. I get some of my best ideas for the future direction of the business when I'm working here, too.'

With this statement carefully delivered, and avoiding the thought that she also came here when she missed her sister the most, Cecilia glanced about the area.

Sunlight streamed through skylights in the roof into a large open-plan area that housed projects in various stages of completion. Old boots with creepers growing out of them...a rocking chair that had been painted orange and black, its seat area filled with a large planter of pumpkin vine... Demand for this kind of repurposed item was growing.

'I didn't know about this.' Linc's gaze moved about the area before it returned to her. 'How long have you been doing this work? Where did you get all these items?'

He wouldn't realise it, but the sun coming through the skylight above had cast his profile into sharp relief. Every strong feature and every subtle nuance was there for her to see. Right down to the length of his dark eyelashes and the way they curled slightly at the ends. And the shape of his lips...

Cecilia struggled to remember his question. He'd asked something about where she got the items for refurbishment. It was one of her favourite aspects of the plant nursery, which showed how easily being around Linc could throw her completely off her guard.

'I find items in all sorts of places.'

She took a step to the side, to break that particular view of him. It was as though she'd jumped back through time six years and all her past awareness of him as a man had returned.

Actually, it hadn't—because she saw him now with a history of working in his employ for six years. She saw him with more maturity. With more certainty in her interest in him...

'I started this operation about four months ago.'

Soon after she'd realised she needed a distraction and a way of letting out her emotions, thanks to the implosions going on in her personal life.

She simply *couldn't* feel a renewed attraction to Linc, let alone a deeper one. Because—because business and that sort of pleasure didn't mix. Because she had enough to deal with in her life without trying to take on a romance. Because she'd learned the hard way, when Hugh had disappeared from her life without a backward glance, that you just couldn't trust romantic attachments once 'real life' interfered with them!

Most of all because Linc had rejected her overtures all those years ago. *Remember?* There was no earthly reason why he'd feel any differently now.

'Any time I'm out and about I visit garage sales and junk shops…thrift stores and car boot sales.'

Perhaps if she made herself sound like a lonely single girl with a craft obsession, she would embarrass herself out of being so conscious of him.

'All the items are ridiculously cheap to buy,' she continued, 'and people leap at the chance to purchase the end product—the repurposed item. There's good profit to be made, and the items appeal to the style of visitor who comes here to tour the maze. Jemmie features them online, as well.'

His strong hands lifted a pottery urn from the bench. It had a chunk missing from one side. 'So a buyer will pay top dollar for this?'

'Once the urn has herbs growing in it, or maybe some flowering cacti, you'll be surprised how quickly it will be snapped up.'

She took the urn from his hands, held it up to the light. She ignored her fanciful thoughts and how it felt to stand so close to him, to measure her smaller frame against his taller, stronger one.

Get over it, Cee. Get over it right now!

Cecilia went on to tell Linc about her repurposing timetable, and then led the way back through the nursery acreage to the maze, quickly showing Linc the upgrades she'd had done to the *fruticetum* at the centre of it. Its circular arrangement combined colourful blooming potted shrubs with evergreen native species.

'Clever work.' He made the declaration the moment they stepped into the central area. 'Those shrubs grouped all around the edges of the circular space will add to the air of mystery for the masked ball.'

She gestured to the picnic tables dotted around the central area as well as the edges.

'Currently, when folks finish touring the maze, they can sit for a while, enjoy the quiet and utilise the screens embedded in the tabletops to scroll through our available stock lists and place orders. They can either take them with them, collect later or have them sent to any address they choose. The night of the ball there'll be a raised dais for dancing. The central picnic tables will be shifted out to the edges of the area and the canopied dais will be assembled on-site the day before the event.'

Something she had told herself was mostly about commerce and exposure for the business suddenly felt quite personal to Cecilia. She could imagine herself on that dais, dancing with a handsome partner.

Well, a girl could buy into a romantic idea, couldn't she? Even if it *was* an idea she had germinated to increase the popularity of her business.

As for that vision of herself on the dais… The man who appeared in it with her looked remarkably like Linc.

Heat warmed the back of her neck. The middle of a working tour was not the time for such flights of fancifulness. Hadn't she allowed herself to be distracted enough by him this morning?

'Will it be an old-fashioned ball?' he queried. 'With waltzing and so on?'

Was his voice deeper than usual? Cecilia glanced at his face but couldn't read his expression.

'There will be waltzes and other simpler dance tunes. I want people at all levels of dancing ability to be able to participate,' she murmured, and then had to clear her throat and strive for a stronger tone. 'I hope to create a night to remember.'

His gaze met hers and, for one breathless moment, electricity seemed to charge the air between them.

'I'm sure you'll achieve that.'

Oh, Linc, do you feel this too?

'I hope you'll be there.' The words came unthinkingly, and the warmth that had started at the back of her neck now rushed into her cheeks.

Had she not learned the last time?

She rushed on. 'What I mean is, it would look good to have the owner here. For business. But I understand you may be busy. It's not an expectation.'

Cecilia *had* asked the question with business in mind. She had!

'I'll have to consider—' He broke off as his cell phone started to ring.

Yet not before Cecilia sensed the hesitation in him. So there. That answered her unspoken question.

Of *course* he wouldn't want to involve himself in a masked ball. She had never asked him to do anything like that before. Why should she start now?

Mortification threatened, because she did *not* want him to see her request as an overture. It didn't matter what she might or might not have felt towards him since his arrival to undertake this review of the business.

Her request had been about *business*, and she needed Linc to know that.

Cecilia ignored the little voice that suggested it had been a little bit about the man himself, as well…

A moment later he'd responded briefly to the caller. He turned to Cecilia. 'I'm sorry. That was the call I've been waiting on. I need to go.'

'You're fine. Go do what you need to do.' Cecilia waved him away as though she had some claim to granting him permission or not. 'And don't worry about my invitation. I understand if you can't make it or don't want to attend. It was a marketing-related thought. That's all.'

Another thought encroached. What if he *did* attend the masked ball and arrived with some beautiful woman on his arm?

Not her business—and she wouldn't care one way or the other!

Linc gave a quick nod and strode off.

Cecilia did *not* watch his departure until he was out of sight, nor did she stand there daydreaming, incapable of remembering what she should do next even though she'd just given herself a stern internal talking-to.

She merely took a moment to gather herself for her next job. Yes. That was what she did.

And that job needed to be a last-minute check of the maze before the flower-show committee arrived.

Cecilia forced her attention to her work. And it was as she inspected the perfect flowerbeds that Cecilia admitted to herself that she really did hope Linc would attend the masked ball.

But only for business purposes.

'You can go ahead and sell off two of the three apartment complexes as whole lots to those investors. It's a good time to do it, and you know the profit margin I'll be looking for.'

Linc gave his agreement over his cell phone to his property broker as he strode from his car to the entrance of Cecilia's plant nursery the following morning.

'The third is to be offered as individual units under the first home-buyer arrangement we have with our partner real estate firms.'

'You know that plan is neither time efficient nor as cost-effective as the investor option.' His broker's voice held the tone of an oft-repeated lament.

Linc treated the warning to the same response he gave it every time. 'Nevertheless, you know where I stand on this.'

'There are times when you're going to give back, whether it reduces your profit margin or not. Yeah, I know. I'm proof of that myself.' The other man gave a wry laugh and yielded the point. 'You gave *me* a great chance when you employed me, and I haven't looked back since.'

'You can fill the time while you're waiting for those units to sell by property shopping for me in Queensland,' Linc offered. 'How does that sound? I've been wanting to buy into that state for a while.'

He gave his broker—suddenly a much happier

man—his instructions, ended the call and set out to find Cecilia.

'She's in the office.' Jemmie, Cecilia's second-in-command, told him as Linc strode across the courtyard.

'Thanks.'

As Linc headed for the office, he acknowledged silently that he really *wanted* to see Cecilia. He *should* want to see her again to prove to himself that this recent and inexplicable sharpening of his interest in her had disappeared as quickly as it had made its presence felt.

Odd that he should feel a lift in his spirits as he approached the door of the plant-nursery office, if that was the case.

The office door stood open. As Linc drew closer, observing Cecilia's concentration and hearing the sound of her voice as she spoke into the phone, he silently acknowledged that she looked beautiful sitting there and that seeing her gave him a warm, happy feeling.

He could live with that without ever doing a thing about it. In a short span of time he'd be out of here and back to his regular world, anyway.

Out of the way of temptation?

'Linc. Hi.' She glanced up after ending her call and offered a welcoming smile.

For a moment Cecilia looked equally happy to see him. Happy and...*interested*? Linc couldn't take his gaze from hers. And blue eyes stared back at him—before she seemed to realise how long their glances had held.

She dropped her gaze. 'I wasn't sure if you'd be here today.'

He stepped over the threshold and let his gaze linger on her face, enjoying the lovely lines, the sweep of her lashes against her cheeks.

'The business with my property guy didn't take long.' Linc gave himself full points for sounding so close to normal. 'I wound it up a few minutes ago on the phone, actually.'

He brushed aside his travelling all over Sydney to inspect his property holdings as though it had barely impinged. Right now it didn't seem to matter. All he could focus on was Cecilia.

What the heck was going on with him?

'Besides, I've got this review to do for you. It still shouldn't take too long if I get a good run at it.'

As though to mock him, his phone rang.

'I think you may have spoken too soon.' Amusement crinkled the skin at the corners of Cecilia's eyes, and her mouth turned up into a soft smile.

Linc lost himself in her in that moment. His breath caught and, still stuck on that smile, he answered his phone absent-mindedly.

He had to run the caller's first few words back through his mind again before he could focus. 'Sorry, Alex. Which export law did you say is concerning you?'

Linc forced his attention to the call.

Cecilia turned her focus to her work while Linc spoke on the phone with his brother. It felt strangely intimate to be in the same room with Linc while he did that, yet she had learned from his brief time here so far that he would step outside if he wanted privacy for a call.

Maybe she should find a reason to step out, anyway. She didn't need to add any extra feelings of intimacy to her connection with this man. She was having enough trouble ignoring her awareness of him as it was.

She started to stand.

'Okay. Tell Jayne I said hi.' Linc's voice softened noticeably as he said his goodbyes on the phone. 'I'll stop by to see you both tonight on my way home.'

The man loved his family to pieces.

Cecilia's heart softened and ached a little at one and the same time. He must be close to his family. That was so appealing. Yet it made her feel sad because she, on the other hand, was experiencing a difficult phase with her sister.

But that was going to get better. It *was*!

Linc ended the call and glanced up just as Cecilia settled back into her chair. 'How did the committee's visit go yesterday?'

'It went well.' She welcomed the distraction from her thoughts more than he could know. 'The committee members were happy with the standard of the maze and with the area that will be used at its centre for dancing. There will only be a hundred guests. Tickets to the ball are being auctioned online, with proceeds going to charity. I'm relieved the committee were satisfied with my plans and with the site itself.'

If the nursery played its cards right, it might get a yearly event out of this. She would definitely hold more balls for special occasions...weddings. The possibilities were endless. Cecilia couldn't help but feel a little excited about the doors this first event might open up.

'It sounds as though you have things well under control.' Linc murmured the words as he sat down to recommence his review.

Cecilia laughed. She didn't mean to, but the sound escaped her. 'All except the fact that Valentine's Day is about to erupt onto my work horizon, whether I feel ready for it or not—and I'm leaning somewhat towards the "not" side of that particular equation right now.'

As Linc turned his attention to his work—with numerous interruptions on his cell phone, despite his desire for a clear run at the review—Cecilia refocused and settled in to finalise stock orders for Valentine's Day.

She worked hard, but she had to admit—to herself, at least—that Linc's proximity was corroding her concentration. He was just so *there*.

And she was so busy. Every time she tried to work on her orders, the phone rang again or a supplier called through directly on her cell phone. There were cancellations of previously established orders, stockists informing her that they'd oversold to other buyers and couldn't fill *her* order, asking if other blooms could be substituted.

Cecilia's answer was always the same. No, they couldn't!

This happened every year—it was part of dealing with this particular day on the nursery's calendar—but that didn't make it any less busy or any less challenging for her to ensure she reached her necessary stock levels.

On top of that the floor staff came in more often than usual, with odd questions that simply couldn't wait. The more that time passed, the busier it became.

'Linc, I'm putting this call on speaker. I'm sorry if it disturbs your concentration.'

She tried not to let frustration colour her tone as she jabbed at the settings on her cell phone. Once she had placed it atop the filing cabinet in the corner of the room, she began to riffle through the cabinet's contents.

'It's fine. I can see you're under pressure.'

Linc's words were calm. He had fielded numerous distractions of his own since he got here today, and he seemed quite unfazed. As though he didn't find Cecilia's presence and nearness at all disturbing.

Not that Cecilia felt agitated due to *his* presence. Certainly not in any personal kind of way. She'd had that conversation with herself earlier. She simply had to get over the nerve-racking, overalert, oh-so-conscious of him feeling.

And she was over it. She 100 per cent totally *was*. Her consciousness could just catch up with that attitude right now!

'Mr Sampson, I have your previous delivery docket, your invoice and a receipt showing a nil balance in front of me.' She gave the reference number, speaking towards her phone. 'If funds are outstanding to your company, they aren't owed from here.'

After a moment the man discovered a mistake at

his end. He agreed to finalise Cecilia's order for the next day and ended the call.

With Mr Sampson sorted out, Cecilia replaced the file in the cabinet and returned to her desk.

Time passed. And when a customer phoned with a special request for a particular style of repurposed item, and Cecilia happened to be able to match it, she decided to take the opportunity to head to the repurposing shed to collect the piece.

She replaced the desk phone in its cradle. 'You'll be okay for a few minutes, Linc? I'll put the phone through to Jemmie, out front.'

'Leave it. I believe I may *just* be able to manage without you for a little bit without having to disturb Jemmie.'

His wry smile brought out every gorgeous manly feature. It also undid every bit of Linc-ignoring effort Cecilia had put in today.

Before she could stop herself, she smiled back. A big, wide, pleased-with-the-world smile that brushed across her face and made Linc grow still before an enigmatic veil came down over his eyes.

Her breath hitched, and just like that it was all there again. The awareness. The *interest.*

She drew in a slightly shaky inhalation. 'Okay. I'll…ah… I'll leave the phone. I'd better go take care of this.'

Before she did something she regretted for the *second* time since knowing him.

Cecilia exited the office and gave herself a good talking-to while she was at it. She wasn't interested in Linc. Such an interest wasn't something she could allow to exist. Just because her boyfriend had dumped her when her issues with her sister had hit crisis point, it didn't mean she should try to pick up the next available—

Oh, get over yourself, Cecilia. And get over Hugh, too.

As if Linc would participate in that possibility, anyway. He was a millionaire, for crying out loud, *so* successful in life. *And* he'd already rejected her once before. Was she trying to line herself up for a second shot at that humiliation?

She wasn't. She just hadn't expected to feel this attraction to and interest in Linc again. It had surprised her. All she needed to do was adjust to that surprise factor and she would be fine.

In minutes she was back at the office.

'Item retrieved and left with the front staff ready for collection.' She spoke as she stepped over the threshold of the office space.

'Great.' Linc was in the process of putting down the office phone extension as he responded. 'I've taken a couple of messages. You'll know what to do with them.'

He didn't break into a big smile. She didn't, either. That earlier moment of blinding connection had passed. So why could she still not seem to be able to tear her gaze from him? And why did he gaze so intently at her? And had she not taken any notice whatsoever of her earlier warnings to herself?

Immersed in those thoughts, she was slow to realise that her cell phone had started to ring.

When she did realise it, she barely gave the caller's identity a thought. It would be some supplier again. However, she wasn't sure where her phone actually was.

Cecilia patted her pockets. Her gaze searched the desk. Then, without any warning whatsoever, the worst possible thing happened for her privacy, and perhaps the most heart-wrenching yet hope-inspiring thing for her emotions.

The phone's voicemail picked up automatically, went straight on to the speaker setting she'd left it on and a tinny prerecorded message from the caller's end began to play out into the room.

'Are you willing to accept a call from the Fordham Women's Correctional Centre? Your sister, Stacey Tomson, wishes to speak with you... '

The revealing words blared across the room as though trumpeted through a megaphone by the world's largest elephant.

'If you do not want to accept this call—'

She'd left the phone on the filing cabinet. She had received only two other calls like this, and questions filled her mind.

Why had Stacey chosen now to phone? Did it mean their rift might be ending or would they argue again?

So many emotions swirled inside Cecilia in that moment. Hurt. Frustration. Disappointment. Love.

Cecilia quickly crossed the room, grabbed up the phone and fumbled to take it off speaker.

One glance at Linc's face told her it was way too late to try and hide this, but she managed to change the setting and get the phone to her ear. She wasn't sure if he'd heard her sister's voice or not, but when she started towards the door, to leave the room, it was to realise Linc had beaten her to it.

The door clicked shut behind his receding back, and Cecilia could acknowledge both the joy and the pain of finally receiving this call when she hadn't known when or even *if* she ever would.

She said hello to her troubled, incarcerated twin.

CHAPTER THREE

'STACEY. HOW ARE YOU? I've been hoping you'd call. It's so hard not being allowed to call you. It's been such a long time. I've missed you so!'

Are you still angry that I said you needed to change your direction in life? I wanted to help you, and it needed to be said!

Cecilia didn't want the gap between them to widen even more, and yet if she hadn't challenged Stacey, who would have?

The man who'd disappeared and left Stacey to carry this punishment alone? Who'd appeared to do nothing but manipulate Cecilia's sister up to that point?

'Are you okay?'

She couldn't make herself say *Are you okay in jail?* Or even, *Are you okay in there?*

'Have you been getting the money orders for extra food and things?'

'Yes, I've been getting them.'

Cecilia thought she heard Stacey swallow hard before her sister went on.

'Thank you for doing that.'

'You're my sister.' Emotion rose in Cecilia's throat.

'Cee, I wanted to ask if you'd be willing to start visiting me again.' Stacey's words couldn't mask her emotion. 'I've missed you. I should have called sooner. I was angry, and it's tough in here. There's been a lot of adjusting to do—'

'Of course I'll visit again. I've been dying to see you.' So much relief coursed through Cecilia that she wanted to laugh and cry at once. 'We can talk about your future, when you're finally out of there.'

Surely that would be something they could both look forward to?

'We can.' Stacey sounded on the verge of tears before she spoke again. 'I don't want to not be talking to you. I guess I felt hurt at a time when I needed you to just love me. But there's been time for me to think, and to realise I've made some really big mistakes.'

'I'm really sorry, Stacey.'

Cecilia had thought she was doing the right thing in pointing out the bad pathway that Stacey had followed. For some reason she'd thought that because Stacey had been so angry at the time her sister couldn't possibly have been hurting. Tears sprang to the backs of Cecilia's eyes again. How could she have been so short-sighted?

'I should have found a better way to deal with your situation than I did.'

'You were worried about me, and with good reason.' Stacey sighed. 'I can't understand now how I was so blind. Joe seemed nice at first—a little rough around the edges, but charming with it.'

'And then the charm wore off.' Cecilia understood that. She'd been there herself with Hugh. At least in this she could try to rebuild some solidarity with her sister. 'We're not very good at finding great men, are we?'

Stacey agreed, and then sounded a little troubled and vulnerable as she went on. 'I need to tell you that if you start coming to see me it will help my chances of gaining parole, because I'll be demonstrating that I have a sound relationship with someone reliable. I want you to know that before you come in, so you don't think I asked just because of it. I've missed you and I'm longing to see you.'

'I believe you, and I want that sound relationship again.' Cecilia had longed for it over the past months. 'I'm so glad you phoned, Stacey.'

'I am, too. I'm *allowed* to have a sister.' Stacey's words were firm, almost defiantly so. '*And* to see you and have a relationship with you. I should have stuck up for that from the start.'

'Of course you are.' Cecilia frowned. 'Who's told you otherwise? Surely not the authorities there?'

'Joe did—constantly throughout my relationship with him and again quite recently before I finally woke up.'

Cecilia clamped her teeth together so she wouldn't speak without thinking first. Finally, she said carefully, 'I thought that after the armed robbery he'd gone underground. Wouldn't he be detained and taken in by the police if he visited you?'

'He found a way to get messages to me in here through another inmate who was about to be released.' Stacey admitted it in a low voice. 'At first I was happy. I thought there must be some explanation for Joe dragging me into what happened that day and then leaving me to pay for being an accomplice to something

I didn't even understand was going to happen until it was too late.'

'I'm guessing that's not what happened?' Cecilia wished she could give her sister a hug.

'No. He wanted me to tell him if I had any secret money stashed anywhere outside of here or any valuable jewellery.' Stacey made a disgusted sound. 'I sent a message back telling him never to contact me again.'

'That was horrible of him, Stacey.' Cecilia could only be glad that Stacey had cut the man off. 'I love you, sis. We've got through life up to this point, and we can keep getting through it.' Cecilia struggled not to choke up again. 'I just want to see you. When can I come?'

'Let me talk to the officers here and find out.' Relief filled Stacey's tone.

'You'll ring again?' Cecilia wanted that assurance before Stacey hung up.

'I will. As soon as I know when you can come.'

They said their goodbyes then, and Cecilia slowly placed the phone into her pocket. They'd never been cut off from each other before. At least now she could see Stacey. Relief and gratitude tugged even further at her teetering emotions.

But right now, somewhere on the other side of the door, Cecilia had to face Linc. What could he possibly think?

Stacey had been unhappy since they were teenagers, but this was the first time she had done anything actually against the law. No one knew about the jail sentence. In fact, no one here had even met Stacey. The sisters had tended to meet up after work, and then when Joe had come on the scene, Stacey had kept contact with Cecilia to a minimum. Cecilia understood why now.

The guy hadn't wanted anyone else to have influence in Stacey's life. Thank goodness her sister had finally sent the man packing.

Cecilia wanted to undo Stacey's history and get her out of there because she'd been tricked. Those wishes were unrealistic, and she knew it, but she hated it that Stacey's life had been impacted so deeply by this whole situation.

Well, for now it was time to face Linc. Cecilia didn't feel ready, but she had no choice.

She forced herself to open the office door and to speak to Linc, who lounged with pseudocasualness against a pillar partway across the courtyard.

'I've finished my call. Thanks for giving me privacy for that.'

'It was no problem.' He started towards her.

Cecilia didn't know what else he might have said. Anything, or nothing at all. But suddenly she couldn't stay there to find out. Not right now. Not until she could get her emotions under better control. If he was sympathetic she might fall apart. She couldn't let that happen.

'I need to do a few things in the repurposing shed.' She blurted the words and turned on her heel. 'I'll be back in a bit.'

She couldn't even speak to him about getting Jemmie to come out of the retail section and cover the office during her absence. Cecilia couldn't say anything more at all. But she had her back turned before Linc reached her, and she walked herself quickly far enough into the rear of the nursery that no one would see her until she could blink back the well of emotion that threatened to overcome her.

It wasn't perfect. She shouldn't walk out on a busy office. But she needed time to gather herself.

Cecilia walked on and set to work on regaining her control—because that was what she needed to do.

Linc wanted to go after Cecilia. To ensure that she was okay. Although clearly he couldn't ensure any such thing, because she wasn't. The heartbreak she must have tried so hard to shore up before she opened the door minutes ago had been etched on her face.

That had shouted more loudly than any voice could have done for her to be given privacy to regroup. Even so, it had taken all his resources not to stride across the courtyard and take her into his arms.

She had a sister.

That sister was in a correctional facility.

Linc hadn't known either of those things.

What had Cecilia's sister done to land her where she was now? How long had Cecilia been trying to cope with this reality?

'Linc, I could use your help.'

The request from Cecilia's second-in-command forced his attention back to his surroundings, to the busy plant-nursery office. He'd called in Jemmie to help out, and the phone still kept ringing. The rest of the world remained unaware of Cecilia's turmoil and wasn't about to grant any concessions.

Jemmie went on. 'Will Cecilia be gone long? I've got an enquiry about one of her orders, and the amount of money involved is too substantial for me to make the judgment call alone. Unless *you* want to decide, Linc?'

'She won't be gone much longer.' Linc would have to go and find Cecilia before he let much more time pass. 'What exactly is the problem, Jemmie? I may be able to resolve it.'

He did just that, but he had no sense of satisfaction—only a gnawing awareness of the passage of time.

Linc frowned, checked his wristwatch again and got to his feet.

As he did so Cecilia stepped into the office space.

'Thanks for helping out, Jemmie.' She spoke as though nothing were amiss. 'You can head back now.'

The office phone rang. Cecilia answered it as Jemmie left. Again, Cecilia's composure seemed rock solid.

Except she was pale, her beautiful eyes looked as though she'd been crying and she wouldn't fully meet his gaze.

Linc waited while Cecilia took the call. When it had ended, he spoke carefully. 'I didn't know you had a sister.' He hoped that by acknowledging this in some way he might help Cecilia to feel less uncomfortable. 'I'm sorry that I heard the start of your conversation. If I'd known—'

'Stacey is my twin.' She searched his gaze. 'I wouldn't have expected you to know anything. This whole situation has been…challenging.'

'I can imagine.' Linc took care to allow that search and to keep his expression as open as possible. Cecilia might feel comfortable enough to confide in him a little more—not because he harboured some morbid curiosity about her difficulties, but because he cared.

He refused to ask himself whether that kind of care should fall within the realms of an employee/employer relationship. It fell within *his* realm.

After a moment Cecilia simply said, 'We hadn't spoken for months. We went through a really bad patch. Both of us were partly to blame, but I—I can see now that I let her down, and I regret that so much. Today was the start of turning that around, at least.'

'I'm happy for you—that there's a chance for you to get things on a better footing with your sister.' His words emerged in a deep tone. Linc hadn't managed to be there for his brothers when they had needed him vitally. For Alex most of all. He'd never forgiven himself for what he'd allowed to happen. His heart squeezed for Cecilia.

He cleared his throat. 'If there's anything—'

'Thank you.' She spoke quickly and seemed to force herself to draw a slow, deep breath. 'There's nothing. And it's busy.' She turned to her computer. 'I should get on with this work.'

Linc conceded to her need to refocus her attention and did the same, but her situation and his own memories from the past remained in his thoughts.

He'd hated the orphanage so much—the discipline and the emotional darkness and the complete lack of love or hope. Alex and Brent had saved him—had given him their brotherhood and let him love them and be loved in return.

Except at one vital point in time when Linc had failed in that charter.

And for that he could not forgive himself.

Linc forced his attention back to his review.

He still wanted to take Cecilia in his arms, but today's revelations had only drawn more attention to the reasons why he must let go of just such thoughts.

He wasn't worthy of her.

He never could be.

CHAPTER FOUR

'LINC. I WASN'T sure if I'd see you today.'

It was the following morning—Valentine's Day—
and Cecilia had arrived at the nursery well ahead of
schedule. She had wanted to be certain everything
was in order for this most lucrative day on the nursery's calendar.

She had wanted time to compose herself before
facing Linc again, if he did come in today, but would
that composure even be possible? Yesterday's phone
call with her sister had brought joy. That was undeniable. But it had also left Cecilia feeling exposed.

Yet when she searched Linc's gaze now, she saw
only acceptance and, as their gazes held, awareness.

Cecilia stood on the outside of her office space,
and Linc stood on the inside. She tried to pull herself
back to the conversation. 'Did you—did you resolve
your business challenge so soon?'

Linc had received a call from his brother late yesterday afternoon and had excused himself to go and
take care of whatever matter had arisen.

'The problem was a joint investment I have with
Alex.' The words were gruff. 'I'm sorry I left so
abruptly yesterday. I had to deal with it quickly oth-

erwise Alex could have lost a sizeable chunk of his portfolio. It is sorted out now.'

'I'm glad everything turned out okay.' She was, but her emotions were still a jumble. 'I had better print yesterday's orders, ready to start checking stock.'

Cecilia grasped the edge of the door and prepared to push it wider so she could enter.

'Actually, I hoped we could talk.' As he spoke those words he, too, reached for the door.

For long, still moments Cecilia felt the touch of warm, strong fingers over hers. *Linc's* fingers.

Aside from a handshake, when she'd first met Linc for her initial job interview, they'd never touched. But now they were, and that one simple touch undermined the slim control she'd had over her seesawing emotions—and over her attraction to Linc.

She wanted to know him better…to explore that interest. Now—today—she felt this. She hadn't shaken off that old interest in him at all. It had lain in waiting, ready to ambush her for a second time. It was a shock to admit that to herself, and as she searched his eyes, she wondered if those thoughts were reflected in hers.

'Cecilia…' Grey eyes searched her face, and his head dipped closer.

Her lips parted and her breath sighed out in a soft exhalation. She leaned towards him, just a little…

In the next moment, shocked at her own lack of control, she pulled back. How *could* she have ended up standing there with her emotions churning, so in need of his kiss?

Would he truly have kissed her? Had that been his intention?

A peek at his face revealed a mixture of surprise and…guilt?

Then his dark brows drew down, and she couldn't see into his eyes any more.

'Today—today will be manic.' She felt rather frenzied herself. Worked up. Freaked out.

You simply touched hands with him. Pull it together, Cecilia!

And he'd wanted to talk. About her sister phoning? About Stacey being in a women's prison?

Cecilia did *not* want to talk about that.

And now they'd almost kissed, and she needed to think about that—to figure out how she felt about that and why, if she'd interpreted it correctly, he should feel guilt over that.

'Delivery trucks will be arriving, and it won't stop after that.'

No sooner had she uttered the words than a truck could be heard, backing up to the loading bay.

The driver leaned on the horn.

The office phone began to jangle.

Linc frowned.

Cecilia raised her hands, palms up, towards him. 'It's Valentine's Day. The customers deserve their happiness. I can't deliver on that if I have to—'

'You're right. Now isn't the time.'

Linc conceded to Cecilia's declaration. He shouldn't have tried to bring up yesterday's shock revelation now, anyway.

But that moment in the doorway, when their hands had touched. He'd wanted to kiss her. He almost *had* kissed her.

Linc operated with a lot more self-control than that in life. He didn't get affected by *hand touching*.

So what was going on with him?

'I'll help out today, if it's going to be frantic. The review work can wait.'

'Th-thank you. I hope that won't be necessary, but I appreciate the offer.'

Her relief was heartfelt. Not because he'd offered to help out, Linc imagined, for he knew she could manage just fine without him and had done so for years. Her relief was patently because he'd backed off on his desire for an in-depth conversation. Who could blame her? If the roles were reversed, would *he* want to talk about it?

Or was her relief because that awkward moment in the doorway had ended?

He waved his hand in the direction of the truck. 'You get that. I'll take care of the phone.'

Apparently, the moment had been saved by the ring of the telephone and a truck full of red roses. For now, at least.

'So how's my brother enjoying this business review?' Brent MacKay asked the question cheerfully while well-ordered chaos reigned all around. 'I have to admit I was surprised when you told me you're thinking of giving Cecilia a share in the business. You've only ever taken on business partnerships with family up to this point.'

'It wouldn't be a gift. She's more than earned it in hard work over the past six years.'

It was later that day. The brothers stood in the busy nursery courtyard.

Linc watched Cecilia stride across the other side of it with a customer at her side and several more trailing at her heels like lovelorn ducklings.

'The review is progressing nicely.'

Except perhaps for today, when all he'd done was watch Cecilia rush to and fro while he'd fielded phone calls and observed the madness and the mayhem.

He'd taken care of some customers as well, to help share the load.

'And Cecilia's different. I'd be comfortable having a shared holding with her.'

Brent's eyebrows lifted. 'Oh, yes? Any reason in particular for that?'

Conversely, Linc's brows lowered. 'Because she's a trustworthy manager, and owning a share of the business would only make her more so.'

Linc started towards the nursery exit, where Brent had his utility truck parked out front.

'You *could* sound happier about that.' A corner of Brent's mouth turned up. He'd drawn level with Linc as they passed through the nursery exit. 'Anyway, I thought you'd be happy to see all this profit occurring right before your eyes—today at least?'

'I am.'

Of course Linc was. Any business owner would be pleased to see money coming in. Unless that owner didn't care just at the moment, because all he wanted to do was take the manager of the business aside and slow her down long enough to—

To do what? Talk to her about yesterday's startling revelation of her sister's situation, when he'd already had to concede that it wasn't the time to have that conversation?

Cecilia had made it pretty clear she didn't want any such discussion at *all* and that no time would be the right time for her.

Is that what you feel miffed about, MacKay? Or is it because she recoiled from that moment your hands touched at the door as though her fingernails were on fire?

It wasn't, either.

Fine—it was both.

Blast it. He didn't know!

'Is there anything else you need while you're here, Brent?' He slung the final bird's-nest fern into the back of his brother's utility truck and turned.

'Another one of those that *hasn't* just had half its foliage knocked off would be a start. I'm quite particular about the standard of plants that go into my landscape garden designs.' Brent said the words in a dry tone.

'Ah, sorry.' Linc glanced at the thing. 'I can replace that.'

'Don't worry. I've got enough to do without it if I have to.' Brent clapped him on the back.

'Did you know Cecilia has a twin sister? Or a sister at all, for that matter?' The words passed through Linc's lips before he could stop them.

Brent was halfway into the driver's seat of his truck. He settled fully and turned a quizzical gaze Linc's way. 'No. Why?'

'I didn't, either.'

How could he have known Cecilia for so long and not know the first thing about her personal life? He'd let her into *his* life. She knew his brothers. She'd been to their warehouse home a couple of times on business matters back when they had all lived there. She'd met Brent's and Alex's wives here at the plant nursery when they'd come shopping for things.

That was a lot of 'letting in' for a man who held his personal matters as close to his chest as Linc did.

He ignored the knowledge of all the things he *hadn't* let Cecilia in about—such as his entire personal life aside from her interactions with his family, most of which had been instigated by those family members rather than Linc himself, if he were honest about it.

Not the point. He hadn't deliberately shut Cecilia out of any of it.

She wasn't trying to shut you out, either, MacKay.

Linc didn't wait for Brent to respond. What could his brother say other than to ask him if he was feeling okay or had received a blow to the back of the head or something? Linc didn't know what to make of his own thoughts, anyway.

He saw Brent off and went back to helping out around the nursery. Sooner or later this romantic day would end. Maybe then he'd finally be able to focus on getting the review done, and then getting out of here and on with his life again.

The thought should have cheered him, but instead it made him feel unsettled and restless.

At the end of the day Linc found Cecilia in one of the auxiliary sheds, sweeping up rose petals. Although the room was empty now, except for those remnants, the scent of roses still filled the air.

'I thought I might find you here. The rest of the staff have gone home.' He'd come to find her and encourage her to leave. 'You should stop. You've pushed yourself hard today.'

His gaze tracked over her, registering the exhaustion stiffening her shoulders, the faint bruises beneath her eyes. A single deep red petal had caught in her hair.

'I wanted to get everything tidied up before I left.' The broom stilled in her hands as she looked up at him. Her face softened, and a weary pleasure lifted the corners of her mouth. 'We sent a lot of people home happy today, at least.'

In this moment she seemed to have found a true and deep contentment that came purely from wearing herself to the bone in order to *give*. Linc couldn't have admired her more.

'*You* did.' He took the remaining steps to her side and gently retrieved the broom from her hold. He placed it against a pillar.

'You contributed, Linc.' Her words were unguarded. 'I saw you helping out that little old lady who wanted roses for all her children and grandchildren.'

He *had* done that and, in amongst the antsy feelings he hadn't understood, Linc had found pleasure in giving that assistance.

But so much more had he admired Cecilia's generosity in doing the same, regardless of her personal circumstances. And now, in her presence, some of his restlessness today distilled into what it had really been. The need for her company, her attention, to focus on her and be with her. He couldn't explain the feelings. He already knew he had to stay away from her. And yet here he was.

Maybe if he tested this interest in her he would

prove to himself that the feelings were no different from those he'd felt towards any other woman who'd passed through his life. Then he could move on.

It was either sound reasoning or the flimsiest excuse of all time. Linc didn't try to discern which.

'There's just one petal remaining.' He reached up, drew the soft velvety petal from Cecilia's golden hair and placed it into her palm.

'Oh.' Her fingers closed over the petal. Her gaze lifted and searched his.

That was all. Just a touch and a glance and he was lost.

'I've wanted—' He searched *her* face, her eyes, and when he found curiosity, consciousness, he kissed her.

The moment their lips met, hers softened.

Oh, so sweetly.

Linc drew their joined hands to his chest and held them there. He wanted to keep kissing her and never stop. He wanted this one moment to last forever so he didn't have to think about it, or about what it meant, why it felt different from any kiss that had gone before it. Why his arms seemed to need so very much to envelop her. Instead, his fingers tightened around hers.

Cecilia had waited for Linc's kiss. She didn't want to admit that to herself, but it was true. She had wanted and needed to know how this would make her feel, and now she was experiencing it.

Against their joined hands she could feel the warmth of Linc's chest through his shirt, the hard wall of muscle. Yet his lips were soft as they caressed hers. She felt cherished and as if she was the absolute focus of his attention in this moment. She felt...*dif-*

ferent inside. As though this was changing her even as it happened.

Oh, she didn't want this kiss to end.

Cecilia curved her other hand against the column of his neck and acknowledged that this was not like it had been with Hugh. This was not like anything or anyone before.

Uncertainty rose then—because how could this touch her emotions so immediately? With this man who dated but didn't seem to look for the same kind of relationship as Cecilia did? The long-term, permanent kind?

'Cecilia…' Linc murmured her name against the side of her face as his lips left hers. He enveloped her in a hug.

She felt again the magnitude of the barriers within herself, wanting so very much to let them topple and fall, to open her heart to at least the hope of him.

Oh, Cecilia. That would be such foolishness. A kiss is a kiss is a kiss. With a man like Linc, how can you believe it means anything beyond the moment?

Hugs weren't kisses, though, and she hugged back and then quickly freed herself, searched his face. Because if there was even a hint of pity for her circumstances…

But all she could read in Linc's expression was bemusement, before he blinked and blinked again.

What had happened to her emotions just now?

They'd kissed, and that had been wonderful and amazing for her, but she needed to find some reality here. Linc's bemused expression might be for a hundred reasons. Hopefully, not because he knew she'd reacted as though her whole world had tilted on its axis when they kissed!

Pride surfaced as she confronted that absolutely untenable possibility. It was Valentine's Day. He'd kissed her. It could easily have been nothing more than a spontaneous act of the moment. Indeed, he could be regretting it even now, because of their business relationship. Remember? What would happen to that now?

It would be reinstated immediately—that was what! And for the sake of her pride Cecilia wanted to be the one to initiate that.

'I—I believe I'll do as you've suggested and head home. There'll be work again, bright and early in the morning, and it's been a long and busy day.'

Maybe Linc would put their kiss—or at least any vulnerability he might have detected in her as a result of it—down to the physical drain of the day.

She didn't wait to find out. Instead, Cecilia turned quickly and left him there to lock up, to secure everything.

'Goodnight.'

For the second time Cecilia abandoned her duty because her heart was in the way.

Not her heart! Her emotions. There was a difference—a really big difference. She had been overwhelmed by the power of the day and her exhaustion and missing her sister.

Oh, yes? And somehow that had made her trip and fall onto Linc's lips and kiss him and feel things she had never felt before? Even now she wanted to turn around, to go back, to extend her time in his company. Because...

Because of hope that shouldn't exist and that needed to be extinguished *now*—before it was allowed to grow any further. How could she feel this way? Be so drawn to him and in some part of herself so willing to leap in and believe he had some kind of emotional investment in her when no evidence whatsoever existed to prove that?

Linc wasn't offering her anything! One stolen kiss that might have happened without forethought or reason did not add up to...*anything*.

He was probably thinking already that it shouldn't have happened. And Cecilia would think exactly the same—just as soon as she could get her emotions unjumbled and back into some kind of reasoning, sensible order.

Maybe she and her sister were doomed to pick out the wrong men in their lives. Well, at least in Cecilia's case Linc would walk away from this moment, and it would fade to oblivion and be forgotten.

The same way Cecilia had 'forgotten' a six-year-old crush?

Fine. *He* would bury it and forget it. She might take a little longer to get to that point, but in the end she would.

She would!

CHAPTER FIVE

'YOU'RE LOOKING AT a classic nineteen-forties pram, luv.' The man selling the item turned the frame this way and that so Cecilia could get a better view of it. 'A bit of paint and you've got yourself—'

'A refurbished carcass missing all its interior parts?' Cecilia softened her words with a smile. 'I *do* concede that the frame is still in decent order. There's not too much rust.'

She named her final offer.

'It's that or no sale, I'm afraid. I have my buying limits, just as you have your selling ones.'

Cecilia was at a used-items fair in an outer suburb of Sydney. Hundreds of sellers had taken stalls both inside the pavilion and outdoors on the grassed area, and there were plenty of browsers and buyers there to enjoy the day.

She was doing her best to focus on her surroundings, but she was struggling. All she could think about was those moments with Linc at the nursery. What was *he* thinking? Had he thought about it at all? Or forgotten it the moment it happened?

Why had it happened, in any case? Had it been a moment of forgetfulness on his part? Had he seen the rose petal in her hair and that had led to an automatic response that might have happened anywhere, with any person? Maybe he'd intended a quick brush of lips or something and she'd prolonged that?

No. They'd both been equally involved. Hadn't they…?

This was what happened when a girl spent too much time revisiting a few special moments. She lost any shred of objectivity she might have had.

'All right, then.' The seller gave a brief nod. A twinkle of approval for her bargaining prowess flitted through his eyes. 'You can have it for that.'

'Thank you.' Cecilia finalised the transaction and told herself to draw a line under her thoughts about that kiss with Linc at the same time.

She had just handed over the money and turned to begin the task of taking the pram frame away when a deep voice spoke.

'I thought I saw a familiar face. Grabbing more items for refurbishment?'

It was Linc. A rush of warmth flooded into her cheeks. Oh, she hoped he wouldn't be able to see that in the dim lighting!

'Linc! I was just think—'

She had just been remembering a kiss that had left her confused and fighting herself, and now Linc was right here. She needed to step past that memory and not embarrass herself or let him see in any way how much those moments had affected her.

'How—how are you? What are you doing here?'

He'd seemed to materialise beside her as though from thin air. In fact, the air *did* seem thin around Cecilia in that moment. She could barely breathe.

Linc, in casual Saturday gear, was—well, he was *Linc*. The man she had kissed with such shattering impact on her equilibrium. And then she'd left him and told herself to forget all about it. But she hadn't managed very well. She hadn't managed at all.

Had it affected Linc in that way or not at all? And what was he doing here right now? *Oh, my.* What if he wanted to talk about it? To make sure she understood it had been a momentary slip in good judgment on his part or something?

Yet there'd been that bemusement in him, so maybe he had been affected by it, too?

And he couldn't have known he'd find her here today.

'I plan to fill the pram with snapdragons and baby's breath and mint.' She prattled the words with a breathless edge.

Get a grip, Cecilia!

She forced herself to slow down and to ask as casually as possible, 'What's brought you to the fair?'

Unfortunately, as she asked the question she allowed herself to *really* look at him. He looked amazing, in a polo shirt that emphasised the breadth of his shoulders and faded jeans.

He'd kissed her, and she'd seen stars and flowers and all manner of romantic things.

Well, wasn't she better off admitting that to herself? At least then she could start fighting the foolish feelings.

'My sisters-in-law plan regular outings for the family.'

His gaze roved her face as he spoke. And in that

moment of examination Cecilia was certain that the memory of their kiss was in his eyes.

'Do—do they?'

'Yes.' He took a half step closer to her. 'They wanted to visit the fair because it has a number of vintage train sets and other vintage toys listed, and Fiona and Jayne know that Brent is mad about those. They…ah…they already have a restorer lined up to work on anything we find today.'

Oh, Linc. What's happening here? Do you feel this?

Cecilia realised in that moment that the hurt of Hugh was over. It had given way to more immediate things.

The thought brought panic with it. Was she allowing those barriers to disappear because of Linc? Surely that would do nothing more than open her up to far greater hurt?

'It's sweet that Fiona and Jayne are doing that for your brother.' And Linc was sweet too—for participating, for caring about his family.

There goes one corner of a barrier.

Fine. So maybe Cecilia *was* changed as a result of their kiss. She would just have to make sure it didn't show in any way that Linc could discern.

'Have you found anything?'

Enlightenment? A desire for us to be together or to find out more about these shared feelings that are so amazing to me?

And that probably didn't even exist for him!

'I've got a few items.' He pointed to the bag in his hand and gave a short laugh, but his gaze still searched hers.

Oh, how she wished she could simply read his thoughts.

'The girls went off together when we arrived, and Brent and Alex and I decided to split up and buy everything any of us came across and sort it out later. I'm not sure whether I've got junk or buried treasure, but at least I haven't come up empty-handed.'

Cecilia laughed. She just couldn't help it. This was a different side of Linc—a family-activities side— and it was adorable.

He smiled, and his gaze seemed to soften as he did so. That softening reminded her of when he'd kissed her.

So now she thought he was adorable, and she couldn't forget their kiss.

Bye-bye second corner of a barrier.

Don't you dare hope, Cecilia.

It was only as she warned herself against hope that Cecilia realised just how much she had allowed it to rise, despite all her warnings to herself.

Yet Linc was here, and she was here. Why couldn't she enjoy a chance encounter without getting bogged down in all kinds of worries and concerns and thoughts about who felt what? Linc wasn't making reference to their kiss, so why should she let it stop her from enjoying seeing him in this simple, every-day sort of way?

There. You see?

This didn't have to be a problem. She had let her thoughts run away with her, but she realised that now and would be able to bring them back into line. She and Linc had shared a kiss—it was over. He didn't seem to be about to mention it. She didn't have to, either. They could just act as though it had never happened.

The completely illogical nature of this decision-making process she simply ignored.

'What about you?' He glanced at the pram frame. 'Are you still looking around, or did you come just for that?'

'I've been here all morning, and I've got more searching to do.' She gestured towards the exit. 'But for now I need to get this pram back to my car and do something about lunch.'

That was fairly normal, wasn't it? She drew a deep breath and caught the scent of his aftershave…not blunted this time from a day's wear, as it had been when they—

'It's later than I thought.' He glanced at his watch. 'I must have got caught up in my browsing. Let me help you.'

As though he dealt with nineteen-forties baby carriages on a daily basis, he lifted the pram frame.

'Would you like to lead the way?'

Yes. Yes, I would. I'd like to lead you all the way to revisiting that kiss to see if I made up my reactions or if they happen again.

No sooner had the recalcitrant thought passed through her mind than Linc shifted his grip on the pram frame. The muscles in his arms flexed.

Had it just got really warm in there?

Not helpful, Cecilia.

'My car is beside the park.'

They left the building, crossed the road and Cecilia led the way to her car, where it stood at the edge of a public park. The vehicle was an old model, red because she hadn't been able to help herself and most importantly a hatchback, with seats that would lie down to make more storage space. She still felt completely flustered.

Linc tucked the elderly pram into her car. As he did so, he glanced at the items she'd bought earlier in the day. 'That's a nice load of junk—I mean *refurbishing items* you've got there.'

'Thanks.' She laughed and pointed to his bag. 'That looks quite bulky, and by the sounds of it you got quite involved in your shopping if you lost track of time. It seems I'm not the only one who has been engrossed in collecting junk—I mean *vintage items* today.'

Seeing shared amusement crinkle the lines around his eyes while his lips kicked up made her smile even more. She tried not to acknowledge that it also made her breathless.

Cecilia pressed the lock to her car and turned her back on it. 'Buying used items is a lot of fun. Maybe you'll want to keep doing it now that you've started?'

'Perhaps I will.' He gestured towards the park. 'My family are gathering for a picnic lunch. Join us. You said you were due for a break, and you can lend your expert opinion on the vintage items we've found.'

The invitation was casual, and yet her heart leapt stupidly and so easily.

Cecilia warned herself to thank him and say no. 'I guess I could take a look—but only if you're sure I wouldn't be imposing.'

'You won't be. They'll love it.' He started moving into the park, clearly expecting her to keep pace with him.

Cecilia did.

Fine. So she'd accepted his invitation? That didn't have to mean anything in particular. Lunch with his family didn't have to be a big deal unless she thought of it in that way. She'd obviously overthought the kiss they had shared, but if Linc could go on acting as though it hadn't happened, then so could she.

They made their way down a beautiful tree-lined avenue, past plane trees and palm trees and boab trees and a children's playground, and strolled up the curved path that skirted a classic fountain. Two soft grey pigeons rested right at the top, their heads close together.

Cecilia's glance remained fixed on them for too long, and she almost lost her footing on an uneven segment of the path.

'Careful.' Linc tucked her hand through his arm as though it were the most natural thing to do. 'It's tranquil here, isn't it?' He turned his head and glanced into her eyes.

'Yes.' She returned his glance before she looked away again. 'There's a sense of peace.'

They walked on in silence until finally she looked ahead and there, seated on a massive picnic blanket beneath the shade of a eucalypt tree, were Linc's family members. Two men. Two women. Each familiar to her.

She'd met them all before, at various times, but never in this kind of idyllic setting. Never while arm in arm with Linc and trying so hard not to make too much of that.

Cecilia dropped her hold of Linc's arm. 'Maybe I shouldn't—'

She thought he murmured, 'Maybe I shouldn't, either...' before he cleared his throat and said, 'I think it might be too late. They've seen you.' He gave his family a wave that on the surface at least appeared casual.

Cecilia forced her attention to the group. She glanced at the scattered bags the family had accumulated, particularly the pile beside Linc's sisters-in-law. 'It will be fun to look at the vintage items.'

'I thought you'd like doing that.' He gave a nod of his head. 'And I can guarantee the food will be amazing and there'll be plenty of it. Our family's housekeeper, Rosa, is an excellent cook.'

His family called greetings and, in the middle of it all, Cecilia found herself swept up into the heart of this gathering where she might have felt like an intruder and yet they made her so welcome that she simply couldn't.

Cecilia wanted to stay on her guard, but instead she relaxed as the family made her welcome. It *was* wonderful to be here, and if Linc's presence at her side contributed to that more than it should—well, she would simply have to worry about that later. She had no answers right now, anyway!

'Isn't it nice to enjoy the sounds of nature and this feeling of open space?' Brent's wife, Fiona, asked the question of the group. She glanced around. 'What a *great* way to relax.'

They all did exactly that. Cecilia examined the vintage train sets and toys they'd found and felt all of them had potential. 'I'm sure that some attention from a restorer would bring them right back to life.'

'That's what I thought.' Fiona returned a set of carriages to their faded box.

Conversation flowed across a range of topics after that and ended up rather randomly in a discussion about pet adoption before Cecilia began to notice the passage of time.

Linc had repeatedly drawn her into the conversation, as though he truly valued her thoughts and opinions. Somehow that made her feel safe.

Great.

That was all she needed—to start feeling *safe* around him. Self-delusion alert! She found the man attractive and interesting, but he was the owner of the business she managed—a millionaire, totally out of her reach. Did she even need to go on? What was safe about any of that?

Yes, but he'd also kissed her.

I don't believe he's not interested, said one side of her thoughts.

She pushed that side down, with the other side called *common sense*, and said in a bright tone as she forced her gaze around the group to encompass everyone there, 'This picnic food is delicious.'

'It is, isn't it?' Alex's wife, Jayne, encouraged Cecilia to take another lettuce cup, deliciously filled with seafood and a spicy dressing.

'It's nice to see you outside of a working environment, Cecilia,' Fiona said. 'We're so glad you could join us.'

'I was certainly surprised to see Linc when we bumped into each other at the fair.' Cecilia glanced at the man in question, where he half reclined in a very unmillionaire-like sprawl beside her.

How could one person look so alluring just by existing?

As she was about to turn her glance away again, Linc's mouth lifted at the corners. Just that and Cecilia's heart lifted right along with the turn of his lips.

She might have made her excuses and left then, but instead she became embroiled in a conversation about her refurbishing. Initially, it was with the whole group, but one by one they dropped out of the conversation to talk among themselves until it was only Linc and Cecilia left discussing the topic and she lost herself completely in it.

'If you outsourced the refurbishment work, that aspect of the nursery might increase its financial viability.' Linc made the statement laconically.

'At the moment it wouldn't,' Cecilia hedged, not really wanting to explain just why that would be the case.

'You're doing some of the work at home, aren't you?' Linc shook his head. 'I might have guessed you wouldn't stop at simply buying items on your own unpaid time.'

'It's a manager's privilege to donate time to the business.' She jumped in quickly to justify this. 'Besides, it's soothing work. I benefit from it as much as I give to it.'

'As much as I want to, I can't really argue with that.' His expression sobered as he went on. 'But I *can* encourage you not to let the work be a burden to you.'

'I enjoy it too much for that to happen.' Cecilia pursed her lips. 'You could be right about the outsourcing, though. Even if one of the lower paid staff took care of some of the basic work.'

'I was only teasing you.' Linc's gaze followed the movement of her lips. 'It's profitable enough as it stands now, and I'm sure part of the charm for customers is your ability to sell the items on as the person who breathed life back into them in the first place.'

'That does help.'

She realised then how close they were to each other, that at some point each of them had leaned towards the other, and her heartbeat skipped. Her breath caught in her throat. She had the sense that maybe he wasn't as impervious as he was making out, and it made her want to test that theory.

But they were here with all his family. This was not the time for her to indulge in a state of superawareness of Linc yet again.

She glanced guiltily around them, to discover that she and Linc were now alone!

'Did we cause them all to leave with our—?'

'Our long-winded work-related discussion?' A spark of devilment danced in his eyes, and this time he *didn't* bank it down or try to stop her from seeing his thoughts. 'Trust me, they're all just as bad—and, no, we didn't drive them off.'

Cecilia fell into those eyes then and there. She simply softened to Linc and that was that.

Something had got into her that she couldn't seem to control. It felt rather too much like anticipation, happiness or maybe even hope.

'I find our discussions very enjoyable.' His words seemed to emerge in a very deep tone.

Before Cecilia could fully register the pleasure in his voice, he went on. 'My family have wandered off to try to find an ice cream parlour somewhere, and then head for their homes. There was some sign language about all that just before they went, but you had your back turned at the time.'

'Going on about my refurbishing without noticing anything around me.'

She still felt a little mortified, but more than that she felt their shared consciousness of each other. She had to be sensing *that* correctly, surely?

'I should get back to the fair, too.' She forced herself to put more distance between them on the blanket and began to gather together the remnants of the family meal. 'Please thank the others for including me when you see them again.'

A part of her wished she hadn't made that belated decision towards self-preservation, but she had courted enough danger around Linc for one day. She didn't know how he felt, and until she could understand her own emotions better, she should keep her distance. The exact opposite of what she'd done today up until now.

Linc watched Cecilia gather plates and napkins and replace them tidily into the wicker picnic basket. With each movement she seemed to gather her barriers more closely about her.

Conversely, Linc's seemed to be slipping further away from him. Even as he watched her, he noted that she had beautiful hands, with slender fingers that were stronger than they looked—somewhat like Cecilia herself.

He'd gained great pleasure in drawing her out today. Knowing that she'd relaxed enough to forget her surroundings pleased him, too.

In all of it he'd told himself he *wasn't* thinking about their shared kiss, that his thoughts *hadn't* turned again and again to those moments and the emotions they had made him feel. Tenderness for her, and interest, a strong desire to know more of her—who she was and what made her tick and everything about her.

Those reactions didn't fall under the category of passing interest. He shouldn't have allowed any interest at all.

In truth, he shouldn't have invited her to this lunch. He'd told himself it would be a way to get them back on to a comfortable footing with each other, to leave that Valentine's Day kiss behind them, but that had been quite delusional—for him, at least.

He wanted even more to kiss her again.

Great going, MacKay.

And then, as though he had no control whatsoever over his own behaviour, he opened his mouth and added to the temptation.

'I'd hoped you might let me tag along this afternoon while you look over the rest of the stalls. There may be more train sets that I can pick up.'

Linc loved his brother. He totally did. And he'd cheerfully continue to buy Brent train sets if Brent continued to enjoy collecting them.

But why would Linc stay all day here, browsing for them, when the rest of the family had already left?

'You'd be more than welcome to join me.' Cecilia said it and bit her lip, but her eyes were luminous.

Immediately, Linc felt ridiculously pleased by that fact.

Fine. So he'd extended the time they would spend in each other's company today. So what?

He did what any good man would do in such circumstances, when he couldn't figure out which way was up or down in his life since a kiss had completely altered his perspective.

He pretended not to notice any of it.

The afternoon proved wonderful for Cecilia. She and Linc wandered the remaining stalls. Linc very quickly worked out the kinds of items that attracted her eye and pointed out several things to her that she would have otherwise missed. In turn she found two more vintage train sets that he purchased for his brother.

They laughed and made silly comments, and Cecilia remained constantly aware of him. Each time they bumped shoulders or had their heads close together over some item, her breath would catch.

Yet still she told herself that this was okay, that things were under control. That her attraction to him and interest in him *weren't* running full steam ahead.

Right or wrong, Cecilia felt happy for the first time in a long, long while, and she let herself relax fully into the feeling.

Maybe that was why at the end of the day, as they stowed the final item into her car and Linc turned to her, she remembered her sister in a sudden guilty rush and words poured out before she could stop them.

'I've had such fun today I forgot about Stacey completely.' Her words were low, almost inaudible and filled with guilt.

How *could* she have forgotten her sister so thoroughly? Especially now, when she should be waiting every moment for the call that would let her know when she could go to visit her?

Linc heard Cecilia's confession and she didn't need to say anything else, because those few words showed it all. The deep love, and the guilt that she had lived her own life for a few hours while her sister was shut away, only half living hers.

But there was a difference between a woman forgetting her sister for a few brief hours, when she couldn't do anything further to help her than she already was, and a man who'd completely neglected his brother's welfare for weeks at a stretch when he'd been charged with looking out for that brother.

While Linc acknowledged that he couldn't change his own past, he could offer comfort to Cecilia now. He opened his arms and pulled Cecilia inside them. 'It's okay. You haven't done anything wrong.'

His lips were in her hair, and for a brief moment her arms stole about his middle before she drew back. 'Thank you.'

Again, he watched her put herself back together, shore herself up and square her shoulders.

A feeling of pride in her welled. It may not be his place to feel it, but he did.

'Linc…'

In her beautiful eyes, and on her face, her appreciation for these moments showed. She seemed to be struggling to find words.

Linc struggled, too—against wanting to draw her close again. He knew he had to fight this awareness of her, that he should have fought it and won before they'd shared that Valentine's Day kiss.

Today he hadn't even controlled his urge to gain as much time with her as possible once their paths had crossed. In no reality could he justify that, when he knew there could be no future in pursuing that interest.

Linc needed to get his own boundaries back in place. That meant sticking to their working relationship. He shouldn't ever have allowed himself to waver from it.

'If there's anything I can do in terms of workload or freeing up your time to help with the situation with your sister, please tell me.'

Cecilia heard Linc's words and tried not to let them hurt her feelings. They came from the perspective of a business owner to one of his managers. She and Linc *were* those things, but even so...

She forced her chin up.

'Thank you. If there is anything I need in that respect I will let you know.' She gestured to her car. 'I must be going. It's been a nice day. I'll see you at work tomorrow.'

She couldn't be any more businesslike than that.

Cecilia congratulated herself all the way home. And if she also felt miserable and confused and unhappy in the middle of that congratulating, she buried those feelings in a flurry of repurposing work from the moment she stepped inside her front door.

It was good that she'd spent the day with Linc, because now she really did know that somehow she had to stop her thoughts and, yes, some of her feelings from running away with her any further when it came to her millionaire boss.

CHAPTER SIX

'HELLO, CECILIA? I'm just calling to seek your response to our invitation to attend the opening gala this evening.'

The words came from the president of the Silver Bells flower show organising committee.

'We don't seem to have heard anything back from you.'

The woman had called Cecilia at the plant-nursery office, and now Cecilia frowned with complete mystification as she registered the request. 'I'm sorry. I haven't received any invitation for the gala opening. I assumed it was for VIPs and organisers only when nothing came through.'

Cecilia *had* wondered but had put the thought from her mind as time had passed and the gala night had drawn nearer and still no invitation had been received.

'Oh, dear. I suspected that might be the case.' The woman's disappointment rang in her words. 'The invitation was to you and the business's owner. I'm afraid we outsourced the sending of our official invitations and a number of them appear to have been overlooked. That's a process that will definitely be changed for next year, but in the meantime we really *did* want to see you and Linc MacKay there tonight.'

'At such short notice I'm not sure—'

'It's *so* important to us, my dear.' The president sounded determined.

Well, the committee hadn't got such an amazing event into its inaugural year by hanging back, Cecilia supposed.

Cunningly, the woman went on. 'The masked ball will be one of our premiere events this year, and as its hosts we'd like to honour you. Surely there's a chance you could both make it?'

'I'll be delighted to be there.'

Cecilia would. This was an opportunity for her to promote the nursery and perhaps to gain some useful insights into the hopes the committee held for the rest of the month-long event.

Would Linc want to attend, though?

Cecilia's glance lifted and sought him out, where he sat at the other desk. As she glanced his way, Linc straightened from his computer, stretched his arms over his head and gave his shoulders a good roll. His head was turned, his gaze focused out of the window, so he wouldn't be aware of her eyes on him.

She was taking in the strong lines of his upper torso before she realised what she was doing.

'I...um...let me check and I'll get back to you. What exactly are the details?'

She scribbled down the return phone number, the start time, all the other information she needed, ended the call and turned to Linc, who was now working at his computer again.

'Linc?'

He looked up. 'Mmm?'

'An invitation that should have gone out asking both of us to attend the opening gala for the Silver Bells flower show was somehow overlooked. That was the president of the organising committee on the phone just now.'

A ridiculous flutter started up in her tummy as she went on.

'They are hoping we can both be there. There's just one problem. It's tonight.'

Cecilia refused to dwell on the prospect of spending an evening in Linc's company, if indeed he decided to attend. This was work related. He would either go or not go, depending on his level of interest and his schedule, and Cecilia wouldn't care one way or another. She had her feelings about Linc completely under control now.

Maybe he had a date with some beautiful woman tonight, anyway.

Worse, maybe he would bring one as his date to the gala!

Cecilia shouldn't care but, oh, she did. She cared about that possibility far too much. Suddenly, she wasn't at all certain that she *did* want Linc there.

'It's short notice. I understand if you have other plans.'

'There's nothing on my schedule that can't be changed.' His gaze showed only businesslike interest. 'If it will be helpful to your cause then I'm happy to make an appearance with you.'

With her.

Okay, so that was good.

In a purely business way.

Right.

So it was agreed that they would attend the event together. As colleagues.

Which was how it came about that just hours later Cecilia stood waiting inside her modest cottage home for Linc to arrive and collect her.

She didn't feel businesslike at all, no matter how much she tried to talk herself into feeling that way.

She wore a rose-pink evening gown with a soft cowl neck and fitted bodice. The gown fell from a high waist in gentle folds. Pearl drop earrings and her hair piled high on her head completed the look, and she had classic white high heels on her feet. Maybe the evening clothes were the problem…causing the flutter of excitement in her tummy right now.

Cecilia glanced again in her hall mirror and couldn't help but note that the person looking back was a far cry from the one who went off to work in casual clothes and sturdy boots most days.

What would Linc make of the transformation?

Not that she cared one way or another.

Indeed, she'd spent hours fussing over her make-up and hair just to please herself.

Outside, a car door closed. Inside her small home, Cecilia held her breath.

Moments later footsteps sounded on the short pathway to her front door.

Breathe, Cecilia.

Somehow the hopes and expectations for this evening's outing had got into her blood before the evening itself had even begun. The lift of anticipation only increased as the doorbell chimed.

She collected her purse, made the short journey to the door and pulled it open.

'Hi, Linc. Thanks for stopping by to collect me.'

She got the words out before she looked at him properly. It was just as well, because when she did, she couldn't drag her gaze away again.

He had on a sleek evening suit in a dark pinstripe grey, a crisp white shirt and a thin powder blue tie. Polished black dress shoes completed the outfit, and as he moved his arm slightly, she caught a glimpse of a gold cufflink.

Oh.

My.

Gosh.

Could *any* man look more handsome than Linc did tonight?

'Good evening, Cecilia.'

Linc spoke the words in slow response to Cecilia's greeting.

His first glimpse of her in a gown of deep pink shimmery fabric had stopped him in his tracks. All he could seem to see was bare sun-kissed shoulders, hair piled high on her head, showing off the lovely lines of her neck, and her beautiful face: eyes made up subtly to draw out their perfect blue depths, lips accented in a soft shimmery pink to match her dress.

'You look…' *Stunning. Gorgeous. Kissable.* 'Lovely.'

Even in saying that he felt like a master of understatement. What she looked was indescribably beautiful.

His intention to behave in a highly businesslike manner this evening seemed to have flown away as he stood there, his gaze caught in the bright blue depths of her eyes.

Linc tried to call that business mood back, but how could he as Cecilia's eyelashes swept down and she thanked him for the compliment?

When she glanced back up again, her gaze moved quickly over him and returned to meet his. A hint of pink tinged her cheeks.

'You look nice, too.'

The words were simple; the appreciation veiled at the backs of her eyes was complication bathed in blue.

'Shall we?'

He held out his hand for her to grasp before he managed a sensible thought. Led her to the car before he registered anything more than the subtle scent of her perfume—not floral this time, but something more complex and very alluring.

Only when he'd closed the door after helping her into the car did Linc take a moment to draw a breath and wonder what had just happened there.

This was not the first time he'd called for a beautiful woman to take her out somewhere. There *had* been women in his life. A number of them up until about a year ago, when it had all started to feel pointless and his dates had become further and further apart.

But seeing Cecilia tonight had literally taken his breath away. How could he deny his attraction?

Yet how could he do anything else?

In this moment he had no answers to any of it.

Linc strode to the driver's side of the car, opened the door and got in.

As Linc started the car, Cecilia stole another glance at him. Tonight he looked every bit the powerful and wealthy man about town. She might have always known it, but seeing him this way really brought it home to her that Linc was indeed a man who'd left his mark on life and would continue to do so.

She felt a little Cinderella-ish at the thought.

This is no fairytale, Cecilia.

In an effort to distract herself, she spoke. 'Did I tell you that tonight will start with a tour of the Gantry-Bell estate gardens?'

At least she'd said something, and furthermore something that didn't relate at all to how attractive she found Linc.

'Apparently, this will be the first time ever that the estate has been opened to the public. Given the name of the charity, and the fact that for a whole month people will be allowed to visit and tour the gardens, the committee must have cut a deal with the owners.'

They entered into a discussion about the flower show. Before she knew it, they'd arrived at the venue. Acres of beautiful gardens surrounded them on all sides, and in the midst of those gardens stood a mansion Cecilia would have expected to see in a fairytale.

'Oh, it's beautiful! Look at the ivy growing all the way up that south wall. There are turrets, too—just like on a castle,' she murmured, and then felt more than a little foolish for showing her awe so obviously.

'And a tower.' Linc stopped the car and handed the keys to a waiting valet, but he opened Cecilia's door himself and extended his hand to help her out. 'Isn't there a fairy story about a woman being trapped in a tower?'

'There's more than one story like that among the classic fairytales.'

In that moment *she* felt rather like a princess in a modern-day fairytale herself. A princess waiting to be swept away by a millionaire prince, perhaps?

Except Linc wasn't royalty, and nor was she and Cecilia was certainly not a damsel waiting to be swept away by a fantasy love in any way at all.

Would that be so bad, Cee?

She must not allow such thoughts even the tiniest space in her mind—and yet hadn't she already started to believe that she and Linc…

So unbelieve it right now—or you might find a pumpkin dropping out of the sky at midnight and giving you a concussion or bringing you a prince who could be a shoe salesman!

Yet they were here, and this *was* rather magical and Cecilia was tired of being practical all the time.

For the second time tonight, she placed her hand into Linc's outstretched one, and she *did* feel just a teensy bit regal as she alighted from his car.

At least until her gaze moved around them and she saw the other couples making their way to the front of the mansion. Couples dressed in similarly glamorous clothing and all looking completely at home in these surroundings.

Couples…

'Look…' She whispered the word to Linc. 'Up ahead. Is that that famous Australian gardening celebrity?'

The tall celebrity with his distinctive features turned and shared a laugh with the woman at his side. Cecilia knew for sure then.

'It *is*. I can remember watching his show when I was just a child.'

Cecilia felt even more out of her depth. A millionaire at her side, famous people all around her… Well, all right. She'd only seen one. But who knew who else might be there?

She on the other hand was just a girl who ran a plant nursery. A girl who happened to be at the side of that very same handsome millionaire just now.

'I can do this.'

She muttered the words beneath her breath, but Linc heard them, anyway.

'Don't tell me you're intimidated by your surroundings, Cecilia?' He asked it with a teasing grin, as though he didn't have a care in the world.

Money would pave the way for that, she supposed.

Actually, Linc would pave the way for himself, whether he had money or not. Instinctively, Cecilia knew this.

So why should she be worried?

'I was a little awed by all this,' she admitted, 'but only for a moment.'

They made their way to the mansion's entrance, where they were met by the president, who'd called Cecilia earlier in the day.

'I'm so glad you're here.' The woman, a tall powerhouse in her late sixties, greeted Cecilia with an air kiss and clasped one of Linc's hands in both of hers. 'The committee are so happy you could both make it. We particularly want to catch up tonight.'

She gestured to a distinguished gentleman at her side.

'This is our host, Mr Gordon Gantry-Bell.'

'It's a pleasure to meet you.'

After a moment's small talk, their host gestured inside.

'Please make your way to the drawing room for light refreshments.'

As they strolled away, Cecilia turned her head to catch Linc's eye. 'I wonder what the committee want to talk to us about. Maybe it's just last-minute questions regarding the masked ball.'

The drawing room turned out to be a huge room, easily capable of holding three hundred people. A curved alcove made up of long sparkling windows looked out onto one aspect of the gardens. A grand piano filled the space in the alcove, and a man sat playing, his tall, thin frame concentrated utterly on producing the lilting melody.

Overhead, a long oval inlay graced the ceiling, and at its centre what must be a family crest in the form of an eagle was featured. Chandeliers hung at intervals along the ceiling. The room was stripped of furniture other than the piano and numerous oval tables spaced about. The pristine tablecloths bore the same eagle family-crest design, embossed into the cloth, while luxurious velvet-covered chairs surrounded each table.

'I really do feel as though I've stepped into another world.' Cecilia whispered the words even as she tried to ensure she had her most confident expression on as heads turned at their entrance into the room.

Immediately, another committee member separated herself from a small group of people near the entry, greeted them and introduced them to a number of other guests.

During a break in the flow of conversation, Cecilia leaned her head close to Linc's and murmured that she supposed they should do as others were doing and divide and conquer. After all, a room full of flower enthusiasts, sponsors and other interested parties allowed endless possibilities for networking. She shouldn't come across as though she wanted to cling to Linc's side.

'Don't even *think* about leaving me.' His low words sounded close to her ear, and her hand was lifted and tucked firmly into the crook of his elbow. 'The only conversation I have to offer about flowers is how to make money out of them.'

This was patently untrue, and Linc would be just fine on his own—Cecilia didn't doubt that for a moment. Still, if he wanted her company…well, that felt good. It shouldn't, but it did.

Minutes later the tour of the gardens was announced. Curtains were drawn back from a sweeping set of doors at the end of the room. These were thrown open with a flourish, revealing a vista of glorious colour and splendour so eye-catching on the other side that it was almost too much to take in.

'I've seen photos.' Cecilia almost whispered the words. She felt spellbound as they entered the gardens. 'But it's so much more when you're here. The perfect symmetry, the arches and blend of colours and shades, the different forms… I think these gardens may have taken some of their inspiration from the Butchart Gardens in Canada. This is so much more beautiful and complex than I realised when we first drove into the grounds.'

She understood now why the event would have

attracted celebrity interest—especially from a renowned gardening identity.

'It is.' Linc glanced into her eyes, and his seemed to shine with pleasure at her happiness. 'Brent and Fiona would love to see all this. Their landscaping and Fiona's artwork would both be inspired by it, I suspect.'

'You *must* encourage them to come during the month the gardens are open to the public, Linc.'

Cecilia herself felt inspired. Without even realising she was doing it, she clasped Linc's hand. His fingers curled around hers and her heart expanded, taking in the beauty and the pleasure of sharing it with him.

They wandered at their own pace. Cecilia barely noticed they had dropped behind the group at first, but after a time she became intensely conscious of the man at her side.

Would he think she had lagged behind deliberately? She hadn't.

But she couldn't deny that she wanted to be with him right now and couldn't be sorry that the rest of the group had moved ahead.

She forced herself to concentrate on this experience, and a thought occurred to her. 'The committee have achieved something quite amazing in getting these gardens opened up. They must be very determined.'

'And connected to the right people.' Linc added this thought as they paused to admire an ancient sundial.

Cecilia gave a contented sigh. 'This makes my efforts at Fleurmazing seem small-scale, doesn't it?'

'Not one bit. Don't downplay your success just because you're seeing something larger.' Linc held her gaze for a moment. 'Let it inspire you.'

'To even greater things?' She liked his philosophy.

'If you like.' Linc sounded relaxed.

Cecilia thought the gardens had worked their magic on him, too.

'My dears, we're about to make our way in. Will you join us at our dinner table?'

The question broke through Cecilia's reverie. The committee president had found them again. Indeed, it appeared the tour was over, because the entire group had dispersed and were making their way back to the welcome of the drawing room.

The president introduced another member of the committee. 'Do call us by our first names. I'm Susan, and this is Agneta. It would be such an honour to spend some quality time with you both.'

'Thank you,' Linc murmured.

'We'd be delighted,' Cecilia added and felt way too much like half of a couple.

She supposed she was—but they were a *business* couple!

They made their way to the table Susan indicated and took their seats. Shallow bowls filled with tea roses graced the centre and filled the air with their lovely scent.

At the urging of their hosts, Cecilia accepted a glass of white wine. The bottle looked French, and she suspected it would have cost her a week's salary. As she took a first sip she glanced at Linc.

His gaze was on her lips, and for just a moment in time their gazes met and held. Even her heart seemed to skip a beat, and then make up for it by beating fast.

'Madam…sir. Your entree.' A waiter discreetly placed fragrant plates before them.

'How long have you been in the plant-nursery business, Linc?' Agneta asked the question and gave a smile that was both coy and a little cheeky all at once. 'If you don't mind me asking, dear?'

Linc responded with the kind of smile and easy response that Cecilia would have expected if he'd been talking to an elderly aunty.

'I got into the business at nineteen after working two jobs and renovating houses until I had enough money to buy my first small nursery.'

Cecilia loved hearing this explanation. She'd never asked him these questions herself and took the opportunity to sit back and allow the older two women to grill him gently for all the information they wanted.

'And you, Cecilia? How long have you worked for Linc as a nursery manager?'

'Oh…' Guilty heat crept into her cheeks, because she knew she'd allowed the conversation to drift over her while she just enjoyed sitting beside Linc and hearing him share information about himself. 'It's been six years.'

They chatted easily with the committee members, getting to know others in the group as the evening wore on.

Cecilia was never unaware of Linc—whether he was talking to the committee member on his right or engaging in conversation with others around the table. She just couldn't seem to distance herself from a sharp consciousness of him.

She tried to focus her attention on the meal and on playing her part in the conversation. As the courses progressed from roasted fennel with blackberries to ocean trout and finally to a tangy lemon sorbet that was made with fruit from the lemon trees in the vast gardens, Cecilia felt tension building in the president and in some of the other committee members.

Tension was building within herself as well, but for different reasons. Sitting so close by Linc had her senses humming. Maybe it was the setting, the glamour or perhaps it was just that in other circumstances this might have been any girl's idea of a dream date. Whatever the reason, those two tensions—the one inside her and the one now being manifested by the committee—shortened her breath.

'No doubt you've both been wondering why we so specifically wanted to speak with you tonight.'

Susan's words brought Cecilia back to earth.

'We have a proposal that we feel will excite you. As you can see from tonight's gathering and our surroundings, the Silver Bells flower show will be prestigious from beginning to end. Now that we've inspected your maze and gained a clear insight into your plans for the masked ball itself, we know that yours will be a wonderful feature event, too.'

Here the woman paused and gave Cecilia an approving glance.

'Cecilia, we were pleased and impressed by your initiative when you approached us to make a masked ball at Fleurmazing one of our feature events this year. We believe it will complement the core activity of the flower show very nicely. Indeed—' here she glanced apologetically at Linc for a moment before turning back '—if the opportunity arose, we'd steal you to work exclusively on helping us with our arrangements for next year. A maze of the kind that you've produced at Fleurmazing, if undertaken here on these grounds, for example, could create a crowning glory for the event.'

Although it was said with a tongue-in-cheek smile, Cecilia didn't miss the keen look that accompanied it.

An opportunity to add to these beautiful gardens? To leave a creation of hers as a legacy to be enjoyed into the future?

'I'm stunned. Thank you. It's very kind of you to say such a thing.'

She glanced quickly at Linc and caught the shocked expression on his face before his brows came down and he quickly masked his thoughts.

'I'm certainly delighted to be holding the masked ball at the nursery this year.' Cecilia wasn't sure what else to say.

The group couldn't have asked her here simply to comment on her maze-making skills. There must be more.

'Regardless of any other possibilities, we'd like to offer Fleurmazing the chance to sign on now with us for future years.' The president drew a document from a satchel on the floor beside her chair. 'This outlines our offer in writing, but if I may elaborate now…?'

Her glance shifted to encompass both of them.

Linc was the one to respond. 'Please do.'

The president straightened in her chair. 'We'd like to bring our relationship with Fleurmazing onto a stronger footing for at least the next five years. We're in the throes of negotiating a contract with our hosts for the same time period, and we feel the two agreements would complement each other.'

She went on.

'Planning has already commenced for our second year of the flower show, of course. Imagine how great it would be to know at this stage that you'd be holding a masked ball for us again this time next year.'

'I'm flattered,' Cecilia said. 'It's wonderful that you'd like to continue the relationship into the future.' Her words were positive. She turned to Linc. 'I think you'd agree we should review the contract with a view to signing?'

'Definitely.'

Linc's response held just the right tone of business interest. Yet did he seem a little disconcerted, as well? Perhaps he hadn't liked it that the committee had all but offered Cecilia an alternative job right under his nose.

Cecilia smiled at the president, and then allowed that smile to encompass all those seated at the table. 'I would very much like to continue a working relationship with your committee, provided it can be done in a way that's workable for all concerned. If you'll allow us to examine the documentation, we will get back to you as quickly as we can.'

Later, as Linc drove her towards her home, she thought again about the committee's offer of an ongoing contract with Fleurmazing.

'That was an interesting way for the committee to handle their approach to us.' Cecilia made the observation quietly. 'I'm not complaining. It was a delightful night.'

As Cecilia spoke, she didn't seem to notice that she had slipped into using *us* rather than *the business* or even referring to herself as its manager. But Linc noticed.

He noticed it and he liked it. In fact, he had liked almost everything about this evening from the moment Cecilia had opened the door of her home and he'd seen how beautiful she looked.

To be so aware of her as a woman and to believe that she was equally aware of him had made it difficult to maintain distance in what had needed to be treated as business. Even in a setting of elegant glamour.

This shift in his interest in Cecilia should scare him. It *did* scare him.

'I guess the committee are looking to really cement their relationship with the Silver Bells owners.'

It also bothered Linc that the committee had all but offered Cecilia a job. He could see now that it had been naive of him, but he had never imagined Cecilia leaving his employ. The thought of it now made him uncomfortable.

Face it, Linc. The dividing line between a business and personal relationship when it comes to Cecilia is now irrevocably blurred. Just what do you plan to do about that?

'I don't blame the committee for wanting to consolidate. It's what I'd do in their shoes.' She nodded her agreement just as he drew the car to a halt outside her home.

Just so long as they don't take you from me in this 'consolidation'.

The thought came without Linc being able to

control it. Suddenly, the tie he'd been wearing all night felt constricting. With a tug he removed it and tossed it onto the console between them. 'At least that's gone.'

'Was it bothering you? You looked quite at home in all your finery.' Cecilia blurted the words, and then fell abruptly silent.

And everything changed, just like that.

No, it didn't change. Linc made himself acknowledge it fully. This need to pursue and build on what they had already shared, to take it further, to know Cecilia more wasn't a change. It was a truth.

'I—I should review that agreement tonight, before I go to— Before I turn in.' Cecilia said it as they alighted from the car. 'Did—did you want to come in, Linc, and look at it with me?'

'I'm happy to trust your judgment on it.'

They were some of the most difficult words he'd ever said. But they had reached her front door, and if he hadn't said those words, he'd have invited himself in and…

Silently, he held his hand out for her key. When she gave it to him, he opened her door and drew the contract from his breast pocket. He handed both to her together.

'You can tell me what you want to do tomorrow.'

Cecilia took her house key and the contract from Linc. Her fingers curled around both, and she felt the contract still warm from the heat of his body. It took will power for her not to hug that warmth to her.

'Thank you for attending the gala with me tonight.' It had been a night she would remember for a very long time. 'It was— I'm sure the committee must have been pleased that you were there. Good—goodnight.'

'Goodnight, Cecilia.' His words were deep.

She didn't know who moved, but somehow they were close, and he bent his head, and she lifted hers and all her good intentions, wobbly as they had been, disappeared.

Their lips met.

Cecilia's resolve, whatever it might have been in the first place, melted away. When his hands held her waist, her free arm wrapped around his neck and their kiss deepened naturally.

There simply was no hesitation—on Linc's part or on hers. Cecilia gave herself to this closeness and this man.

He tasted of lemon sorbet. She probably did, too. But more than that he tasted of Linc. Appealing and sensual and wonderful.

She said his name against his lips. 'Linc—'

'Cecilia.'

He spoke at the same time. His tone was low, and it let her know that he had been equally moved by their kiss.

One tiny shred of self-preservation surfaced within her. 'I have to go in—'

'I have to go—'

Again, he spoke at the same time, and she was glad then that she'd not asked him to come inside with her again, because he would have rejected her, and she'd been there before and it wasn't nice.

He stepped back and away from her, and she pushed her door open and stepped over the threshold.

'Goodnight, Linc. I'll see you at the nursery.'

She went inside and closed the door behind her, listened as Linc's steps faded away and his car door opened and closed. She heard the soft start of his car's engine.

He was gone.

CHAPTER SEVEN

'I'VE EARNED THIS TIME. Just fifteen minutes before I leave for the day.' Cecilia said it aloud, though there was no one there to hear her.

She was in the repurposing shed. She opened a can of paint, stirred it and carried it to an unfinished project.

Linc hadn't come in to the nursery today. He'd called to say he had to deal with the fallout from an overnight crash in the commodities market, and she'd been both relieved and disappointed by the news.

She'd prepared herself to see him, to acknowledge the kiss they'd shared last night and to say that it would be best if they focused on their professional relationship and didn't go there again. That was the sensible choice, and she needed to protect herself… to make sure she didn't get hurt again.

Couldn't you trust that this might be different from the disappointment you experienced with Hugh?

Actually, she was over Hugh. What she was really worried about was that she might allow herself to start to care deeply for Linc. It was her own developing feelings that scared her.

It would be for the best when Linc completed the

review and they could both just get on with their normal lives again—as they had done before this started.

Good. Fantastic. That was exactly what she wanted, and she 100 per cent believed they could go back to exactly the way they'd been before.

'Sure. Why *wouldn't* we be able to do that?'

She slapped the paintbrush against the side of an old crate with a little too much vigour. Spots of paint spattered onto her shirt and shorts.

When her cell phone rang moments later, she answered without even looking at the caller ID.

It was her sister.

'I know this is short notice, but is there any way at all that you can come in to see me tomorrow?' Stacey asked the question in a rush of words. A hint of excitement crept through into her tone. 'I've got approval for the visit, and I've made a booking for you in the morning group in the hope that you can make it. I understand if you can't come. I can book it for the following week. I just thought I'd ask.'

'Yes. I'll be there.' Cecilia didn't hesitate for a second. Emotion tightened her throat. A chance to see Stacey after so long... She would make it work! 'Oh, I can't wait to see you.'

'I'm so glad you're coming.' Stacey gave an audible sigh of relief.

They talked for a few minutes more before Stacey reluctantly ended the call.

Cecilia turned back to her painting, but her thoughts were filled with the upcoming visit to her sister.

She was deep in thought when she heard a footfall behind her. She swung around and there was Linc— and he looked so dear.

'Linc.' Here was her chance to talk about what had happened last night. 'You…ah…you gave me quite a start.'

'Is something wrong?' He stepped forward. Concern laced his voice. 'If it's about—?'

'No, no. Nothing's wrong at all.'

Instead of bringing up the matter of *them*, as she should have, Cecilia shied away from even mentioning it. Well, she had a major family matter on her mind right now!

'I just had a call from my sister, asking if I'd visit her tomorrow. I'll have to check that Jemmie can cover for me. I—I can't wait to go.'

The last sentence surprised her by being tougher to say than it should have been. Cecilia *did* want to see her sister. *So* much! It was just that it would challenge her emotions. The place itself and all that it represented… Her having to leave her sister there when she left… Having such distance from the reality of what Stacey was going through…

'That's great news.' His expression softened with happiness for her but also with a more sober emotion. 'Although I can't help feeling concerned about you going into that environment,' he said carefully. 'Even though I know you have no other choice if you want to see your sister.'

He had spoken the very concern that she felt deeply herself. But she couldn't speak of it, because it might make her sound selfish or unwilling.

Oh, Linc. You don't make it easier for me to stop caring for you when you show this caring side yourself.

The thought crept in, unannounced, and then it was

too late. She couldn't deny it. She *did* care for Linc. Her feelings had developed without her even wanting to allow it to happen.

What if those feelings continued to develop? What if she couldn't control them and...?

Why didn't you take the chance to say something just now, when it was right there in front of you? You should have drawn that firm line and given yourself the chance to get those emotions under control.

'It—the visit—will be fine.'

She would cope with how challenging it felt to pass through all those self-locking doors, the checkpoints, to feel hidden gazes upon her and not know who was looking or what they were thinking, because it meant a chance to see and be supportive to her sister.

Cecilia had visited Stacey just one time, and that had been such a disaster of a visit that she hadn't let herself think too much of how confrontational it had been in and of itself.

Well, Cecilia *had* to be fine.

'There are plenty of staff on duty in the visiting room. I'm sure if anything...worrying happened, they would know what to do.'

'Right. That's good.' He paused, and then couldn't seem to hold back his questions. 'What time is the... uh...the appointment? Fordham, isn't it? What amount of contact do you...ah...do you have with the other prisoners there when you visit?'

His questions about all the practical aspects of the visit were...well, they were adorable, actually.

Oh, Cecilia, you are in so much trouble with your feelings.

Perhaps, but it wasn't as though she loved him or anything. That would be beyond foolish.

She explained the details he had asked about. 'There will be other prisoners in the visiting room, where I'll see Stacey, but people keep very much to themselves. Fraternising with other groups is not allowed.'

Linc listened as Cecilia explained about her upcoming visit to her sister. With every fibre of his being he wanted to insist that Cecilia did not step foot into that place.

Surely there was some risk involved in being exposed to other prisoners and their visitors? What if someone decided to start a riot?

What if you let your mind run away with you a bit more, MacKay?

Yet at the same time he wanted Cecilia to go. This was her family, so of course she had to go. In the same circumstances—

In the same circumstances he had failed, in a way that had left his brother Alex paying the price. Linc had sworn an oath to himself that he would never let anything like that happen again.

He watched now as Cecilia turned and quickly closed up the paint can, tidied the area.

They'd kissed last night, and Linc had not been able to get those moments out of his mind. When he thought about her, his chest squeezed and he had an overwhelming need to…to be wherever she was— just so he could look up and she'd be there. What did *that* mean?

'I'd better call Jemmie and ask if she's happy to step in tomorrow and continue with the preparations for the masked ball.'

Cecilia's words broke through Linc's reverie.

She went on. 'I have an action list she can follow, but it's a really busy time.'

Linc welcomed this distraction from his thoughts, even though it brought him back to Cecilia's trip to visit her sister tomorrow. 'Everything is well in order, because you're such a good operator, so it will be fine. I'll come back to the office with you now.' He fell into step at her side. 'It's late to be starting, but I want to put some work in on the review.'

I stayed away from here all day but gave in and came looking for you, anyway.

He just hadn't anticipated that seeing her would fill him with warmth and something that felt rather like happiness.

'I hope that commodities crash didn't impact too badly on your businesses?' Cecilia made the statement to Linc and knew she should have done it earlier.

Did Linc want to work late like this because he couldn't wait for the review to be finished? Cecilia tried not to feel hurt at the thought.

He thanked her for her concern. 'It wasn't great, but these ups and downs happen.'

As they stepped inside the office, Cecilia brought up the flower-show committee's proposal. 'They're offering next year as a fairly solid proposition for Fleurmazing to host the masked ball again, with the proviso that the Silver Bells charity would still need to sign off on the overall plans for it all to go ahead.'

'That sounds reasonable.'

Linc took his seat at the second computer. He looked at home there now…as though he belonged.

The thought crept up on Cecilia and she frowned.

Linc didn't belong here. He belonged in his high-flying corporate world, running all his business interests and never giving her a thought.

She'd pushed for a review, and he'd rewarded her dedication by conducting it himself. Once it was done, that would be it.

But would it? Or had things changed for him, as well? Maybe he'd want to keep seeing her?

'The flower show committee want exclusive rights to the Fleurmazing masked ball for the next five years. I'm willing to give them that, but I'll want the contract updated first to spell out that Fleurmazing *can* conduct other celebrations and activities utilising the maze.'

'Well done.' His gaze met hers over the tops of their computer screens. 'It's clear you've considered this from all angles.'

She felt so proud in the face of his praise that it was difficult to keep a pleased smile from her face.

Tell him now that you want to be careful there's no repeat of what happened last night. Tell him. Because you can see for yourself that you're all but hanging off every word he speaks. You need to do something about your out-of-control and ever-developing feelings towards him before they truly get you into trouble.

'Thanks. I'd…um…I'd better make that call to Jemmie and then do my tidying up here for the night so I can get going.'

'Good idea. You'll need to get some rest tonight, too.'

Linc wanted to say more, to say that he enjoyed her company and didn't want it to end, but he stopped himself. An attraction that should have been easy for him to control seemed to be getting the better of him. Linc wasn't accustomed to that, and he didn't know how to address it.

Get his work here finished and remove himself from her life as much as possible, he supposed.

He ignored the knowledge that it wasn't only a physical awareness of her beauty and appeal that had him in its thrall and tried to focus on his review work.

Linc succeeded, somewhat, but his thoughts kept returning to Cecilia's upcoming visit to her sister at the correctional centre the following morning. To the kisses that he and Cecilia had shared. To this whole situation and how it was making him feel.

He needed to start working out just exactly *why* Cecilia was impacting on him the way she was and put a stop to it.

Yes, sure—he would work all that out and get it under control in no more than a blink of an eye and with a few minutes of careful thought and concentration.

He'd probably find the answer to world peace while he was at it…

CHAPTER EIGHT

'I'M READY. It's okay to leave early. There's nothing else I need to check or make sure about. It's time. I'm going to see Stacey.'

Cecilia said the words aloud as a means of stopping herself from fussing any longer, checking and rechecking that she was prepared for her visit to her sister.

It was 7:50 a.m. She had a lengthy drive to get to the facility, so leaving sooner rather than later made sense.

And if she was struggling to breathe through an onslaught of anxiety, if her heart was thumping—well, it was with hope and excitement, too. Stacey had realised she'd made mistakes, and she was choosing to set a better path for her life for the future. One that included her sister in it.

Cecilia pushed back the sudden surge of emotion—relief and hope for Stacey, and worry and pain for where her sister had landed herself already. She couldn't indulge such things right now.

She stepped outside, closed and locked the door behind her, and made her way along the short path.

Out on the street a man leaned against the back of

her car—a very familiar man, who removed his sunglasses and straightened as she approached.

Oh, how her emotions leapt in that moment of recognising him.

'Linc! What are you doing here?'

She didn't know what to think. In fact, her mind seemed reluctant to process more than how the sight of him made her heart ache a great deal less, and more, all at the same time.

'I know you won't have been expecting me.' His words were roughened, as though pushed past emotion. 'There might not be anything else I can do that'll take some of the strain off you, but I want to drive you there and back today. If that's okay with you?'

It wasn't pity. She knew that immediately. But had this come simply from an employer's sense of duty towards his employee?

She searched his face and saw the way his jaw clenched. As their glances locked and held, the deep steel grey of his eyes softened.

No. This wasn't about work. This was personal—a man wanting to help a woman he cared about. Cecilia was certain. That *had* to be what she was seeing!

Her emotions wanted to take hold of this and run with it. But she cautioned herself that any measure of affection that Linc now felt could be *any* measure. She did not need to set herself up to expect more and then be hurt.

So don't go hoping too much about Linc's feelings towards you. In fact, why are you even pondering that when your focus needs to be on your sister?

It was easy for Cecilia to use that thought to push aside any need to trust Linc beyond that. She didn't

make any correlation to the impact of Hugh desert-
ing her, and the blow that had given to her self-worth
as a partner, but it was there in the back of her mind.

'Thank you, Linc, for coming here for this.'

His offer to drive her to the facility did mean a lot.
She would thank him and say she would go on her own.

But Cecilia knew that she wouldn't do that. His
company today, his willingness to be there for her…
She simply couldn't turn her back on that, caution
and past history or not.

'I would be grateful for your company, to tell the
truth.'

As though to confirm her earlier hope about his
feelings for her, he took an involuntary half step towards her and lifted one hand.

*Oh, Cecilia, are you sure you want to believe that
he really cares about you in an emotional sense?*

Because that was what she was trying to do right
now—to imbue Linc with a deep and personal caring
feeling towards her when he could just as easily be
feeling concern for a colleague he happened to have
kissed a couple of times.

But sometimes people denied that they were emotionally entangled when in fact they really were, so
could he be?

Was she saying that *she* was emotionally entangled in Linc?

No.

Maybe a little.

*Can't you just accept his help today, just this once,
because it will make the trip there and back easier
for you, and not think about the rest of it? Focus on
Stacey. That's more than enough to worry about.*

'So if you really do have the time, Linc, I'd love the company.'

'I do, and I'm glad to hear it. I need—'

He cut himself off, but his shoulders eased.

Instead of finishing his previous thought, Linc simply said, 'Do you prefer that we go in your car or mine?'

'I'd rather it be my car. The parking area is underground, so you'll be able to wait there if you want, or you could come with me to the reception area and stay there while I—while I go in. You can't bring a cell phone with you, though, not even in the car.'

'That won't be a problem. My phone is in my car, and it can stay there until we get back.'

Linc took the driver's seat of Cecilia's hatchback car. He had to push the seat right back to fit his legs in comfortably. In truth, he'd deal with any amount of discomfort to ensure Cecilia didn't have to face this day on her own.

He'd known yesterday, when she'd first told him she was going to the correctional centre today, that he would want to go with her.

Linc hadn't understood the fierceness of that need at the time, and he had fought it because he hadn't known what she would make of it if he *did* ask to go with her. He had fought right up until he'd woken at five this morning, and then he had stopped fighting it.

He still didn't completely understand the strength of his feelings for Cecilia, but he could no longer go on pretending they didn't exist. Linc needed to know.

Somehow, yesterday, when Cecilia had told him she would be coming to visit her sister, something inside him had changed. He hadn't been able to let her face this on her own. That hadn't simply been about wanting to protect another person. If it had, he'd have been able to explain it away. He couldn't bear not to be a part of this with her. Linc needed this for himself.

All he could do right now was accept the need and be grateful she was allowing him to act on it—hope that a greater understanding of what was going on inside him would come.

'I'll give you the directions.'

She proceeded to do exactly that as they began their journey.

'Tell me about Stacey.'

I would love to know more about your family, your past, all the things that matter the most to you.

'What was your favourite thing to do together when you were little?'

He hoped, too, that talking would help take her mind off the more confrontational aspects of the day ahead.

Cecilia shared some memories from her childhood. Playing games with her sister…finishing each other's sentences.

'Our mother wasn't very loving towards us, but having each other helped. We look significantly alike even now, but we aren't identical, so we couldn't get away with switching places with each other. We used to daydream about it, though.'

Sharing those childhood memories now had brought a smile to Cecilia's strained features, but when she had first stepped out through her front door that morning, anxiety had radiated from her.

Linc felt it himself—on her behalf. He also felt the disappointment of knowing that she hadn't been surrounded by a loving family all her life. Every person deserved that, in his opinion. And now she had another hurdle to get over.

'I wish I could go in with you this morning.'

'Stacey would raise her eyebrows a bit if you did that!'

Cecilia managed the quip and even a laugh to go with it. Linc had done her a world of good by coming along this morning. Oh, how her heart had lifted when she'd seen him—but she couldn't tell him that!

'Unfortunately, you have to be booked in advance to visit, so it wouldn't be an option today, anyway.'

'And you'll want your sister all to yourself.' He said it in a matter-of-fact tone. 'I wouldn't expect anything else.'

They covered the rest of the trip speaking intermittently of matters of no importance. It helped her fight off the nerves until they drove into the underground parking area.

Rather than dwell on her unease at the upcoming visit, Cecilia got straight out of the car when Linc stopped it. He alighted, too, and she had to confess— silently, at least—that she was rather glad he would be with her for as long as possible before she went in.

After that it was identification, registration, the wait while names were called, until finally it was her turn and she got up. Linc quickly pulled her tight against his chest and released her again.

Cecilia made her way through all the security processing. She was electronically scanned and had to pass a drug-detecting dog's assessment. A band with a number on it was affixed around her wrist. The officers were professional, but she couldn't help a feeling of being just that number to them.

Did her sister feel that way? Of course she would.

An officer checked her wristband. 'You're at table twenty-three.' The woman pointed towards a separate building and gave some other instructions.

Cecilia drew a deep breath. 'Thanks.'

Once seated inside, Cecilia fixed her gaze on the inmates' entry point and waited. She wished Linc were there with her and was comforted to know he was waiting for her outside.

After what felt like hours but was probably only minutes, her sister stepped into the room.

'Stacey. Oh, I've missed you so much.'

Cecilia stood and hugged her sister and felt relief rush through her as Stacey hugged back just as hard. When they drew apart and took their seats, Cecilia looked carefully at her sister.

Stacey wore a dark green T-shirt and matching pants, with trainers on her feet. Around her neck was a chain with a tag on it. Had she lost weight? Or was it stress giving her that lean look?

Cecilia pasted a big smile on her face. 'I brought coins for the vending machine. Would you like something?'

'Maybe in a little bit.' Stacey's hands fidgeted together on the tabletop until she stopped herself.

'Would you rather just talk first, Stace?' Cecilia wanted to take her sister's hands but had to settle for hoping her love for her sister shone from her eyes.

'I made such a stupid mistake.' Stacey said the words quietly before looking up to meet Cecilia's gaze. 'Running around being an idiot with Joe and not getting out of the situation when I realised I'd got myself into something I didn't like and wanted nothing to do with. I wish I'd never met him. I'm not saying this is all his fault. I made the choice to be with him. But I don't want anything to do with him now. Not ever again!'

Cecilia drew a deep breath. 'I'm glad you've decided not to have any part of him now.'

Stacey glanced around them briefly, and then returned her gaze to Cecilia. When she spoke, it was in a quiet tone. 'He put me in a scary position—led me to believe that whole situation was very different to what it turned out to be. And when it all went wrong, he left me there to face the consequences while he disappeared.'

'It's not always easy to see what people truly are, Stacey.' Cecilia knew that from the time she'd spent with Hugh. 'Sometimes it's not until they let you down that you can see it. Anyway, I'm glad you've left him behind you. That's good.'

'It is.' Stacey gave a wan smile. 'And now I can find my way back from how I've messed up my life. I'm going to have to.'

Before Cecilia could respond, Stacey went on.

'I got in the habit of being rebellious years ago, because it helped me to feel better about the way Mum gave up on us.'

'That wasn't our fault. The problem was with *her*.' Cecilia had carried her own anger and hurt over it. To some degree she probably always would. 'It's up to us to choose how we let that influence us now.'

'I'm choosing to do what I can to get out of here on good terms and follow a better path once I do.'

They talked about Stacey's future then and about Cecilia's life too—the plant nursery and the upcoming masked ball, but not about Linc. The time disappeared so quickly. Before Cecilia knew, it they were being told that the visit was over and Cecilia had to leave.

Reluctantly, Cecilia got to her feet and hugged her sister goodbye. 'I love you so much, Stacey.'

'I love you too, Cee.' Stacey used her pet name for Cecilia, and for a moment her eyes shone with the sheen of tears before she resolutely blinked them back. 'I—I'll see you at your next visit, but I'll call you. I'll stay in contact now—that is, if you'd like—?'

'Yes!' Cecilia smiled past her own emotion, and then she was on her way back through all the checkpoints until she arrived in the waiting room.

She couldn't help but feel happier. She would come back and visit again soon. They could talk again. Stacey would call, so they could stay in contact. Cecilia felt as if a missing piece had finally been replaced back in her life.

Linc wasn't in the waiting room, and the clerk informed Cecilia that he'd been sent to wait in the car. 'We don't allow people to remain in the waiting room if they have no reason to be here.'

Cecilia was on the pathway outside, still some distance from the parking lot, with her thoughts on the future, when Stacey could live her life again outside of this place, when a man suddenly came up beside her.

He grabbed her wrist in a punishing grip and lowered his face close to her ear. It all happened so fast she wasn't sure what was going on.

'What did you say to your sister to turn her against me? What did you say to her in there just now? Tell me!'

Fear and adrenalin shot through Cecilia. Who *was* this? What was going on? Her head whipped around. She caught a glimpse of largeness, tallness, of a face tightened by anger and hair the colour of wheat, cropped close to the man's skull.

This had to be Joe. It couldn't be anyone else.

'Let me go.' Cecilia said it in a low tone as she tried to pull free.

His grip around her wrist tightened. 'I know where you live, Cecilia. I know lots about you.' His voice was harsh. 'Trust me, you don't want a visit from me. So stay away from Stacey. Stop putting ideas in her head about getting out early and anything else you might have in your mind. She's better off doing the full term. When she gets out that way, she's free. No one will be watching her, checking her every move. She can go back to supporting—' He broke off.

'She shouldn't have ended up in there in the first place.' Cecilia forgot to be afraid as protectiveness for her sister drove the words from her. 'What kind of man leaves a woman to pay for his crime?'

'I make my own rules—and you've just pushed me too far.'

He started to pull her forward, and Cecilia wasn't strong enough to hold back. Fear ripped through her as she stumbled and fell into him.

And then Linc was there, breathing hard. 'Get your hands off her!'

For a moment Cecilia didn't know if Joe would obey, but then he uttered a curse, let go of her and ran off. He leapt into a car at the end of the parking lot, and the car roared away.

'I'm driving.' Linc spoke the words as he pulled open the driver's side door of her car.

Cecilia hadn't even been aware of them making their way back there. Her ears were buzzing and she felt light headed.

Don't you dare hyperventilate or faint.

'What just happened?' Linc rapped out the question. 'What did that guy say to you before I got there?'

Cecilia climbed into the passenger seat and noted that her hands were shaking so much she had to try twice to fasten her seat belt.

'That was Joe—the man who was with my sister when she got caught committing a robbery. Stacey's told me that Joe was the mastermind, and I've no reason to doubt that. Aside from some teenage rebellion, my sister never did anything criminal before she became involved with that man. He's been sneaking messages in to her. But she's seen his true colours and wants nothing more to do with him, and he...he isn't happy about that.'

'Why would he be here this morning? He can't visit her. He'd be picked up as soon as they recognised who he was.' Leashed power echoed in each word Linc spoke as he drove the car through the parking lot. 'We have to report this to the police. There's a station not far from here. We'll go straight there.'

'Yes, I think we'd better.' Cecilia laced her fingers together tightly so their trembling wouldn't show. 'I don't know how he knew that I'd be visiting this morning, but I believe he was waiting specifically for me. He basically implied just then that he would harm me if I didn't stay out of Stacey's life.'

'Is that what your sister wants? For you to stay out of her life?'

'No!' Cecilia said it with vehemence. 'We may look at life differently at times, but we love each other. We…well, we really did mend our issues just now. I promised I'd keep coming to see her, and she promised she'll call me when she can.' Cecilia drew a deep breath.

'I'm glad to hear that.' His tone of voice underlined the truth of this before he went on, 'You could have been really harmed just now.'

'You could have been hurt too, Linc.' Her words were low as remorse began to fill her chest. 'I shouldn't have asked you to come with me today.'

'I asked if you'd let me. There's a difference. And this is not your fault.' Linc's jaw clamped into a tight line. 'If I hadn't got there when I did—'

'He would have dragged me into his car, and I dread to think what would have happened to me.' Cecilia suppressed a shudder. 'Thank you for being there and for acting so quickly to scare him off.'

They made their way to the police station, spoke to the police, looked at images, and found out in the process that Stacey's Joe was operating under an alias. He was wanted not only for the armed robbery in Australia, but for a string of other crimes in his home country of New Zealand—some of them very serious.

The police over there had been trying to catch him for two years.

'I don't think Stacey knows any of that.' Cecilia spoke as Linc drove towards her home after the interview with the police. They would meet officers there to ensure her house was safe.

Linc shook his head. 'The police said he can lay the charm on when he tries. He must have hidden a lot of the truth about himself from her.'

'He must have. It makes me scared for her, as well as for myself.' She pushed the words past a lump in her throat.

There was a long pause while Linc's hands maintained a death grip on the car's steering wheel. The street was quiet. Then he pulled over into a parking space, unclipped his seat belt and hers and pulled her into his arms.

The strength of Linc's hold let Cecilia know how concerned he had been for her safety.

Barriers Cecilia had tried to keep propped up fell away. Her arms tightened around him.

He didn't say a word. Neither did she. But, oh, it felt good to be held and to hold him.

'That situation ranked right up there with some of the worst moments I've experienced in my life.' The words were almost wrenched from Linc as he held Cecilia close. 'If he'd harmed you—'

He drew back, and his gaze searched her face, travelled over her. He lifted the wrist the man had gripped. Red marks showed on the delicate skin. Everything inside Linc cried out for justice, for the man who had done this to her to pay for it. In those few moments in time, he let his eyelashes sweep down, because he didn't want Cecilia to see his roiling emotions.

'There will be a bruise, but that's all.' Her words were soft, hushed almost and edged with a need for reassurance that she probably didn't realise was there.

Linc lifted her hand and pressed it against his chest, laying his own over it. His need to give to Cecilia won out over his memories and the guilt from the past. The emotions he felt, this need for connection, just couldn't feel wrong to him in this moment.

The knowledge sent a warning signal through him. But with so many other emotions churning, that signal quickly faded and disappeared. He gently kissed her, and then there was no thinking at all—just experiencing.

Cecilia's lips parted beneath Linc's as she gave herself to kissing him. Her lips softened, yielded to him and received from him at one and the same time. Her defences were down and she needed this.

They kissed softly and gently, exploring each other and healing the fear of those earlier moments.

And then a thought came to Cecilia.

She'd reconciled with her sister.

Surely that meant that anything could be possible.

She and Linc could be possible...

Once that last thought surfaced, there was no taking it back. It changed her. It infused her with hope. And while the common sense side of her warned that such hope was not wise, she couldn't heed it.

When they finally broke apart, Linc seemed to let her go reluctantly.

He sighed and restarted the car. 'We'd better get moving. Now, talk me through the layout of your home.' He cast a quick, apologetic glance her way. 'I'd like to know before we get there. I remember from this morning that there's no place in the front that a person could hide. I could see all of it while I was waiting for you. What about the sides and the back? Would it be easy to break in from any of those points?'

'I've never thought deeply about any vulnerabilities there in that way.' Cecilia forced herself to think about it now. She'd forgotten the threat of Joe during those moments in Linc's arms.

Oh, how easily she had forgotten.

'The back door is deadlocked, and all the windows have locks, but the house isn't alarmed. It backs onto a neighbouring property, but I guess that wouldn't really stop anyone. A person could also enter from the front yard and walk down the left side. The bathroom window is halfway down on that side.'

When they were several blocks away from her home, Linc spoke again. 'The police suggested you don't stay there for the time being. I'm holding you to your agreement to that advice.'

'I know I might not be safe.'

In a way she'd been waiting for this—and also dreading him bringing it up, because it forced her to think about the implications. The thought of being forced out of her home and looking over her shoulder until this situation could be resolved was hard to take.

'There's work, too. That will have to be managed so no one is placed in any danger. Oh, goodness! The masked ball. What am I going to do?'

'That isn't upon us yet, so let's worry about one thing at a time. We'll sort this out, Cecilia. I promise you.'

His calm words helped.

'For now I want you to wait in the locked car while I let the police in so they can check your place. Once I'm sure it's safe, you can gather some things together.

The police said they'll have a car there watching until further notice, in the hope that Joe *does* follow through and turn up.'

Linc stopped the car two doors down from her home.

She identified her front door key for him.

He reiterated that she was not to get out until he came back and gave the okay.

'How do I know you'll be safe?' The question burst from her at the last moment.

The smile he gave had an uncompromising edge to it. 'I'll be careful. You don't need to worry about my safety.'

She worried anyway, and it seemed he was gone for endless minutes before he returned to the car and told her he was satisfied she could safely enter her home.

Cecilia entered, retrieved her phone and started packing an overnight bag. It was reassuring to have Linc with her and to know that the police were watching from across the road in their unmarked car.

'Pack for several days.' Linc made the suggestion from the living room. It was the one place where he could see both her and the front and back doors. 'Since we don't know yet exactly what will be happening, I think that would be best.'

She packed. They left quickly.

Cecilia let herself think then about where she should go, and realised Linc seemed already to have a plan in his mind, if his confident driving gave any indication.

Rather belatedly, she asked, 'Where exactly are you taking me?'

CHAPTER NINE

'YOU'VE LEFT YOUR car at my house.'

Cecilia not only didn't know where Linc intended to take her—she didn't know what might happen to his vehicle if he left it outside her home.

'I made a couple of calls when I retrieved my phone out of it. Alex and Brent are on their way to collect my car.'

Linc's words were matter-of-fact, as though he called in his family to sort out other people's problems on a daily basis. As though he didn't find it strange at all to be helping Cecilia deal with this entire issue.

'The police will be watching, so I've let them know Alex and Brent will be doing that.'

'Okay. That's good to know.'

She couldn't deny that it was reassuring to have Linc's level-headed input just now. Was this what people experienced when they entered into a truly meaningful partnership? This alignment of emotion to the needs of each other?

Not that she and Linc had entered into such a thing.

She, however, *had* entered into believing it could be possible.

Not a smart way to start thinking, Cee.

Yet she couldn't undo the thoughts. They were a part of her now, and they did not want to be denied. She needed time to consider them, to think it through rationally and ask herself whether there really might be a chance and what that might entail.

Could she see Linc for a period of time, enjoy wherever it might lead them and then let it end with no regrets? Because wouldn't that be all Linc would offer?

'It's good of Alex and Brent to help.' She knew she was dodging her own question. 'Please thank them for me when you can.'

'Not needed, but I will.' He drew a deep breath before he spoke again. 'I want you to stay with me tonight, Cecilia.'

For a moment she felt as though he'd read right inside her mind just now, and her heart fluttered, but then she realised there must be a different motivation for his statement.

'It's good of you to want to keep me safe.'

If you'd asked me to stay for other reasons, I'd have agreed instantly.

Maybe it was just as well that he hadn't!

She cleared her throat. 'But I'd planned on going to a hotel.'

'I don't feel that would be safe enough.' His response was immediate and firm. He went on, 'We're heading for my place in the city. The building has excellent security. I realise I didn't ask you first. I should have. That scene back there left me more shaken than I care to admit, I guess, but I know I do need your agreement. I'll take you to a hotel if you insist, but please don't.'

Any problem she might have had over him not seeking her agreement first evaporated in the light of that final request.

Oh, Linc, you become more lov—likeable by the minute.

'I've only ever seen your warehouse building.'

That near slip-up in her thoughts shocked Cecilia so much she struggled to maintain an even tone of voice. It was one thing to contemplate seeing where a relationship might go with Linc in the short term, but to almost think the L-word about him was a whole other matter!

'I maintain both. The family all get together at the warehouse regularly. Rosa keeps everything ready for us.'

He shrugged his shoulders—a wealthy business-man with a busy lifestyle and the financial capacity to make that lifestyle as workable as possible for him-self and for those around him.

'I guess that would make sense for someone in your position.'

She'd known he had other properties and that both brothers had moved out of the warehouse to other homes. But knowing she was about to enter another one of Linc's properties did remind her of the dispar-ity in their circumstances.

Well, from Linc's perspective it would be the height of practicality to have a place in the city. If Cecilia wanted to think about anything, it should be how she was going to manage the rest of her commit-ments while this was all going on.

Yes, Cecilia. Maybe you should be thinking about

*the actual circumstances that have brought about this
temporary change in your place of residence.*

And she should also be thinking about what she
could do, if anything, to try and help get that man
caught, so she could get back to her normal life and
be totally sure Joe was out of Stacey's life for good.

'I appreciate your offer, and I'm grateful to accept the security measures that will go with it.' She
forced her voice to remain as steady and even as his
had been. 'I need to figure out how to manage things
at work. I have to get back there. There's so much to
be done, and I also need to make sure the staff are
safe. What if this guy knows where I work, as well?'

'There are certainly measures that need to be
taken, and the police don't have infinite resources.'
He said it carefully, as though feeling his way.

When he went on, Cecilia understood why.

'I've asked Alex and Brent to arrange a security
firm to provide around-the-clock surveillance at the
plant nursery until further notice.'

Rather than contesting or questioning this, Cecilia
simply expressed her gratitude.

'Thank you.' She would worry about what that
would do to the business's bottom line later. For now
the important thing was that everyone would be safe.
'That will help when I return there, as well.'

With a suppressed sigh she changed the subject.

'I need to make that phone call to the centre now. I
know the police were going to alert the staff to what
happened in the parking lot, but I need to put a request
in for Stacey to call me. I haven't even had the chance
to tell you that we had a genuinely wonderful recon-

ciliation this morning.' Cecilia fell silent for a moment. 'I hope this happening won't undo that progress.'

'I'm glad you got that result with your sister, and I'm sure she will want to continue being closer to you.' Linc drew the car off the street, and his words rang with sincerity. 'We've arrived.'

'I didn't notice we'd come so far.'

They were on an affluent street in one of the city's most sought-after suburbs. A beautiful multistorey building loomed before them. It had secure underground parking. Other cars must also park there. Yet Cecilia saw only Linc's private parking area as they drove in.

At least by focusing on those details she could distract herself away from her softening emotions towards Linc.

Yes, Cecilia, but those emotions are still there. What are you going to do about that?

Fine. Maybe there *were* emotions. But it had been an emotional day. She didn't need to do anything about…anything.

So she stated the obvious instead. 'You're the owner of the whole building, aren't you?'

'Yes, it's one of my investment properties.' He said it without any particular inflection. 'Holding an apartment here works well for when I need to meet with my business broker or take care of other business without the trouble of going in to the office.'

Yet he and his brothers had created their own return-to-the-family oasis out at the warehouse building after the other two had moved out. Cecilia liked that concept, too. It spoke of a close-knit family who, while they went about their individual lives, still needed to reconnect on a regular basis.

That was what she'd had with her sister when they were younger, and now she believed she would have again. She *did* believe it and felt better for giving herself that reminder.

Minutes later they were safely ensconced in Linc's apartment on the top floor. The harbour views were magnificent, and the apartment was furnished in elegant yet comfortable style. A squashy black leather sofa and matching chairs dominated the lounge area. The kitchen shone in chrome, with a white marble workstation in the middle.

'This is—'

Opulent. And yet it was still Linc. A demonstration of his vast wealth, and yet it felt welcoming. Maybe that came from the clutter of kicked-off male shoes and boots inside the door, or the scatter of financial magazines tossed down beside one of the armchairs.

'It's a great place, Linc.'

Linc might wear jeans and work boots and look like a regular working man much of the time, but he *was* a millionaire—a self-made success story. This apartment certainly testified to that fact.

'I'm glad you like it.' He shifted her bag in his grip. He'd insisted on carrying it in for her from his car. 'There's a guest room through here.'

They passed a room that must be his, and an office, and came to the guest room. With her bag stowed inside the door, and Cecilia determinedly refusing to think about Linc's bedroom just an office space away, she followed him back into the living area.

'I don't know what to do.' She'd murmured the words before she realised she had spoken aloud.

About my feelings, about that threat, about anything at all right now!

'It will be okay, Cecilia.' Linc spoke the words from the open-plan kitchen.

He was boiling the kettle and had mugs, coffee granules and a teabag at the ready. Right there, in that chrome and marble masterpiece, Linc MacKay was preparing a fortifying cup of tea for her and making coffee for himself while he was at it.

Who was he, really? Which man was the real Linc? The one dressed in work boots and casual clothes who would drive a woman to a correctional facility first thing in the morning so she could see her sister? Or was he the man in this apartment, entertaining high-brow corporate colleagues? Was he the business magnate, or the loving, protective brother? Was he Cecilia's boss, or the man who would have fought today to ensure her safety?

He was the same Linc and yet not the same—because the Linc of six years ago had rejected her interest in him. *This* Linc had kissed her, held her and he was letting himself care about her. He *was*!

Cecilia told herself he must be all of those people, all of those things. His complexity had caught her attention from the first day they'd met, and it intrigued her more and more now as she came to know each new layer of him in a more personal way.

Cecilia made her call to the correctional centre then, and they surprised her by allowing her to speak to Stacey.

'Cecilia? What's going on? Are you okay?' Panic

rang in Stacey's tone when she came on the line. 'People don't get called to the phone here unless it's bad news, and on top of that they moved me into the strict protection section here today!'

'I'm afraid it *is* troubling news, Stacey.' Cecilia drew a breath and explained what had happened. 'I've been to the police, and obviously the staff there at the centre know about it as well now. I'm glad they've moved you. I was trying not to worry about whether harm could come to you. '

'It won't. Not in that way, now that I've been shifted. But this is still my worst nightmare.' Stacey's words were low. 'And I've brought it down not only on myself but on you. I'm so sorry, Cecilia.'

'We're going to be okay, Stacey. We can get through this together.' She had to tell her sister what she'd discovered about this man. 'There's more you need to know. Joe has warrants out in New Zealand for offences the police described as "both violent and serious", as well as for the robbery here.'

'Are you completely sure about this?' Stacey's voice shook as she asked the question.

Cecilia's heart ached for her sister so much in that moment. 'I'm quite sure.'

'He needs to be caught.' There was a pause and then Stacey spoke again. 'There are things I can tell the authorities that might help them to track him down. Cee, I know you may not believe me, but I thought he and I were going to have a life together. That sounds ludicrous now, but I thought he was someone different.'

'I understand, Stacey. Please don't give up on yourself because this has happened.'

'I won't.' Determination fuelled Stacey's words. 'If I do that, then I'll be letting him get away with how he used me.'

Cecilia was grateful to hear the words but knew her sister would need to hold on to her determination as hard as she could. 'I love you, Stacey.'

They talked for a minute or two more, until Cecilia was finally able to put the phone down.

She turned to Linc, and all the pent-up emotion surfaced. 'She's going to work with the police to try and help them catch him.'

'That's good.'

He handed her the cup of tea and settled beside her on the sofa with his coffee. His calmness helped her to centre herself again.

'She's not a criminal.' It was a relief to say it and to let it sink into her own heart. 'Stacey has a great deal of passion for life, but deep down she has a good heart.'

'Something tells me that with you to help her, she'll find her way back to the best of herself in time.'

'Thank you, Linc—for helping me with these issues.' She went on, 'Most people wouldn't even want to try to understand what it's like to have to deal with a person you care about being incarcerated, let alone today's problems.'

'I understand more than you know.' His words were low.

'What do you mean?'

How could he understand more? For a moment she wasn't sure if he would answer, but then he spoke.

'My brothers and I had a great deal of our freedom taken from us when we were growing up.' His gaze fell to his hands for a moment. 'Being stuck in an orphanage, with no option to get away until we were old enough to leave under our own steam. Scant meals, and all of them identical. I know it's not the same as your sister's situation, but it had a strong impact on each of us.'

'How did that happen to you—to them?' She knew Linc and the other two weren't blood brothers, yet their love for each other was as strong as hers for Stacey. His brothers even carried his last name now.

'Brent's father thought he was a disappointment.' Linc's words were low, edged with harshness, as though even to say it, let alone reveal that it had happened to Brent, infuriated him. 'In my case my mother had died and my father was an alcoholic. He didn't want the responsibility of raising a child so he dumped me at the orphanage.'

'Like our mother leaving Stacey and me…' There was an oddly comforting affinity in knowing that she and Linc held this common bond. 'In our case she waited until we finished school, but even that much was a strain for her—and she didn't hold back in letting us know that.'

'Regardless of their age, no person deserves to be treated that way.'

Linc said this with finality, just as his brother Alex buzzed to come up, and Linc got up and punched a code into a number pad on the wall to allow Alex access.

Minutes later Linc's youngest brother stepped into Linc's apartment, clapped his brother on the back and turned his attention to Cecilia. 'You're all right? Linc said there was a bit of a shake-up with some guy threatening you.'

'I'm fine. Thank you, Alex.'

In that moment Cecilia knew that Linc hadn't exposed any more of her story than had been necessary. She valued Linc for that but couldn't help wondering why he'd left Alex out of his explanation about the orphanage.

Cecilia forced her attention back to Linc's brother. 'It was good of you and Brent to go to my home and collect Linc's car.'

The brothers might have grown up in difficult circumstances, but it appeared to have brought out the best in all of them.

Cecilia's glance shifted to the man holding her thoughts, and her heart softened despite herself.

Linc's gaze locked with hers, and for a moment she thought she saw deep emotion churning in his eyes.

Seconds later he'd looked away, and Alex's calm words filled what Cecilia hadn't noticed yet was a silence.

'So you're okay, big brother?' The younger man glanced from one to the other of them. His gaze finally settled on Linc. 'There's nothing else I can do for you? I could ask Jayne to come over for a while to visit with Cecilia. Brent's waiting in the parking area, but I can get him up here now, too, if needed.'

'I've got it covered.' Linc's face softened. 'But thanks.'

'You'll both be safe here for as long as necessary. I know nothing will happen. It's just—' Alex headed for the door. 'Aw, well, you know… Anyway, if you need anything, you know I'll come in an instant.

As will Brent. Keep us informed of developments, please.'

Linc stopped him before he got through the door and clasped his shoulder for a long moment. 'I know, and I will. Say hi to Jayne.'

Alex's glance drifted to Cecilia for a moment and then back to his brother. 'See you later.'

The day passed. There were further conversations with the police, and then Cecilia and Linc prepared an early evening meal together. Linc proved a dab hand with pasta and confided that he'd worked for a time in a restaurant when he'd been trying to amass enough resources to get his brothers out of the orphanage and make his business empire strong enough that he could afford to support them.

He seemed sad as he spoke.

'You never mentioned how Alex ended up in the orphanage.' Cecilia carried her plate to the outdoor dining seating on Linc's balcony.

'We never knew.' Linc pushed his food around on his plate.

Cecilia tried to give her attention to the meal. The food was delicious, the wine Linc had poured to go with it beautifully refreshing. Yet she really couldn't do the food justice. Linc seemed to be struggling, too.

'Not hungry?' Linc asked of Cecilia and wished he could take the strain from her slender shoulders.

She shook her head. 'It's delicious, Linc, but I keep thinking about all that's happened today and about families and the difficulties they face. I hate thinking how hard it must have been for you and your brothers.'

'For you and your sister, too, by the sounds of it.'

He set down his fork and, by silent mutual consent, they moved back inside. This time when she settled on the sofa, he sat right beside her.

He went on. 'It sounds as though both of you needed your mother's support and missed out on it.'

'Yes.' That was certainly true. 'I ended up trying to be a mother to Stacey, and that hasn't always worked out well for our relationship with each other. You know, this has been a rough day, and I'm worried about what's ahead. I *have* to go back to work tomorrow. There's just too much to be done.'

'You would have managed on your own today if you'd had to, but I'm glad to have been able to help. And we'll see how things are going tomorrow when tomorrow arrives.'

His fingers threaded through hers. It was just that—such a simple thing—but Cecilia sighed and closed her eyes and he drew her head onto his shoulder as they sat there side by side.

She needed this comfort more than she ever would have wanted to admit. So she took it and let herself absorb the healing it brought.

That it would shift from comfort to something more than that was inevitable. Cecilia knew it, and when Linc turned his head, she met him halfway— wanting this, wanting *him*.

Outside, night was falling over the city, and there was a man on the loose somewhere who'd threatened her and who had to be caught.

But here in Linc's apartment Cecilia was safe, and she lost herself in Linc's kiss. That kiss became another. And another.

As their lips meshed, tenderness for him swept

through her and she received tenderness from him. That tenderness brought healing from the most over-whelming aspects of the day they had both shared. Fears receded to a more manageable level. Gratitude was registered and remembered, and then placed aside to allow her to focus wholly on these precious shared kisses with a man who was perhaps also becoming precious to her.

She'd asked herself where a relationship between them might go. Tonight there was desire and need and tender emotion, and she wanted all of those things with Linc. She wanted that beginning. Cecilia didn't let herself think of where such a beginning might lead.

'I have longed for this more than you can know.' Linc's words were low.

His fingers sifted through her hair, and his hand came to rest on the nape of her neck. A shiver of plea-sure followed his touch.

She cupped his cheek and, when the kiss deepened, gripped his strong upper arm and allowed delight and need to blend in the giving and returning of each breathless moment. Cecilia could have continued like that forever, and yet she wanted more. So much more.

'Cecilia…'

Oh, so much was expressed in that simple speak-ing of her name, in a voice that had deepened and mellowed with all they had shared.

Yet there was a question there—a silent seeking of agreement.

Yes, Linc. Yes, with all that I have and all that I am. Yes.

The response was deep within her soul, surpass-ing any conscious thought of warning to herself that she might have formulated. She couldn't have denied that 'yes' if she'd tried.

And there were no thoughts of warning or caution or 'what ifs' or concerns. There was this and only this, and her heart was engaged.

She acknowledged that in this moment she should gently extract herself, end this here, cherish these shared kisses and seek nothing more. But Cecilia could only focus on the desire for her that glowed in the depths of Linc's eyes, on all the emotions she felt within herself, both named and unnamed, and on the soft and gentle expression on his face. On the touch of his hands that now cupped her shoulders and stroked her face.

'Take me to your room, Linc.'

Linc heard Cecilia's words, saw the need and longing reflected in her eyes, and faced a watershed moment deep within himself.

He had turned his back six years ago, for her sake, because he'd known he would never truly commit. Now Linc knew that his emotions *were* invested in Cecilia, that his feelings were real and only for her.

Linc wanted to give her those things, but would she be able to receive them and let it end there without being hurt? For that matter, could he give in that way and end it without hurt to his own emotions?

Too late, Linc. You're already there.

Deep down he knew that, and he hoped for this chance to just this once do all that he could to show her those feelings.

'I need you, Cecilia, and I need this night. But I can't… In terms of the future…' His chest hurt and he struggled to go on.

'I don't care, Linc. I need—' She broke off, and her gaze was clear and determined as it held his.

Thank you. With all my heart and soul, thank you.

Linc took Cecilia's hand and drew her from the sofa. It felt like the most natural and right thing to lead her to the door of his room.

He drew Cecilia inside with him, turned her into his arms and lowered his mouth to hers once again, knowing that now there would be more. There would be the fulfilment of all the desire that hummed in the air surrounding them, the opportunity to cherish and give and revere.

He gave himself to making it the most special experience for her that he possibly could. Valuing her with all he could invest in that valuing. Expressing without words the emotions running through the fabric of his soul.

If you don't say it, it's not real.

The childhood words were silly, because these emotions were entirely real, whether they were verbalised or not. Yet they couldn't be spoken because he couldn't look for a future.

Linc didn't ask himself in that moment just what those deep emotions meant. He wasn't sure he could afford to know. Instead, he breathed deeply and inhaled Cecilia's closeness and let it fill him.

Linc gave himself to these shared and treasured pleasures, this precious giving and receiving. He was all of himself and yet more within himself than he had ever been. That was all Linc knew—that and the deep, resonating need to demonstrate to Cecilia how much sharing this with her meant to him.

His breath caught as she melted wholly into his

embrace. His arms trembled with how deeply he valued holding her. Chest to chest, warmth shared, soft lips against caressing lips, they explored as people who knew each other but didn't really, and now they needed so much more.

Today had acted as a catalyst for him. He felt as though layers had been peeled from his soul and that he could finally acknowledge that he *did* long for Cecilia. That he did not simply *want* but *needed* to carry their closeness to this inevitable conclusion.

Linc needed this with everything within him. Just once…and only with her…

'Linc…' She whispered his name against his lips.

He swept her closer and gave all his being to the *sense* of her—the soft loveliness of her arms about his neck and the delicate arch of her spine where his hands held her. She pressed closer still. She seemed unable to be near enough.

Something inside Linc, in some place that he hadn't known before, felt *right* for the first time in his life. *This was right*—holding her, sharing these precious moments.

His chest rose and fell on a deep breath. He pushed away the thought that there could never be this again—pushed it far, far away, where it couldn't tighten its grip until he could no longer breathe, where he might not feel it even existed any more.

'Cecilia…' He murmured her name against her lips and grounded his emotions in this giving.

'Oh, Linc…'

My heart is so full of emotion for you right now.

Cecilia couldn't speak the words, but they rose in her mind as she embraced Linc and he embraced her.

Everything about these moments imbued her with thoughts and emotions so deep she couldn't fathom how she could feel so much.

Impossible to try to stop herself, to protect those emotions. So she told herself not to label them, not to give them names—because while they were nebulous and unnamed she could have this and not think about tomorrow...

Linc's hand rose to stroke her hair. 'Your hair is beautiful. It's so soft.'

He murmured the words before his lips touched hers again.

'I want this.'

Conviction echoed in her quiet words. Her hand rose to his chest, felt its strong rise and fall as he registered her words.

She went on. 'I want to share this—with you. Everything there is to share...' Everything that could be shared from her emotions to his.

He'd made no promises, had been careful that she understood there would be no tomorrow. And Cecilia did understand, and it made this easier. One chance to give and receive and close a chapter. She would feel happy because of that.

Surely she would...

His hands stroked her arms reverently, with the lightest touch against her skin, and she let go of the uneasy thought.

As clothing fell away she felt only a sense of rightness so strong and so comforting that it was infinitely beautiful finally to become one with him. Every barrier was removed and only this existed.

He held her tenderly and his gaze locked with hers.

Each touch seemed to value her deeply, each moment of delight seemed to bring them closer.

Time ceased to exist. Nothing existed but the two of them. His touch. Their shared kisses. And more...

A crescendo built—until finally she looked deep into his eyes and felt that their souls must have merged as they yielded together.

Held in his arms in the afterglow, Cecilia asked herself how she could feel as though her world had stopped still and as if Linc held the key to all that she was and would ever be. This didn't feel like 'closure' from her six-year-old feelings.

Inside her was a burgeoning emotion. It spread through her heart until she felt overtaken by it. She realised in that moment that she had fallen deeply and irrevocably in love with Linc. Rather than having closed the chapter, she had unleashed this.

The knowledge was so large, so all-encompassing, that she thought he must surely sense it. She tensed, and her breath stopped. Because he mustn't know. Not now. Not until she could come to terms with this and know how to deal with it.

She *loved* him! Loved him in a way that would dictate her wanting to be with him and be part of his life forever. No, not just part. She would want to be right there in the centre of his world, and him in hers, living out life *together*.

Linc gave a deep sigh and drew her gently closer, encouraging her to curl into his arms. He seemed close to sleep as he placed a soft kiss in her hair.

'*Your hair is beautiful. It's so soft.*'

The echo of his earlier words reverberated.

She thought he'd also whispered that she humbled him, that he didn't know himself right then.

She realised that Hugh was the chapter that had been closed completely. That had been a weak shadow of real emotion in the first place, and it was now so completely gone. She had wanted true love, but Hugh had not been that.

Cecilia understood this now because of the man who held her and the love she held for him.

How would she face tomorrow?

She closed her eyes and willed the thought away.

Exhaustion won out at long last.

She slept.

CHAPTER TEN

'I SHOULD BE at the nursery, making sure my staff are safe and continuing with preparations for the masked ball.'

Cecilia spoke with emphasis as she addressed her words to the small group gathered in the rooftop garden area at Linc's family's warehouse building the next morning.

'How can I hide myself away and leave them vulnerable?'

It was still early. Linc had called this family meeting to put the situation to his brothers and sisters-in-law and seek their collective input.

Cecilia had agreed to the meeting. In truth, it had seemed easier than trying to deal with her new-found emotions alone with Linc at his city apartment. But those emotions were still there, and so were the demands of the rest of her life.

It was clear Linc wanted to gain his family's support in convincing her to stay out of the limelight. Linc had said as much when he'd woken that morning and joined her in his kitchen, where she'd been already showered, dressed and waiting to tell him she *had* to go to work.

All the shock and uncertainty she had been too exhausted to process late last night, in those incredulous moments when she had realised she'd fallen in love with Linc, had awoken her before dawn, determined to make themselves well and truly known again and demand that she work out what to do about them.

As she'd showered and dressed, a need to be by herself and process this new knowledge had overwhelmed her to such a degree that she hadn't known how she could even face Linc.

She loved him.

There could be no future for them.

Her heart was breaking.

All her heart and emotions, everything she had inside her, had fallen in love with one amazing man. That was the beautiful part...the wonderful, incredible part.

But Linc hadn't expressed those emotions—had not at any point in time led her to believe that he had fallen for her. On the contrary, he had tried not to yield to the deepening attraction and interest between them, and last night he had warned her...

She had to acknowledge that if they'd not been through such an emotionally charged day yesterday, in all likelihood he would have continued to avoid taking things further between them.

And his succumbing to temptation did not mean that his emotions had changed whatsoever. That part shattered her heart all over again.

Cecilia caught his gaze. Oh, it was so hard now to look into the grey eyes that had looked into hers in the very moments before she'd realised she loved him!

The only thing Cecilia could think of to do was

hiding herself in her work and finding distance from him so she could shore up her defences.

'Linc, you said yourself that you've assigned a security team to the nursery, so there shouldn't be any problems with me going back to work today.'

You have to let me go. I can't be in your company—especially not just the two of us, shut away from the world. Not yet. Not now. Not ever. And I can't think of that right now, either!

She needed to gather her strength and figure out how to go forward from here.

'I should be safe enough at the nursery with a security detail in place. And if I'm not, then my staff aren't, either!'

This was a genuine concern, and it made complete sense to her.

Until Jayne spoke.

'I have to agree with Linc.' Concern for Cecilia shone in Jayne's eyes. 'At least for today allow the security team at the nursery to monitor things and give some feedback as to whether anything odd or unusual occurs. It would be better if you didn't go back to your workplace, Cecilia. You'd be distracting them from being able to watch the others as well as they would without you there.'

Cecilia's hopes fell. 'I hadn't considered that...'

She *should* have considered that. It should have been completely obvious to her.

Linc heard Cecilia respond to Jayne's comment and silently thanked his sister-in-law for voicing the concerns that he shared. But Cecilia looked so crestfallen as she acknowledged Jayne's point, and—as they had done since he'd first woken that morning—

Linc's emotions churned. He'd thought that he could give himself last night. That if he made sure Cecilia understood there would be no tomorrow it would be okay. He'd convinced himself he could do it without causing hurt, provided he was honest about it at the start.

If all that was true, then why did he feel so empty inside right now? Why did he feel that he'd lost something wonderful? And Cecilia… She didn't look happy and fulfilled—as though she'd been able to answer a question that had been in her mind and now could happily move on. She looked as though she wanted to run as far and as fast as she could.

What if she did? What if she took up the offer from the Silver Bells committee and left him?

You mean if she left working for you.

Either would have the same result. She would disappear out of his life, and he wouldn't see her any more.

Panic tightened Linc's chest. He couldn't let that happen!

So help her sort out these issues and, the first chance you get, talk to her about last night. Tell her how it made you feel. Tell her you want more.

But Linc couldn't *have* more. He glanced across the room at his brothers. He could *not* have more.

'It's still early.' Linc offered the words quietly.

There was still the situation of a dangerous man who had threatened harm to Cecilia, and that situation had to be managed, whether Linc had other things preying on his mind or not.

So he waited until Cecilia finally raised her gaze to his, and then he said, 'We have time to contact Jemmie, to let her know the basics of the situation and ask her if she'll be comfortable taking charge for today while the security team do their thing. I am confident she and the others will be protected if anything does transpire.'

'I have to work.' Cecilia's words held an agitated edge. 'It's not that I believe the nursery can't get along without me—certainly for one day, anyway—although the timing isn't great. I just can't spend the day in idleness with nothing to do but think.'

The others would believe she wanted to avoid thinking about the man on the loose, her sister's plight and of course those things *would* be causing her worry and stress. And she *would* think about them if left to her own devices.

Somehow Linc had lost sight of that for a bit—had failed to remember all the pressure that would be weighing on Cecilia's shoulders today.

He felt selfish in that moment, to have believed all her thoughts would be of what they had shared. Last night he could have controlled that situation—not allowed it to reach the conclusion it had.

Yet even as he thought this, Linc knew it wasn't true. For the first time in his life he had *not* been able to fight his way out of core emotions that had been so strong.

Cecilia sought his gaze and held it. 'You know I need to be at work. I can't possibly— I need—'

'Whatever you need, you will have. I will make this work for you, Cecilia.'

He simply made that commitment to her. Linc was a man who'd struggled, triumphed, lost, loved, given and been blessed beyond anything he'd imagined his life could be. The family he, Alex and Brent had built out of the ashes of abandonment had saved Linc.

If Cecilia needed space, he could give her that and still keep her secure. He could help her, even while he tried to sort out his own emotions.

Linc felt a degree of calmness return as he realised he could do this.

Cecilia heard Linc's words and felt the kindness and care in them. Oh, she wanted so much to believe that those words came out of a deeply held love for her, but she knew Linc would do this even if they had never shared so much as a kiss.

Don't think about it. Not yet.

She glanced about at the gathered group. 'I'm grateful to all of you. None of you needed to weigh in on this but you did so without hesitating, and that means the world to me. I just—' For one panicky moment she thought she might choke into tears in front of them all. 'I need—'

'Not to have everything taken away at once?' Brent broke in.

'Not to feel overwhelmed with pressure?' Fiona added. She turned her gaze towards Linc. 'You're quite certain everyone at the nursery will be safe?'

'I don't believe anyone could get past the teams that are in place.' Linc's words were resolute. 'But I still have to take every precaution, and because the guy threatened Cecilia directly, made it clear his grudge is towards her specifically, I can't make that same guarantee for her.'

When he went on, it was as though he had focused inwardly.

'I've made the mistake in the past of letting a bully

harm someone—' He broke off and his gaze rested on Alex. 'That was unforgivable, and I will not ever allow it to happen again.'

'That was a long time ago, and it wasn't even your—' Alex got halfway to his feet.

'Worry about it later, Alex.' Brent cut him off almost sharply. 'We need to focus on the current issue.'

What had Linc meant? And why had his words caused Alex to respond in that way, and Brent to cut the conversation off completely?

Brent spoke again before Cecilia could think any further. 'We've established that the security team should be able to cope and that they'll need at least today to observe without the bulk of their attention being on keeping Cecilia safe.'

'Yeah. We have.' Linc turned his gaze to Cecilia. 'I'm sorry, but that's where I stand on it. I'd shut the place down rather than have you there today.'

She knew that he would, and she paused to consider and then reject that option. 'I'd rather avoid that, if possible. It would only draw more attention to the fact that there's a problem.'

'I have what I hope will be a tolerable second option for you.'

As Linc spoke the words he could only be grateful for his family and for the support they'd given by rallying around this morning. Last night had thrown him so far off balance he'd been concerned that he might miss something or make a poor decision.

Linc didn't feel worried about that any more, but he was still thankful.

'I'll bring some of your repurposing items here. You can work on them today and stay for as long as is needed. You'll have access to the phone and internet, so you'll be able to give support to Jemmie remotely, as well.'

This apartment was large. They could work all day and barely see each other if they chose.

'Great idea.' Brent nodded his approval.

'We can take turns coming here if you need to go away anywhere, Linc.' Alex added his thoughts.

'I'll agree to that plan—for today at least.' Cecilia didn't love it, but if she could busy herself that would help. She caught each person's gaze in turn. 'Thank you all for—for caring.'

At least by accepting this today, she would ensure that Linc's relatives didn't do dangerous things such as turning up at the plant nursery, where protection would be more difficult, wanting to express their support for her. Given their care and concern this morning, she wouldn't put it past them!

'Being able to do my repurposing here would be ideal—just while we're waiting to see how the security team are feeling about things.' She filled her tone with determination.

'Thanks, everyone. Why don't we make a start on breakfast?' It was Linc who made the suggestion. 'I'll head to the nursery to collect some of Cecilia's items. I've got the truck downstairs. I haven't had it out for a while. It will be a good chance to give it a run and for me to check in with the security team at the same time.'

'You'll keep safe?'

Cecilia wanted to go with him but knew that he wasn't inviting her and that he wouldn't do so. She had to stay out of the limelight, whether she wanted to or not.

'I'll phone Jemmie and bring her up to speed.'

'Remember that you don't have to tell her about anything more than the threat itself if you don't want to.' Linc turned the grey-eyed gaze on her that was now so familiar and dear. His words were protective, but perhaps only she could hear that? Or was she making it up because she wanted to believe it?

A moment later Linc had gone, and Cecilia was left with his loving, amazing family, all examining her with interested gazes.

'Will you excuse me if I step away to make the call to my assistant manager?' She grasped at this plan a little desperately and hoped her emotions—the ones that related to Linc, at least—weren't all over her face.

Hopefully, Linc wouldn't be gone too long.

Hopefully, Cecilia would soon get control over these new feelings for Linc that had thrown her so profoundly off balance. Maybe she only *thought* she felt this way due to the stress of the current circumstances?

Dream on, Cecilia.

Fine—then she would focus on what had to be done today, one step and one moment at a time, until sooner or later she would get some time to herself and figure out how to deal with these feelings, protecting herself from heartbreak in the process. There had to be a way.

Cecilia stepped away and phoned Jemmie.

CHAPTER ELEVEN

'THEY NEED TO catch this guy.'

Cecilia spoke the words after jumping when the fridge in Linc's kitchen gave a shuddering sound at the end of its auto-defrost cycle.

She went on. 'Either that or I'm going to turn into a complete, neurotic mess.'

It was the following evening. They'd agreed that they would go in to the plant nursery for the day that morning.

Doing so hadn't been as easy as Cecilia had thought it would be. She'd spent all day looking over her shoulder and worrying. Was everyone safe? Could the security team really cope, no matter what happened? Was Stacey truly safe in the correctional facility? What if Linc was holding off talking about the night they'd shared because he didn't want to let her down when she was relying on staying at his home until she could be safe elsewhere?

And so it had gone—all of yesterday and even more today—until finally they'd returned to his apartment to a dinner prepared and left for them by Linc's housekeeper, Rosa.

Cecilia was once again only picking at her food.

There seemed to be a permanent lump lodged in her throat.

Linc watched Cecilia push food around her plate and couldn't deny the relief of having her back here, where it was a whole lot easier to keep an eye on her. All except for the fact that they were now alone, and he'd had all day today and all of yesterday to think about what they'd shared, and all he'd been able to think was what if he'd made such a mess of things that he couldn't turn that around?

'You've got every right to be jumpy.' He stood, cleared their plates and they made their way to the living room.

'I had a call from Stacey today.' She settled into an armchair as he took his place on the sofa. 'It came through while you were doing a check with the security team.'

'How was she?'

'She's okay. She's had several conversations with the police.' Cecilia paused and worried at her lip with her teeth. 'It's been done discreetly, and she's really hoping what she's told them will help them catch the guy.'

'You never stop thinking about her, do you?' It was an observation as well as a question.

'Only when—' Cecilia stopped and shook her head. 'Stacey's very important to me,' she said instead. 'That will never change. I know it's the same for you with Brent and Alex. You love them deeply.'

Her voice held a hint of wistful longing, but all Linc heard was praise for his caring nature. He didn't want to tell her the truth, and yet he couldn't withhold it.

You'll lose her. She won't want you if you tell her what happened. It will be one more rejection in your life, and this time you'll deserve it.

'I *do* love Brent and Alex.' At least he could say that much with absolute assurance. He forced himself to go on. 'But there was a time when I abandoned Alex. He suffered because of my self-interest—because I put what I wanted before making sure he was okay.'

'I can't imagine that, Linc.' Surprise tinged her words.

Linc felt ill. He'd been asking himself how he could hold on to Cecilia, but he knew he didn't have the right to that kind of wonderful relationship. He shouldn't have allowed himself to ignore that fact. Not for a moment.

'I ignored him for weeks on end when he was at his most vulnerable and needed me to be there for him.'

'What—what happened?' Concern filled her expression.

'I was the oldest, and as a result the first to leave the orphanage—though I was able to get Brent out soon after. I got Brent a job. Alex, because he was younger...'

'He had to wait before he could join you?' Her expression showed empathy. 'It must have been tough, having to leave him there?'

'It wasn't as tough for me as it should have been.'

Linc had never discussed this. Not even with Brent, back when it had all unfolded. Not his emotions about it. He hadn't needed to say anything. He'd done something profoundly selfish and wrong, and he'd shoved that acknowledgment deep down inside himself where it would never leave him. Where it belonged.

'I was so focused on making money as fast as I could. Instead of paying attention to what was happening to Alex, I let weeks go by without checking on him.'

He'd allowed the old adage of 'out of sight, out of mind' to take hold in him.

Cecilia's expression sobered. 'Go on.'

'Brent had been keeping closer contact with Alex, but he got some work that took him away for a month.' Here Linc's eyes clouded over, as though in remembered pain. 'He came and saw me one night and asked me to make sure I visited Alex often. Brent was worried about a new employee the orphanage had taken on. He thought the man could be violent. With him going away, he knew he couldn't keep an eye on him.'

'Oh, Linc…' Cecilia wasn't sure that she *did* want to know the rest.

'I checked on Alex just once—asked if he was doing okay.' Linc shook his head. 'I asked him if he'd mind if I didn't come in much because I was so busy. He didn't want me to worry or feel I had to leave my work because of him, so he told me everything was fine.'

'But it wasn't?' Cecilia almost whispered the words.

Linc forced the rest out. 'When I finally visited Alex again, he was trying to hide that his ribs were bruised.' Linc closed his eyes for a moment. 'That man had beaten Alex where he knew no person would be able to see it. He'd done it because he was mean and because he could—and I'd allowed it to happen.

I didn't listen when Brent expressed his concerns, and I put it on Alex to tell me whether something was wrong or not. And he didn't want to stop me being able to work.'

The self-condemnation and the agony of what had occurred while Linc should have been on watch were rife in his tone as well as in his words.

'Oh, Linc. You must have been devastated.' She offered the words carefully, and she had to add, 'But surely you know that might have happened even if you *were* visiting? Unfortunately, there are people in this world who do such things any chance they get.'

'I took Alex straight out of there, of course.' Linc said it as though there couldn't possibly have been any other option. 'I walked him out on the spot and consequences be damned. Brent and I kept him hidden until he was old enough that the authorities couldn't take him from us. It was only a few months. Why didn't I do that in the first place?'

'Because you didn't know.'

Cecilia could only imagine how he must have felt—how hard it must have been for Linc to face Brent as well, knowing that he'd failed to give the situation the attention he should have at the time.

'You removed Alex from the threat as soon as you could. That was a *good* thing.'

'Yeah, but way too late.' Linc shook his head, as though that just hadn't been enough. 'He'd been beaten for trying to protect one of the smaller kids.'

'You know, none of us are infallible—'

'Not like this.' His tone was harsh and filled with self-directed censure. 'I left my brother there to be harmed—and I did it even though Brent had brought his concerns to my attention. Thanks to me, Alex ended up being preyed on by that guy. And it wasn't just about the physical beating. There are emotional scars from things like that, which last much longer.'

Had Linc and Alex talked about this? Did Alex blame Linc? Cecilia couldn't imagine that. In fact, she was convinced that Alex not only would have forgiven him long ago, but that he would never have blamed Linc in the first place.

'It sounds to me as though Alex had the bravery to step in where a lot of other young boys wouldn't have to protect the other children.'

'I guess that's the irony.' Linc glanced at his hands before his gaze met hers again. 'Brent and me, we raised him well in there. His ethics were rock solid.'

Yet Linc couldn't let himself experience anything that resembled forgiveness for his own actions. Cecilia could see that very clearly now.

His words as he went on confirmed it. 'It was way too easy for me to forget about him. I've had to conclude it's a character flaw in myself.' He drew a breath. 'There's something wrong—wrong in me— to make me able to do that. They chose to become my brothers, and I let them down. I don't deserve the kind of happiness they've found.'

Cecilia realised in that moment that this was Linc's morning-after talk. He'd gone away and thought about what they'd shared, and he'd ruled out the possibility of any kind of a future for them because this part of his history was insurmountable for him. He couldn't forgive himself. He believed there was a flaw in his make-up that made him unworthy.

Oh, Linc. How could you believe that about your-self when you're such a good person?

Yes, he'd made a mistake—but people did that. He'd been young! He'd also been breaking himself, trying to secure things so they could all be safe, so he could make a life for all of them outside of their horrid upbringing.

Had Linc thought about and longed for a future with Cecilia as she had with him? Was that why he was saying all this now?

Cecilia couldn't let herself think that he was saying it because he'd realised how she felt about him.

As she hesitated, trying to formulate words, trying to know what to say, to understand where she stood and try to figure out what to do, Linc got to his feet.

'I had to tell you.' He seemed to be experiencing a deep pain but also to be resolute. He drew a breath. 'The time we shared together was the most precious I've experienced in my life, but I shouldn't have allowed it to happen and…and I can't let it happen again. You understand why now. You deserve more. I hope you'll forgive me.'

Linc left the room.

'We may still have no news on our wanted man, but I *can* give you some good news about the nursery.' Linc spoke the words the following day as he sat back from his computer.

They were in Cecilia's small office at the plant nursery. Cecilia wasn't as jumpy as she'd been the day before. Maybe she should have been, but she'd had very little sleep…and her heart hurt. She suspected that if she let herself feel everything to the depths that she could at the moment, she might break down.

She'd made her decision. There was no other choice that she could see. Her love for Linc would never be returned. She was trying to accept it, to be grateful that he didn't know how she felt. But mostly she was just trying to hold a great wall of pain at bay.

What news could Linc have? They were going ahead with the masked ball. They hadn't told anyone other than their staff about the issues going on. If need be, they would bring in the biggest contingent of undercover security any place had ever seen, but they *would* go ahead.

Cecilia couldn't actually think of any other good news to do with the nursery. She had news for Linc that would affect the nursery, but she doubted he would want to hear that. Then again, maybe it would be an answer to his prayers.

She forced her gaze up and away from her inspection of the catering lists spread across the desk in front of her. It wasn't easy to look at Linc, but she did it.

'What is it?'

'I've finished the review, and it should be no surprise to you that everything's fine.' He drew a breath. 'I'm more than happy to agree to the percentage share in the nursery that you proposed when you initially approached me about doing this review.'

For a moment she simply didn't comprehend his words—and then they sank in.

'I'm grateful for that, Linc, truly I am…'

She fought to say the rest of the words that needed to be said and to keep her chin up while she did it. Now was the perfect time. So she went on.

'But I won't be taking the offer up after all.'

She couldn't stay here—be here while Linc reverted to stopping in periodically, expecting her update calls as he'd done before this review had started. It wouldn't matter whether those visits took place weekly or were months apart. Or that those phone calls would be all about business. She would hurt a little more each time she saw him. Because loving someone who didn't share those feelings would do that to her.

Cecilia understood his self-blame over his brother, his belief that he wasn't deserving of love. But she *did* love him. And it hurt her every single moment to know that in the end he simply didn't share those feelings.

If he did, he would fight for her, whether he regretted his past or not.

'I thought you were just keeping a presence here today because of the safety issues—though I am pleased about the review results.' She met his gaze. 'It's just that I've decided to take up the offer from the Silver Bells flower show committee. I'm going to work for them. Actually, I'm planning to leave here as soon as the masked ball is over. In the end…it's best. I'm— It's an exciting new opportunity for me, really.'

She felt like two people. The one sitting there, saying those words and trying to appear calm, as though this was what she wanted to do, and the one who loved Linc and was being torn apart by that love.

'If this is because—' Linc's words were strained.

'I've just realised I'm ready for a change.' She pushed the lie past her teeth. This was harder than she had thought it would be, and she prayed that she wouldn't break down.

Linc got to his feet. 'I—I wish you well. Would you excuse me, Cecilia? I need—'

He didn't say what it was that he needed. Linc simply left the room.

CHAPTER TWELVE

'IT LOOKS GOOD, LINC.'

Alex made the comment as he and Linc stood back from the area in the centre of Fleurmazing's signature maze, which now held a fully constructed and functional raised and canopied dais, in readiness for the masked ball that would commence three hours from now.

'People are going to love it. And you can relax now, knowing that guy has been caught.'

When Alex had learned that Linc was planning to assist with the construction of the dais, he'd put his hand up to come along and help. Linc hadn't really wanted the company, yet Alex's presence had done him good.

Now the construction was finished, and it was just the two of them admiring the result of their handiwork.

Linc glanced at Alex. 'He was picked up in New Zealand. He'll face charges and do jail time over there. It's looking like at least a decade of accumulated charges.'

'He won't be allowed back into Australia after that.' Alex said it with certainty. 'How's Cecilia taking all of this?' His gaze focused on the maze beyond the dais as he went on. 'She must feel as though she's been put through a wringer, one way and another.'

'What do you mean by that?' Linc asked the question too quickly before he realised Alex probably meant nothing at all beyond the comment itself. 'Sorry. It's been a tense time. Cecilia is visiting her sister this afternoon at the correctional centre. I'm sure she's relieved the guy's been caught.'

'You don't sound real convinced about her state of happiness, brother.'

Those words drew Linc's gaze to Alex, and he saw his younger brother was looking right at him now.

Alex searched his face. 'Yet seeing the two of you together just days ago, I would have thought maybe both of you were on the brink of something special.'

Linc didn't even ask himself how Alex had discerned that. 'I'm not enough for her. She's better off without me.'

'That's the most foolish rubbish I've heard in all the time I've known you.' Alex's words were sharp. 'Give me one good reason for that belief.'

'When the chips are down, I just think about myself.' Linc fired the volley straight back.

He wanted to tell Alex to keep out of this and mind his own business. His heart hurt, and Alex prodding around in his emotions wasn't helping. Instead, he flayed himself with their shared past.

'You of all people ought to know that—considering you were the one who suffered thanks to my self-interest.'

Instead of backing off, Alex took a step closer to Linc to emphasise his response. 'It wasn't until recently that I even realised you blamed yourself for what happened way back when I was still in the orphanage. Brent and I always believed you were so locked down about it at the time because you were rightly angry—infuriated that such a piece of scum existed and had got into that place to smack around little kids. Just as we were.'

'He preyed on you because I failed to keep watch. I failed to protect you—'

'You're not to blame. *You* weren't the person who bullied me, who had been bullying other kids, as well.'

'I should have made time to visit you. You and Brent let me into your lives.' Linc said it with all the pain he'd carried for so long. 'You chose to accept me as a brother. I was the oldest. I had a responsibility to look after both of you, and in your case I failed.'

'You mean while you were working yourself into the ground so you'd be able to provide for me once I was old enough to leave?'

Ah, don't make me out to be a hero, Alex.

'I don't think you and Brent realise,' Linc said slowly. 'You saved me. I don't believe I could have handled that place without you both.'

He'd have died from lack of love without them. Maybe not immediately, maybe not for all his lifetime, but inside he'd have died.

Alex's gaze held his as he responded, 'We all saved each other. Do you think I shouldn't have married Jayne because I wasn't good enough for my parents to want to keep me? Or that Brent shouldn't have found happiness with Fiona because his father shoved him into that place just as yours did you? Do you think we're not good enough? Because it seems if you think that way about yourself, that's how you think about us.'

'It's not like that. You're twisting the situation.'

And yet...

'This can't just be about me punishing myself.' Linc said it slowly. 'If it is, then I've been using it as an excuse—'

To avoid something?

To avoid letting himself love in case he wasn't loved in return?

'I love her.' He uttered it with complete knowledge. 'I love Cecilia.'

And he'd pushed her away. Shoved her away hard in case—God forbid—she might love him in return. She'd handed in her resignation. After tonight she would be cut off from him.

Alex gripped his arm for a moment, and then let go. 'Brent and I both love you, Linc. We want you to be happy. Neither of us blame you for the past. You held the three of us together and you should be damn proud of that fact. Just know that the past is the past. If we can both let go of it, so should you.'

As Alex started to leave the area, he turned and a satisfied smile came over his face. 'Remember how we all went back to the orphanage the night after you got me out? It was probably wrong of us, but we were going to dish out a bit of justice of our own to that guy?'

'Yeah.' Linc remembered. 'The police were there. One of the little kids you'd protected had sneaked into the office and made the call before we could— had told them the guy was there, beating everyone.'

'The orphanage was shut down and the kids got

shifted into better situations. Most of them got placed into loving families.' Alex raised his brows. 'Do you think that would have happened if I hadn't been beaten that one time? For me, personally, I reckon that was worth it.'

Alex left then.

Linc felt humbled. And he had to ask himself: *had* he been hiding behind the guilt from his past in order to refuse to let himself look ahead and hope for the future? Had he been afraid to love because he hadn't been loved by his father?

If that was the case, had he left it too late to do something about it? Had he lost Cecilia forever?

Because in his heart of hearts he knew that he loved Cecilia with everything in him. That the idea of a life without her in it filled him with pain. That he wanted happiness with her if he could find it, and if she would be willing to take him on and try.

The masked ball was hours away.

Linc needed a plan.

He strode from the nursery.

CHAPTER THIRTEEN

'THANKS, JEMMIE, for all your help.'

Cecilia couldn't believe the evening of the masked ball was here at last. But everything was in place. Jemmie had stayed after hours to give Cecilia time to go home and change in readiness for the ball itself, but now Cecilia was back, the guests would arrive within the hour and Cecilia's heart was so torn she didn't know where to start.

Jemmie said her goodbyes and left the office. At the entrance of the nursery, members of the Silver Bells flower show committee had started to gather. They would greet the guests and send them into the maze to begin what Cecilia hoped would prove to be a magical adventure for each of them.

All Cecilia had to do was get through this night, hold it together and then...

Leave.

Make a complete new start somewhere she'd have some hope of forgetting Linc.

The pressure for tonight to be perfect was even greater because she knew she would be leaving. She wanted to give Linc this one last thing and do it really well. Not that he would see it. With the way things had gone, there was no way he would be here.

But he would hear about tonight and know she'd done a good job.

With a sigh, Cecilia stepped out into the courtyard area, locked the office door after her and made her way into the maze. It was time to go to where the dais had been raised, to check everything one last time and then, as the guests finally began to arrive, to smile and make sure each of them had a night to remember.

Cecilia lifted the delicate mask she held in one hand and placed it over her face.

Maybe it would hide her heartache.

Linc shifted from foot to foot where he stood at the edge of the dais area. He straightened his bow tie and hoped he would be able to carry this off when Cecilia arrived. It was difficult not to feel foolish wearing a mask that the woman in the shop had said made him look like—what was it?—*some swashbuckling hero*?

He just wanted to see Cecilia and to let her know that he loved her. He hoped with all his heart that she might be able to return those feelings, that he hadn't messed things up so badly he couldn't come back from it. But this night meant a lot to Cecilia, so he wanted to be sure that he looked the part.

Linc had told Cecilia about Alex. The guilt Linc had felt had been very real, but Alex had shown Linc that he'd been holding on to that past experience and blaming himself for being human. That he needed to let go of it and reach out for his own happiness. That he had to trust that he could be loved and accepted— just as Brent and Alex loved and accepted him and were themselves loved and accepted.

Behind Linc the string quartet finished tuning up

and began to play a soft, haunting melody. He had asked them to come earlier, to be ready to start playing and keep playing once Cecilia arrived.

Rosa had given him a crash course in waltzing. She'd patted his face and hadn't asked why. She was the closest thing to a mother that Linc could remember.

The rows upon rows of lights in the canopied cover above the dais came on, lending a soft glow to the fading twilight.

In that moment Cecilia stepped out of the maze and he saw her—and, oh, she looked so beautiful. A shimmering deep gold gown made her seem as one with her surroundings. Gold sandals covered her feet, and her hair was piled high on her head. Her mask of gold and blue highlighted her beautiful eyes.

She also looked fragile, as though the weight of this world sat on her shoulders.

Could she love him?

Linc's chest expanded with all the love he felt for her.

She spotted him standing there and, for just a moment, her step faltered and surprise made her eyes round.

Linc stepped down from the dais and quickly walked to greet her.

Don't leave. Don't walk away before I've had a chance to tell you—

'Cecilia. You look beautiful.'

She did. He wanted to see her in all her stages of beauty, all throughout their lives.

Her gaze searched his face. 'Thank you. I didn't think you'd be here.'

Along with the strain, did her gaze show pleasure that he was there? Or did Linc just long to see that?

'I had to come.'

As he looked at her, he knew he wanted—no, he *needed* to wake up beside her every day, forever. He needed that as much as breathing. And he hoped with all his might that she would give him that chance.

'Will you dance with me, Cecilia? Now? Before the guests start arriving?'

He held out his hand.

The string ensemble began the strains of a waltz.

Cecilia searched his face. He thought she would say no, but after a long moment she silently put her hand in his.

Linc released the breath he'd been holding and led her onto the dais. He drew Cecilia into his arms, and they circled the floor together. His arms had hurt from the lack of holding her, and now there was this symmetry, this beauty of touch and music and movement. She matched his steps perfectly, and it was effortless and so right.

He looked down into her upturned face, into the dark blue pools of her eyes, and knew that he could trust his heart in her care just as much as he wanted to care for her heart forever.

Cecilia gazed into Linc's eyes as they moved around the dance floor. She heard the quartet playing, but she saw nothing but Linc, felt nothing but the touch of his hand holding hers, his other hand against her back.

The scent of flowers kissed by the cooling night air surrounded them. Everything was perfect. She wanted to cry and never stop crying, and still she hadn't been able to deny herself this.

Oh, she had not expected to be held in Linc's arms, to be whisked about the dais as though she and no one else meant the world to him.

Please don't break my heart all over again, Linc. I don't know why you're doing this.

Why had Linc come here, asked her for this dance? She wanted to hope—and that was the most dangerous and heartbreaking thing she could do!

She'd prepared herself to leave him, to try and mend her heart away from him and, when this dance was over, that was still exactly what she had to do.

Eventually, the dance came to an end. Linc led her off the floor. 'Will you walk with me in the maze for a minute? I need to talk to you.'

'All—all right.' His serious tone made her heart thump.

'This is where I found you that first day of the review.' Linc spoke the words quietly.

She looked around her and realised they were in front of the statue of the sun goddess. Her favourite part of the maze. All of a sudden the affinity she felt with this place, with the work she'd put in, her vision and seeing her dreams come true here all welled up, and that sorrow added itself to the sorrow of unrequited love.

She started to speak before she could stop herself. 'I'll miss—'

'You remind me of her tonight.'

He spoke at the same time, and his gaze briefly rested on the statue before it returned to Cecilia.

'It's not just the colour of your dress.' He seemed

to search for words to express his thoughts. 'It's how you are inside yourself. You spread light. You warm people.'

The words weren't flattery. They were far deeper than that.

She searched his gaze. 'That's a lovely thing for you to say.'

Linc had his chance now, and he didn't want to blow it. He pulled the mask from his face and gently removed hers, dropping them both at the foot of the statue. There were some things that just couldn't be said with barriers in place.

'We've known each other for a long time…'

He started there, because that had been the start of their journey.

'Back then, when we first met…' She'd shown an interest in him and he'd rebuffed her. 'I was convinced I didn't deserve love and a happy-ever-after. I didn't know it at the time, but I was using it as an excuse.'

Linc paused for a moment. He took her hand in his and cherished the connection, the simple sense of rightness the touch gave him.

'I've realised that I *wanted* to blame myself.'

Her fingers tightened on his for an instant, and she frowned. 'Why?'

'Because it let me hold back from people other than my brothers.' He'd been afraid of being hurt. The big, strong millionaire Linc MacKay hadn't known how to protect his emotions, so he'd used that as an excuse to hold them at bay from the world. 'I didn't want to risk being given up on again, as my father gave up on me.'

'How others behave towards us can have a profound impact.' Cecilia's words were open and honest, and she knew she had to go on. 'Our mother telling us repeatedly that we were a burden on her not only harmed Stacey and helped her along the path of self-destruction that led her to where she is today, it also harmed me.'

It had. More than Cecilia had ever wanted to admit.

'I had very little faith that a loving relationship could be built and could last. When I tried to form one with…with Hugh, and he disappeared out of my life the moment things got challenging, it not only damaged my faith in others but my belief in myself that I was worth sticking around for.'

'And I added to that—both six years ago and recently.'

Linc's words were low, filled with remorse. Yet as he spoke, his expression became determined and his grip on her hands firmed.

'I'm in love with you, Cecilia. I'm worried sick that I've left it too late to tell you, but I love you with all my heart and I want us to be together.'

Cecilia stared at Linc mutely. All her breath seemed to have escaped from her lungs. She dragged in air. 'Wh-what did you say?'

'I love you.' The truth of it shone from his eyes. 'I'm *in love* with you. Is there any chance, Cecilia? Any chance at all that you might come to return those feelings? I want to spend the rest of my life with you. When you said you were leaving, I felt as though my world was ending.'

'Six years ago I was attracted to you…' Cecilia said it slowly, remembering that time, the immaturity of her emotions. 'But it took coming to know you closely for me to…to totally fall in love with you.'

Linc's gaze searched her face. 'I want to marry you—have children, God willing—and grow old together. I want to love you for the rest of our lives. Please tell me there's hope for that.'

Cecilia might have hesitated on the brink of Linc's proposal but, oh, she wouldn't. She simply would not—because this was worth the risk. This was worth reaching out for.

Linc was worth it.

'Yes.' She broke into a smile that was full of love and relief and happiness. 'Oh, yes, Linc. That is what I'm saying. I want all of those things, too. With *you*. It's what I want more than anything.'

'You've made me the happiest man in the world.'

The relief and acceptance in his voice showed his belief in those words. And the kiss they shared was filled with all the hope and relief and joy they both felt. Cecilia finally believed then—and, oh, it felt good to do so!

As they finally drew apart, Linc asked her, 'Will you still go to work for the Silver Bells committee?'

She searched his gaze and thought for a moment. 'Do you know, I think I will? But if you don't mind too much, I might like to take that on part-time and work on my refurbishment projects the rest of the time.'

'From our home?'

As she nodded, a smile spread over his face.

'I already do a lot of my work from home.' He looked a little sheepish. 'I'm not all that keen on the idea of working out of an office full of staff. We could work from home together...take coffee breaks and do what we liked. The warehouse—'

'Would make a perfect home for us.'

Happiness welled up inside Cecilia, and she couldn't contain it. She reached out for him, and they hugged each other for long moments before they once more drew apart.

Linc reached into his pocket and brought out a small velvet box. He dropped to one knee. His fingers shook as he opened the box and held it out to her.

'Will you marry me and accept this ring as a token of my love for you?'

Cecilia understood his vulnerability then. Knew that they could walk through life together and strengthen each other, that they truly could be stronger and greater together than either of them could ever have been on their own. Her heart opened up to all they could have and be, and she gently received the box from him.

Inside nestled a solitaire engagement ring. The band was white gold, its design cut low, to give all the attention to the glittering jewel it held.

'Oh, Linc, it's lovely.'

His quiet exhalation held both satisfaction and a hint of relief.

He got to his feet and clasped her left hand in his own. 'I'm glad you like it. I bought it today. When I saw it, I thought it was the right one for you. I had to plan, to hope you'd say yes, that it wasn't all too late. I had to put my faith on the line.'

She closed her eyes. 'Oh, Linc. I love you so. I thought I would never have the chance to tell you, let alone to think about a future together.'

'And I thought I'd lost any chance with you by being buried in fears from the past.' He blew out a breath that seemed to let the last of his tension go.

And then he slipped the ring from the box and onto her finger, and she realised it was possible that she could adore him even more.

'It fits perfectly, Linc. Like it was meant to be there. I will be proud to wear this, and every time I look at it I will remember this night and this moment.'

'The start of our future together.' Linc liked the thought a great deal.

Beyond them, they heard the murmur of the first guests entering into the beginning of the maze and knew that the masked ball was truly about to begin.

'Shall we give everyone—and ourselves—a night to remember?'

Linc retrieved their masks from where they rested at the foot of the statue.

Cecilia donned her mask and smiled a little to herself as Linc donned his and immediately took on the persona of a man of mystery.

He was *her* man now, not at all a mystery to her any more, and she liked that fact just fine.

'Yes, Linc. Let's make this a night to remember.'

They made their way back to the dance floor and, as other people arrived, one after another, the first thing they saw was a couple obviously deeply in love with each other, circling the floor in each other's arms to the strains of a beautiful waltz.

It was indeed a night to remember.

EPILOGUE

'DO YOU, LINC MACKAY, take this woman, Cecilia Anna Tomson, to be your lawfully wedded wife?'

The celebrant's words rang out in the beautiful country chapel. She went on, adding words of love and fidelity, commitment and forever.

Cecilia stood before Linc in her wedding gown and knew that her love for him was written all over her, and she didn't care one bit that it was!

Linc's words were low and heartfelt as he responded, 'I do.'

It was Cecilia's turn then, and she saw her sister's hands shake where she stood to her left, holding Cecilia's bouquet of perfect creamy roses and baby's breath along with her own bouquet of deep red blooms. To have Stacey here, so happy herself, added to Cecilia's joy.

When the celebrant had finished her words, Cecilia smiled and saw her love reflected back in Linc's eyes, and she said, with all the conviction in her heart, 'I do. I *do* take this man to my heart, and I will keep him there forever.'

They kissed, and the strains of the 'Wedding March' rose through the church and filled it.

The party made its procession outside onto the steps, facing a field of spring flowers. Linc and Cecilia, and behind them Brent and Fiona, Alex and Jayne, and then Stacey and a man by the name of Brendan Carroll, who seemed to have some special history with Alex. And, of course, Rosa—the family's wonderful housekeeper, who was so much more.

There were other guests—friends and colleagues from the plant nursery and from elsewhere. The family sent them on to the wedding reception, but instead of staying at the church for hours of wedding photos, they took just a handful in front of the chapel and in that field of spring flowers.

At the end of it, Cecilia glanced about the group. 'I couldn't be happier—and especially to be sharing this day with all of you.' She reached out her hand and clasped her sister's in hers for a long moment. 'I'm so glad you're here, Stacey.'

It wasn't just about the day, and they both knew that. It was about the fact that Stacey had stuck to her word and turned her life around. She'd even managed to be civil about their mother making an excuse for not being there when Cecilia had got her courage together and invited her. It really didn't matter. Cecilia *had* her family, and deep in her heart she knew it.

Linc. Stacey. The others. And...

'Oooh!' Jayne rested her hand over her abdomen and a look of surprise came over her face. She turned to Alex. 'The baby just moved. It was like butterfly wings! That's the first time I've felt it.'

Cecilia's love and happiness expanded even further as she observed the quiet joy shared by the couple.

She saw Fiona glance into Brent's eyes, and they both looked sheepish as they broke into smiles.

Cecilia gave a soft laugh. 'Do you two have something you want to share?'

'We're pregnant, too.' Fiona's smile burst right across her face. 'We weren't going to say anything until after the wedding.'

At this, it wasn't Cecilia who laughed but Linc, who unexpectedly threw his head back. But he quickly sobered and clasped Cecilia's hand, and all his hope and love were in his eyes, too.

'We were waiting for Stacey to be here for the wedding...' he began.

'To tell you all that we also may have pre-empted the baby part,' Cecilia finished for him.

'Oh, my God!'

'That's wonderful!'

'That's the best news!'

'I'm going to be an uncle once more than I thought.'

Everyone broke into happy speech at once, and then Stacey spoke quietly into the midst of it.

'I will guarantee you're having twins.'

She said it with such conviction that Cecilia's eyes widened.

'So it's just as well I'm around now, because you're going to need me once they come along.'

Brendan Carroll, the man at Stacey's side, gave a low laugh. 'Double the trouble? I like the sound of that.'

Stacey looked startled and a little intrigued. 'Are you planning to be in Sydney for a while?'

'Actually, I just opened a gallery in the city.'

Cecilia looked at her sister's glowing face, at all

the happiness around her, and suspected that Stacey was going to be just fine.

And her sister was probably right about the possibility of twins, too. Cecilia had a feeling about that herself.

Whether one baby or two, Cecilia would indeed want her sister to be a big part of her life from now on.

'Shall we go to this reception?' Linc whispered the words into her ear. 'The sooner we arrive, the sooner I can sneak you away so I can have you to myself. I want to discuss the possibility of twins…' Love and warmth and desire mingled in his gaze. 'Among other things.'

And so Mr and Mrs Linc MacKay led the family—*their family*—towards the cars that would take them to the reception.

As Linc settled beside Cecilia in the back seat of their chauffer-driven car, he couldn't believe how happy she had made him and went on making him in every single moment.

'I can't imagine life without you now, and I'm longing for this child or these children to join us. Do you think your sister is right?'

Cecilia's contentment flooded over, and she blinked to dispel the sudden rise of emotional tears to her eyes.

She glanced down. 'It would explain why I've had to have this dress let out three times in the last month, even though I'm so early along in the pregnancy.'

Linc gave a delighted laugh. 'Cecilia MacKay, I love you with all my heart and I always will. Did you know that?'

And, actually, Cecilia did!

* * * * *

THE UNFORGETTABLE
SPANISH TYCOON

CHRISTY McKELLEN

This story is dedicated to my super-smart friend Erica, who talked me through the different types of amnesia and their symptoms, then patiently listened to my rambling and slightly bonkers story idea and still pronounced it something she'd love to read.

I really appreciate the time you took to help me shape it into something workable.

And thanks for always being such a good friend.

CHAPTER ONE

IT WAS UNSEASONABLY hot in Barcelona for February and, what with the adrenaline-spiked blood rushing through her veins and the brilliant sunshine that beat in waves at her back as she alighted from the cab outside Araya Industries' ultra-modern offices, Elena Jones was just about ready to combust in her made-for-English-weather woollen suit.

After giving her name in the wonderfully cool air-conditioned reception area, she was shown into a meeting room by a rather anxious-looking PA, acutely aware of the sound of her heels clicking loudly on the highly patterned ceramic tile flooring.

Swallowing down a twinge of nerves, Elena accepted the offer of a drink of water from the young woman, who for some reason didn't seem to be able to look her in the eye, then chose a chair at the head of the imposing twenty-seater frosted glass-topped table, carefully hanging her suit jacket over the back of the sharply stylish but rather uncomfortable-looking chair so it didn't get crumpled. She wanted to look her absolute best today in the hope it would provide her with the boost of confidence she needed to get a positive result from this meeting.

What was making her most nervous was not knowing how Caleb Araya was going to react to seeing her again after all this time. She was actually annoyed by just how anxious she felt about being out of her comfort zone. After running her own company for the last five years she'd become far better at taking risks and getting a grip on her fear of the unknown, and it took something rather exceptional to faze her now.

Apparently the thought of coming face-to-face with Caleb again was to be one of those things.

Would he have forgiven her by now?

Her heart gave an extra hard thump in her chest.

He had to have done, surely? What happened between them had been fifteen years ago; he couldn't still be holding a grudge. He was a businessman after all, a hugely successful one by all accounts, who wouldn't pass up the opportunity to get in on a profitable deal just because they had a bit of a rocky past.

Would he?

Staring out of the floor-to-ceiling windows at the busy street below, she remembered how she'd felt the very first time she'd met him during her second year at the University of Cambridge. At the tender age of twenty she'd thought Caleb Araya was the most arresting, ambitious and charismatic man she'd ever met.

They'd been good friends once, able to talk for hours about their passion for engineering and their hopes of making a mark on the world after they'd gained their degrees.

They'd made a strange pair, the two of them, so much so that their classmates had found their friendship a great source of amusement: she a petite, middle class, inner-city-living bookworm and he a hulking bad boy from the wrong side of a small Spanish town.

But away from other people the formerly laconic, gruff Caleb had been playful, gentle and animated. He'd fascinated her with his passion and drive, not to mention his dangerous sex appeal, and had excited her in ways she'd never experienced before.

What she'd most loved about him was that despite having a tough start in life Caleb hadn't let it beat him down. He'd been determined to better his situation through sheer hard work and making intelligent decisions.

Looking around her now, she could see he'd certainly achieved his goal, and then some. According to the articles she'd read on the Web, his was now the most successful technology and engineering company ever to come out of Spain.

The door in the remarkably fingerprint-free wall of glass that divided the room from the large, plush reception area swung open, letting in the sound of Spanish chatter, and she stood up, taking a deep breath and preparing herself to face Caleb with a cool head and a warm smile.

She was determined not to let her shame about the heartless way she'd treated him in the past get in the way of her objective here today.

Hopefully, he wouldn't let any residual antipathy to-

wards her get in the way of a promising business partnership either.

A wave of nervous tension made her skin prickle as
the man himself strode into the room with his PA hot
on his heels.

Caleb was just as captivating as she remembered, probably even more so now that he'd grown into his darkly arresting looks and six foot five, broad-shouldered frame.
It seemed he'd only built on the animal magnetism she
remembered so keenly too. With his dark, hooded eyes
and jet-black hair slicked away from his strong-boned
face he looked fierce, indomitable and rather dangerous.

No wonder his PA seemed so afraid of him.

The scowl currently marring his craggy features as
he approached was so intimidating it made Elena's heart
leap about in her chest.

'Elena Jones,' he drawled in that same beautiful gravelly Spanish accent she remembered so well, his voice
sounding not so much friendly as vaguely amused.

Her stomach jumped with nerves as he came to a
halt in front of where she stood.

Instead of holding out a hand in greeting, he folded
his enormous arms, making his shirt sleeves tighten
over his bulging muscles, and looked down at her with
one dark eyebrow raised, as if waiting for her to explain how she could possibly have the nerve to show
her face here.

He hadn't forgiven her then.

She swallowed hard, wishing she could take a quick
sip of water to loosen her suddenly dry throat, but she

didn't want to weaken her position by breaking eye contact with him so she ignored the impulse.

'It's good to see you again, Caleb. Thank you for agreeing to this meeting.'

His mouth twitched at the corner as if he were suppressing a smile. 'My former PA made it without my knowledge,' he said, glancing quickly towards his current PA, who seemed to shrink into herself a little, as if afraid she was about to take the fall for her predecessor's mistake. 'But when I saw your name in my diary I couldn't help but be curious about what you could possibly want from me after all this time.'

His presence seemed to grow, crowding out the light in the room as he dropped his arms and drew his shoulders back, pulling himself up to his full height. 'I'm guessing you're only here because you need something from me—rather desperately, judging by the power suit and heels.'

Damn, his dispassionate attitude was going to make her job here so much harder. But there was no way she was giving up that easily. Just because he wasn't prepared to be friendly it didn't mean she couldn't persuade him to agree to give her what she needed. She was going to have to play this meeting carefully though. Apologise—again—if that was what it took.

Just not yet.

It was probably best to keep things on a purely business tack for now.

'I'm here to put a proposition to you,' she said, forcing herself to keep her gaze firmly fixed to his. 'Although to say I'm "desperate" isn't at all accurate,' she lied.

If she knew Caleb at all, and she thought that she did, showing any kind of weakness at this point would be a huge mistake.

'A proposition?' he said, a hint of incredulity colouring his voice.

Elena nodded jerkily, cursing her churning stomach. 'Yes. I'm sure it's something you're going to be very interested in.'

There was a heavy pause while Caleb ran his piercing gaze over her face—perhaps looking for signs of a set-up, or even a joke—before appearing to decide that she was absolutely serious.

'Then I suppose we'd better sit down,' he said, gesturing towards the chair she'd vacated and taking another one two places away, which he turned around so it was facing her.

'You won't need to take any notes,' he said to his PA, waving his hand dismissively. 'This won't be a long meeting.'

Trying not to show how much his glib assumption riled her, Elena took her own seat and smiled encouragingly at the PA, who gave her a nervous nod in return before scuttling out of the room.

Poor woman.

Biting her lip to refrain from saying something to Caleb about his ogre-like behaviour, Elena sat up straighter in her chair and fixed him with a serious stare.

He looked back at her with one eyebrow raised in

apparent curiosity, though the look in his eyes was still hard enough to cut diamonds.

'I don't know whether you know, but I'm the Managing Director and owner of a company in England called Zipabout,' she began, leaning forward a little in her chair.

His expression gave no hint as to whether he'd known that or not so she decided to just forge ahead with the pitch.

'We've designed an electric car specifically suited for a single person to make short trips around towns and cities. It's safer than riding a bike and easy to park in small spaces, but the overarching benefits are that it'll help cut down on air pollution and unnecessary fuel usage.' She took a breath. 'Right now we're looking to source a large rechargeable battery to run it. The one that your company makes would be a perfect fit for our design.'

The smile he gave her made her think of a wild animal about to pounce.

'You're asking me to partner with you?' he asked with dry amusement in his voice.

She cleared her throat to try and defuse the tension that was building there.

'That's exactly what I'm proposing.'

He nodded slowly, his intense gaze never leaving her face.

'Why did you choose my battery?'

'It's the best one on the market.' She held back on revealing that it was the *only* one that would work with the design now that their previous choice was no longer viable.

When their former supplier had called a meeting at the eleventh hour to let her know there was an unfixable fault with the battery they'd planned to use in the car, Elena had done some frantic research, only to come to the uncomfortable conclusion that Caleb's company was the only other manufacturer of a battery compatible with the design. If she didn't get him to agree to supply her company today it was quite likely the car's product launch would be perilously held up and they'd lose all the pre-orders they'd worked so hard to accrue.

'And I think a partnership would be highly beneficial for both our companies,' she went on, hoping to goodness that her nerves weren't beginning to show. Her whole body was rigid with tension because, most crucially, if he didn't agree to supply the battery Zipabout could go under and her entire workforce, who had become like family to her over the last five years, would all lose their jobs.

Tamping down on the dread that sank through her at the thought of it, she widened her smile. 'I sent some information over to your PA this morning in case you had a chance to look at it before the meeting, but I'm guessing from your reaction that you haven't. I have a short presentation on my laptop with me though; perhaps you'd like to see it?'

He regarded her without speaking for what felt like minutes, his dark eyes narrowed in thought. There was something else there in his expression that she didn't like the look of. Something cold and hard.

'No, I don't think I would,' he said finally.

She stared at him, wondering whether she'd mis-heard. Surely he couldn't be dismissing the idea without at least looking at her proposal?

'What—?' she whispered, giving herself a little shake, then leaning in closer to him. 'Caleb, at least look at the sales projections—'

But he cut her off with a wave of his hand. 'I'm not interested in partnering with you, Elena.' He stood up. 'Now, if you'll excuse me, I have a busy day—'

'Wait!' She raised her hand with all but her pointing finger clenched into a fist so he wouldn't see how sweaty her palm was. 'I haven't given you all the salient details yet,' she said desperately.

'I don't need to hear them; I've already made my decision.'

'But—' She could feel panic rising from her gut. 'Why, Caleb?'

He took a step towards her, his face completely devoid of emotion. 'Because, Elena, I don't do business with people whose word I don't trust.'

She shook her head in disbelief. 'That was a long time ago, Caleb. I can't believe you're still angry with me for that.' Getting shakily to her feet, she took a step towards him. 'Please know I still feel bad about the way I handled it all, but we were both so young and naïve—'

'You were naïve,' he cut in angrily. 'I wasn't. I'd experienced far too much ignorance and cruelty in my life for that to be the case.'

'And you're really still harbouring bad feelings about it? It was fifteen years ago! Surely you've experienced enough happiness in your life now to get over it?' She swallowed down her regret. 'I read that you got engaged last year.'

He batted away her questioning look, his gaze finally slipping from hers. 'It didn't work out.'

Something twisted and tightened in her chest, making it harder for her to breathe. 'I'm sorry to hear that.'

His expression darkened. 'Are you? Since when do you care about my love life?'

'I—' She didn't know how to answer that. The truth was she'd kept tabs on what he'd been up to over the intervening years because, despite the fact their friendship had ended badly, she still cared about him. Not that she thought telling him that right now would do anything to strengthen her case. He'd probably just see it as more weakness.

Caleb used her hesitation to push the knife in deeper.

'How *is*—what was his name?—Johnny, was it? Are the two of you still living your safe, comfortable life together?'

Heat raced to her cheeks. 'His name was Jimmy and, no, we're not together any more. We split up a number of years ago.' Which was yet another painful regret. She still felt guilty about backing away from her and Jimmy's wedding, even though she'd known it was the right thing to do at the time.

The main problem had been that the memories of Caleb had never left her, even though she'd tried her hardest to forget him. He'd stayed with her, buried deep in her heart.

There wasn't a flicker of reaction on Caleb's face at

this news though, not even a twitch of an eye. Clearly he didn't care a jot about her any more. But then, if that was true, why was he being so pig-headed about not listening to her?

Because he was punishing her for hurting him *fifteen* years ago.

Frustration surged through her. 'I can't believe you're still holding a grudge, Caleb. Surely someone of your standing and success has no need to be so small-minded.' She could hear the anger vibrating in her voice and it seemed Caleb did too because he widened his eyes a little before replacing his flash of surprise with an amused smirk.

'Is this the controlled, cautious Elena I knew all those years ago? My, how you've changed.'

'For the better, Caleb. I'm not the naïve young girl you used to know.' She refrained from saying *and love*, knowing that would be taking things a step too far. He'd never said such a thing to her, he'd been too proud for that, though it had been implied in his every action.

Unless she'd read him wrongly.

Which was quite possible.

She'd been wrong about a lot of things.

There was a quiet knock on the glass door and Caleb's PA crept, hunch-shouldered, into the room.

Before she could speak, Caleb let out a growl of frustration and snapped, 'I thought I told you I didn't want to be interrupted!'

Because Caleb had spoken to her in English, and perhaps in deference to Elena's presence there too, his PA replied in English. 'I'm so sorry, but I thought you'd want to know about this straight away. Apparently there's a problem with the meeting with the Americans on Monday. Señor Carter's PA is saying he's having second thoughts—'

Caleb held up a hand to stop her speaking, his gaze flicking momentarily to Elena before returning to his PA, his expression thunderous, as if furious that Elena had been a party to hearing about the setback.

This time he replied in Spanish and, even though Elena didn't understand a word of it, not being a Spanish speaker, she could see that his words had cut his PA deeply when she backed out of the room with tears glinting in her eyes.

'How can you be so cold? So *mean*!' she blurted when he turned back to look at her. 'That poor woman was just doing her job.'

Mouth dry, she reached for the glass of water but when she saw how much her hand was trembling she quickly dropped it to her side again.

'How could you treat her like that, Caleb?'

'Like what?' he growled.

'Like nothing. Less than nothing. I would have thought you'd have made every effort to make sure your subordinates were treated with kindness and respect after what you went through when you were young.'

Anger flickered in his eyes. 'I'm respectful to people when they work hard and make good choices.'

'But people won't learn from their mistakes if you don't nurture them. They become afraid to take necessary risks and everything grinds to a halt.'

'Is that what's happened to your business, Elena?'

he asked quietly. 'Did you drive it into the ground with your inept handling of your staff so you were forced to come here, begging for my help? What a fall from grace that must be for you.'

Hot rage rushed through her body. How could the smart, compassionate man she remembered have become so hard and mean? 'I knew you could be a bit on the curt side, Caleb, but the man I knew was never cruel. Or a bully!'

Shock flashed momentarily across his face before it was replaced with a stony scowl. 'Enough! This meeting is over. I don't need you coming in here, telling me how to treat my staff. Go home and run your own business—' he leant in closer to her so she saw the conviction plainly in his eyes '—without my battery.'

With that closing shot, he turned his back on her and strode out of the room, leaving the glass door swinging in his wake.

Caleb Araya paced the floor of his corner office, his blood pumping frantically through his veins.

Who did Elena Jones think she was, turning up after fifteen years of silence and presuming to tell him how to run his business and treat his staff?

The woman certainly had some nerve.

And a skewed sense of priorities.

Not that he didn't already know that from experience.

To his utter frustration, and despite the fact they hadn't seen each other in a very long time, as soon as he'd seen her standing there in his meeting room he'd been hit hard by that same immediate connection they'd always shared.

It had put him on the back foot.

It had always been like that with her—she affected him like no other woman ever had. The moment he'd met her at the beginning of his Erasmus exchange year to the University of Cambridge he'd found himself drawn to her.

Her cool integrity and assertive sense of self had set her apart from the other immature, entitled female students that had swarmed around him, believing him to be an ideal candidate for the bad boy fling they were so keen to tick off their list before settling down with their rich, boring husbands.

They hadn't bothered to get to know *him* at all.

Elena, on the other hand, had made him feel as if he didn't need to pretend to be somebody he wasn't when he was with her. She'd liked him for his erudite conversation and refreshing views on the world. Or so she'd said.

After growing up as the poor, pitied son of a woman who was infamous in the small town where he lived for being the mistress of a married man and a woman of loose morals, he'd promised himself he'd make sure his adulthood would be very different.

Because of the disgrace that surrounded his family, his early life had been pretty tough by all accounts: friendless, violent and isolated. But after he'd been threatened with expulsion from the elite school that he'd later found, to his chagrin, that his mother's sugar daddy had funded, he'd pulled up his socks and es-

chewed everything and everyone for a life dedicated
to study so he could get away from the small town and
its even smaller mentality.

He was going to be someone that people looked up to
and respected, and Elena had made him feel as though
he'd achieved that—for a short time anyway.

To his shame and regret, it had turned out he'd been
very wrong about how much she'd actually cared about
him and she'd been the first and last person he'd ever
trusted.

The memory of her betrayal had stayed with him
over the years, tarnishing every relationship he'd had, as
if she were a devil on his shoulder, judging his choices,
prodding at his conscience, reminding him he could
never truly trust anyone with his heart.

When he'd seen her name in his diary this morning it
had sent a shock of such intense regret-fuelled nostalgia
through him he'd had to sit down and take a few deep
breaths to regain his composure. He'd been on the cusp
of telling his PA to cancel the meeting, but curiosity
and a deep-seated urge to regain some sort of equilibrium over past hurts had stopped him at the last minute.

He wanted to feel as though he finally had a handle
on his feelings about Elena Jones.

It had been going well, with him feeling in control
of the meeting until she'd caught him out by accusing
him of being a bully.

It had shocked him to his core.

Was that really what she thought he'd become?

It had been such a long time since someone had stood
up to him like that, he had no idea whether his behav-

iour was out of line or not. The thought that it might have been had rattled him. *She'd* rattled him, despite his determination not to let her get to him.

He stabbed at the buzzer on the phone to summon his PA.

Benita hurried into the room, her hands tightly clasped in front of her and her gaze lowered as if she was afraid she'd get another dressing-down for what had just happened.

He'd been furious when she'd let it slip in front of Elena that things weren't exactly going to plan with the Americans. He'd not wanted her to know that things weren't running as smoothly as he'd wanted to project, for the sake of his professional pride, but he was aware, now that he'd calmed down a little, that he'd perhaps been a bit too harsh on the woman. She'd not been working for him for long, having stepped into the role after his usual PA had gone on maternity leave, and they hadn't found the right rhythm for working together yet.

But he wasn't a complete monster, as Elena had so brazenly suggested. He was firm and expected total professionalism at all times, but he made sure to reward those who did a good job for him.

'Benita, I wanted to say good work on putting that file together for me yesterday. It was very helpful in my meeting.'

His PA stared at him, as if in shock.

Surely it wasn't that surprising that he'd offered her a compliment.

Was it?

No. He was letting Elena Jones get into his head and

that was the last place he wanted her to be. He was over his feelings for her. It had taken him years to get rid of the ache he'd carried around after she'd rejected him, but he'd finally managed it.

'Thank you.' Benita paused, a worried frown now pinching her brow. 'Are you okay? Is there anything I can get you?' she asked with hesitation in her voice.

He opened his mouth to dismiss her misplaced concern, annoyed that she'd noticed his agitation, but pulled himself back at the last second, now hyper-aware of Elena's comments.

Damn the woman!

'I'm fine,' he muttered, forcing his mouth into a smile.

But, instead of seeming reassured by this, his PA took a hurried step away from him as if suspicious about his sudden change in attitude.

He sighed and ran a hand through his hair, pacing to the window to look down at the street below and collect himself.

What was happening to him today? His head was a mess.

At least he was free of Elena now though. His outright rejection of her proposal would surely mean she'd never darken his door again.

The street was busy with people milling about between office blocks and cafés and he watched them scurrying around for a moment, his thoughts jumping between relief and dissatisfaction. He knew he'd been petty, not even agreeing to look at the proposal she'd brought all the way from England, but she'd humiliated and hurt him once and he wasn't prepared to let her get anywhere near him again.

A partnership between them—their *companies*, he corrected himself—could never work.

For a second he wondered whether his mind was playing tricks on him as a familiar lone figure on the street opposite his building caught his eye. His stomach lurched as he watched her pace back and forth, then throw her gaze up towards Araya Industries and frown, as if hatching a plan to get back in here and torment him again.

Apparently he couldn't have been more wrong about having chased Elena Jones away for good.

Well, he wasn't having it.

'Hold my calls for a while longer,' he said to his PA as he swept out of the room past her and headed towards the lift that would take him down to street level.

Apparently he hadn't made it clear enough to Elena that there would be no further opportunities to meet with him, so he was going to rectify that right here and now. He was going to tell her to go home and that he wanted nothing more to do with her.

Storming onto the street, blood pulsing feverishly through his veins, he called out her name and she turned to meet his eye, her expression registering first surprise then hope.

Hope away, cariño—*you're not getting a thing from me except a wave goodbye.*

The street was quiet as he drew level with where she stood on the pavement opposite and he glanced quickly left, not seeing anything coming his way, anger at her audacity buzzing in his head.

Elena's eyes were fixed firmly on him as he began to cross the street towards her but, as he stepped into the middle of the road, something made her glance away then quickly back to him again.

This time there was an altogether different expression on her face.

Panic.

Blood thumping in his ears, he swivelled to look at what had spooked her and time seemed to slow down. There was a motorbike coming towards him at speed and he knew in that moment, with absolute certainty, that there was no way he could get out of its path in time.

Memories flashed before his eyes: of him and Elena laughing together after one of their classes at university, of her sitting in his room telling him she was thinking about splitting up with her childhood sweetheart, and all the blood rushing from his head as he realised he finally had a chance to have what he'd wanted for so long, of the look of abject hurt and distress on her face just now when he'd told her he wouldn't partner with her.

Lights and colours danced before his eyes and a strange kind of euphoria lifted his senses, making his surroundings hyper-loud and vividly real.

And then the bike hit him, the impact throwing his body into the air, knocking all the breath from his lungs. In a panic he flailed his limbs wildly as he tried to grab hold of something, anything, to anchor him as he spun through the void. A moment later his body made rough, painful impact with the ground, quickly followed by his head.

And everything went black.

CHAPTER TWO

ELENA STOOD IN SHOCK, her arms still outstretched as if she'd thought she could do something, some kind of magic perhaps, to stop Caleb from being hit by the motorbike that had sped round the corner just as he'd stepped into its path.

She felt light-headed and displaced from reality, as if this was all some horrible dream—though the heavy thump of her heart in her throat and the adrenaline that roared through her body told her otherwise.

The rider was picking himself up from the ground after coming off his bike and miraculously seemed not to be injured in any way, but Caleb's slumped body, which had been flung at least ten feet, was still lying half on the pavement and half on the road. And he wasn't moving.

A cacophony of noise suddenly rushed in on her as people began running towards where Caleb lay, finally shocking Elena out of her dazed state. She stumbled towards him, falling to her knees by his side, barely registering the rough ground biting into her skin, and put her shaking hand onto his torso. His eyes were closed, but she could feel his chest rising and falling with his breathing.

So he was still alive. *Thank God.*

She could feel tears pressing at the back of her eyes but she blinked them away, determined to keep it together for his sake.

'Caleb? Can you hear me?' she whispered, leaning in closer to him and breathing in the distinctive scent of him that had haunted her throughout the years, usually at the most inopportune moments.

Somebody—a woman—asked her a question in Spanish and Elena shook her head, mouthing back ineffectually, totally unable to summon even the basic Spanish phrase for *I don't understand.*

The woman frowned, then asked, 'Are you English?'

Was it that obvious?

Judging by the fact she was wearing a highly inappropriate woollen suit for the weather and had skin so light it was almost translucent, she guessed it must be.

'Yes!' Elena said, relief flooding through her that the woman would be able to help her. 'I don't speak Spanish.' She swallowed hard. 'I need to call an ambulance. Can you help me?'

'Don't worry,' the woman said, gesturing behind her. 'My husband has already called them.'

Caleb let out a low groan and Elena swivelled back to look at him, her heart leaping with relief. 'Caleb? Are you okay? I'm so sorry—this is all my fault.'

At least it felt like it was her fault, even though rationally she knew it had been an accident. But it was also another thing for him to hold against her.

She should have left this area and gone to regroup somewhere else—to give Caleb a chance to calm down—then come back again once her head was clear and her plan fully formed, instead of pacing about in front of his building like a lunatic. He must have seen her prowling around out here and decided to come out to ask her what the hell she thought she was doing.

When she'd heard him call her name from across the street her first thought had been that he'd changed his mind and decided to listen to her after all and her heart had leapt with excitement and relief. But as he'd crossed the street and she'd seen the look of frustrated fury in his eyes it had become powerfully obvious that she'd been very wrong to suppose that.

He hadn't wanted to turn back the clock. He'd wanted her gone.

The woman laid a hand gently onto her back, dragging her out of her distraught reflection. 'He'll be okay, don't worry. The ambulance is on its way.'

Elena nodded gratefully, this time unable to stop tears from welling in her eyes. 'He was crossing the road to meet me and didn't see the bike.'

'It's okay. Not your fault,' the woman said in a soothing tone, rubbing Elena's arm in sympathy.

If only that were true. She already felt guilty enough about the anguish she'd caused Caleb in the past and now she'd hurt him again, only physically this time. He never would have been out here if it wasn't for her.

A moment later the sound of a siren broke through the low murmurs of the crowd that had gathered around them and an ambulance sped round the corner and parked up nearby, its flashing lights bouncing off the windows of the buildings opposite.

The paramedics jumped out of the cab and ran towards where Caleb lay, pushing their way through the large group of bystanders that had gathered to ogle the drama playing out in front of them.

The helpful woman disappeared from Elena's side as the paramedics came to kneel next to Caleb and check his vital signs. The female paramedic turned to ask Elena a question in Spanish, indicating towards Caleb, and Elena guessed she must be asking whether she knew him.

Novia meant friend, didn't it? It sounded like a friendly kind of word.

'*Sí, sí!*' she said, her voice sounding shaky and weak from shock. The woman nodded and gave her a reassuring smile, then turned back to help her colleague tend to the now silent and deathly still Caleb.

A short while later he was lifted onto a stretcher wearing a neck brace, then into the back of the ambulance.

Elena stood there stupidly, watching as they secured the straps to keep the makeshift bed from rolling around in the back of the vehicle, her chest tight with worry.

What if he died?

No. She couldn't think like that. He'd be fine. The paramedics weren't rushing around shouting and wielding scary-looking equipment as if they were worried that he was in grave danger. Mercifully, there was hardly any blood on the ground where he'd lain, just a little from where he'd cut his temple.

Perhaps he'd just been knocked out and not badly hurt. Just a bit bruised and battered.

Please.

Please.

Elena didn't realise the female paramedic had said something to her until the woman waved a hand in front of her face and spoke again, her expression registering sympathy. 'You come. To hospital.'

Elena nodded dumbly, not entirely sure it was appropriate that she should be the one to go with Caleb, but no one from his company had rushed out to be here with him. It looked as though the paramedics wanted to get him straight to hospital now so there wasn't time to go into his building and find someone.

She should just go with him and call his office from there to let them know what was going on. Then she'd leave him be and go back to the hotel to get her head together.

One thing was for sure, going to pieces was not going to help anyone right now.

Mind made up, she gave the paramedic a wobbly smile and climbed into the back of the ambulance.

There was something wrong with the light in his bedroom, Caleb thought fuzzily as he woke up from a deep, dreamless sleep. And his cleaning lady seemed to have used a different kind of product than usual because he didn't recognise the smell in here either.

'Ah, you're awake,' came a voice from somewhere to his left and he wondered wildly who he'd gone to bed with the night before.

He couldn't remember.

In fact, now he thought about it, he found his mind was strangely blank, as if it had been wiped of details. How much had he drunk last night to wake up in this state? It must have been a lot because he had the unsettling feeling that he wasn't at home at all. In fact, he realised with a lurch as his vision cleared, he had no idea where he was or how he'd got here. The walls were painted an institutional green colour and were disturbingly free of any kind of decoration. Turning his head, he saw with a shock that he was lying next to some kind of flashing, beeping, monitoring machine with wires and drips hanging from it.

Which were attached to him.

He tried to sit up and felt his whole body complain, pain shooting through his abdomen.

'No, no, don't try and get up. You had an accident and you've cracked a rib and banged your head so you may feel dizzy and disorientated for a while.'

'An accident?' he asked, shocked by how rough and raspy his voice sounded. His throat was so dry it felt as if he hadn't had a drink in days.

'Here,' the voice said and he turned towards where it came from to see a middle-aged woman in a crisp white uniform standing next to the bed where he lay, pushing a straw towards his mouth.

He sipped gratefully from the drink, feeling the cool liquid soothe his throat and begin to refresh him.

'Your girlfriend's very worried about you,' the nurse said, taking the cup away once he'd finished and putting it on the nightstand next to his bed. 'She saw you get hit by the motorbike and is blaming herself for the accident because you were crossing the road to see her when it happened, so be nice to her when she comes in to see you.'

'My girlfriend?' He didn't remember having a girl-friend.

His heart began to race as panic swept through him, nausea welling in his stomach as the room started to slowly spin. He shook his head, trying to clear the feel-ing, determined not to give in to it.

He didn't do panic, dammit.

Not appearing to notice his disorientation, the nurse helped him sit up a little so she could fluff up his pil-low and he gripped the rail at the side of the bed hard, racking his brain for the memory of how he came to be here in an attempt to centre himself. The nurse had said a motorbike had hit him but he had absolutely no recollection of it.

How could he not remember something so serious?

'I think she needs a hug and some reassurance that you don't hate her,' she said, smiling at him. 'Judging by the way she's been pacing the halls and badgering us every ten minutes for updates on your condition, she obviously cares about you very much. You're a lucky man to have someone who loves you like that.'

He just nodded, not wanting to let on that he had no idea who she was talking about, or that he was becom-ing more and more aware of other rather worrying gaps in his memory. He knew his name and that he owned a company called Araya Industries, which he'd built up from scratch, and that he lived in the L'Eixample district of Barcelona. He even knew what the inside of his penthouse looked like, but things like where he grew up and who his friends were seemed to have escaped him. And he definitely didn't remember being hit by the motorbike. The last thing he did remember was getting into work this morning and turning on his computer, but after that it was all a blank.

This disjoin in his memory made him feel sick if he thought about it too much, so he decided to put it out of his head for now. It would all come back after he'd been awake for a while and had got his bearings again. And he didn't want any fuss; he just wanted to get out of here, back to his home. Maybe once in familiar surroundings his mind would catch up with everything else.

'I'll let her know you're awake so she can come in and see you,' the nurse said, coming over to him and smoothing down the sheet that was covering him up to his armpits. It seemed they'd stripped him of the rest of his clothes, perhaps to check him over for injuries.

'Who?' he asked distractedly, still trying to get a handle on the anxiety that stubbornly surged through his body.

'Your girlfriend, Elena.' The nurse frowned, as if beginning to suspect that all was not entirely well with him.

He shot her a quick smile and said, 'Okay, good, I'd like to see her.'

Perhaps as soon as he saw this Elena he'd recognise her right away and the rest of his memory would come flooding back with it.

The nurse nodded curtly, clearly still a little suspicious about his well-being, but then turned and left the room.

A moment later there was a tentative knock at the door. He sat up a little straighter in bed and called, 'Come in.'

A woman with ice-blue eyes and long blonde hair hanging loosely around her slim shoulders entered the room and walked towards him, coming to a stop a couple of feet away from the bed. Her movements appeared graceful and controlled, but he could see from her strained smile that she was tense and worried.

Something about her shot a bolt of intense sensation through him, almost like déjà vu, though he could have sworn he'd never set eyes on her before in his life. He had vague memories of relationships with other women, beautiful, smart women, but there was something about Elena, something almost untouchable, that unnerved him. Or was that just his addled brain playing tricks on him? He'd obviously banged his head pretty hard if he'd forgotten he was having a relationship with a woman as attractive as this.

'How are you feeling?' she asked in English, which for some reason seemed absolutely right and totally expected.

'I'm okay—a bit banged up, but I'll live,' he said, patting a space on the bed next to him, wanting her to come nearer so he could study her closer. He had the strangest feeling that if he touched her he'd feel more grounded.

She looked at him warily for a moment then visibly

swallowed before stepping up to perch on the edge of the mattress, as if worried about getting too close and knocking him and causing him pain.

Desire shot through him as the scent of her perfume hit his senses and he closed his eyes for a moment, feeling another wave of déjà vu sweep through him.

Come on brain, catch up.

'It's good to see you awake. I was really worried about you,' she said, her voice sounding a little croaky.

'You're trembling,' he murmured, reaching out to touch her arm, feeling her practically vibrating under his fingertips.

'I wasn't sure what to expect when I came in here,' she said, her gaze darting away from his face to look down at where his tanned hand rested on her pale skin.

'Well, you don't need to worry. I'm fine,' he stated vehemently, hoping to reassure her—and perhaps himself a little too—though, judging by the tremble in her bottom lip, it didn't appear to have worked.

He *was* fine though, he told himself hazily, just a bit disorientated…that was all. Just because the sight of her hadn't brought his memory back, it didn't mean it was gone for good.

Perhaps if he kissed her, it would spark something in his brain.

She certainly looked as though she could do with some proof that he was still the man she knew and cared about. What was it the nurse had said? That she blamed herself for the accident because he'd been crossing the road to see her at the time? Was that the problem here—was she worried he was angry with her?

'Come closer,' he said, moving his hand up to slide his fingers under her jaw, feeling a strong urge to wipe the concern from her beautiful face now.

She stilled under his touch and her eyes widened as if she was surprised by what he was doing.

'Stop worrying,' he murmured, then drew her towards him and pressed his mouth firmly to hers.

She sucked in a startled-sounding breath but he paid it no mind, pulling her closer to him, ignoring the twinge of pain this caused in his damaged rib and hoping against hope that this would make everything right again.

Her mouth felt wonderful against his but he was blurrily aware that the kiss wasn't having the effect he'd hoped for. Determined not to give up that easily, he opened his lips and slipped his tongue into the heat of her mouth. As he'd suspected, she tasted incredible, like honey and harmony and sex...

And then his brain seemed to switch gear and suddenly he couldn't get enough of her. It was like having that first drink of water all over again, his body reacting with a forceful relief that shook him to his very soul. Her full mouth was soft but not as pliant as he would have liked, so he kissed her harder, feeling the pulse in her neck racing against the heel of his hand where he cupped her jaw.

A deep growl rumbled in the back of his throat as he began to lose control of his restraint and she let out a breathy moan in reply and dug her nails into the flesh of his upper arms.

He sank into the possessiveness of her grip, lost in

the sensual taste of her, feeling the strangest mixture of comfort and desire and relief—until he suddenly became aware that she was trying to pull away from him.

Reluctantly, he slid his hands away from her jaw and let her go.

'What's wrong?' he ground out, frustrated that she'd cut the kiss short when he'd been enjoying it so much.

It had been the first time he'd felt anything like himself since he'd woken up here.

Her eyes were wide and her expression a little wild. 'Why did you kiss me?' Almost absent-mindedly, she brushed her fingers against her lips and his body reacted with such erotic force he very nearly dragged her back to him again for another round.

But the look in her eyes stopped him.

He could see now that she was shaken by the kiss and not because she'd enjoyed it as much as he had.

'Why shouldn't I kiss you?' he demanded, feeling panic begin to work its way back under his skin again.

She blinked at him, looking utterly bewildered, her cheeks flushed with colour and her brow creased. 'Because of what happened this morning. We had a row.'

He frowned, his mind spinning with confusion. 'You mean before the accident? Look, I'm sure that wasn't your fault; I can't have been looking where I was going.'

Getting up from the bed, she took a step away from him, crossing her arms and frowning hard as if she didn't understand what she was hearing. 'Caleb, don't you remember what happened?'

He wanted to say yes, that he remembered everything, but he knew, with a slow sinking feeling of dread, that there was actually something very, very wrong here.

Throwing up his hands in frustration, he said, 'No! Okay! I don't remember!'

She flinched in surprise, then stared at him in horror, her mouth forming a perfect O shape.

Closing his eyes, he attempted to pull his focus back and took a long, deep breath. Fighting to keep his voice steady this time, he said, 'The truth is my memory's been a little fuzzy since I woke up.' He ran a hand over his face then looked up at her. 'I don't remember anything between getting to work this morning and waking up in the hospital and anything before my life here in Barcelona is a little difficult to pin down—'

She was still staring at him in dismay. 'Oh, no, Caleb. That's not good.'

He flapped a hand dismissively, hating the idea of her pitying him. 'It's fine; it'll come back to me soon. It's probably just the drugs messing with my head.'

Taking a step closer to him, she said with a shake in her voice, 'Caleb, do you remember who I am?'

'Yes, you're Elena, my girlfriend,' he said airily, hoping it sounded more convincing to her than it did to him.

Her eyes grew comically wide. 'What makes you think I'm your girlfriend?'

Confusion swirled through his head again. 'Because… I thought…' He paused and frowned. 'The nurse told me you were, and I *know* I know you. You're very familiar to me.'

Elena shifted on the spot, looking uncomfortable now. 'I don't speak Spanish so I must have misinterpreted the paramedic's question when she asked me about my relationship to you,' she muttered to herself, staring down at the floor. 'Or perhaps the nurse got the wrong end of the stick or something.' She looked up at him again, her brow pinched into a frown. 'Anyway, however it happened, I'm not your girlfriend.'

He looked at her for a moment and got the distinct impression there was more to this than she was telling him.

'So we're what?' he asked slowly, one eyebrow raised. 'Just friends?'

Elena knew that lying to Caleb was the last thing she should do right now but she didn't want to add any unnecessary stress to the situation, not when he'd only just woken up from an accident with a head injury and seemed to be rather confused.

And the thing was, they *had* been friends once, very good friends, and if she had any say in the matter she'd make sure they got past their differences to become friends again.

But that would be all. Just friends.

Even though the kiss they'd just shared had rocked her world. Her whole body still buzzed from the after-effects of the feel of his firm mouth on hers—her pulse jumping in her throat and her nerves on fire with a wild, almost frightening demand for more that she'd not felt the like of in years.

Not since the last time he'd kissed her.

'Uh-huh. We haven't seen each other for a long time though. We knew each other at university.' She waited for him to recall the fact that they weren't exactly friends any more but his expression remained blank. It seemed he really didn't remember her.

'I'm just visiting from England for a few days and dropped in to see you,' she added, wondering if that would help jog his memory, but it didn't appear to. He was looking at her with such an intense expression in his eyes now, as if he was thinking about kissing her again, that she had to drag her gaze away and look down instead at the sheet that was tucked up against his rather impressive bare chest. She tried not to stare too hard at it, or at the dark bruises marking his skin. Apart from those, he was in really good shape, his limbs strong and muscled, his torso toned and hard.

Stop gawping, you fool!

'I'm sorry if I've made you feel awkward,' Caleb said, frowning and shaking his head, then closing one eye and squinting as if the movement had caused him great pain.

She went to put out a hand to touch him, then withdrew it. 'Is your head hurting?'

'Like crazy.'

'I'll get the doctor.'

She started to walk away, then paused and turned back to face him. 'Is there someone else you want me to call to be here with you?'

He looked at her in surprise, before frowning. 'No, I don't think so. To be honest, I can't think of who I would call.' He looked so uncomfortable she couldn't help but feel a rush of sympathy for him.

She was just about to offer to stay until they were

able to contact a friend in Barcelona for him when his expression cleared and he said, 'Could you ring my office and ask my PA to come here?'

'I've already called her,' she told him. 'She's on her way over. I asked her who your emergency contact is but she wasn't sure. Apparently she hasn't been working for you for long.'

'No. My regular PA has just had a baby.'

'It's not yours, is it?' she quipped, then regretted it when she saw a look of panic flash across his face.

'I'm just joking, Caleb. Sorry, that was tasteless of me considering your state of mind at the moment.' She squeezed her eyes shut and wrinkled her nose. 'I'm still a little shaken up after what just happened.'

But, instead of giving her a piece of his mind, he gave her a slow, wry smile instead, like the ones he used to give her back when they were friends. It was such an incredible sight and something she'd not seen for such a long time it stopped her in her tracks.

'I'll…er…go and find a doctor,' she said hurriedly, swallowing down the lump that had formed in her throat.

Turning away, she strode out of the room on rather shaky legs, relieved to be able to get away from his befuddling presence for a moment so she could figure out how the heck she was going to handle this situation from this point on.

Just as she reached the nurses' station Caleb's PA hurried around the corner and, spotting her, gave a little wave of recognition.

'Benita, thank you for coming,' Elena said as the

woman came to a breathless halt in front of her. 'Caleb's okay, but he's banged his head and is having trouble re-membering which friend to call to come and look after him. Has he mentioned anyone to you that he's close to?' she asked.

Benita shook her head, biting her lip and looking a little anxious. 'I've only been working for him for a few days and he never talks about anything of a personal nature. I checked his computer and his work mobile— which he'd left on his desk,' she added a little defen-sively, as if Elena might accuse her of snooping, 'but there was no one obvious I should call.' Turning away, she began rifling through her bag, her movements be-coming increasingly desperate as she failed to locate what she was looking for. '*Caramba!* I forgot to put his phone in here.'

Elena put a steadying hand onto the woman's arm. 'It's okay. He's in no state to be using his phone right now anyway. In fact, it's probably better if he doesn't have it right away. Less stress.'

She nodded, though the expression in her eyes re-flected her worry. 'I'll drop it round to his apartment later.'

'I'm sure that would be fine,' Elena said in an at-tempt to soothe the poor woman.

Sighing, Benita shook her head. 'Carla would never have forgotten it.'

That gave Elena an idea. 'Hey, would Carla know of a friend of his to contact?' she asked hopefully.

Benita shook her head again. 'I called her but she said the same thing. He never gave away much personal information about himself. He had a few girlfriends over the time she worked for him but she never met any of them and he's not seeing anyone now, as far as she knows. He doesn't have any family left either, now his mother's passed away.'

Elena experienced a pang of sorrow on his behalf. She knew from their time at university that he'd always been a bit of a loner and that his mother had been his only family, not that they'd been particularly close. He'd been angry with her for continuing to have a long-term relationship with a married man. He didn't know who his father was either; his mother had refused to tell him, saying he was just a man she'd met in a bar one night. Unfortunately for Caleb, that had been a well chewed over piece of gossip in the town where he'd grown up, which had followed him round like a bad smell.

It was really no wonder he was so keen to keep his private life private these days.

'When did his mother pass away?' she asked.

'About six months ago, I think. Carla mentioned something about it because he'd actually taken some time off work for once to be with her in the hospice. It was cancer, apparently, that took her.'

The two women stood quietly for a moment, reflecting on this.

'Well, I'd better get back to the office now I know he's okay,' Benita said suddenly, smiling, as if Elena's presence there had released her from her own duties to Caleb. 'I'll let the other managers know what's happened and that he won't be in work for the rest of the week. Please tell him everything's under control. I know he'll worry otherwise.'

'Don't you want to go in and see him?' Elena asked, a little shocked by the woman's intention to withdraw without even saying hello to Caleb.

Benita shook her head, taking a step backwards. 'No, no. Just tell him I hope he feels better soon.'

'Well, perhaps someone else from work could come over and sort out who can look after him—' Elena said rather desperately, but Benita was backing away now, clearly keen to get out of there and return to the sanctuary of a Caleb-free office.

'I doubt anyone there will know any more than me,' she said, giving one last tight smile, then turning and rushing away.

Sighing, Elena rubbed a hand over her face, her insides sinking with a mixture of sadness for Caleb at his apparent lack of close friendships and nerves about exactly what she'd got herself into here.

The sad fact was, it looked as though the only person available to take care of him right now was her.

As she thought about this a crazy idea began to form in her head and her stomach gave a nervous little flip. Maybe if she could show him she was happy to be here for him, and prepared to help in any way she could, it might go some way towards rebuilding their friendship— without the prejudice and anger he seemed to be holding on to from the past getting in the way—and help her reconnect with the man she knew was in there, hiding behind that hard shell she'd seen earlier. Otherwise, once his memory came back she might never have the opportunity to speak to him again, especially when he remembered why he'd been crossing that road, but if she could be a good friend to him now and prove how much she cared about him, perhaps he'd think twice before pushing her away again.

It was worth a try.

Anything was worth a try at this point.

But if she did stay to look after him there would be no more kissing, she told herself firmly, setting back her shoulders and heading towards the desk to ask the staff there to contact his doctor.

Definitely not.

CHAPTER THREE

THE MEMORY OF Elena's captivating ice-blue eyes and her long slender legs with their dirty, scuffed up knees remained stubbornly imprinted in Caleb's mind as he lay back in bed and waited impatiently for her to return.

Just friends, huh? What on earth had stopped him from pursuing more than friendship with her? He'd very much like to know that. He found her intensely attractive and she was clearly a smart, compassionate person—qualities he valued highly.

An English rose.

The phrase floated into his mind. Yes, that summed her up perfectly.

A moment later the door opened and she strode back into the room with a tall dark-haired woman following closely behind her.

'Sorry I was away for so long; I bumped into your PA out there—she said to tell you she hopes you feel better soon and that she's got everything under control at work so you can rest without worrying—and then it took me a while to locate your doctor.' She gestured towards the woman she'd entered with.

'Señor Araya,' the doctor said, walking over to his bed and picking up the clipboard that hung at the end of it, 'how are you feeling?' She scanned the paperwork quickly before replacing the clipboard.

'I feel fine,' he said confidently. He didn't want to give her any reason to keep him here unnecessarily. He was uncomfortable with being in hospital; it made him feel vulnerable and edgy for some reason. He'd be much better off in his own home with his things around him. Maybe then his memory would come back.

The doctor pressed her lips together. 'So it seems you have a cracked rib and a bump on your head, but apart from that you got off pretty lightly, considering you were hit by a motorbike travelling at speed.'

'Can you speak English so Elena can understand?' he snapped, riled by the doctor's officious manner and not wanting Elena to feel ignored when she'd been good enough to stay and check on him. Unlike his PA.

'Yes, of course,' the doctor said, switching easily to English and giving Elena an indulgent smile before turning back to fix her scrutinising gaze on him again.

'I'd like you to stay here tonight. Head injuries can be serious and I'd like to keep you under observation for a while longer to make sure you're okay.'

The thought of staying here any longer filled him with a sinking dread. 'No,' he stated firmly. 'I want to go home. Now.'

'I don't think that's advisable—' the doctor began, a concerned frown pinching her brow.

'I feel fine. I don't want to take up a bed unnecessarily when someone who's really sick could use it. I'll be okay at home,' Caleb said gruffly. He wasn't used to people telling him what he could and couldn't do and it rankled.

'I really don't think—'

'I don't care what you think. I'm going home,' he said, levering himself up and readying himself to swing his legs out of bed.

The only way he was staying here was if they called Security and tied him down.

The doctor sighed as if she'd seen this scenario before and knew there was no way to stop someone like this once they'd made up their mind.

'I can't prevent you from leaving, Señor Araya, but I must insist you don't go home on your own,' she said sternly. 'You'll need someone responsible there to keep an eye on you in case there are any after-effects from the head injury. The CAT scan we gave you didn't show up anything worrying, but it's better to be safe.'

Frustration rattled through him. He just wanted to be at home now, without people fussing over him any more.

'I'll be fine. I can call my GP if I start to feel ill,' he bit out.

The doctor shook her head. 'That's not good enough. You need someone there with you full-time for the next forty-eight hours at least.'

Elena must have sensed his unease because she stepped forwards and said, 'I can stay with him, at his home.'

The doctor studied her for a moment. 'Are you his partner?'

There was an infinitesimal pause before Elena said, 'Yes.'

He glanced at her in surprise but she didn't turn to catch his eye, just kept her steady, confident gaze trained on the doctor.

The doctor nodded, seeming to decide that Elena was a sensible and trustworthy sort of person.

He could see why. She certainly gave that impression. Caleb really liked that about her. She was no-nonsense, just the kind of person he liked to have around. He couldn't do with women who simpered and flapped about ineffectually. Having her at home with him for a short while would be fine by him. It might even give him more time to try and figure out the real state of their relationship. He was positive there had to be more to it than 'just friends', as she'd claimed.

Turning back to Caleb now and fixing him with a steely stare, the doctor asked, 'Have you been sick since you woke up or had any dizziness? Any memory loss?'

Out of the corner of his eye he saw Elena stiffen and waited for her to tell the doctor about his elusive memory, preparing himself for a fight, but when he turned to look directly at her she just gazed back at him with those bright, intelligent eyes of hers, her mouth firmly shut. A strange kind of unspoken agreement seemed to pass between them and he realised she was letting him know that she was on his side.

She wasn't going to give him up.

Well, that proved something at least; she must care about him if she was willing to twist the truth to help him get out of here. The thought warmed him.

'No, I feel fine,' he said, tearing his gaze away from her to look at the doctor again, feeling the weight of anxiety begin to lift from his chest.

The doctor nodded, apparently convinced that he was telling the truth. 'Okay then, I'll go and fill out the paperwork. You'll need to come in next week for further tests though, Señor Araya, to make sure we haven't missed anything.'

Caleb nodded but didn't say anything. He'd deal with all that later. He just wanted to get out of here now.

'I'll let you get dressed then. Your clothes and personal effects will be in the cupboard at the side of your bed,' the doctor said, moving towards the door. 'You might need a bit of help getting dressed because of the pain in your rib. I can call a nurse if you like,' she said, turning back with an expectant look on her face.

'I don't need a nurse,' he said dismissively.

'I can help him if he needs me to,' Elena chimed in, throwing him a chiding look.

The doctor just nodded briskly.

'Thank you, Doctor,' Elena added, giving the woman a warm smile.

Once the doctor had left the room, Elena busied herself by pulling all his things out of the bedside cabinet and laying them out on the bed. Picking up his shirt, she looked at it with her nose wrinkled. 'I'm afraid there's some blood on this from where you cut your head.'

'I don't care about that. Pass it to me, will you,' he said, reaching out for the clothing and wincing as his cracked rib made itself known.

She batted his hand away, frowning. 'I'll do it. If you can just sit up a bit more—'

Ignoring his huff of frustration, she put one hand carefully behind each shoulder and pulled gently, forcing him to sit up enough so she could slip the shirt around his back and hold it out for him to slide his arms into the sleeves.

Her hands had been cool and the sensation of her skin on his hot flesh lingered there while she leant in to do the buttons up for him.

Her nearness made him want to pull her in for another kiss but, despite his still rather woolly-headed state, he was aware that it would be a highly inappropriate thing to do.

He growled with irritation, hating how weak and vulnerable he must appear to her right now. 'This is ridiculous. I'm not a child. I can do my own buttons up!'

A small smile lifted the corners of her mouth and she raised an eyebrow at him. 'Stop being so proud and let me help. If you won't let me take care of you I'm going to have to tell the doctor that I can't go home with you after all and you'll have to stay in the hospital with the nurses fussing around you instead.'

He let out a harrumphing noise, but let her do the rest of the buttons up. Despite feeling annoyed that she was using his injuries against him, he was impressed that she hadn't been upset by his shortness and obviously wasn't about to let it put her off coming home with him.

Most women would have let him have his way and backed off, but it seemed that Elena wasn't most women.

He drew the line though when she tried to help him

get out of bed and firmly batted her outstretched hand away as he swung his legs out. He pulled on his suit trousers over the boxers he was mercifully still wearing, managing after a moment or two of pained fumbling to pull the zip up and hook the fastener, then sat for a moment to catch his breath.

'Is this your address?' Elena asked as he slowly levered himself up off the bed, fighting back a wave of nausea as he stood up and felt a heavy weight of darkness pressing down on his head.

He must have moved too quickly.

Blinking hard to clear his vision, he stared at the driving licence she was holding up, which was sandwiched behind a clear plastic window in his wallet.

'That's it,' he said, taking a long breath to steady himself.

'Okay, I'll go and arrange for a taxi to take us home,' she said, giving him a pointed glance that said, *Take it easy until I get back.*

He got the distinct feeling that this was only the beginning of his time being ordered around by this woman.

To his surprise, he found he didn't entirely hate the idea.

The cab drew up in front of the building where Caleb lived and Elena swallowed hard, her stomach doing a slow somersault now they'd reached their destination.

It had been fine in the hospital while she was distracted by the practical aspects of getting Caleb home, but now they were finally here, and were going to be totally alone for the first time since the disastrous meeting this morning—where she'd had a worrying amount of trouble keeping her emotions under wraps—she was beginning to regret her rash promise to look after him for the next couple of days.

She was determined to follow it through though—because she owed him. If it hadn't been for her he never would have had the accident in the first place.

The moment she'd sensed how determined he was to get out of hospital she'd made a snap decision. Not calling out his lie to the doctor about his memory being sound had almost been a step too far for her, but she'd told herself that if she stuck with him around the clock she'd be able to alert the doctors the moment he seemed to be even vaguely struggling. In the busy hospital he could have been left alone for long periods of time, but here in his house she'd be there to keep an eye on him every second of the day.

Unless he suddenly remembered that he hated her and sent her away, of course.

Her stomach did another sickening flip.

If that happened he'd be left alone in his apartment without anyone there to look out for him. And what if he passed out or fell and hurt himself once she'd gone?

She took a steadying breath then blew it out towards the sky, imagining it was her fears she was expelling as they exploded into a million pieces in her mind.

No. She wasn't going to worry about that right now. Hopefully, if he did remember what had happened between them, the fact that she'd helped bail him out of hospital and offered to stick around to take care of him

would at least make him pause before chucking her out.
If she was really lucky, her presence here might even
prove to him that she was genuinely sorry for what had
happened in the past and that she was serious about
wanting to make amends for hurting him.

That she still cared about him.

Not that she'd ever really stopped, even when she'd
pushed him away.

'Elena?' Caleb said beside her and she could tell
from the tone of his voice that he was wondering what
the heck she was doing, still sitting here like a lemon
when they'd reached their destination.

'Are you sure you want to come in with me?' he
asked brusquely. 'You don't have to, you know. I can
take care of myself from here.'

She turned to fix him with a stern glare. 'No, you
can't, Caleb; you heard what the doctor said. You need
someone around, especially if you're still feeling a bit
confused.'

He shrugged as if it was neither here nor there to him
whether she stayed or not, but she could have sworn she
saw a flash of a smile in his eyes.

'Okay, let's go,' she said, opening the cab door and
telling herself that the best thing all round was just to
take one step at a time and deal with any consequences
as and when they came.

Caleb's penthouse apartment was breathtaking, and
exactly the sort of place she would have expected him
to choose to live. Light poured in through the large
warehouse-style windows, bathing the stylish but
comfortable-looking furniture in soft spring sunlight.

The colours he'd chosen to furnish the place were earthy and muted in a warm and comforting way, with terra-cotta tiles on the floor and dark tan leather and stained wood sofas and tables gathered in the middle of the vast space. It was a really restful room to be in and Elena let out a breath as she felt herself relax a little.

She was still acutely aware that she was here under false pretences, but she reassured herself that this was about making sure Caleb was safe and cared for; it had nothing whatsoever to do with her trying to persuade him to listen to her business proposal. She'd deal with all that once he was fully well again. There was no way she'd take advantage of his lapse in memory.

She was here as his friend, nothing more.

His only friend, by the sounds of it.

Judging by the fact he didn't have anyone obvious to call upon when he was in the hospital, she guessed she wasn't the only one he'd kept at arm's length.

The thought of how alone he was made sorrow well heavily in her gut.

She knew she should have sought him out before now. She'd wanted to, had for years, but she'd never quite plucked up the courage to face him again—until it had been absolutely essential. That made her a coward, she knew that, but she'd always been afraid of how out of control Caleb made her feel and she'd needed every ounce of strength over the intervening years to build a successful career for herself. It wasn't easy being a woman in a male-dominated arena.

At least that was what she was telling herself.

The passion of his kiss earlier came back to haunt

her as he walked past her into the living area and she caught the unique scent of him in the air.

Moving quickly away from him, she marched into the kitchen diner at the other end of the large room, aware that her heart was racing, and pretended to be admiring the high-tech gadgets he had in there to give herself a moment to pull herself together.

'Can I make you something to eat? Or drink?' she asked, turning back to look at him. He was standing by the largest sofa, watching her with a perplexed sort of frown.

'You don't need to mollycoddle me, Elena—I can fix my own food. In fact, I should be cooking for you to say thanks for bailing me out at the hospital.'

She held up a hand. 'Not a chance. Unless your cooking skills have improved since university?' she said with a slow grin.

He threw her a look of mock offence. 'Was it that bad?' He frowned. 'I don't remember.'

'It was passable,' she said, her mouth still twitching with mirth at the memory of it.

In truth, it had been terrible. The one time he'd cooked for her, when she'd gone over to his place to study for an exam, she'd pulled such a face after the first mouthful that Caleb had scraped the lot into the bin and called for takeout pizza instead.

'Well, like I said earlier, you don't have to stay here with me; I'll be fine,' he said, sitting down carefully on the sofa and wincing a little as his rib appeared to give him trouble.

She folded her arms. 'Like *I* said, there's no way I'm leaving you alone.'

She'd always stood up to him like this, refusing to be intimidated by his gruff demeanour, but deep down his dominating personality had twisted her into knots, threatening her carefully constructed cool.

Fifteen years ago he'd made her question everything she'd thought she wanted in a man. He was bold and charismatic, but he also seemed exactly the sort to smash her heart to pieces should things go wrong between them. At the time she wasn't prepared to put herself in danger of that happening, not after working so hard to get into her first choice of university and make her first move towards the kind of life she'd always dreamed of building for herself.

But she hadn't been able to stay away from him.

Struggling to keep her feelings under control, she'd found the safest thing had been to pretend that they didn't exist. It had been the only way to protect herself.

Except that somewhere along the line that had stopped working.

Caleb could sense that Elena wasn't altogether comfortable being here in his apartment with him and he wondered again what it was she wasn't telling him.

'If you're worried about where you're going to sleep, you're welcome to take one of the guest rooms.' He pointed towards a door that led to the corridor of four bedrooms.

'Okay, thank you,' she said a little distractedly.

'Is there somewhere else you need to be today?' he

asked, concerned now that he was keeping her from something important. The last thing he wanted was to be a burden to her.

'No, nowhere,' she answered, coming to sit down on an armchair opposite where he sat, finally giving him her full attention.

A sense of relief took him by surprise. He was still feeling pretty woozy and disorientated and it was soothing to know she'd be staying there with him for a while. Even if she did feel like a total stranger to him at the moment.

'So, *friend*, I guess I need to get to know you all over again. Do you have a partner? Husband? Boyfriend in England?' he asked.

She recoiled a little, as if the question had caught her by surprise. 'Not at the moment. I've been too busy recently with work to hold down a serious relationship.'

'When you say recently—?'

She flashed him a self-conscious smile. 'For the last few years.'

'You haven't had a serious relationship for a *few years*?'

She shrugged as she smoothed her hands down the sides of her skirt. 'I've dated, but I've not clicked with anyone.'

'I find that hard to believe.'

The air between them seemed to throb with tension and she gave him a strained smile, then glanced away.

He was making her uncomfortable. But why?

'Elena?'

She looked back at him, her expression now impassive, as if she'd pulled a mask back into place. 'Do you mind if I make myself a drink?' she said suddenly, slapping her hands onto her knees. 'I'm dying for a cup of tea.'

He frowned at the sudden change of subject but didn't press her on the reason for it. Perhaps she was just tired after the stress and strain of the day. He was pretty tired himself now, even though he'd slept for a lot of it. 'Sure, help yourself,' he said.

She got up and walked over to the kitchen. 'Would you like one?' she asked, reaching for the kettle on the work surface.

'No, thanks.' He sat forward in his seat. 'I should take a shower.' He sniffed at his shirt, inhaling the institutional smell of stringent cleaning fluid and decay and, just like that, a memory flew to the front of his mind and he knew why he'd wanted to get out of that hospital so quickly.

His anguish must have shown on his face because Elena said, 'Caleb? Is everything okay? Did you remember something?' her voice sounding breathy with concern.

'Just why I wanted to leave the hospital. My mother died about six months ago and I spent an awful lot of time visiting her in one.'

The expression on her face changed from worry to one of sympathy. 'Your PA told me. I'm so sorry for your loss,' she said, her bright blue eyes soft with compassion.

He nodded, accepting her condolences, and ran a hand over his face, feeling stubble rasp at his palm.

There was something more to the memory of losing his mother but he couldn't put his finger on what it was. Some kind of underlying emotion bubbling under the surface, not quite clear enough for him to fully grasp.

'I don't seem to be able to remember a lot about her at the moment. I know the time I spent with her at the end of her life was…difficult…but I'm not entirely sure why.'

Elena folded her arms and leant against the counter top. 'From what you've told me about her, I don't think you were particularly close, at least not when you were younger. You were keen to move away from the place where you grew up and she didn't want you to.'

She looked at him, as if expecting this to jog his memory, but nothing new came to him.

Sadness swelled in his chest.

What was wrong with him? Why was he getting maudlin all of a sudden? Perhaps the trauma to his head was somehow affecting his emotional state. That had to be it. He knew it wasn't his usual way to discuss how he was feeling with anyone, particularly not a woman. It was one of the things that had contributed to destroying his relationship with his ex-fiancée. Her constant need to try and get into his head and fix him had caused him to feel both hounded and suffocated.

There was something about Elena that invited confidences though.

But what was it?

A half-formed answer flitted around the edges of his mind, just out of reach, and he pushed an unnerving resurgence of panic away, telling himself there was no point in trying to force his memory to come back; it would reappear in its own good time. Perhaps after he'd had a good night's sleep in his own bed.

He stood up carefully, relieved to find his dizziness had subsided, and started to make his way towards the door to the corridor that led through to his bedroom and en suite bathroom.

'Where are you going?' Elena asked, dashing out of the kitchen to intercept him.

He bristled at her bossy tone. 'I told you, I need a shower.'

'Not on your own. What if you get dizzy and fall?'

'Are you offering to join me?' he asked with a teasing smile, feeling his pulse pick up at the thought of it.

She visibly tensed, then shot him a cool, reproving smile. 'I'll wait in your bedroom, just in case you need me,' she said, turning on the spot and striding away from him, her body language looking a little stiff and awkward now.

He wanted to call after her that he wouldn't need her, that he didn't need anybody, that he was fine on his own. But he had the oddest feeling that that wasn't the case at all.

CHAPTER FOUR

CALEB MANAGED FINE by himself in the shower, despite the sharp pain that shot through his chest every time he moved his left arm. Checking over his body now that he was naked, he was shocked to see how much of it was covered in angry-looking bruises. It made him realise just how lightly he'd got off considering he'd been hit by a motorbike.

Or so he'd been told.

He still couldn't remember a thing about it.

Tamping down on the now familiar swell of unease, he wrapped a towel tightly around his waist and stared at himself in the mirror, tentatively touching the raised bump in his hairline where he'd hit his head. Perhaps all his errant memories were trapped in the bump and when it went down they'd be released back into his brain.

He shook his head at himself, wondering where his normally sane self had disappeared to. He really didn't feel like himself at the moment. There was a strange sense of having lost something heavy from deep within him, as if a weight he'd been carrying around had lifted from his body and was hovering somewhere over his head.

Or perhaps the accident had just knocked all the sense out of him.

Whatever it was, the best thing he could do right now was carry on as normal. There was no way he was letting a slight blip in memory and a small fracture stop him from functioning properly.

Giving his reflection a firm nod, he turned away from the mirror and left the en suite.

He expected to find Elena waiting there for him and was preparing to bat away any help she tried to offer and prove to her he wasn't as frail and vulnerable as she clearly suspected he was, so was surprised—and, if he was honest, a little disappointed—to find the room empty.

The sound of voices floated in through the open bedroom door and he heard the swish and click of the front door closing, then the gentle pad of feet on the hallway tiles as someone walked towards the bedroom.

'Oh, you're out,' Elena said as she emerged in the doorway, her cheeks flushing with colour as she eyed him standing there with just a towel slung around his hips.

He suppressed a smile as she averted her gaze and pretended to be studying a picture on the wall next to her, as if making a point of not staring at his half-naked body.

'Who was at the door?' he asked.

'Benita.'

'What did she want?'

'She brought your mobile phone over, which you'd left on your desk. She thought you'd want it, but I told her you wouldn't be dealing with anything work-related today because you need to rest.' She turned to look at him now, her expression serious. 'I also said that you wouldn't be back in the office for a while.'

'You did, huh? Well, unfortunately, I don't have time to be off work right now.' He held out his hand. 'I'll take the phone.'

When she flashed him an I-don't-think-so expression he added a determined, 'Thank you.'

'Caleb, I really don't think you should—'

'I'm not interested in what you think,' he said, feeling irritation prick at the back of his neck.

But, instead of handing the phone over like most people would have done when he used that tone of voice, she crossed her arms and fixed him with a hard stare.

'There is no way I'm giving you this phone tonight. You need to rest and get a good night's sleep and you're not going to do that if you're worrying about what's going on at work without you. I'm sure you've hired an exceptional team of staff and they're more than capable of handling things there without you for a couple of days.'

He glared at her in disbelief. No one ever talked to him like that and it was rather shocking to have her facing off with him, especially here in his own home. In his own bedroom.

'How do you intend to stop me from taking it from you?' he asked, putting on an amused smile to cover his incredulity.

She didn't even blink. 'By doing this,' she said, lifting open the front of her blouse and sliding the phone down inside the neck, so that it nestled in between her breasts.

He swallowed hard. There was no way he could physically try to take it from her now. Even though he ached to. Very much.

'Cute,' he growled, his frustration coming over loud and clear.

She smiled serenely. 'Someone has to save you from yourself.'

'I don't need saving,' he ground out, folding his arms.

'I beg to differ. I know you, Caleb; you'll work all night tonight to make up for the time you lost in the hospital.'

He frowned. 'How would you know that?'

'Because you regularly worked through the night when we were at university to make up for any time you lost.'

'That sounds like me,' he said slowly, as the unsettling feeling of not remembering his university days bit at his nerves again.

'So I'm staging an intervention. Again.'

'Again? What else have you kept so close to your chest from me?' he asked, raising a suggestive eyebrow.

Her jaw appeared to tighten and she frowned. 'I mean it's not the only time I've had to point out that you work too hard, that's all,' she said, looking a little uncomfortable now.

Despite the fact he could probably have held both of her wrists in one hand and easily retrieved his phone, he could tell from the steely look in her eyes that she wouldn't tolerate such behaviour.

Frustration pinched at him. He was going to have to let her win this one.

'Right, well, now that's settled I'll leave you to get dressed,' Elena said, her mouth twitching at the corner with what looked like suppressed amusement.

She was enjoying ordering him around. Damn her.

As soon as she'd walked away he strode to the door and swung it shut with a little more force than was entirely necessary.

Okay, so he was grateful to her for helping him get out of the hospital, but he had the unsettling feeling he would have been better off staying there if this was the kind of treatment he was going to have to put up with for the next couple of days.

Elena walked out of the room with blood rushing loudly in her ears. She couldn't quite believe she'd just hidden his phone down her top, but it had been obvious he wasn't going to allow himself to rest if she didn't force him to. After an accident like this he needed time to recover and heal. Especially as it appeared his memory still hadn't fully returned—even though he was clearly trying to brush that tiny detail under the carpet.

She was painfully aware that she'd know the moment it all came back to him because she'd probably find herself out on her ear.

Though hopefully that wouldn't happen any time soon.

The phone pressed uncomfortably against her breastbone as she walked away from him and as soon as she reached one of the spare bedrooms she removed it and stuffed it under the mattress at the side of the bed she always slept on. If he came into the room to look for it while she was asleep—just the thought of *that* gave her the jitters—he'd have to lift both her and the mattress up in order to get to it.

Not that she believed for a second he'd actually do that. He was too proud. She had wondered for one panicked moment earlier though whether he'd ignore her insistence that he took the evening off work and stuff his hand down her blouse to grab his phone, but luckily decorum had prevailed. She gave a little shiver. That would have been altogether too much to handle. She'd already been struggling to hold it together in his half-dressed, badly bruised presence, and his touching her like that would have tipped her right over the edge. Into what, she wasn't quite sure. But it was definitely better not to find out.

Flopping back onto the bed, she ran her hand over her eyes, which felt gritty and sore with tiredness. She was exhausted now after all the stress of the day, not to mention the tension she was carrying around with her, worrying about her staff and the fate of her business.

There was a loud rap at the door and she sat up quickly, smoothing her hair away from her face, not wanting Caleb to see any kind of chink in her armour.

He strode into the room, thankfully dressed now in a pair of faded jeans and a casual shirt, which fitted him so well she suspected they must have cost a fortune, despite their lived-in appearance.

'Will you be okay sleeping in here?' he asked, his

eyes scanning the room as if checking for anything that might be wrong with it.

'Yes, thanks, I'll be fine.'

'Okay, well, if you're not going to give me my phone back I'm going to watch TV in the living room for a few minutes, then go to bed. You're welcome to join me—' he shot her a wicked grin '—watching television, I mean.'

'Er…no, thank you. I have a bit of work to catch up on, so I'll stay in here so I don't disturb you,' she said, giving him a strained smile back and trying to ignore the warmth blooming between her thighs at the mere suggestion of sharing his bed. The most disconcerting thing was that she wasn't entirely sure whether he was genuinely flirting with her, or just teasing her to get his own back for her phone-hiding stunt.

She guessed the latter, knowing from experience how much he struggled with not being fully in control of every situation.

'How's your head now?' she asked, keeping her hands folded in her lap so he wouldn't see how nervous she was having him loom over her while she sat on the bed.

'It's fine. I have a low-level headache but pieces of my memory seem to be coming back now.' He looked away from her as a strained expression flitted over his face, proving to her that she'd been right about him trying to hide how unsettled he really felt about it.

She wanted to reach out to him, to somehow soothe away his worry with her touch, but she was acutely aware that it would be entirely inappropriate considering their former relationship.

'I'm sure it'll all come back soon, perhaps after a good rest.'

He nodded, his expression now coolly nonchalant. 'I hope you'll be comfortable in here,' he said brusquely. 'There are some T-shirts in there if you want something to sleep in,' he added, waving towards a wardrobe on the other side of the room.

'Thank you,' she said, touched that he was concerned about her comfort. 'Is there anything I can do for you?' she blurted as he began to turn away from her.

His slow, loaded grin made her insides swoop but she ignored the feeling, continuing to look at him steadily until he shook his head.

'Nothing, Elena. I'm fine. I'll see you in the morning.' And, with that, he turned on the spot and exited the room, leaving his tantalising, clean scent hanging in the air behind him.

Flopping back onto the bed again, she took a deep calming breath, willing her heartbeat to slow down. It was so unnerving, being here in Caleb's house as a guest. She almost didn't want to go to sleep in case she woke up to find him back to the beast of a man she'd encountered this morning in his meeting room.

She'd enjoyed seeing the small flashes of his personality coming through since they'd left the hospital though and part of her ached to join him in the living room and push him to show her some more of them.

But she knew, deep down, that that could be a dangerous game to play.

No, she'd leave her door open to keep an ear out for him in case he needed her, but it was probably best to give him a bit of space now.

After getting washed in the en suite in her room and changing into one of the large, soft cotton T-shirts Caleb had loaned her she slid beneath the sheets and lay listening to the low murmur of the television in the other room, feeling exhaustion dragging at her eyelids until she could no longer keep them open.

She slept fitfully, her dreams punctuated with disturbing images from the accident.

Waking up in the early hours with her heart racing, she had a sudden panic that Caleb might have had a turn for the worse in his sleep and she slipped out of bed to tiptoe silently to his room to check on him. Pushing the door open quietly, she was confused to find his bed empty and looking as though it hadn't been slept in all night.

Where was he? Had he left the apartment without her knowing?

Blood pulsed hard in her head as she moved quickly down the corridor, checking the other rooms, which all appeared to be empty, then ran into the living area, her heartbeat erratic now.

Relief rushed through her as she spotted him lying on the sofa nearest the windows with a laptop perched precariously on his lap, breathing gently, his face smoothed of its usual fierceness in repose.

She stood and watched him sleeping for a while, letting the still and silent darkness envelop her as she tried to get a handle on the intense rush of feelings that cascaded through her.

She'd cared so deeply for him once, had thought at one point that her future would be with him by her side, but then she'd blown it, naïvely choosing the safe—boring, as Caleb had called it—option instead.

Looking at him now, she realised with a surge of emotion that she missed him. So intensely it hurt. Over the intervening years she'd been able to quash the waves of regret she'd experienced in her weaker moments, but she knew now that she still craved the elated, excited way he'd made her feel, like a habit she couldn't kick.

She wasn't here to get him back though, she told herself sternly, forcing herself to unclench her fists as she walked quietly over to where he lay to lift the laptop off his lap so she could take it back to the bedroom with her—just in case he woke up and decided to keep working. It was highly unlikely he'd ever trust her again, not after the way she'd let him down.

He was altogether too proud for that.

But she was determined to make it up to him somehow. Perhaps, if she was lucky, once he was better he'd remember this time they'd spent together and decide it was worth giving their friendship another chance.

Tiptoeing out of the room, she glanced back briefly to where he lay sleeping, his chest rising and falling in a steady rhythm.

All she could do now was hope for the best.

Caleb woke bleary-eyed from such a heavy sleep it took him a few moments to figure out where he was.

As the room came into focus he realised he was lying on the sofa in his living room.

Huh, strange.

Levering himself up to a sitting position, he felt a twinge of pain in his chest and the memory of waking up in the hospital yesterday after an accident came flooding back. As did the baffling appearance of the beautiful woman who had turned up to take care of him. A woman he couldn't remember ever seeing before in his life.

Though he knew her. He *knew* her.

And why did he feel as though there was something more to their friendship?

Feeling his heart rate begin to rise, he forced the perturbing question out of his head for now and turned his attention to what he usually thought about upon waking instead.

His business.

He hadn't intended to work for long last night—just wanting to make sure he hadn't missed anything important whilst he'd been at the hospital—and had brought out the laptop he'd had stashed under the coffee table, feeling a sense of relief that Elena hadn't noticed and confiscated that too. After skimming a number of things that didn't require his urgent attention, the words beginning to blur together in front of his tired eyes, he'd come across a message from Benita that had made him start with worry, causing him to wince with pain as his cracked rib complained.

He'd turned the problem over and over in his mind for a while, desperately trying to keep his attention focused on solving this hiccup, but his tired brain had had other ideas, insistently pulling him into a deep, overpowering sleep.

He was awake now though.

Reaching down onto his lap where he'd left his laptop, he was confused to find it wasn't there. He sat up carefully, mindful of his damaged rib, and felt along the floor next to the sofa, guessing it must have slipped off his knee whilst he was asleep.

'Looking for this?' came a softly chastising voice from the other side of the room and he turned his head to see a woman—Elena—standing there with his computer held between her hands. Her brow was creased and her expression guarded.

'I thought you were going to give your poor brain a rest last night so it had a chance to recover.'

He shrugged and swung his legs off the sofa, then stood up carefully, turning to face her. Twisting his body was not at all comfortable at the moment.

'Like I said, I don't have time to take a break right now.'

She huffed out a sigh. 'Why not?'

He threw up his hands in frustration, wincing at the twinge of pain this caused. 'Because there are things going on that need my immediate attention.'

'Like what?'

Clearly she wasn't going to give up her questioning. He wasn't entirely sure he could trust her with details about his business, but something in him, something he couldn't identify, told him it would be okay to talk to her.

He sighed. 'I need to convince a potential American supplier of my small appliance-sized battery that I'm an easy and reliable person to partner with,' he muttered, folding his arms and rocking back on his heels as he thought about the problem again.

'Apparently he has concerns and is considering backing out of a meeting I've taken great pains to set up while he's over here in Spain. He's supposed to be coming to Araya Industries on the last day of his visit and I'd hoped to persuade him to include one of my rechargeable batteries in their product range.'

Walking over to the kitchen, he opened the fridge and extracted a carton of orange juice, which he held up towards her to ask if she'd like some. When she nodded, he grabbed two glasses and poured them both a good measure of it.

'According to Benita, his PA let slip he'd heard a rumour about me being a difficult man to work with and is considering taking a meeting with one of my competitors instead—who is apparently the stable, patriarchal type that Carter prefers to work with.' He put the carton back into the fridge and slammed the door shut, noticing her jump a little at the forcefulness with which he did this.

Taking a calming breath, he picked up one of the glasses and handed it to her, then grabbed his own and took a long drink from it.

He really needed to keep his cool here if he was going to get on top of this problem. Especially as he was still having a bit of trouble thinking straight after the accident.

'The fact that I don't have a partner, let alone a wife, is troubling to him,' he said, running a hand over his face, trying to wake himself up a bit. 'But if I can convince him I'm a good bet it could be a hugely lucrative deal that would give us a strong foothold in the American market.'

'How are you going to do that? Convince him, I mean,' Elena asked, looking at him from over the rim of her glass.

'I'm going to offer to take him and his wife out for dinner tonight and show them I'm not the ogre they seem to think I am,' he said decisively.

'You're going to meet them on your own?'

He hesitated, thinking about this. 'It's better if I don't make it too business-formal, so I don't think I should take anyone else from the office,' he said slowly. 'It needs to be a more laid-back affair.'

'But you're concerned it might confirm his suspicions about you if you turn up on your own.'

His gaze snapped to hers. How did she seem to know what he was thinking? It was as if she could read his addled mind.

She shrugged a shoulder. 'I know you don't remember, but I run my own manufacturing engineering company in England and I've been in a similar situation before. In my experience it's better to have someone else to make up a four, especially if he's bringing his wife.'

He ran a hand across his jaw, frustration needling him. 'I don't have a girlfriend at the moment and I haven't worked with Benita long enough to build up a convincing rapport with her.'

'No,' Elena said, making it sound as if taking Benita would be the last thing she'd suggest.

'And it would be helpful to have someone who knows something about the industry and how to behave in business meetings already,' he said as an idea began to form in his head.

'That's true, especially as your memory isn't exactly at its best right now.'

'So that only leaves one person,' he said, folding his arms and giving her a pointed stare.

'Who?' she asked, frowning at first, then widening her eyes as she caught on to just what he was suggesting.

'That's right, Elena. *You.*'

CHAPTER FIVE

'*ME?*' Elena's heart leapt into her throat.

Caleb gave her a firm smile, as if the matter had already been decided.

Though, to be fair, she guessed it had.

There was no way she could refuse to help him, of course. For one thing, she couldn't let him go out on his own when his head injury was still an issue, and for another she was keenly aware that this could be the perfect opportunity to atone for the way she'd treated him in their younger years. She could really help him here—do something of substance.

'It's the ideal solution,' he said, nodding sagely.

'How are we going to convince them we're a couple when you don't remember a thing about me though?' she asked, her nerves biting a little.

He waved a hand, dismissing her concern. 'We'll do a cramming session before the meeting.'

She swallowed, feeling tension building in her throat. She was going to have to be careful what she told him if she was going to avoid the small matter of her being his number one enemy.

'Okay, well, I'll need to dash over to the hotel where I'm staying first and fetch my bag so I can change. I'll need something more appropriate to wear to dinner,' she said, gesturing to her now rather crumpled suit.

And she could do with a few minutes on her own to get her head together.

'Which hotel are you staying in?' he asked.

'The Barcelona Gran Mar, near the beach.'

He looked at her long and hard for a moment. 'Okay, I'll come with you. We can walk from here; it's not far.'

Her stomach sank. 'No, you should stay here and rest.'

'I'm fine,' he said in that no-nonsense manner she knew so well. 'Anyway, how are you going to keep your beady eye on me otherwise?'

She sighed and shook her head at his droll expression. The man had an answer for everything. It had been the same when they were younger too.

'Okay, fine, come with me then. Perhaps you can point out some of the famous landmarks on the way. I've not had a chance to see any of them since I arrived.'

She waited while Caleb put in a call to Benita, asking her to get hold of Carter's PA and arrange a dinner meeting for that evening. Once he'd hung up, they shrugged on their jackets and left the apartment, Elena's heart beating at twice its usual speed as she contemplated the idea of spending the whole day with Caleb by her side.

Gaudí's mesmerising art nouveau Casa Milà building was only a couple of streets away from Caleb's apartment, fortuitously in the right direction for her hotel near the Nova Icaria beach, so they strolled past it, Elena admiring the strange, cave-like curves and outlandish quirks of the architecture. The whole building looked as though it had been hand-carved out of an enormous piece of rock by prehistoric man, looking truly anachronistic next to its more modern neighbours.

'He really was a genius,' she said in wonder, gazing up at the breathtaking façade. 'Such a visionary.'

'Unparalleled,' Caleb agreed, using his hand to shield his eyes against the bright glare of the sun as he squinted up at it. 'You know, I'm a little embarrassed to admit this, but I barely notice it's there any more. It's become part of the street furniture to me after all my years living here.'

'That's terrible,' Elena said, frowning up at the building.

'I'm so busy getting from one place to another I forget to look up,' he murmured.

She glanced at him. 'I do the same thing in London,' she said, feeling a little rush of poignancy that their lives had followed such a parallel path, despite the distance between them. 'It's very easy to take beauty for granted,' she added.

'Yes.' He paused then said, 'It's funny, but losing big chunks of my past seems to have brought the present into sharper focus.'

When she looked round at him she experienced a little frisson at the intense way he was looking at her.

'Are you happy with your life?' she blurted, her nerves getting the better of her.

His brow furrowed as he thought about this. 'I'm satisfied with the way my business is growing and I enjoy living in Barcelona.'

There was a heavy pause while she waited for him to continue. 'And, for the purposes of our dinner this evening, I'm very happy with my love life.' He flashed her a wolfish grin, making her tummy flip over.

He gestured for them to start walking again and she fell into step with him as they made their way along the pavement, feeling even more jumpy now than when they'd first started out.

'Speaking of which, I guess we ought to decide how long we've been an item, for the purpose of tonight's charade,' Caleb said, a wry grin turning up the corner of his mouth.

Elena took a breath, feeling her pulse jitter. 'Yes, I guess we should get our story straight. How about we tell them that we met at university but were just friends then, and bumped into each other again a year ago at a business conference and things progressed from there.'

'Dull, but believable, I suppose,' Caleb said with a thoughtful nod.

A coach had parked a little way down the street and as they approached it the pavement suddenly became overrun by a large tour group that filed off to look at the famous building they'd just left.

She felt Caleb slip his arm protectively around her as they began to be jostled by the crowd moving past them and she allowed herself to sink against his strong body for a moment, her heart beginning to race as she breathed in his zesty, familiar scent.

Once they were clear of the crowd he let her go and

she dazedly rubbed at her arm where his hand had gripped her, her skin feeling tingly and sensitive where their bodies had connected.

'You're going to have to get used to me touching you,' Caleb said in a low voice, looking at her arm where she was rubbing it. 'Or they're not going to believe we're a couple.'

Elena swallowed hard, balling her fists. 'Yes, of course. You just took me by surprise then, that's all.'

He looked at her with one eyebrow raised. 'Were you always this jumpy around me?'

'No, no! I'm just a little off balance today. This is all a bit strange, to be honest.' She flashed him a strained smile. 'You have to admit, we've got ourselves into a rather odd situation here.'

She tried not to notice the puzzled look he gave her and strode on confidently, looking deliberately around her, at anything but him, to give her some time to pull herself together.

Good grief, if she couldn't even act normally around him when they were on their own how was she going to manage it when they had an audience tonight?

She needed to get herself into a more relaxed and *friendly* mindset.

A little further on they walked past Gaudi's Sagrada Família, which rose majestically into the sky like a discarded giant elf king's crown.

'It makes me think of something from the *Lord of the Rings*,' Elena said in wonder as she took in the arresting quirkiness of it. 'We spent a whole weekend at university once, working our way through the trilogy of films. I could barely keep my eyes open at the end of it and I dreamt about it intensively for the next few nights.' She glanced at him speculatively. 'Do you remember?'

He shook his head, agitation flashing in his eyes. 'I have no recollection of ever seeing those films.'

Her heart went out to him. It must be so distressing for him to lose so many of his memories—though, now she thought about it, the hard shell she'd witnessed at their initial meeting had definitely softened a little since they'd been gone. Perhaps the absence of deep-seated anger that had driven him for most of his life was finally allowing his true nature to emerge from the dark place where it had been hiding.

'Well, perhaps you should think of it as a good thing,' she said with forced jollity, in an attempt to lighten the sombre atmosphere that seemed to have fallen between them now. 'You get to experience the excitement of watching them afresh. I wish I could do that.'

His eyebrow shot up. 'Losing the first twenty-five years of your life is a high price to pay though, don't you think?'

She shrugged. 'I think it's worth taking every positive you can out of an experience. Even if it is a testing one.'

'You're quite the optimist,' Caleb drawled, raising a derisive eyebrow.

Her skin prickled with annoyance. 'And you're a cynic! Life's too short to dwell on the negative.'

Although perhaps she should learn to take her own advice, she thought wryly, considering how much anxiety she seemed to be carrying around with her at the moment.

Caleb looked taken aback at her outburst, but after a moment his features softened and he let out a low laugh. 'Maybe you're right,' he said. 'I have little enough "life" outside of the business as it is; I guess I should spend it enjoying what I work so hard to have.'

They walked on again in silence for a minute, their arms swinging at their sides.

'To be fair, I'm just as bad about spending too much time working and not enjoying all life has to offer,' Elena said after a while. 'I can regularly spend up to ten hours a day at work and sometimes carry on into the evenings if I need to. I've lost count of the number of parties and get-togethers I've cried off recently. My friends despair of me.'

'You don't go out much?' he asked.

'Not as much as I should. There's no wonder I'm single; my personal life could definitely do with some TLC.'

'Why have you *really* been on your own for so long?' he asked in such a casual tone she felt sure he'd been waiting for the right opportunity to broach that question.

So this was it then—time to be totally honest with him.

'Well, the thing is, I nearly got married some years ago, to a guy called Jimmy,' she said, bracing herself in case the mention of his name jogged Caleb's memory, but he didn't react, just looked at her with interest. 'And I needed some time on my own after the relationship finished to get my head straight and then I got so busy at work I let things drift,' she said.

'Why did you split up with him?' he asked brusquely.

She sighed, feeling the old familiar tug of guilt in her chest. 'I changed my mind about whether he was the right guy for me and called the wedding off at the last minute.'

He blinked, but his expression remained impassive. 'Do you regret it now?'

'No. It was the right decision. It wouldn't have worked out. He was a really nice guy, but being married to Jimmy would have stifled me in the end, killed my spirit.'

Caleb nodded as if he understood exactly what she was talking about.

'I think I felt the same about my ex-fiancée,' he said, surprising her with his direct honesty.

'She was a beautiful woman, incredibly smart and very driven, but there was something missing for me. I thought for a long while that it wouldn't matter, but as soon as we started to talk seriously about arranging the wedding it became apparent it wasn't going to work for me. There was something else wrong too, but I can't remember what it was.' He squeezed his eyes shut as if trying to bring the memory to the fore.

Don't let this be the moment when he remembers everything, she prayed silently—not when they were just starting to get on so well.

'I think my problem's always been that I was brought up by two parents who argued all the time and I found my life growing up incredibly stressful,' she jumped in, hoping to divert his attention back to her story in order to impart the whole sorry tale, just in case she found herself suddenly talking to the pre-accident Caleb—who she was sure wouldn't be quite so interested in her reasons for letting him down so badly in the past.

'They seemed to be on the verge of divorce all the time and I hated it. It made me so anxious I used to lock myself in my bedroom and turn my music up really loud so I didn't have to hear the constant bickering. It made me crave stability, so when I met Jimmy a year before I left for university I thought he was the perfect person to give me what I needed.'

Caleb just looked at her as if to tell her to carry on, so she continued.

'He was such a calm and well-balanced person—the embodiment of a safe, solid future in my mind. Exactly the sort of man I wanted to settle down with. The complete opposite of my dad.'

And you, *Caleb.*

She cleared her throat nervously. 'Somehow the relationship survived through our time at separate universities—with a small blip—' She glanced at him then hurried on, 'And he proposed to me a couple of years after we graduated.'

It was nearing midday now and the sun was out in full force. Elena was beginning to feel increasingly stifled in her suit so she slipped her jacket off, looping it over her arm to carry it instead.

'I thought I wanted a relationship like that at the time, but as it got closer to our wedding day this strange kind of panic engulfed me. I was terrified I was heading for a life of middling satisfaction and settling for someone I didn't feel any true passion for. I loved him, but I realised it was only as a friend.'

And she knew this because she knew what real passion felt like. After meeting Caleb at university her feelings for him had crept up on her, day by day, until she could barely see straight with confusion. She'd wanted him, so much, but the sensible side of her brain had told her that Jimmy was a much better bet for a future partner. Caleb was fierce and impulsive and somewhat wild: the kind of man who scared her with his dominating intensity and passion, not to mention his overwhelming sex appeal.

Something that was still powerfully evident today.

'I hurt Jimmy really badly and I still feel awful about it, but it was for the best. He's fine now. He met someone else and they've just had a little girl. I hear they're getting married next year.'

When she finally turned to look at him again, Caleb was nodding thoughtfully as if he understood where she was coming from.

They'd reached her hotel now, which had views from the city's beach across the sparkling blue of the Balearic Sea.

'It won't take me long to grab my bag; I'm on the first floor.'

To her surprise, he followed her to the lift.

Shrugging off a twist of nerves, she pressed the button and waited for the lift to arrive.

She guessed he was following her mandate to keep him in her sights at all times to the absolute letter.

Typical Caleb.

Once up on her corridor it took her three attempts to make her key card work in her door and she finally stumbled into the room, flushed in the face and her skin prickling with awareness as Caleb followed her inside.

'Okay, I'll just be a minute. I need to grab my things from the bathroom and wardrobe then we can go.'

He just nodded, watching her as she shoved her meagre possessions into her suitcase then strugged to zip it up.

'Here, let me do that,' he said, putting his hands on her shoulders and gently but firmly guiding her out of the way so he could get to the case.

She saw him wince with pain as his cracked rib protested when he bent down and started tugging at the zip.

'Caleb, stop! I can do it.'

Without thinking, she pressed her hand against his chest, feeling the dips and peaks of his muscles shift under her touch as he tensed with surprise.

It suddenly felt too seductive in that small room— the two of them standing so close together, only inches away from the bed. She could feel the heat from his body throbbing against the palm of her hand and his enticing scent flooded her nose, making her senses reel.

When she looked up into his face he was gazing at her with such intensity in his eyes she thought she might melt under the heat of it.

Little shivers of excitement raced over her skin and she drew in a shaky breath, feeling her blood pulse thickly through her veins.

No, no, no, this shouldn't be happening. She shouldn't

be looking at the full firmness of his mouth and thinking how wonderful it would be to feel it on hers again, or about how much she wanted the comforting strength of his arms around her, or how she longed for him to guide her over to the bed and lay her down, trapping her underneath him so she could experience the feeling of their bodies pressed closely together.

She shouldn't be wanting all that.

But she was. She was.

Denying herself was almost too much to bear.

But she *had* to.

Withdrawing her hand from where it still lay over his heart, she forced her mouth into a wobbly smile.

'I don't want you in pain because of me,' she muttered, the tormenting subtext of the words not lost on her.

He frowned, his eyes dark with confusion.

'Let's get out of here,' she mumbled, turning away and hurriedly zipping up the final side of the case, not daring to look at him again in case he saw how much she ached for him to touch her reflected in her expression.

They didn't say a word to each other as they left the room and walked side by side down the corridor and into the lift, the air around them throbbing with a strange new tension.

Once back on the street, Elena stood blinking in the bright afternoon sunlight feeling as if they'd moved into some kind of parallel universe up there in the hotel room.

'Let's grab a bite to eat from that café on the beach,'

Caleb said, pointing to the place in question, his voice sounding a little rough.

'Okay, sure. I could eat,' Elena said, deciding the best thing to do was just pretend the incident in the hotel had never happened. That was the only way she was possibly going to get through the next twenty-four hours.

After locating a suitable table, she watched him stroll over to the counter and place their order for food and coffee. The woman serving him gave him a coquettish grin and leant forward in a seductive manner to ask him a question and Elena experienced a pinch of jealousy as she saw him return her smile.

She put her hand over her heart where it hurt the most and gave a gentle rub there.

Oh, no.

She was in such trouble.

He returned a minute later, balancing a couple of plates of food in one hand and grasping the handles of two mugs of coffee in the other.

'Here, let me help you,' Elena said, rising to take the plates from him so he could put the mugs down on the table without spilling the hot liquid everywhere.

She was horrified to find her hands were shaking and sat down quickly, placing them in her lap before he noticed.

When she looked up to say thanks for the drink he'd put in front of her she saw he was frowning, as if something was bothering him.

'Did we spend a lot of time together at university?' he asked.

The memory of her and Caleb sharing a bottle of

wine in his room after a study session flitted across her vision, stealing her breath away. It had been on that night that everything had changed between them.

That fateful night, in a drunken haze, when she'd admitted her true feelings for him and he'd dragged her into his arms and kissed her, making her insides melt and her blood fizz with excitement.

Forcing herself to unclench her now sweaty hands, she gave him as composed a smile as she could muster.

'Yes, we were pretty close back then. We were doing the same course so we had a lot in common. Our tutor put us together as partners on a project at the beginning of the first term and found we worked well together.'

The memory of her broken promise to Caleb that she'd return to university after the Christmas holidays a free woman after breaking up with Jimmy, ready to commit her newly unchained heart to him, pressed heavily on her.

Picking up her drink to give her restless hands something to do, she took a tentative sip of the hot liquid.

'So why haven't we seen each other for so long?' Caleb asked, the look in his eyes so searching she choked on her drink.

'Are you okay?' he asked with amusement in his voice as he reached over to pat her gently on the back.

'I'm fine,' she gasped, taking the opportunity to wipe her eyes with the napkin that had come with the sandwich so she didn't need to look at him while she answered.

'I guess life just got in the way. We've both been so focused on our careers.'

When she finally looked up at him again he nodded slowly. 'Tell me more about our time together at university,' he said, giving her the impression that he needed to hear about it to help him understand something.

So she did. She told him about the way they'd met on the first day of term and how grumpy he'd been with her when their tutor had paired them up.

'I was so annoyed with you I gave you a real dressing-down at the end of that lesson. I think I said something about how just because I was a woman it didn't mean I couldn't beat your arrogant arse at engineering.' She smiled at the memory, remembering how it had taken a lot of guts to say that to him, and how proud she was of herself afterwards that she hadn't let him just walk all over her.

He'd been taken aback by her defensiveness at first, but once he realised she meant every word he'd challenged her to a quiz on engineering terms.

'And I won,' she told him, smiling at his raised eyebrow. 'But you were a good loser. You just gave me this respectful kind of nod and then offered to take me to the nearest pub to toast my win. We ended up staying there all night and by the end of it we were firm friends.'

He snorted with laughter, clearly amused by this, though the expression on his face told her he was impressed by what she was telling him.

'We spent a lot of time together after that,' she continued, warming to her theme now, 'and talked about a lot of personal stuff too, especially the things we found tough growing up. Like you being brought up in a single-parent household and being bullied at school, and me living with parents that constantly rowed or sniped at each other. I think we felt a certain kind of affinity with each other after that.'

He continued to look at her with a frown pinching his brow now, but didn't comment. Clearly he had no memory of any of that.

'We liked the same kind of movies too—sci-fi and fantasy,' she said, to fill the silence that had fallen between them.

He nodded in agreement, a relieved sort of smile playing about his mouth as if this made total sense to him.

'Most of our other friends weren't interested in them so we often went to the cinema together to see them and stay up late dissecting them afterwards.' She smiled, trying to hide how sad those memories made her feel now. 'Good times.'

'It sounds like we had fun together,' he murmured, his eyes never leaving hers.

She gazed back at him, remembering how happy they'd both been then, how full of vigour and positivity and excitement for the future—a future she'd hoped would have him in it in some way—and felt her spirits plummet. Would he have been a happier, less angry man today if they'd stayed together then?

'We did,' she said quietly, swallowing past the lump in her throat.

He opened his mouth to ask her something else but, before he could get the words out, his mobile began to ring, mercifully diverting his attention away from her rapidly heating face.

'That was Benita,' he said once he'd concluded the call and put his mobile down on the table. 'She managed to get hold of Carter. He's agreed to meet for dinner tonight and, as we anticipated, he's bringing his wife with him.'

He raised both eyebrows. 'Looks like we're on, girlfriend.'

She covered a resurgence of nerves with a smile. 'Great.'

Once they'd polished off their food, at Elena's request they spent the walk back to his apartment going over any relevant points about Araya Industries that might come up in conversation with the Americans, making sure she was fully briefed—or at least as much as a girlfriend working in the same industry might be.

It was fascinating to hear how he'd chosen to run his business, but Elena experienced a twinge of guilt at being trusted with detailed strategies and projections when Caleb had been so keen not to allow her anywhere near his business operation only the day before.

This was all to help him though, she reminded herself firmly. She wasn't going to take advantage of it at any point.

'So tell me about your business,' he said once they'd covered all the salient points about his.

His question caught her off guard and she stumbled a little, feeling him grab her elbow to right her, and gave him a strained smile.

'Er...well, I run a company in England called Zipabout. We make single-person electric vehicles to be used for short trips around towns and cities.'

He raised his eyebrows with interest. 'And what sort of battery are you using to power them?'

She thought about telling him the truth, somehow bringing the conversation round to the fact she was hoping his company would be the one to supply it, but her conscience wouldn't let her. It would be totally inappropriate to mention it when he didn't remember the row they'd already had about it.

With a sinking heart she said, 'We're looking into that at the moment. I have a few leads.'

Darn, darn, darn! And it could have been such a good opportunity to find out whether he'd be interested in supplying his battery to her without the angst and anger from their past getting in the way. But it was too much of a morally ambiguous move for her to do that.

Caleb was nodding slowly, looking as though he was going to ask something else, and she held her breath, poised to fudge an answer, but, as luck would have it, at that moment his attention was diverted as he looked round to fully take in their surroundings and said, 'We need to take this turn for my apartment.'

It was just the distraction she needed in order to redirect the topic of conversation without it seeming strange.

'So how long have you lived on this street?' she asked, waving her hands around expansively. 'It's a lovely area.'

As they walked out onto his street, with him telling her he'd been here for the last four years and how he came to find it, it suddenly struck her how businesslike the area was. The apartments were large and expensive-looking, but didn't give the impression of being held together by a cohesive community. It was a district for people who liked to live alone within a bustling major city.

It made her spirits sink to think of Caleb like that. But then he'd always been fiercely independent and protective of his personal space and she guessed this was just a grown-up extension of that, she reminded herself.

As soon as they walked into his apartment she excused herself, saying she needed a rest before they went out for dinner, in desperate need of some space away from him in order to regroup before their meeting tonight.

Shutting her bedroom door firmly behind her, she took the opportunity to check her email. Her stomach lurched as she saw a message from her Sales Director asking her how it was going with Caleb and checking whether there was any news about being able to use his battery in their car yet.

Closing the laptop with a snap, she resolved not to look at her messages again until after the meal this evening. She was going to need her wits about her tonight, not only for the sake of Caleb's business but also in order to keep her cool whilst looking as though she was intimately acquainted with the man. He already turned her insides to goo every time he so much as looked at her and if he was going to be touching her all night too she was going to need every ounce of strength she had to remain unflustered and in control. The last thing she wanted was for Caleb to suspect she was enjoying his company as more than a friend.

That was a complication neither of them needed at the moment.

CHAPTER SIX

CALEB TOOK A long shower, feeling energised by the time he'd spent getting to know a bit more about Elena today.

The intense moment they'd shared in the hotel room, where the air had positively crackled between them, had convinced him that there had to have been more between them than just friendship during their time at university.

Judging by her jumpiness around him afterwards, she'd definitely felt the same weight of possibility that had hummed between them as they stood gazing at each other with her hand pressed against his heart.

Having the space to think about it now, he realised he'd been aware of an odd kind of tension between them all day, as if she was trying to suppress something—or hide something, maybe. Had they not taken their relationship further because she'd been seeing that Jimmy guy? Had he, Caleb, been the blip she'd mentioned?

Perhaps this connection he felt had always been there, but even though they were both single now Elena didn't think it appropriate to act on it when he was just out of hospital after the accident.

Well, to hell with that. Why should a bang on the head stop them from exploring this thing between them? He wasn't an invalid. He knew his own mind.

Pulling on a smart shirt and trousers for dinner with a determination to find out whether he was right later, he walked out into the living area to discover Elena was also dressed for their meeting and was waiting for him.

The pale pink dress she had on was beautifully understated but entirely beguiling at the same time. It had a halter top, which tied behind her long, elegant neck and showcased her pale, slender shoulders. He couldn't help but notice how the bodice of the dress dipped in under her full breasts then gently curved against her slender waist, perfectly emphasising her hourglass figure.

Feeling her watching him, he dropped his gaze to look at the skirt instead, which was slim-fitting and narrowed at the knee, making her legs look as if they went on for miles.

Forcing himself to snap his mouth shut and pull his gaze up to her face, he gave her a nod of hello and went into the kitchen to get himself a very cold drink of water.

Right now wasn't the time to explore his theory. He had more immediate things to deal with, in the shape of persuading Jonathan Carter to take his business.

'Will you be ready to go in five minutes?' he asked, placing the glass carefully into the sink with an unsteady hand.

'I'm ready when you are,' she replied, but he could have sworn he saw a flash of concern on her face. Perhaps she was nervous about the charade they were about to embark on. It suddenly occurred to him that every time Elena saw him after a break she seemed a little more tense, as if she was expecting him to do or say something she was afraid of. But why?

He remembered with a jolt that she'd mentioned at the hospital that they'd had a row right before his accident, but in his befuddled state he'd not asked her what it had been about.

'Elena?'

She looked round at him as she went to grab her handbag from the table by the door.

'What did we argue about before my accident?'

Her face seemed to blanch a little.

'Er…' Wrapping her arms around her body, she fixed him with an awkward smile. 'It was an old argument from when we were at university. I don't think it's a good idea for us to talk about it now though. We need to be totally focused on the meeting.' She looked so stricken he decided not to push it any further. Especially when she was doing him such a favour by attending this meeting with him.

But why was she so tense? Perhaps she was still feeling responsible for him being hit by that bike. He wished, not for the first time, that he could remember it.

'Fair enough,' he said, 'but, whatever it was, stop worrying that I'm going to bite your head off every time I see you. We're friends after all.'

'Uh-huh,' she mumbled, not looking at him now.

Walking slowly over to where she stood, he put his hand on her bare arm and felt her quiver under his touch.

She took a quick step away, breaking their contact and folding her arms across her chest.

'We should go. We don't want to be late.'

'Of course,' he said, forcing himself to remain where he was and not touch her again, just to see what she'd do. The urge to provoke more of a reaction was intoxicating.

Grabbing his warm weather overcoat, he slid his arms carefully into the sleeves. He was going to have to be careful not to let Carter see he'd been in an accident or it might serve as another mark against him, especially if the man thought he was in any way mentally incapacitated as well at the moment.

It was funny but refusing to show any physical weakness felt like something he was well acquainted with, but he couldn't quite put his finger on why. It eluded him, like something flittering on the edge of his vision. He knew something important was there, but he couldn't fully grasp what he was looking at.

Damn memory—it was playing havoc with his self-assurance.

But it would all be okay; he'd make sure it was.

As for Elena, he'd get the full story from her eventually, but for now she was right—he needed to keep his head in the game.

The restaurant that Benita had booked them into was on a small, winding side street off the famous grand La Rambla, a tree-lined pedestrian mall in the oldest part of the city.

On Elena's request, the car that Caleb had ordered dropped them in the Plaça de Catalunya, next to the magnificent fountain and the looming Francesc Macià monument—that looked to Elena a bit like an upside-down staircase—so they could soak up the buzzy atmosphere on their way to the restaurant.

They walked together, close but not touching, along the busy street bustling with tourists and locals alike, then detoured down one of the small side streets and through a labyrinth of roads crowded on both sides with a mixture of brightly lit pavement cafés, designer clothes shops and trinket stalls, until they reached the Gothic Quarter, where their final destination was located.

According to Caleb, El Gótico had served its famous fusion of Spanish and Mediterranean fare for the past ten years and was a favourite with Barcelonans, as well as the handful of tourists that occasionally stumbled across it.

The décor was a mixture of warm, earthy colours with rustic wooden furniture and a tiled terracotta floor which contrasted sharply with the angular metal and glass of the staircase and bar. Bright splashes of primary colours were picked out on the back wall, which were also reflected in the small lamps and glass water carafes on each table, giving the place the impression of chic modernism. The whole effect was both comforting and uplifting.

The delicious smell of the place wrapped around Elena's senses, making her mouth water as they made their way to the bar, where the greeter stood waiting to welcome them.

Caleb spoke to the woman in rapid Spanish and a

moment later they were whisked towards the staircase leading to the upper mezzanine of the restaurant, which had a long glass balcony affording diners views of the lamplit tables below.

Just as he was about to mount the stairs, Elena put her hand on Caleb's arm to stop him. She wanted to make sure they made the most of this opportunity to charm the Americans and for that to happen Caleb was going to have to rein in his more dominating side for a while.

'I'm sure I don't need to say this, but go easy on the man tonight, okay? Just until everyone's had a chance to find their feet here.'

Caleb's eyebrow shot up. 'You think I'm going to dangle him from the balcony if he doesn't agree to a partnership?'

She batted a hand at him, suppressing a smile. 'No, of course not. But I know you; you'll want to go in all guns blazing. I recommend a lighter touch. If he's here with his wife he's not going to take too kindly to being bullied and harangued.'

'I wouldn't—'

She put up a hand to pre-empt his angry rebuttal. 'Not intentionally, I know, but you can come across as a little bit abrasive and intimidating until someone gets to know you. Show him a bit of your soft side too, that's my advice.'

Caleb blinked at her, his brows drawn into a tight frown as he appeared to consider what she'd said. After a moment he nodded slowly, his frustrated expression clearing and being replaced with a wolfish grin. There was something else in his eyes too that made her tummy flip and her blood begin to race. She stared at his mouth, wondering erratically how she would react if he leant forwards and kissed her right now.

'Okay, I'll be nice,' he murmured.

Shoving away her lustful urges, she nodded. 'Good.' She let out a gasp of surprise as he suddenly slipped his hand around her back and drew her closer to him.

'Just relax, *cariño*. You seem tense and that's going to look strange to our guests.'

Swallowing hard, she gave him a jerky nod, her heart banging hard against her chest and her nerves jangling due to their intimate proximity.

'Perhaps I should practice my soft side on you before they get here,' he murmured, his dark eyes boring into hers.

'How are you going to do that?' she asked, but before she could draw breath he leant in towards her and brushed his mouth against hers.

Fireworks seemed to go off deep inside her body and she wondered wildly for a second how the other diners would react if she suddenly burst into flames in front of them.

Caleb's lips were warm and firm, his mouth fitting perfectly with hers. She stood frozen to the spot, too befuddled to react, as a crazy surge of desire unfolded deep inside her, spiralling out to the very ends of her fingers and toes.

His hands slid into her hair and instinctively she sank against him, her body craving the hard press of his against it.

A moment later she was left gasping for air when he drew away from her, giving her a strange knowing kind of smile and nodding towards the upper mezzanine, his arm pressing into her back as he encouraged her to mount the staircase with him.

'Let's go and find our seats, ready for the show,' he murmured into her ear, his breath tickling the sensitive skin on her exposed neck and making her shiver with longing.

Oh, goodness, it was going to be impossible to keep her cool if he was going to be this physically attentive all evening.

Somehow she managed to make it up the stairs on rather wobbly legs and had just settled herself into a chair that Caleb held out for her when Carter and his wife arrived and she had to stand up again to greet them.

In a fit of continued nerves at Caleb's proximity, Elena managed to knock her knife onto the floor, which then skidded under the table, causing a flurry of amused response as they all tried to locate it so she could retrieve it, apologising profusely as she did so, which fortuitously broke what could have been an icy start to the meeting.

There was something so healthy and vibrant about the couple, Elena thought dazedly as she smiled a more composed hello to them once she'd straightened up after her little mishap. She guessed that was what people who had incredible wealth and an inclination to take care of themselves looked like—polished and dauntingly self-assured. They put Elena in mind of a high-powered couple from the eighties' American soap operas she used to watch for guilty pleasure late at night during her university days.

Mrs Carter, who must have been in her early fifties, wore a flattering shift dress with wide shoulders and her hair was so coiffed it looked as though every strand had been sprayed separately into place. Mr Carter, who looked to be of a similar age, was just as polished in a dark grey double-breasted suit and blindingly white shirt to match his blindingly white teeth.

Caleb took the lead by holding out his hand for them to shake and introducing Elena as his girlfriend—which only added to the fluttering sensation in the pit of her stomach—then gesturing for them all to take a seat.

The atmosphere was a little awkward at first; Mr Carter appeared to be on the defensive, as if waiting for Caleb to become angry about the fact he was considering walking away from the partnership they'd been discussing, but after a few minutes of attentive questions from Caleb about how he and his wife liked Barcelona and being given a few pointers on the places they must visit whilst here, he appeared to relax a little.

The waiter came over and they ordered a bottle of local wine and a selection of food for the table on Caleb's recommendation and the conversation turned to business.

At first Elena sat back, drinking her wine a little too fast and watching Caleb lead the discussion with something close to awe. She found his clear handle on the market and technical, as well as fiscal, knowledge truly breathtaking and he seemed to be impressing Carter too, because the man was actually sitting back in his seat now and had taken his hand off his wife's lap, where they'd been holding hands.

Putting down her glass, Elena gave the woman a smile and was rewarded with a genuinely warm grin back.

'So how long have you two been together?' Brie Carter asked her with an inquisitive glint in her eye as the two men expounded on the state of the recharge-able battery market in the States.

Elena's stomach lurched. 'Er…well, we've known each other since we met at Cambridge. Caleb was doing an Erasmus exchange year and we became good friends.'

'And that turned into more, I see,' Brie said with a hint of a plea for some juicy gossip to break up the work talk.

Elena glanced at Caleb to check whether he was lis-tening, but he seemed to be deep in conversation with Jonathan Carter. Taking another large gulp of her wine and feeling its warming effect steady her nerves, she leant forward in her chair and said, 'To be honest, it was a love-hate relationship for a long while, but we met again recently and worked things out and we're a strong couple now.'

'I guess that's what makes powerful men so exciting to be with,' Brie said with a glimmer of recognition in her eyes. 'The unpredictability of them.'

Elena smiled. 'Yes, I've always had trouble working Caleb out. He keeps his emotions close to his chest and can come across as a bit of a prickly character, but he's actually an intensely kind, passionate and caring man.'

It wasn't just the alcohol warming her veins now, but also the recognition of the truth in her words. She'd never met anyone else like Caleb and she suspected she never would again. He was one of a kind.

'That's good to hear,' Brie said with a thoughtful nod.

Sensing an advantage in convincing Carter's wife about Caleb's suitability for a working relationship with her husband, she took the opportunity to endorse him some more.

'He's the most brilliant, focused and hard-working person I've ever met and he'll be the best business partner your husband's ever had,' she said, throwing the older woman a conspiratorial smile. 'He never fails to excite and inspire me, both in a business sense and on a personal level. Always has.'

She felt Caleb shift next to her as he slid his arm across her back to rest gently on her shoulders. She nearly jumped out of her seat as she felt his fingers brush against the exposed skin of her upper arm, sending little electric currents rushing across her nerve endings. Turning her head, she saw he was looking at her with that dark intensity in his gaze again and her cheeks flooded with heat as panic rose in her chest. Had he heard what she'd just said about him?

If so, did he realise she was telling the truth and not just putting on an act for the Americans?

But his expression gave nothing away, his attention seemingly focused on the complex business discussion he was involved in as he asked her to qualify an answer to something about the market for rechargeable batteries in the UK. She forced herself to relax her rigid posture and answer as clearly and succinctly as possible while her pulse raced and her palms grew hot with worry that he'd overheard her gushing admiration of him.

But when she'd finished he nodded his thanks, removed his arm and turned back to Carter, as if he'd not noticed a thing.

It seemed he hadn't heard what she'd said about him and he was just playing the part of attentive boyfriend.

Thank goodness.

It could put them both in a really difficult position if he knew how she really felt about him, especially as their relationship was such a tangled mess. Her stomach lurched as she allowed herself to consider how it might feel to pursue a real relationship with him. It was a disconcerting yet also unnervingly exciting idea, but she'd be a fool to even entertain it. She'd come to Barcelona in the hopes of being his partner in business only—which, of course, she'd thoroughly messed up—and to hope, even for a second, that anything of a romantic nature might develop with Caleb now, when he couldn't remember what had happened between them, was completely reprehensible.

Pushing the notion to the back of her mind, she made sure to keep the conversation focused on Brie after that and they spent the rest of the meal chatting happily about her daughters and the wedding that she was helping to plan, which was taking place in Boston that August.

Elena tried her best to concentrate on what Brie was

saying but she couldn't help but tune in to what Caleb and Jonathan were discussing, especially when their voices became more animated. Thankfully, it seemed it was just friendly rivalry, and the two men became more and more relaxed with each other as more wine was consumed and the evening wore on.

Despite her worry about Caleb struggling due to his head injury, he'd coped admirably with the questions that Carter fired at him. It seemed he'd done it; he'd kept his cool and turned the American's opinion of him around. In fact, to Elena's delight and relief, he appeared to have returned to the man she remembered knowing all those years ago at university.

The idea of it made her heart flutter.

She'd become increasingly aware of him sitting only inches away from her throughout the end of the meal, his heady, clean scent in her nose and the heat from his body warming her side, so it was something of a relief to her addled senses when Jonathan pronounced it time for them to go back to their hotel.

The four of them stood and the two men shook hands firmly, Carter's initial wariness nowhere to be seen now as he clapped Caleb jovially on the back.

'Good to meet you, Caleb. I'll get my team to contact you about moving forward with this partnership as soon as we get back to the States.'

Brie leaned in to give Elena an elegant air-kiss near each cheek, then drew her close on the pretext of giving her a hug to whisper in her ear. 'It's wonderful to see how Caleb inspires such genuine loyalty in you. I can tell by the way you look at him how much you care about him.'

She drew back to look Elena in the eye. 'It's heartening to see, especially after the rumours we've heard about what a hard character he is to get on with,' she murmured. 'But, after meeting the two of you tonight, I sincerely think my husband's going to find working with him a positive experience.'

Jonathan Carter turned from listening to Caleb's assurances he'd be primed for the next point of contact to give Elena a dazzling smile. 'It was wonderful to meet you too, Elena. Caleb here's a lucky man.' He slapped Caleb on the back again and Elena had to hide her frown of concern when she noticed him wincing in pain from his injured rib.

'Thank you for preventing my wife from dying of boredom with all our business talk,' Carter went on, not seeming to notice Caleb's physical discomfort. 'It looked like the two of you had a lot in common, no doubt swapping tales about the two of us!' he boomed, gesturing between himself and Caleb, then sliding his arm around his wife's waist and giving her a hard squeeze which made her gasp and slap him gently on the chest in retaliation.

Elena's breath caught in her throat as she felt Caleb slide his arm around her waist and pull her closer to him, as if wanting to mirror the American's loving behaviour.

As part of the act, Elena reminded herself fuzzily.

Heart thumping in her throat, she watched the couple as they weaved away through the tables towards the stairs leading to the ground floor, then carefully extricated herself from Caleb's hold on the pretence of grabbing her jacket from the back of her chair.

'Well, that went well, I think,' she said, looking up into Caleb's face to find him frowning, as if perplexed about something.

Because she'd moved away from him so deliberately? Probably.

She felt pretty sure he wasn't used to women rejecting his touch.

It made her wonder again whether he'd heard her gushing praise of him.

'You did a great job, Caleb; it sounds like a partnership is in the bag,' she said, shrugging her jacket on awkwardly. She couldn't quite look him in the eye now. Not after she'd seen the way he was looking at her a moment ago.

As much as she wanted him to know she was sorry for the way she'd treated him in the past and wanted to make amends, she also didn't want to give him the wrong impression here tonight.

She needed to be more careful.

'Yes, he seemed to be on board,' Caleb said, his voice a low, seductive rumble that sent a shiver of unwelcome longing down her spine.

'Shall we go?' she asked, her voice sounding prim and strained as she overcompensated for her body's inappropriate reaction.

'Sure. Lead the way,' he said, gesturing for her to leave first, with a somewhat unnerving glint in his eyes.

* * *

As they walked away from the Gothic quarter, Caleb finally allowed himself to think about what he'd overheard Elena saying to Carter's wife about him.

She could have just been playing the game of being his lover, of course, but there had been something in the way she'd said it that had made his breath catch in his throat. Clearly she'd thought he wasn't listening because when he'd turned to catch her eye she'd looked almost—shifty.

So there *was* something more than friendship between them, just as he'd suspected. But if that was the case, why was she pretending that there wasn't?

He had no idea.

What he did know was that he was going to make sure to find out before she left for England and do everything in his power to smooth things over with her.

The kiss they'd shared before Carter and his wife had arrived had made his body hum with tension all evening. When he'd seen the look of concern on her face he'd wanted to do something to reassure her he was going to do whatever it took to win the Americans over, but as soon as his mouth had met hers he'd been lost in a great surge of hunger for her. The sounds and sights of the restaurant had faded away until all he was aware of was the gentle sway and press of Elena's body against his and the sweet, exotic fragrance of her. Her mouth had felt so good against his it had taken a monumental effort to drag himself away from her and not grab her hand and run with her out of the restaurant and jump into the next cab to take them home.

After that, watching her charming Carter's wife and dazzling the couple with her wit, intelligence and profound beauty—he'd found it almost impossible to keep his mind solely on the business conversation.

Throughout the entire evening he'd been intensely aware of the connection between them, taut and alive, as if it was a tangible thing drawing them ever closer together.

He wanted to know more about what was going on between them—*had* to know, for the sake of his sanity.

Yes, he assured himself, he wasn't going to let her go until he'd got the full measure of Elena Jones.

CHAPTER SEVEN

THE CAR PICKED them up a couple of streets away from the restaurant and took them straight home to Caleb's apartment, the two of them sitting in a buzzing, tension-filled silence as they looked out at the wide city streets flashing by.

'You were great tonight,' Caleb said after his driver had pulled up outside his building and he'd helped Elena out of the car, feeling her cool, small hand in his and marvelling at how good it felt to have it there. 'Carter's wife really seemed to like you.'

She flashed him an equable smile as she straightened up. 'I liked her; she was a really lovely woman, very focused on her family.'

'Well, I owe you big for what you did for me tonight.'

There was a loaded moment where they stood and looked at each other, the gentle, far-off sounds of the city at night making him feel as though they were trapped in a bubble together. Caleb broke the strange energy by smiling and saying, 'Anyway, thanks, Elena. I really appreciate your help.'

She shuffled a little on the spot and nodded, her

bright eyes gleaming in the light thrown out from the streetlight above them.

'It was my pleasure. Anything for a friend.'

The emphasis she put on the word 'friend' made him bristle.

It suddenly struck him that by tomorrow her forty-eight hours of observation of him would be up and she might well leave and return to England.

And he found he really didn't want her to go.

He wondered where this intense need to keep her here longer had sprung from. Okay, he found her really attractive and was impressed with her business acumen and how smart and savvy she was, but he never normally felt this sort of draw to a woman.

There was something different about her, something *compulsive*.

He had to explore what this thing was between them, or it would haunt him for ever.

Turning back to look into her hooded eyes, he was intrigued to see she seemed to be having her own non-verbal debate with herself. Was she only holding back because she thought he was still incapacitated? *Weak?* Frustration surged through him. Well, he wasn't. He was completely in his right mind and he knew damn well what he wanted—her, and now.

Pulling his key card out of his pocket, he let them into his building and they stepped into the lift that would take them up to his apartment, Elena swaying gently in her heels beside him.

Being around her felt *right*, dammit—as if she were a missing link in his life.

And he was going to do whatever it took to have her back in it.

'Elena?' he said, turning to face her once the lift had begun its smooth ascent.

'I know what happened between us at university. I know we were more than just friends. And I know we didn't act on it because of Jimmy.'

Elena swallowed hard as blood rushed to her head and her stomach did a backflip.

His memory had finally returned.

'You remember?' she whispered through lips that would barely form the words.

He nodded, his beautiful mouth curving into another of its wolfish, dangerous smiles.

The lift came to an abrupt stop, making her stomach do an extra flip for good measure. She could barely breathe with worry about what he was going to say now he remembered what had happened all those years ago. Would he be angry with her? Shout and swear at her, or just be coldly dismissive again?

Her pulse throbbed in her head. She really hoped he wouldn't go ballistic and chuck her out on the street now, not after what they'd just been through together. Not now she'd finally met the real Caleb again. She couldn't bear it.

The door of the lift swished open and he strode out and straight over to his door without another word, slipping the key into the lock then holding the door open for her to walk through it.

She strode into his apartment with her head held resolutely high, determined to keep her cool, to restate her case and hopefully prove to him once and for all that she was sorry about how their relationship had ended.

Her heart hammered in her chest as she watched him shrug off his jacket and hang it up before finally turning back to face her.

His expression was impassive as his dark gaze bored into hers.

'We've wasted a lot of time leading our separate lives and I think it's time to remedy that.'

She stared at him in shock. Had she misheard? It sounded as though he was talking about pursuing more than friendship with her. 'I'm sorry?' she stuttered, aware that her hands had begun to shake at her sides.

'What happened was a long time ago, and we're both free and single now,' he continued, apparently oblivious to her befuddlement. 'Without anything standing in our way. No partners, no memory loss—'

'Do you remember everything that happened between us?' she asked, her voice sounding shaky with anticipation and hope.

There was a flash of something in his eyes, remembered pain perhaps, but it quickly disappeared. 'Yes.'

'And you forgive me for it?'

He took a deliberate pace towards her and raised his hand to touch her face, smoothing the backs of his long fingers gently over her cheek.

'I'm not going to let some stupid argument from the past get in the way of what we have here—right now. We're good together, you and I. We fit.'

'Caleb—are you sure?' Her voice came out as a low

breath of air as sensation rushed over her skin at his touch. Had she really done it? Made up for the hurt she'd caused him in the past? Her spirits soared as the heavy weight of guilt began to lift and she finally felt as though she could breathe properly again.

'Yes, I'm sure,' he said with a conviction she felt deep in her chest.

Letting out a breathy laugh, she said, 'This is all happening so quickly. I don't know what to think—'

'I understand why you might be unsure about restarting something between us,' he murmured, cutting her off. 'We live in different cities, live different lives, but we can work around that.'

She swallowed hard, her thoughts spinning wildly. Could she finally be about to get her Caleb back?

'This would make me happy and I think it would make you happy too—you and me, here together, tonight.' His mouth curved into a seductive smile, making her insides quiver and her heart leap about in her chest.

Heat rose to her face as a strange sort of panic settled in her stomach. Was she ready for this? After all this time, regretting what had happened between them and hoping, wishing she could do something to make it better—that she could go back in time and do it all differently—now that she was actually here in the moment, a moment where her whole life could change, she was afraid. Terrified.

What if it all went wrong again?

'It seems too soon to be jumping into something, especially after your accident—' she hedged.

He shrugged away her concern. 'I'm fine now. You

don't need to worry about me any more.' He moved even closer, making the air crackle around her. 'And I thought you were the one who liked to take every positive out of a situation.'

There was no comeback for that.

'I *know* you, Elena.'

'You do?' she asked breathlessly.

'Yes. And I know we still want the same thing.'

The look of desire in his eyes made her whole body shiver with longing.

'And what's that?' she said, knowing exactly what he was going to say, but hoping he wouldn't because then she'd have to make a really difficult decision.

'That you still want me as much as I want you.'

He was so close now, the feel of his soft breath on her skin making her lips tingle with the craving to feel his mouth on hers again. Somewhere in the back of her mind she was aware that she should stop this, draw away and be the sensible one, insist they talk about all that had happened between them first, point out that it was too soon for them to fall into bed together. That she didn't think it was a good idea.

But that would have been a lie. And she wasn't going to lie to him any more.

So instead she said, 'Yes, I want you.'

Before she could qualify that with 'but I still don't know if it's a good idea *right now*' he'd closed the tiny gap between them and pressed his mouth hard to hers.

Her body responded without conscious thought, her lips opening against his to allow his tongue to dip into her mouth, tasting her, possessing her.

Being careful not to crush his broken rib, she pressed herself against him and felt his arms slip tightly around her back, holding her close to him. His strength enveloped her, making her senses reel with pleasure, and she stumbled backwards as he moved forwards, guiding her gently but purposefully towards the corridor where his empty bedroom waited for them.

They reached the bed in a tangle of limbs, with her grabbing at his clothes with a frenzy and a need that took her by surprise.

Elena had never felt so wanted, so worshipped, as Caleb tugged his shirt over his head, not seeming to care that he was ripping buttons off in his haste. She almost stopped when she heard him grunt as his broken rib must have twanged with pain but, before she could say a word, he shook his head and said, 'I'm fine,' grasping the straps tied behind her head to release the halter neck of her dress then tug at the zip so the silky material fell open and glided down to pool at her feet.

'So beautiful,' he muttered as he bent to kiss her again, sliding his hands down her back, tracing the lines of her body with his fingertips and sending her into raptures of ecstasy. Just the feel of his hands on her was enough to make her shudder with joy.

'There's nothing like making up for lost time,' he murmured against her mouth and all she could do was smile and nod in agreement, her brain too fuzzy with lust to help her form anything like intelligible words.

He guided her gently backwards until her legs hit the side of the bed, but she knew she'd have to be the one to lead this because of his injury, so she wrapped her hands around his arms and steered him round so the bed was behind him instead and used the momentum of him being slightly off balance to make him first sit, then lie down.

Then she climbed carefully on top of him, kissing him hard and covetously, the sense of finally being allowed to have him back after all these years of yearning for it making her frantic and greedy.

And some time shortly after that her brain shut down completely and all that was left was the feel of their two bodies moving together and sweet, sweet fulfilment.

The next morning Elena woke to find sun pouring in through the large warehouse-sized windows of Caleb's bedroom.

Blinking blearily, it took her a moment for the events of the night before to rush back to her—and remember exactly what had happened between them.

She'd slept with Caleb.

And it had been amazing.

In the heat of the moment, with his mouth on hers and his body pressed so close they'd almost become one, she'd completely lost herself in him, hazily justifying her easy capitulation by telling herself she owed him some happiness, though in truth she knew deep down she'd done it for her own purely selfish reasons. She'd wanted him so much it had caused her physical pain to imagine tearing herself away from him and stopping it.

And it had been such an incredible night, so full of passion and pleasure.

But it all felt like a surreal dream now.

Turning to look at Caleb lying next to her, she felt her insides flutter and heat with pleasure.

In truth, she was still confused about his sudden change in attitude towards her, especially after he'd been so vociferous at their first meeting about not wanting to have anything to do with her again, but she guessed that after helping him turn Carter's opinion of him around he must have felt she'd paid her dues.

Not that she'd done it for that reason alone. She'd wanted him to be successful with the meeting; she could sense how much it meant to him to win the partnership deal and keep his business thriving—the company he'd worked so hard to build from nothing, just like she had with hers. She wanted him to be happy. To be the man she remembered again.

Trying not to think about how precarious the future of her own company still was, she watched him for a while, his eyelids flickering gently in REM sleep and his wide brow smooth now without his regulation frown creasing it.

She'd been happy too last night, happier than she could remember being in a very long time. Because of him. The guilt and regret that had followed her around for so long that it had felt like an intrinsic part of her seemed to have vanished, leaving a strange, yearning ache in its wake. One she hoped to satisfy with something new and positive and exciting.

A relationship with Caleb, perhaps.

Pushing away a strange nervous sensation in her chest, she slid out of bed and went into his en suite bathroom to take a quick shower, lathering herself all over with his zesty-smelling body wash.

The way he'd looked at her last night when they'd arrived back in his apartment had shaken her to her core. There had been such heat in his eyes, a little like the carnal ferocity she'd seen during their first meeting, although this time it had been driven by desire rather than anger.

He'd looked at her like that before—the night she'd told him how she really felt about him at university— and the impression it had left on her had stayed with her for the rest of her life.

That feeling of being so coveted, so *wanted* was a hard one to forget. She'd craved it over the years, desperately trying to find a way to feel like that again, but she'd not been successful.

Until now.

She knew she was being reckless here, jumping into something so intense with him so quickly, but she was sick and tired of being sensible. It had brought her nothing but pain and stress in the past and it was high time she started being brave and taking some risks with her heart. Otherwise her life would only ever be half lived and what a waste that would be.

After drying herself, she pulled on an oversized towelling robe that she found on the back of the door and padded quietly back over to the bed.

He was lying on his side facing away from her, towards the wall, apparently still asleep if his regular breathing pattern was anything to go by. Moving to stand by his side of the bed, she looked down at him, at his strong, arresting face, with his usually neatly swept back dark hair mussed and falling over his forehead, making him look younger and less fierce.

She jumped in shock as his eyes sprang open and he grabbed for her, wrapping his arm around her legs and pulling her roughly towards him so she lost her balance and toppled onto him with a squeal of surprise. He kissed her hard before rolling her over, so he was on top now, his brow momentarily pinched as he remembered his damaged rib.

'What are you doing, you maniac?' she spluttered, laughing at his self-reproachful grimace.

'Just saying good morning,' he replied, flashing her a grin before he kissed her again so thoroughly it made her toes curl.

'Well, okay then,' she purred, cupping his jaw in her hands, her whole body buzzing with the joy of finding herself in his arms again. 'I'm so glad we're friends again.'

He frowned, looking a little perplexed. 'Friends? Do you do this with all of your friends?' he asked, nuzzling her neck and placing soft, sensuous kisses against her hyper-sensitised skin.

She laughed, then sighed, running her hands into his bedhead hair. 'No, just you.'

Pulling back, he looked straight into her eyes, his gaze unflinching and determined.

'I know you don't need to be here with me any more, but I want you to stay for a bit longer. We should go to Gaudi's Park Güell today. It's an amazing place. I'd like to show it to you.'

'I don't know, Caleb; perhaps you should rest today—'

He held up a hand to cut her off. 'You can't come all the way to Barcelona and not visit all the places of interest.'

'Places of interest? You sound like a tour guide,' she said with a tease in her tone.

'There's no one better than a resident to show you all the best bits of a city,' he said with a seductive lift of his eyebrow. 'I know all its secrets,' he murmured, lifting his hand to trace the line of her jaw and sending little currents of sensation down her throat, which joined with the ones already humming deep inside her body.

She gave him a dazed sort of smile, barely able to concentrate as he slid the backs of his fingers down her throat, then lower to skim over the swell of her breasts.

'Well, that would be…really…amazing…' she murmured, her voice coming out broken and husky as she struggled to concentrate on forming the words.

Lust twisted her insides as he leant forwards and kissed her hard again. She responded instinctively to his touch, sliding her arms around his back and wriggling closer to him.

Pulling her underneath his strong, hard body, he murmured, 'Okay, but we'll go later. Much, much later.'

They spent the rest of the morning in bed, only getting out of it for a minute to fetch some food from his fridge for lunch, which they ate right there, sitting naked on top of the covers.

'This reminds me of all those meals we ate sitting on

my bed whilst working on our project at uni—though of course we were fully clothed for those,' Elena said, grinning at him with one eyebrow raised. 'I found breadcrumbs in my sheets for days after that. Who knows where we'll find them after this.'

She laughed and he smiled back at her, wishing he could remember the time she was reminiscing about. It was getting harder and harder to pretend he knew the stories she relayed without it seeming suspicious that he didn't bring up some of his own recollections.

He felt a little guilty about lying to her last night, but he'd been so sick of her holding back and wasting time when it had been so clear they were destined to end up like this anyway.

Anyway, she seemed much happier now, and if she was happy then so was he.

After they'd finished eating she left the room and returned a few minutes later in a pair of jeans and a loose-fitting, soft pink T-shirt with her hair scraped back into a ponytail, her lips shiny with some kind of clear lipstick that he wanted to kiss off immediately. She didn't need make-up; she was just as beautiful without it.

'Come on, lazybones, get your carcass out of bed. I thought you were going to show me some of your secrets,' she said, giving him a wide grin.

He rolled out of bed with a grunt and stood up. Pulling her towards him, he kissed her until she squealed with pleasure, but she pushed him away when he began to drag her back towards the bed.

'No, no, you said we should go out and I think you're right; we can't spend all day in bed.'

'Why not?' he murmured, thinking it would be more than okay with him. He couldn't get enough of her—the scent of her soft skin, the feel of her strong legs wrapped around him, the little breathy moans she made in his ear as they moved together...

'Caleb, seriously, get dressed so we can go out.'

He shot her a grimace of annoyance. 'Okay, okay, but it won't be as much fun as staying here,' he ground out. 'I have plenty more secrets I could show you right here in the bedroom.'

'Later,' she said with laughter in her voice.

He loved it when she smiled like that—like she couldn't have stopped herself even if she'd wanted to.

He took her to Palo Alto, an enclosed old manufacturing complex situated a few roads back from the beach, which was like a hidden island of industrial-style buildings festooned with brightly coloured creepers and greenery that had turned it into a wonderful garden oasis. The buildings had all been converted over the years into light, open workshops for businesses focused on regeneration and rehabilitation of the city and beyond.

'No tourists know about it, only the residents of the city,' Caleb told her as they walked through the alleyways between the buildings, soaking up the effervescent but peaceful air of the place. 'I love wandering around here; I find it a really inspiring place to be. You know Araya Industries started out in one of these workshops so it'll always be a special place for me. It's where I realised my dreams.'

'It's wonderful. Thank you for trusting me—an outsider—' she winked at him '—to see it. I'm honoured,' she said, turning to kiss him next to a cascade of fuchsia flowers and russet-coloured leaves.

Then afterwards, at Elena's request, they took a cab out to the spectacular multicoloured Park Güell, which had been designed by Gaudi. He watched her run her hand along the top of the wave-shaped benches that had been decorated with millions of pieces of brightly patterned broken tiles, enjoying her delight at the eccentricity of the design.

After sitting for a while, looking out over the picturesque views of the city and the fairy tale–style gatehouses that looked as if they could be made from gingerbread and icing, they went down the steps to see the forest of Greek Doric columns underneath, which had been designed to house an old marketplace beneath the plateau of the park.

He watched her as she wound her way through the pillars, tracing her fingers over the smooth stone and gazing up at the colourful cornices on the ceiling, and it hit him that for the first time since he'd seen her in that hospital room she looked truly relaxed.

The idea that he could be responsible for that made him feel heady with pleasure, as if he could deal with anything life threw at him right now, as long as Elena was here with him. She made him feel light and positive, buzzed and excited…and what was that other sensation…?

Happy.

His breath caught in his throat as the word pierced through him.

It was a feeling that had been missing from his life for far too long now. And Elena was the catalyst—because he knew without a doubt that she was his ideal woman—smart, sexy and so beautiful it made his chest ache to look at her.

And then, out of nowhere, something strange happened.

A memory flashed through his mind: of Elena's face, cold and hard with indifference, just before she slammed a door in his face.

It left him winded, gasping to drag air into his lungs again, his head swimming and thick, as though too heavy for his body to hold up. A slow trickle of horror-tinged despair slid sickeningly through him and he had to lean against the nearest pillar to stop himself from sliding to the floor.

A moment later the real Elena was there next to him, her hands on his shoulders and a look of deep concern on her beautiful face.

'Caleb! Are you okay?'

The face that looked into his now was so different from the one his mind had conjured up a moment ago he felt relief flood through him. Had it just been his subconscious warning him not to get too carried away with what was developing between them? Not to get too close in case it went wrong like all his other relationships had over the last few years?

Well, to hell with that. He wasn't going to let her go

away because he was afraid of this thing between them failing. He wouldn't let it.

'I'm fine,' he said, forcing his mouth into a reassuring smile. 'My rib's just giving me a bit of pain, that's all.'

She nodded, still frowning. 'Okay, then let's get out of here. You're probably pushing yourself too hard.'

'I'm fine, Elena,' he growled, annoyed at her fussing around him, not wanting this one small blip to ruin the wonderful day they'd been having.

She seemed to sense the agitation with himself behind his snappiness because she gave him a knowing smile and said, 'Okay, then let's go and get something to eat. I don't know about you but I could eat a horse right now.'

He nodded his agreement, grateful to her for not making a big scene. He didn't want the remainder of their time together marred by his minor ailments.

Pulling her towards him, he placed a firm kiss on her mouth, wanting to prove to her how happy he was to have her here with him and that he hoped there would be much more of it to come.

She kissed him back with a fervour that rocked him to his soul, proving to him the connection he felt to her wasn't one-sided.

They were going to need to have a serious conversation soon about how to make a relationship work when they were living so far away from each other. Because he knew now that was what he wanted.

He so wished he could remember the relationship they'd had when they were younger. Perhaps it would give him more insight into how to solidify their connection now.

That damn accident had been such bad timing—though it had at least prompted her to stay in Spain a bit longer, and in his apartment too, for which he knew he should be very grateful. It had brought them together after all.

It was disconcerting though, not having all that information about her available to him. Still, more things seemed to be coming back to him in dribs and drabs now so perhaps his brain was beginning to heal.

Pushing away his lingering unease, he kissed her once more before taking her hand to lead her out of the park.

It would all be fine once the rest of his memory came back.

CHAPTER EIGHT

THE NEXT MORNING Caleb rolled reluctantly out of bed, leaving a sexily rumpled and tantalisingly warm Elena in it.

'Do you want me to come to the hospital with you?' she murmured sleepily as he strode towards the en suite bathroom for a shower.

He stopped in his tracks and looked back at her. She was smiling at him in that earnest, intent way that always made his heart turn over.

In truth, he loved the idea of spending the whole of the day with her by his side, but he definitely didn't want her coming to the hospital with him just in case something happened there that made it obvious his memory hadn't fully returned yet.

'No, it'll be boring for you. You stay here, or go shopping or sightseeing or something. I need to go into the office to make sure everything is running smoothly without me but I'll be back here to spend the afternoon with you.'

She gave him a pained look. 'Okay, but don't get

caught up in the office and forget the time. You should really be resting at home still.'

He walked back to the bed and sat down on the side of it, brushing a rogue strand of hair away from her forehead. 'I tell you what, why don't you just spend all day naked in my bed—that'll give me all the incentive I need to come home as soon as possible.'

Laughing, she pulled him down for a kiss and he gave in to her demand and kissed her back, pulling the sheet that separated them away and rolling on top of her, telling himself he still had plenty of time to make his appointment.

He was late for his appointment.

Luckily, the doctor was also running late with his last patient so Caleb didn't need to apologise for his tardiness as he strode into the consulting room. The extra time he'd got to spend with Elena would have been totally worth missing the appointment for anyway. He was fine, still a bit blurry about the events in his past, but, as he told the doctor, who looked at him with a mixture of concern and perplexity at his attitude, he didn't care—he was alive and he had a beautiful, compassionate woman waiting for him back at home and that was what mattered.

Life was good.

After being put through some rather over-the-top extensive tests by the consultant and agreeing reluctantly to come back later in the week for additional testing, he finally managed to escape the hospital, intent on dropping in at Araya Industries for the barest of moments to satisfy himself that everything was running well there before heading straight back to Elena's warm smile and comforting embrace.

Striding through Reception, he greeted a couple of the PAs who worked for his colleagues with a smile, both of them blinking at him in surprise before hurriedly returning his cheery salutation.

Up on his floor he found a rather bemused Benita sitting at her desk outside his office, and he flashed her a smile in greeting then asked her if she could please come in once she'd finished the email she was typing. She stared at him in surprise, also seemingly unnerved by his new jovial attitude, before nodding jerkily, the expression on her face remaining wary as if worried he was just lulling her into a false sense of security before putting the boot in.

Clearly he had a lot of work to do on his people skills.

He'd always been aware that he came across as intense and forthright, but he'd never considered it to be a failing before, too caught up in the running of his business to pay it much mind. Elena's appearance in his life and her bravery in challenging him about it had opened his eyes to it though. It was as if she'd drawn out something that had been buried for far too long within him. With this in mind he made a firm resolution to review the way he dealt with his colleagues in the future.

Sitting down at his desk, he turned on his computer and was just about to look over his email when there was a tentative knock on his door. He called, 'Come in,' and a moment later Benita's head appeared around the door, her face set in a circumspect smile as if she was a little afraid to enter the room in case he was waiting in there to bite her head off.

'Benita, come in,' he said kindly, giving her an encouraging nod.

She shuffled into the room, keeping a good four feet back from the desk where he was sitting.

'How are you feeling?' she asked with trepidation in her voice.

'I'm fine,' he said, wincing inside as he caught the brusqueness in his tone. 'Thanks for asking,' he added and almost laughed at the look of incredulity on her face.

'So, did Carter's people get in contact?' he asked.

She nodded, moving closer to the desk now as if she was beginning to trust his new upbeat attitude. 'I've put the minutes of the Skype meeting onto the DRM and the relevant account managers have been briefed.'

'Good, good,' he said, nodding. 'Thanks.'

She cleared her throat. 'It's good to see you back, Señor Araya. We were worried when we heard about your accident. It looks like your friend took good care of you though.'

'Yes, she did,' he said, the thought of Elena lying naked in his bed waiting for him distracting him for a moment.

'Did you work out your differences about partnering with her business?' Benita asked.

He stared at her like an idiot for a moment, wondering whether his wandering thoughts had somehow made him mix up the words Benita had said to him.

'What did you say?'

She looked a little taken aback, as if she might have put her foot in it. 'I just meant—it seemed as though you were getting on well again—after your meeting didn't go as smoothly as you'd hoped.'

'Our meeting?'

'With Señorita Jones. On the morning before your accident.'

She was looking at him as if she was worried that he'd gone insane.

He batted a hand at her, his thoughts swirling and confused as a strange sinking feeling appeared out of nowhere and slid through his chest. 'Yes, yes, I remember.' He thought hard for a moment. 'Benita, did you forward me the supporting documents for that meeting?'

'Er…no, you asked me not to. I got the impression you weren't very keen to partner with her company.'

That was strange. Why would he have thought that?

'Well, send them over to me now, will you? I need to take a look at them.'

'Yes, of course.' She paused. 'Is there anything else I can do for you?'

He shook his head, his confusion about what was going on making his brain hurt. 'No, no, that'll be all. Thanks.'

She gave him a nod, then slipped out of the room.

Caleb booted up the DRM programme and clicked on the links that Benita sent through, which connected to a presentation Elena had apparently sent over before a meeting they were meant to be having on Friday.

A meeting he had no memory of.

He read through her proposal with interest, wondering why the hell he'd not jumped at the opportunity she'd put to him. She needed his battery for her cars and it looked to be a very lucrative deal for both of them.

What was wrong with him? Had he really been so blind or so busy with the American deal that he'd not recognised such a good prospect when she brought it directly to him?

When she'd helped him clinch Carter's business at the meeting the other day he'd been hugely impressed with her knowledge of the industry and her insight into what he did, so much so, he'd made a mental note to look up the company she ran in England, so why had he said no?

He remembered with a sting of conscience that she'd not wanted to discuss the row they'd apparently had right before they'd left for their meeting with the Carters. Had the argument been about him turning the possible partnership between their companies down?

And what had made him do it.

Now he thought about it, whenever he'd pressed her for more information about her business she'd changed the subject. This had surprised him at the time, but he'd written it off as her not wanting to discuss work during her time off.

Or perhaps she'd not wanted to discuss it while she thought he was mentally challenged.

Shutting off his screen, he decided it was time to go home and ask Elena some direct questions before she walked away and went to find someone else to partner with—an idea that filled him with anxiety. Afte all she'd done for him over the last few days he felt he owed her a debt of gratitude and perhaps this would be the perfect way to repay it.

Walking past Benita's desk, an idea occurred to him.

'Benita, could you book a table at Restaurant Hora for tomorrow night for two people? I know it's Valentine's night,' he said before she could say the words of warning that were clearly on her lips, 'but I know the owner. Just tell him it's for me and he'll find a way to fit us in.'

'Okay, consider it done,' Benita said with a reverential smile, something he'd not seen on her face before. 'Your friend's a lucky lady,' she called as he walked away.

'She is,' he threw back over his shoulder with a wry grin.

Though I think we've moved well past the friends stage now, he thought determinedly to himself as he made to set off home.

His apartment was quiet when he arrived back and he wondered whether she'd decided to go out and sightsee on her own after all, but as he strolled to his bedroom his spirits lifted when he saw she was sitting up naked in his bed with just a pair of glasses perched on her nose, tapping away on her laptop.

She was so absorbed in what she was doing she gave a little start when she finally noticed him standing in the doorway watching her and quickly snapped her laptop shut.

'Did you miss me?' he asked, shedding his clothes and dropping them on the floor as he moved towards her.

The expression in her eyes softened as he climbed onto the bed next to her and she twisted away for a second to put the laptop carefully by the side of the bed before turning back to face him.

He kissed her hard, feeling her sink against his body as he dragged her closer, the heat and softness of her skin soothing away his tension from being away from her.

'You were only gone a couple of hours,' she chided, but couldn't seem to help herself from smiling and saying, 'but yes, I missed you.'

'Good,' he said, sliding his hands down her body so she made a soft little sighing noise in the back of her throat.

It felt so right having her there in his arms, like nothing he'd ever experienced before. And it wasn't just lust driving that feeling, it was a sense of belonging too. She *belonged* here in his bed. He just needed to find a way to keep her there indefinitely now.

'So, Elena, tell me more about why you need my battery for your car?' he murmured into her hair as she kissed the spot at the back of his jaw that always sent him wild.

Whipping her head back, she looked at him, startled

'What...er...what do you want to know?' she asked her expression suddenly guarded.

The wariness in her eyes gave him pause.

'Why are you so jumpy? What aren't you telling me? Every time I've asked questions about your business you've changed the subject.'

Closing her eyes, she let out a long, frustrated sigh

then seemed to give herself a little shake and pull herself together.

'It seemed wrong to discuss business when you weren't well.' She looked down at her fingers, which were plucking nervously at the sheet. 'And the truth is, I didn't give you the full story then about what's going on with it. I was afraid you might see it as a weakness.'

Ah, so, as he'd suspected, there was more to it than she'd initially let on.

'Okay, I'm listening and I promise not to judge.'

She nodded and he saw her swallow hard. 'The truth is, we used to have a supplier who had designed a battery specifically to fit in the car. Initially we wanted to use an English company so we could say the car was fully manufactured in the UK, but very recently they've let us know that there's a fatal flaw with the design of it and they can't figure out how to fix it. So we're in a precarious position now. We have a lot of pre-orders and the shell of the car ready to go, but no battery to power it.'

He frowned, comprehending now why she'd be so panicked. It could be catastrophic for her business if she didn't find a replacement battery.

He nodded, thinking hard. 'Well, from what you've told me, and the documents I looked at today, it seems to me like it could be a mutually beneficial partnership. I don't see why it would be a problem to let you have the battery for your car.'

She stared at him, her eyes wide with surprise. 'What?'

He smiled at her bemusement. 'I'm saying I'd be happy to let your company use my battery in the car.'

To his consternation, instead of flinging herself into his arms with joy she continued to stare at him with a mixture of confusion and reticence. 'I don't know if that's a great idea now, Caleb.'

'Why not?'

Folding her arms, she fixed him with a hard stare. 'Because of what's happened here, with us. To be honest, I'd be a little nervous about mixing a business partnership with a personal one. What if things went wrong between us? It's a risk.'

He shook his head. 'You can't worry about that. We're adults. We can keep the two things separate. I can't imagine anything that could tear us apart now.'

Moving closer to her, he put his finger under her chin and tipped it up so she had to look right into his eyes. 'I think I've got a pretty good measure of you, Elena Jones, and I want us to move forward—together. What happened in the past doesn't matter any more. I want you to believe that.'

'I do believe that,' she murmured, tears welling in her eyes.

'Then trust me. Trust us.'

After a small pause filled with almost painful expectancy, she smiled and said, 'Yes, okay. I trust us.'

He nodded, feeling his heart turn over with relief. 'I'll talk to the team tomorrow about working out a partnership agreement.' He held up a finger. 'On one condition.'

Blinking away the tears, she raised her eyebrows in anticipation.

'That you agree to stay here for the rest of the week and go out with me tomorrow evening for Valentine's night. I've booked a table at Hora; it's the best Michelin-starred restaurant in town.'

Elena gazed at Caleb, her heart hammering hard in her chest, barely able to believe that her fortunes could have changed so significantly in the space of a few days. Blessed relief at the thought that she might now have a way to save her business and the livelihoods of her workforce cascaded through her.

Pulling him roughly to her, she dropped kisses all over his face until he started to laugh. 'I'd love to go to dinner with you. I've never been out on Valentine's Day before. Jimmy thought it was just a big marketing ploy to pressure men into spending ridiculous amounts of money on their girlfriends just to boost the big businesses' coffers.'

'Hmm, no wonder you left him—what a loser,' he said, running his fingers into her hair and looking deeply into her eyes. 'You deserve to be worshipped in every way possible, Elena Jones.'

The last of the worry she'd been carrying on her shoulders finally lifted, leaving her euphoric and light-headed.

Could this really be happening? Was it possible she'd not only found a way to save her business and quite likely propel it into a hugely successful venture with

Araya Industries' help, but that she'd also got Caleb back into the bargain?

A small voice in her head told her not to get too excited about that last part just yet. It was still early days, and it had all moved so fast. While he seemed intent on rebuilding their fractured relationship right now, she was aware that he might change his mind once the first flush of excitement had worn off.

Although, perhaps the accident really had made him reconsider his whole outlook on life. Maybe he was tired of carrying around the anger and resentment that had broken their connection in the first place and was genuinely taking her advice about being more positive.

But she still couldn't help but worry that it could all change again in the blink of an eye.

She'd just have to be careful.

Though she knew deep down that she was probably far too late to rein back her feelings now.

She knew exactly what this feeling was that warmed her heart and lifted her soul.

She was in love with him.

And always had been.

When she zoned back in she realised he was looking at her with a mixture of concern and amusement.

'Are you okay? Have I blown your mind?' he asked with laughter in his voice.

A shiver of delight ran through her. It was so wonderful to see him happy again.

'Yes,' she said, returning his smile, 'but in the very best way.'

'Good.'

She took a breath and clapped her hands onto her knees. 'Well, if I'm going to stay here for a bit longer and go out for a fancy meal to celebrate with you tomorrow I'm going to need to buy more clothes. I only brought enough for a couple of days.'

'Okay. I can recommend a few places in the city to look for some,' he said, shifting closer to her. 'There are some great independent boutiques in the Gothic Quarter. But for now,' he murmured, reaching out a hand to trace the dips and hollows of her throat and shoulder blades with his fingertips, sending waves of pleasure rushing through her body, 'I think we should celebrate our partnership in a very different, but just as appropriate, way.'

'Sounds like a wonderful idea to me,' she said with a smile, then pressed her mouth hard to his, sinking into the heady reassurance of his embrace.

CHAPTER NINE

THE BOUTIQUE CLOTHES shops that Caleb had recommended were exactly what Elena was looking for and she spent a happy couple of hours browsing through rails of perfectly tailored dresses in a range of delicate, lush materials, heartened by the knowledge that he was so tuned in to her taste. There was something rather wonderful about being so well understood.

It had been a long time since she'd felt this excited about picking out new clothes for a date; in fact, it had been a long time since she'd even gone shopping like this, preferring to buy her clothes over the Internet for speed and efficiency.

Her friend Hannah had often tried to get her to join her at the weekends to browse through the stores and go for long, lazy lunches, but Elena had always been up to her eyeballs in work and had felt that going shopping would be a waste of her time.

How could she have allowed herself to become so practical? So insular? So narrow-minded? It was such a waste of her younger years, spending all her time focused on work instead of enjoying the friendships and opportunities for fun that she had at her fingertips. This time she'd spent with Caleb had really brought that to the fore for her and she challenged herself to make more of her time outside of work from now on.

Hopefully with Caleb there to enjoy it alongside her.

She didn't like to think about how they were going to make a long distance relationship work when they were both so busy with their businesses, but she guessed if they were both fully invested in it they'd make it happen somehow. In fact she rather liked the idea of moving to Barcelona to be near him. Once the Zipabout car had its battery and had been released onto the market she'd be looking for a new project to start on anyway. The rest of her team could handle the day-to-day running of the sales and marketing side so she could work on new ideas remotely, at least to begin with.

But she was getting ahead of herself here. Caleb hadn't talked about continuing their relationship past the end of this week and she'd be a fool to start planning her whole future around him.

Even if she wanted to. Very, very much.

She'd never felt more alive and excited about life than when she was with him. He had a way of bringing out the very best in her.

After choosing some new outfits and underwear to last her for the rest of the week she popped into a perfumery, which she'd spotted on one of the small side streets on her way there, sniffing at each of the bottles with delight and trying to identify the main ingredients in them.

Something shifted strangely inside her as she picked

up a small, dark bottle in the shape of a swan. There was something incredibly familiar about it. Lifting it to her nose, she realised with a shock that she recognised the fragrance. It was one that Caleb had bought for her for a Christmas present, before they'd fallen out with each other. It had been the most exquisite thing she'd ever smelt and the revealing gesture of him taking the time to pick out and give her such a personal and intimate present had been the thing that had pushed her to finally admit how she really felt about him. She'd worn it on her skin for the whole week leading up to the last day of term, after they'd had their heart-to-heart about how they were perfect for each other and she'd promised him she'd finish her relationship with Jimmy as soon as she got home.

After she'd failed to come through on that promise and Caleb had made it clear he wanted nothing more to do with her she'd felt sick with shame and sadness every time she smelled that scent and had thrown it away.

She'd regretted that rashness for a long time afterwards though. In the end it was the only thing she'd had left to remind her of him. Despite repeated attempts to contact him and apologise, once he'd gone back to Spain she'd never heard from him again. It had been as if he'd never existed.

Smelling the scent again now brought back her intensely confused feelings of desperation to be with him, despite her fears that they just weren't practically suited. A memory of him drawing her close, leaning in on the pretext of smelling the perfume on her neck and instead brushing his lips against her skin, flashed across her mind. It had been one of the happiest, most intimate, most electrifying moments of her life.

She'd often wished she could have bottled that feeling to remind her of happier times.

And now she had it, right here in her hand.

Striding over to the counter, she handed the perfume to the sales assistant and drew her purse out of her bag.

'I've been searching for this for years,' she said, giving the woman a delighted grin. 'I'm so happy I've finally found it again.'

Caleb spent the day at work after calling his colleagues into a meeting to discuss how they'd move forward with both the partnership with the Americans and also with Elena's company.

He'd set the tone at the very beginning by being more friendly and relaxed than usual and had smiled to himself as he'd caught the looks of bemusement and surprise that had passed between his colleagues.

There had been a real buzz of excitement in the room as he laid out what had happened in the last few days. He'd made a point of taking a step back so that the project managers had a chance to take the lead, even though he itched to stay fully in control, and it had yielded great results. They were all smiling and buoyed up by the time the meeting concluded, which, he realised with a shock of sudden insight, was an unusual occurrence. Before he would have left the roomful of people a little subdued after he'd demanded their best from them. Today he'd let *them* decide to do the best job they could, and it seemed to have paid off.

He'd learnt an important lesson recently about taking a less aggressive attitude towards business and he knew he had Elena to thank for that.

She was good for him—helped balance him somehow.

He showered and changed at work, putting on his best casual suit for dinner, aware of a low level of excitement about seeing Elena again this evening that had buzzed through his veins all day.

The traffic was bad and he tapped his fingers impatiently against the armrest of the car as his driver wound slowly through the early evening traffic.

'It looks like everyone's out for Valentine's night, clogging up the roads,' the driver muttered.

Caleb smiled at his grumpiness, thinking how great it was to be one of the people looking forward to an evening of romance for once.

Striding through the entrance of the restaurant, he bumped into a couple of people he knew socially who were also there for a romantic meal and they exchanged pleasantries, Caleb's pulse jumping with impatience to see Elena again after spending the day away from her.

He appeared to have turned into a teenager again. Not that he could remember those years clearly. Bits and pieces had come back to him over the last couple of days, mostly feelings of not having fitted in to a small, close-knit community in the small town where he'd been raised, a few miles west of Barcelona.

It was strange, but he was aware that this bothered him much less now—now he knew he'd made something of himself and proved all those naysayers wrong about him. Now that he had Elena.

Finally finding an out in the conversation so he could say a polite farewell to his acquaintances, he made his way towards the maître d's desk, where he was greeted with a smile of reverence and a warm welcome before being shown towards his table where, he was told, Elena was already waiting for him.

He'd chosen this restaurant because he liked its clean lines and no fuss décor, with its wall of glass which looked out onto a courtyard of flowers and olive trees, which were lit up tonight like some magical grotto. The simple wooden spoke-back chairs juxtaposed sharply with the pristine white tablecloths and blank walls, giving it all an understated but refined air. It was classy without being showy and he knew from experience that the food here was out of this world.

The perfect place to celebrate with Elena.

The table where she'd been seated was right next to the glass wall and the candle that flickered in front of her threw shadows onto the reflective surface, making it look as though she was sitting next to her ghostly double.

When she spotted him she stood up and smiled and his pulse skittered then began to jump in his throat. Gazing at her now brought home to him just how truly beautiful she was. Tonight she was wearing a fitted cocktail dress in a deep turquoise colour that made her iridescent eyes glow with warmth. Her pale golden hair flowed around her shoulders in waves, looking so lustrous in the soft light he ached to run his fingers through it.

In fact his overriding instinct right that second was to drag her into his arms and never let her go.

As he reached the table she stepped to the side and opened her arms for him to walk into her embrace, a wide smile playing about her lips and pleasure flashing in her eyes.

He dragged her roughly to him, burying his face in her hair and whispering, 'I missed you today.'

'I missed you too,' she murmured back.

He dragged in a deep breath, desperate to fill his senses with her soft, familiar scent—

And suddenly everything felt wrong.

His vision swam in front of him and a slow sinking sensation began to pull him down towards the floor.

That scent.

He knew it.

He *knew* it, but he didn't know why.

There was something completely wrong about it, but also completely right.

Elena and that scent went together.

But not in a good way.

Images began to cloud his mind's eye: of the two of them at university, studying in each other's rooms, laughing together. He felt flashes of happiness, then insecurity, then a cold hard rage that swelled up from somewhere deep inside him, dragging the breath from his lungs.

'Caleb? What's wrong?'

He heard Elena's voice as if it was coming to him

from a distance. Nausea welled in his gut and he pushed her away from him, needing to be free of her hold, to get away from the smell that was causing his mind to rebel against him. His head pounded as if his brain had suddenly swollen and was pressing against the walls of his skull, the pain so intense he stumbled forwards, grabbing a chair to steady himself.

He felt her hand on his shoulder but he shrugged her off, not wanting her to touch him.

Then, like a floodgate opening, it all came rushing back: the soul-crushing disappointment and the hurt and humiliation he'd endured after he'd opened himself up to loving her back then. The way he'd trusted her implicitly with his heart and she'd taken it, played with it for a while then smashed it to pieces at his feet.

He'd made a total fool of himself for her.

After leading him to believe she cared about him as much as he did her and promising to come back after the Christmas holidays free to be with him, he'd gone home to Spain for the holidays, actually feeling happy for once to be going back there so he could tell his mother about the woman he'd fallen in love with.

She'd been so pleased for him; in fact it had been the first time they'd connected on any kind of emotional level since he'd been a young boy, perhaps because he finally understood how she could love someone so much she would do whatever it took to have them—that loving someone would be worth being estranged from others for.

After what had seemed like an interminable amount of time at home he'd gone back to Cambridge, desperate to see Elena after having promised not to call her whilst she was at home, to give her the time and space to deal with breaking up with Jimmy in a gentle and kind manner, only to find she was avoiding him.

He'd thought he was being paranoid at first, that it was bad timing when he kept missing her at her college. Until he'd finally tracked her down, panic surging through his veins, and she'd been visibly reluctant to see or speak to him. The cold distant look in her eyes had sent shivers of horror through him, which only increased when she'd told him in a toneless voice how she'd decided to stay with Jimmy after all, how she felt that he, Caleb, was too wild for her, too dangerous a proposition, too unpredictable. She needed to be with someone like Jimmy because she needed stability and calm in her life.

He'd felt belittled, rejected, foolish, but most of all heartsick at losing the woman he'd felt so sure felt the same way he did.

Taking a deep, much-needed breath, he finally straightened and turned to look into Elena's beautiful, deceitful face, feeling a deep, hot rage overtake him.

It hadn't been an undeniable romantic attraction that had connected them with such intensity over these last few days: it had been hatred.

'I remember, Elena,' he said, his voice raspy and strained as he forced the words past his throat. 'I remember why we stopped being *friends*.' He spat the last word out, feeling disgusted with himself for allowing her to take him in like this.

She'd used his memory loss against him to wheedle

out what she wanted from him. And he, like a fool, had
fallen for it. Fallen for her. Again.

'What are you talking about? Caleb, I don't understand. What just happened here?' She looked panicked
by his pronouncement, as well she should.

He crossed his arms. 'I know exactly what's been
happening over the last few days. You've been using
the fallout from the accident to get close to me.'

She stared at him, her cheeks flushed with colour
and her brow pinched so tightly white lines formed on
her skin.

'Did you invite me here tonight to humiliate me in
public? To pay me back for what happened fifteen years
ago?' she whispered, blinking as if trying to hold back
tears.

He pushed away a sting of misplaced concern, forcing himself to remember that she was the one in the
wrong here. 'No, of course not! I only remembered it
all just now. The perfume you're wearing... It triggered
something.' His head gave another throb of pain and he
squeezed his eyes shut until it receded.

'Caleb? Are you okay?' The worry in her voice hit
him straight in the chest, winding him.

'I'm fine,' he growled, not wanting to feel the way
she was making him feel with her concerned, soothing
act. The only person she'd ever cared about was herself
and he needed to remember that.

'I see you for what you really are now, Elena,' he
bit out angrily.

She swallowed hard, her face blanching, and glanced
around her anxiously.

He suddenly realised that the room had become awfully quiet. When he looked round he saw that all the diners near them were staring their way in morbid fascination.

'Look, shall we sit down and talk about this rationally?' Elena said with a quaver in her voice, pulling out her chair with a shaking hand and sitting on it.

After a moment of indecision he pulled out his own chair and sat down opposite her, folding his arms. He was interested to hear how she was going to try and explain her self-serving actions away.

'What do you mean, you've only just remembered what happened?' she hissed, leaning forwards and putting her hands onto the table between them. 'You said your memory had fully come back!'

He shrugged dismissively. 'No. I lied about that. I didn't want you to think I was weak.' He leant back in his chair and narrowed his eyes at her. 'I pieced a story together from what you'd said about us and...' he paused, struggling to unclench his jaw to force out the name '...Jimmy. But I remember now. I remember the way you led me on then pushed me away when you changed your mind about who would serve your needs best.'

She held up both hands towards him in a halting gesture. 'I thought you understood how sorry I was about that. How I knew it had been the worst mistake of my life. I've been trying to make amends for the way I behaved then.'

'So you could manipulate me into getting what you wanted.'

Her hands bunched into fists now. 'No, Caleb, it wasn't like that.'

'So why did you stay after I'd told you I didn't want anything more to do with you and your business? Why were you so keen to look after me at the hospital?'

'Because I care about you, Caleb!' she shot back passionately. 'And there was a misunderstanding between the hospital staff about who I was to you that I got caught up in. But I was there because I felt awful about you getting hurt.'

'Because you were responsible for it.' It all made sense now. Cold, cruel sense.

'No! At least not directly. You were crossing the road to talk to me and you didn't look properly.'

'And why was that?'

She didn't seem to be able to meet his eye. 'I guess you were distracted.'

'You mean I was angry with you for not taking no for an answer?'

She visibly swallowed. 'Yes.'

'And then you stuck around when you thought I couldn't remember what had happened.'

'I was trying to make things right between us.'

'You mean when you realised I'd forgotten all about it you thought you'd be able to get what you wanted by pretending to care about me. By charming your way into my bed!'

Her eyes widened in dismay. 'What? No—!'

'I know exactly what you've been doing, Elena— you've been playing me this whole time, hoping to seduce me into giving you what you needed when I'd already told you no,' he bit out, anger and humiliation and heartache making his voice shake.

She gaped at him in stunned surprise, her face now bleached of colour. 'No, Caleb.' Her voice came out as a ragged whisper. 'That's not what happened!'

Elena felt sick.

How could he suddenly be acting so coldly towards her after the closeness they'd shared?

Who was she kidding? She knew how, because she'd done exactly the same thing to him fifteen years ago.

She swallowed hard, her mind whirring, trying to think of some way to convince him that she'd meant well by staying here to look after him and that she genuinely cared about him, but before she could say anything else he frowned, then shook his head as if another revelation had just struck him.

'You only went to that dinner meeting with Carter with me so I'd feel compelled to say yes to your own partnership.'

Gritting her teeth, she let out a moan of frustration. 'You asked me to go with you and I wanted to help you! Not for my own benefit, but for yours!'

He was nodding now though, as if he wasn't listening to her and things were suddenly making sense in his head. 'You guided me towards asking you to help me, planting the idea about me needing someone who understood the business. You manipulated me.'

'I did not,' she said as calmly as she could manage, trying like mad to control the shake of anger and hurt in her voice. 'It was your idea and there was no way could refuse to help and leave you alone with your head injury. And I wanted to help, Caleb. Genuinely.'

He let out a low, disdainful laugh. 'Being genuine is not one of your strong points, Elena.'

'Maybe not fifteen years ago but, I promise you, it is now.'

'They why didn't you tell me everything when we had all our heart-to-hearts? There were plenty of opportunities.'

'Because I was afraid you'd kick me to the kerb. I was worried about you—about the fact you didn't seem to have anyone else to look after you. From what I've seen, you still seem intent on pushing away anyone who gets even vaguely close to you. I don't want you to end up old and alone. You deserve more than that. You deserve to be loved. And to be happy. You're a good man; you just need to believe it.'

He snorted. 'I know my own worth, Elena.'

'Do you?'

'Yes. *I* would never have slept with someone who couldn't remember the callous way I'd treated them in the past.'

She shoved her fingers into her hair in frustration. 'You told me you'd remembered.'

'Did you really believe I'd forgive you for the way you treated me back then, just like that?' He snapped his fingers, shooting her a look of disgust.

Dropping her head into her hands now, she let out a long, low sigh. 'I guess I knew deep down that something wasn't quite right, but I really wanted to believe things were okay with us again so I pushed any misgivings I had to one side.'

When she looked up again he was staring at her as if he didn't believe a word of it, his expression dark and unyielding.

'Yes, okay, I was being naïve,' she said, frustration making her belligerent now. 'It was wrong of me to let it happen.'

'So why did you?'

His question brought her up short. 'I—'

'You could have stopped me.'

'I couldn't. I didn't want to.'

'Why not, Elena?'

'Because I wanted you, all right!' she blurted, furious with herself for losing her cool.

'You wanted my battery, you mean,' he bit out, leaning towards her.

'No!' She took a breath, trying to calm her raging emotions. 'Well, yes. Okay.' She leant forwards too, fixing him with what she hoped was an honest and open expression. 'I need your battery because I have a lot of good people relying on me to find a way to save their jobs, but sleeping with you was a totally separate thing. I wanted to do it for me. For us.'

'For *us*?'

'Yes! I've missed you over the years and I didn't realise how much until I saw you again. How unhappy I was without you.'

There was a heavy beat of silence where they stared at each other, their breathing rapid and the body language tense.

She thought she saw a flash of vulnerability in his eyes, but the next second it was gone, replaced with cool indifference. 'If you're saying that because you're worried I'm going to back out of the partnership then don't bother. I'm not that much of a monster,' he growled, reaching into his jacket and withdrawing a sheaf of papers, which he tossed onto the table in front of her. 'It's a contract I had drawn up earlier today which agrees to a partnership with your company.'

She stared at it in shock for a moment before dragging her gaze back to his.

'Caleb, thank you—'

But, before she could finish her sentence, he cut her off. 'My colleagues will be handling it from here so we won't need to have any more contact. I hope that makes you happy.'

She glared at him, her heart thumping against her chest and her jaw tight with frustration. 'Don't be ridiculous—of course it doesn't make me happy to not have any more contact with you!'

He huffed out a disdainful laugh, the expression in his eyes hauntingly distant, then without another word he went to stand up.

'Please, Caleb, stay,' she said desperately, reaching out a hand in an attempt to stall him. 'We need to talk more about this.'

'There's nothing left to say,' he stated coldly, brushing away her attempt to touch him and standing up, and before she could utter another word he turned and walked swiftly away from the table without looking back.

Elena sat there, numb with shock, battling down a

painful ache deep inside her, afraid that once she let it rise to the surface she wouldn't be able to stop the tears that would inevitably come with it.

Everything might have just gone to hell but there was no way she was going to blub in the middle of a restaurant.

Gesturing to a passing waiter, she asked him to bring the bill for the champagne that she'd ordered and that neither of them had touched. She paid with her credit card, her movements jerky with anguish, then got up shakily and brushed herself down, setting back her shoulders before walking out of there, hyper-aware of the fascinated looks she was getting from the other diners.

Dumped on Valentine's night. It didn't get much more humiliating than that.

Once outside, she walked quickly down a side alley, away from prying eyes, and leant against the wall, burying her face in her hands.

But she refused to let herself cry.

She'd known, of course, on some subconscious level that Caleb had been lying about getting his memory back—that he'd been swept up in the excitement of closing the deal with the Americans and had wanted to celebrate with her the best way he knew how. And, to her shame, she'd let him, pretending to herself she believed that he remembered her even though he'd not remotely reacted in the way she'd been expecting.

Because she'd wanted him so badly she'd ached with longing.

The truth was, she'd been utterly selfish. She *had* taken

advantage of his memory loss after the accident, not admitting it to herself at the time, but hoping—praying—it would never come back.

She'd brought all this on herself.

Just like she'd done fifteen years ago.

Caleb had trusted her implicitly then too, so much so he'd opened himself up to her—the first person he'd ever done that with after enduring such a punishing and isolated childhood—and she'd thrown his love and trust back in his face, deeming it worthless.

Then she'd hidden, like a coward, avoiding him at every turn until he'd been forced to come to her dorm room and practically break down the door to speak to her. She'd been afraid to face his disappointment in her so had put up a wall of ice to protect herself, telling him she'd made a mistake, he was too wild, too unpredictable for her, they could never be happy, not in the long run. She needed someone more stable, like Jimmy. He'd looked at her as if his world had just crashed in around him, before turning and walking away.

And that had been the last time he'd ever spoken to her. From that point on he'd acted as if she didn't exist. He'd looked through her as if she was nothing— a waste of space.

And she'd known deep down that she'd deserved it.

He'd practically gone to ground after that, skipping the lectures where she'd normally see him and never seeming to be at his dorm room when she dropped in, hoping to catch him and apologise and explain her horrible behaviour. And then he'd gone back to Spain as soon as the last lecture had finished, pushing past her when she'd tried to talk to him as if she meant nothing to him any more.

It had left an aching hole in her that had never closed over, even fifteen years later.

Because he'd been the love of her life.

It had tormented her more than she'd wanted to admit to herself over the years, chipping away at her self-respect, causing her to find fault in every man she'd dated, leaving her to wonder whether she'd ever be happy in a relationship again.

Until now.

But just when she'd thought she'd paid her dues and things were finally good between them again she'd lost him all over again.

CHAPTER TEN

CALEB MARCHED INTO his apartment, slamming the front door so hard behind him the angry sound of it reverberated around the space for a good few seconds.

How could he have let this happen? He'd known there was something strange going on but he'd blamed it on his memory loss instead of looking harder at the woman who had appeared out of nowhere like a ray of sunshine on a dark day.

Slumping onto the sofa, he winced in pain as his cracked rib reminded him that he'd been weakened by the accident in more ways than one.

But then hadn't he known, deep down, that there was more to her story than she was telling him and he'd let himself fall for her anyway?

Because he had—hard and intensely. The thought of being with her had consumed him over the last few days, just like it had when he was younger. He knew why he'd not wanted to look too closely at what was going on. It was because he'd wanted her to be genuinely interested in exploring a relationship with him—wanted it more than he'd ever wanted anything in his life.

So he'd allowed himself to trust her, to begin to care about her—no, who was he kidding, he'd fallen in love with her and she'd used that to get what she wanted from him.

Once again she'd played him for a fool.

He felt as though his heart had been ripped from his chest. All that emotion that had been building inside him from the moment he'd seen her again swelled to an almost unbearable size, closing his throat, crushing his lungs, filling his head with unbearable pain.

No doubt she was already at the airport, ready to head home, happy in the knowledge that she'd achieved her objective here: to get him to sell her his battery, no matter what she'd had to do to get it.

Anger flashed through him, propelling him off the sofa and towards his bedroom where her things were still hanging in his wardrobe and sitting on his shelves.

Well, he wanted them gone. He didn't want a trace of her left in his house now. He couldn't stand the pain of thinking about what he could have had if only she'd really wanted *him*.

Grabbing her small suitcase from where she'd stashed it in the wardrobe, he stuffed her clothes roughly into it willy-nilly, not caring how much it hurt his rib to do so—in fact, welcoming the pain it brought because it momentarily overrode the ache in his heart—then went to the bathroom and scooped all her toiletries into it too, forcing down the lid and roughly zipping it up.

Picking up the case, he strode to the front door, opened it, then tossed it into the hallway, where it bounced a couple of times before coming to rest on its side, looking battered and forlorn in the grandiose, brightly lit space.

Pushing away a rush of anguish, he slammed the door on it and strode into his kitchen, grabbing a glass tumbler out of the cupboard and splashing a good measure of whisky into it.

He knocked it back, feeling the burn in the back of his throat and registering the warmth as it hit his stomach, though deriving no pleasure from it whatsoever.

Pouring himself another large shot, he took it into the living area and slumped down onto the sofa again, staring out of the window at the dark night sky, which had become stormy with wind and rain that lashed against the glass, trying not to think about how painfully alone he was here in this big echoing apartment.

Despite the way Elena had treated him, his traitorous body still ached for her. His throat was tense from holding back the urge to rage and swear at the world, his chest tight with sorrow and frustration.

He knew, with ringing clarity now, why he'd deliberately sabotaged his engagement to his ex, Adela. He'd been afraid to trust her love for him for this very reason. His survival instinct had kicked in and he'd pushed her away before she could do it to him first.

Because he'd been afraid of something like this happening to him again.

The sad truth was he'd fallen for Adela in the first place because she'd reminded him of Elena. Adela had exhibited many of Elena's traits; she'd even looked a bit like her, but of course he knew deep down that she could never be her. That was why he'd broken off their engagement. It wouldn't have been fair to Adela to have always been second best in his heart.

Perhaps he was destined to always be alone. It would at least be easier that way. Like it had been when he was younger.

He was also acutely aware now that keeping his relationship with his mother at arm's length had had a serious effect on the way he dealt with all his close relationships to this day.

At least after her cancer was diagnosed he'd made sure to visit her more and they'd brokered a kind of unspoken peace between them. He'd never totally understood the life choices she'd made, but he'd come to finally accept them, and her. During those sad, desolate hours at the end of her life she'd made it clear to him that she'd always loved him and that she regretted the distance that had always been between them.

It had torn him up inside, the futility of it, because she was gone now and all he was left with was a sense of deep sorrow for the time he'd wasted spurning her instead of loving and accepting her for who she was.

And now he'd lost the woman he'd hoped to spend his future with too.

The woman he loved.

Knocking back the second whisky, he closed his eyes and tried to blank his mind of her—to shut out the pain and grief that made him feel as though someone had stripped him to the bone—but it was no good; he knew there was no forgetting Elena Jones.

* * *

Elena paced the streets, barely noticing the rain as it began to fall steadily from the sky, seeping into her new dress and plastering her hair to her head.

How could things have gone so wrong so quickly? She'd known before, of course, that there was a chance they might when she'd thought his memory was still missing, but for him to have lied about remembering her, then shown her how wonderful they could be together, only then to regain his memory and reject her was devastating.

Lightning flashed overhead, shocking her out of her frustrated, meandering thoughts, and she ducked under a nearby awning of a restaurant where a few other tourists had gathered, taking shelter from the storm. What was she doing? Moping around Barcelona in the rain wasn't going to solve the problem; the only way she was going to get him to listen to her was to turn up at his apartment and refuse to leave until he did.

She wasn't going to run from him again, not this time. She was going to do what she should have done all those years ago—be brave and fight for what she really wanted, no matter the consequences. She'd never be able to forgive herself if she didn't, not now she knew what she'd be missing—a positive, life-affirming partnership with the man she loved.

Seeing an available taxi driving down the street, she ran back out into the rain and hailed it, jumping into the back seat and giving the driver Caleb's address in a voice shaking with nerves and determination.

She would not give up on them. Not this time.

The journey seemed to take an age as they joined the slow-moving traffic and more and more people jumped into taxis to shelter from the rain. Elena tapped her foot anxiously, wondering what sort of reception she'd get when he opened the door and found her standing there. Would he be angry, cold, indifferent? Or, now that he'd had some time to calm down and reflect rationally on it all, would he be relieved to see her?

She hoped so.

Oh, how she hoped.

The taxi finally drew up outside his building and she shoved the fare towards the driver, telling him to keep the change in her haste to get to Caleb, and dashed across the pavement and up to the entry door to his block. Pulling out the spare key card that Caleb had lent her that morning, so she could get in and out while he was out at work, she pressed it against the pad and sighed with relief when the door lock clicked open. She wouldn't have put it past him to have the code reconfigured to keep her out.

The lift was already at ground level and it took her straight up to his apartment. Walking into the hallway, she came to a surprised stop when she saw a suitcase lying haphazardly in the middle of the floor. She frowned at the incongruity of it, wondering absentmindedly what it was doing there. And then it hit her like a fist to the gut.

It was hers.

Caleb must have packed her things and thrown them out here in case she had the gall to return for them. Well, she wasn't going to let that deter her. Marching up to his door, she hammered loudly on it, her heart thumping in her throat as she stood there listening for his heavy footsteps coming towards her. It occurred to her wildly that she wasn't exactly looking her best at the moment—a lot like a drowned rat, in fact—but she shoved the thought away, knowing this was no time for vanity.

The door swung open and she looked up into Caleb's handsome face, forcing herself not to take a step backwards as she registered the anger in his expression.

'Your things are behind you in the hall,' he said curtly, the bitterness in his voice making her stomach roll.

'I'm not here for my things; I'm here for you,' she stated baldly, keeping her gaze locked with his and her chin determinedly up.

A range of expressions passed over his face: from bemusement to resentment and finally, and most worryingly, to incredulity.

'Let me in, Caleb,' she said calmly, but with a determination that rose from her very soul.

'You can say what you need to right here,' he said, folding his arms in front of him, effectively blocking her way past him with his enormous bulk.

The coldness in his eyes shook her, but there was no way she was going to let him scare her off now. She knew that the kind, compassionate man she'd got to know again over the last few days was still in there somewhere; she just needed to get him to hear what she had to say then maybe she'd be able to draw him back out again.

'Okay, fine, if it has to be said here in your hallway then it will be.' She took a breath and set back her shoulders.

'You were right; I wasn't honest with you and I should have been from the very start, but I was afraid you'd push me away and I desperately wanted to make up for the way I treated you in the past. I was selfish and cruel then but, please believe me, I'm not that same self-absorbed girl I used to be. I'm a different person now. A better one, I hope. Surely you've seen proof of that over the last few days.'

He didn't give any indication that she was getting through to him, his posture remaining stiff and his expression impassive, so she decided just to get it all out in the hope that something she said would strike a chord with him.

'I know I told you that I decided I couldn't marry Jimmy because our relationship was staid and—boring.' She winced at how awful that sounded. What a terrible person she'd been, to them both.

Caleb still didn't say anything, his expression remaining indifferent.

She took another steadying breath, then let the words rush out. 'But the truth is, I broke up with him because I realised I'd never feel about him the way I felt about you.'

There was a flicker of something in his eyes and she held her breath for a moment, praying for a reaction, but he steadfastly refused to give her one.

Swallowing hard, she bunched her fists for courage.

'Back then I was afraid of how unpredictable you were, how you didn't fit into the way I'd envisioned my life turning out, but mostly how I still wanted you—desperately—despite all of that. After years of keeping a tight control over my life, that completely rattled me. So I stuck with Jimmy, the safe bet, the man I could control. Because I was a coward.'

He wasn't looking at her now, but staring off into the distance. Folding her arms, she steeled herself to hold it together.

'I realised later on, of course, once I'd grown up a little, that a certain amount of conflict can be good for a relationship. I guess it gives it the edge it needs to keep things exciting and fresh. As long as there's enough love between a couple... I think I mistook passion for dysfunction in my parents' marriage but they're still together today, so it shows what I know.'

She was aware that she was dripping water onto the floor now and that she'd begun to shiver with cold, but she pushed aside her discomfort, feeling it was probably a fitting state for her confession.

'I think I've really been single for so long because I stopped trusting my judgement when it comes to relationships. I was ashamed of the way I'd acted in the past and avoided getting close to anyone again in case I made the same mistakes. But after spending this incredible time with you here I realised that if I want to be happy it's time to stop being afraid of what might go wrong.'

She took a step closer to him. 'And embrace what could go right. Because I'm so happy when I'm with you.' Her voice broke as she took another step forwards and saw him tense, then tighten and raise his arms like a barrier.

'You really think I'm going to be able to trust you again?' he muttered.

'I do. Because I think you want to; it's just your pride getting in the way.'

'My *pride*? You broke your word to me and you lied; why should I believe you won't do that again?'

'Because I'm not the girl you remember, Caleb. I'm older and wiser now.' She took a deep, shaky breath. 'I was so ridiculously naïve back then, I had no idea what I really needed.' She gave him a beseeching smile, holding her breath as she waited to see whether she'd finally got through to him.

'You have to understand that you scared me at the time. You were so full of anger and bitterness I didn't know whether I could handle you. I wasn't a very strong person then.'

'I didn't need your strength, Elena. I needed your loyalty and respect.'

It felt as though his words had slapped her in the face. She knew he was right; she'd disrespected him in the worst possible way. He trusted her with the whole of his already damaged heart and she'd toyed with it for a while, then thrown it back at him, broken and be-yond repair. It had been the worst thing she could have done to him; no wonder he'd turned into the hardened character she'd first met here last week.

'I don't blame you for being reluctant to trust my word after I made such a mess of things last time, but please, Caleb, *please* give me another chance.'

Her heart started to race and her body flushed hot

with trepidation as she looked up into his hooded eyes and said, 'I love you.'

He stared at her, a deep frown marring his face.

'You *love* me?' His tone was so troubled her heart went right out to him.

'Yes, and I want us to make this relationship work.'

He shook his head, the expression in his eyes a little wild as if he was fighting with himself about how to respond.

Her chest gave a little jolt of hope at the thought that perhaps she might finally be getting through to him.

Turning away from her, he began to pace up and down the hall, raking his hands through his hair and making it stand on end. He looked troubled, anxious—but *encouraged* maybe?

'I don't know, Elena. It's a lot to process. I thought I knew you—'

'You *do* know me. Everything I've told you about myself is true. Everything we've done together has been genuine and came from a place of love and respect for you.'

Still he shook his head, as if not daring to believe it.

'I understand why you're feeling this way. It has to be so confusing losing your memory like that,' she said in desperation. 'Then finding out you were missing a big chunk of important information.' She walked to him now and put her hands on his arms, gripping them hard and using the whole of her strength to stop him from pacing.

'Listen to me, Caleb Araya. I am not letting you push me away again. I know I was in the wrong fifteen years ago, but everything that's happened between us in the last week has been real. And I think you feel the same, though you're too stubborn to admit it.'

Caleb stared at this brave, fierce woman in front of him and felt the heavy weight of unhappiness lift a little from his chest.

He knew what she was saying made sense; she'd been nothing but kind and caring towards him since leaving the hospital and he was acutely aware that he was letting his fear and panic get in the way of common sense. His chest gave a sharp throb as he accepted that if it hadn't been for her courage to stand up to him and assert her steadying influence at the meeting he would have lost Carter's business. She'd done that to help him. Because she cared about him. He knew that really, deep in his heart.

In reality, it had been his fault this had all turned into such an awful mess in the blink of an eye because he'd lied about his memory coming back so they could take their relationship further; and it had definitely been him who had asked her to go with him to the meeting with Carter. He remembered the look of wary uncertainty on her face now when he'd suggested it. That, he knew without a doubt, had been absolutely genuine.

He could recognise all that now—now he'd started to see through the fog of fear and panic that had engulfed him earlier.

Looking inside himself, he knew he'd forgiven her a long time ago for what had happened between them. Really, he'd hated himself for being so weak and proud but until now he'd been too afraid to admit it to himself because it was easier to hate someone than to admit how much you loved them. How much it tore you apart to not have that love returned.

A small defiant part of him still wanted to hang on to the animosity he'd hidden his feelings behind, to keep himself safe from any more pain and uncertainty, but he knew he couldn't do that. Not after she'd been brave enough to turn up here, dripping wet and bedraggled, to lay her heart at his feet when she could have just got on a plane with her signed contract and never had to face him again.

He wouldn't do that to her because what he wanted most in the world was a real and honest relationship with her, even if their journey together was likely to be littered with obstacles and challenges.

She made him happy.

He loved her and she loved him and when it came down to it that was all that really mattered.

Seeming to sense a softening in his attitude, she moved closer to him and tentatively raised a hand to his face. The warmth of her touch heated his skin, starting a fire in his chest which radiated out through his body until every centimetre of him ached to hold her against him again.

'Please, Caleb, please forgive me. Let me back in,' she whispered.

The crack of pain and desperation in her voice broke through the very last of his reserve and he felt the final tendrils of his anger leave him, washed away by the dizzying elation of her presence here—the place where she belonged.

Cupping her jaw in his hands, he smiled at her, drawing her closer. 'There's nothing to forgive. I've been wrong to hold what happened between us all those years ago against you, but it was easier to hate you than face what I'd become: a bitter, cold-hearted fool.'

She opened her mouth as if to disagree but he held up his hand, asking her to wait until he'd finished.

'Being with you has brought me alive again. I love being around you; the world feels like a better place when you're here.'

He frowned as he remembered the horrified look on her face in the restaurant just before he'd stormed away in angry confusion. 'When my memory came back earlier this evening I think I panicked. I suddenly had all these conflicting thoughts and feelings racing through my head, and I didn't know what was truth and what was fiction any more. My natural instinct was to push you away to protect myself. I was afraid you didn't really care about me the way I'd hoped you did and it scared the hell out of me.'

He stroked his thumbs across her cheeks, brushing away the tears that had begun to streak down her face.

'Because I love you, Elena,' he murmured, holding her gaze with his for one precious moment, seeing relief and love light up in her eyes, before bringing his mouth down to hers with a kiss that took his breath away at the utter perfection of it.

He felt her finally relax against him and he pulled her closer, wrapping his arms around her and pressing their bodies tightly together, feeling the strongest compulsion to never let her go again.

'Caleb, your rib,' she muttered against his shoulder where her face was squashed by his encircled arms.

'It's fine. Don't worry.'

'I don't want to hurt you,' she said, pulling away to look up into his face.

'You won't,' he said with conviction.

'You know, we're probably going to be one of those couples that constantly strikes sparks off each other,' she said with a hint of worry in her eyes.

'I hope so,' he said, dipping down to nuzzle her neck and feeling great satisfaction in the little shiver of enjoyment she gave. 'It will keep life exciting.'

'So we'll have to make sure our kids know how much we love each other,' she said with determination in her voice.

He drew back and raised both eyebrows. 'Kids?'

She nodded firmly. 'Yes. I want three.'

'That's brave,' he said, adding a wry lilt of humour to his voice, though deep down he knew that having children with her would make him the happiest man in the world. She'd be an incredible mother: caring, brave and compassionate, and would fight tooth and nail for her children's happiness and security, making sure they knew how loved they were, how wanted.

'I am brave now,' she said. 'I refuse to be afraid of the future any more. We'll take life as it comes, you and I, and deal with anything it throws at us together.'

'I like your style, Elena Jones,' he murmured, bend-ing to kiss her hard and let her know just how much he meant that.

'And I like yours, Caleb Araya,' she said once she'd got her breath back.

And with that sentiment lifting his heart he took her hand in his and led her out of the cold empty hallway and into the shelter of his home.

EPILOGUE

Two years later

IT WAS UNSEASONABLY warm for London in February as Caleb strode through Green Park on his way to meet Elena by the Tube station and he loosened his tie and undid the top button of his shirt, finding relief as the gentle breeze hit his heated skin. He was taking her out for high tea at The Ritz to celebrate her recent design award for her Zipabout cars and was running a little late after a meeting in the City had gone on longer than he'd anticipated.

They'd both been astonished and delighted by the huge impact that the Zipabout cars had had on the electric car industry and Elena was already deep into the design and pre-manufacture of a new model on the back of its success. He was ridiculously proud of all she'd achieved and infinitely delighted to be able to say he'd played some small part in it.

He saw the cars everywhere he went now, both here in England, where they spent big chunks of time in order for Elena to keep in close contact with her company, and also in Spain, where they'd made a permanent home together in the Pedralbes area in the district of Les Corts, which they'd chosen for its wide avenues and green open spaces as well as the spectacular views towards Barcelona.

He hadn't needed much persuasion to move from his rather sequestered, cavernous flat in L'Eixample and into a comfortable four-bed house set within a friendly community of families and professionals, and for the first time in his life he felt truly settled where he lived. Content.

As he rounded the bend near the station his gaze alighted on a figure walking towards him, her long blonde hair glowing in the soft winter sunshine and her cheeks flushed with colour.

The most beautiful woman in the world.

His wife.

She waved when she saw him, her mouth curving into a beatific smile that both melted his heart and made his pulse race. Despite all the time they spent together now, he still hated being separated from her, rushing at the end of each day to get back home. Not a day went by when he didn't thank his lucky stars for the accident that had brought them together, even if it had been in the most dramatic and extraordinary of ways.

Blessedly, he'd been physically fine after all the bruising had finally gone down and after a few more weeks the rest of his memory had returned in full, along with a sense of regret for all the time he'd spent hanging on to the anger from his past that had kept him so isolated from the rest of the world.

But there were no regrets about his life now.

There were times, of course, when he and Elena butted heads but, instead of being afraid of the conflict they embraced it, getting any bottled-up feelings out into the open and using it as a kind of catharsis. They found as long as they kept communicating they were able to work through anything that crossed their path and Caleb made sure to tell Elena every day just how much he loved her.

Returning her smile, he glanced down in love-struck awe at her belly, which was straining against the trench coat she was wearing. In about three months' time there would be someone else for him to love with the same kind of fierce abandon too. Their child.

'Hello, beautiful,' he said as they reached each other and he drew her towards him for a kiss, savouring the feel of her mouth on his and breathing in her reassuring scent.

'How was your meeting?' she asked with a breathy laugh when he finally let her go.

'It went well, I think, though they were more impressed by the fact I'm married to you,' he said, gently brushing her hair away from her face to gaze into her eyes. 'My incredible, talented wife.'

She raised both eyebrows in an expression of wry modesty, then smiled, unable to keep a straight face. 'I couldn't have done it without you,' she murmured, sliding her hands up to cup his jaw and leaning forwards to kiss him firmly on the lips. 'So let's go and celebrate our perfect partnership.'

And with that they linked hands and walked together to their next destination, driven on by the excitement of all the new adventures they had lying ahead of them.

* * * * *

COMING SOON!

We really hope you enjoyed reading this book. If you're looking for more romance, be sure to head to the shops when new books are available on

Thursday 21st February

To see which titles are coming soon, please visit
millsandboon.co.uk/nextmonth